DESIRÉE M. NICCOLI

HAVEN COVE, BOOK 3

ENSNARING
THE SIREN

ENSNARING THE SIREN

DESIRÉE M. NICCOLI

City Owl
Press

ENSNARING THE SIREN
Haven Cove, Book 3

CITY OWL PRESS
www.cityowlpress.com

Cover Design by MiblArt. All stock photos licensed appropriately.

Edited by Tee Tate.

For information on subsidiary rights, please contact the publisher at info@cityowlpress.com.

Print Edition ISBN: 978-1-64898-467-9

Digital Edition ISBN: 978-1-64898-468-6

Printed in the United States of America

ALSO BY DESIRÉE M. NICCOLI

Haven Cove Series:
Called to the Deep
Song of Lorelei
Ensnaring the Siren

Standalones:
Follow Me to the Yew Tree
Given to the Ghoul

PRAISE FOR THE WORKS OF
DESIRÉE M. NICCOLI

"Deliciously sharp, *Ensnaring the Siren* is as intelligent as it is vicious. Niccoli is a skilled storyteller with an eye for details and the wit to delve deep. Romantic and sexy, *Ensnaring the Siren* is a story with as many layers as there are mermaid scales. Clever and creative, it's a read you can sink your claws into. Her mermaids will have you both fearing and falling in love with them." — *Rania Hanna, author of The Jinn Daughter*

"Murderous sirens, steamy romance, and the return of lovable characters as Niccoli brings us back to the glorious seaside town of Haven Cove. *Ensnaring the Siren* is a captivating and delectable romance you won't want to put down!" — *Melissa Karibian, author of the A Song of Silver and Gold duology*

"A fantastic addition to *Haven Cove's* engrossing mermaid world. Dangerous, sexy and thoughtful, you're in for a page turning ride." — *Agatha Andrews, host of the She Wore Black Podcast*

"With chemistry-filled banter, a reluctant allies-to-lovers dynamic, and delicious slow burn romance that is believable and swoonworthy, the third installment in Niccoli's *Haven Cove* series does not disappoint. Add in a nod to real-world issues and rich underwater and small town settings, and this becomes a story that will ensnare you in a familiar yet fantastical world that you'll never want to leave." — *C.W. Rose, author of Oceansong*

"A dark romantic delight that gives the idyllic mermaid fangs and claws. Niccoli has a wonderful talent for reeling readers in and grounding them in a world that feels like ours." — *Azalea Crowley, author of Odd Blood*

"Completely enthralling. I loved the mermaid lore, the Coast Warrior and his Starfish, and the real world consequences effortlessly interwoven within this steamy mermaid romance." — *Dana Evyn, author of The Other Side of the Mirror.*

"Atmospheric, romantic, scorching, and at times terrifying, Niccoli welcomes us home to the hauntingly familiar *Haven Cove*, where flesh-eating mermaids walk among us in plain sight. *Ensnaring the Siren*, just like its heroine, takes no prisoners in its dissection of what makes us both vulnerably human and wonderfully monstrous." — *Ingrid Pierce, author of Not You Again*

"Sizzling chemistry, endearing characters, and careful, thought-provoking world building make *Ensnaring the Siren* a delicious treat not to be missed!" — *Megan Van Dyke, author of The Musician and the Monster*

"The stakes are higher than ever for the *Haven Cove* mermaids and their human companions in this breathtakingly poignant tale of love, survival, and found family. Packed with action, witty banter, and moments of sheer beauty, *Ensnaring the Siren* is a smart, sexy page-turner you won't be able to put down. Niccoli has established herself as one of the most sophisticated voices in modern romantic fantasy, and her coterie of charmingly vicious mermaids will steal your heart!" — *Paulette Kennedy, bestselling author of The Witch of Tin Mountain*

"*Ensnaring the Siren* is an absolutely perfect blend of atmospheric ocean horror and cozy coastal romance. Desirée M. Niccoli packs every page with thrills, chills, and some truly earth-shaking spice. I would read this whole series over and over!" — *Lily Riley, author of The Assassin and the Libertine*

"Captivating, deadly, and delicious! *Ensnaring the Siren* is an enthralling mix of romance, action, and activism. An absolute must read!" — *Jessica S. Taylor, author of The Syren's Mutiny*

For Kyle, my Coast Warrior.

AUTHOR'S NOTE

You should always feel confident and safe when reading a book. As such, I've included a list of content information available on my website at: dmniccoli.com/books/haven-cove-series/ensnaring-the-siren/

If you have any concerns about the contents of this book, please be sure to check that page first. Thank you and enjoy!

CHAPTER

ONE

REID KRUETZ DIDN'T FEAR THE OCEAN.

It was a brutal, deadly force to be reckoned with, yes, but no matter the danger, it had always called him to its cold, unforgiving embrace. Tonight was no different.

Helicopter blades whirled overhead, drowning out all sound, save for a steady stream of radio chatter inside the cockpit between Reid's aviation team and sector command. There was a fishing boat sinking sixty miles offshore, its emergency beacon pinging them with its location. Word, too, was that it was going down in hostile mermaid territory, and they should proceed with abundant caution.

Sharks, mermaids, whatever the danger, he had a damn job to do. Save lives if he could, recover those lost if he couldn't, and get the hell out of there.

Sky and ocean joined as one in their inky blackness as Reid and his team raced in the dead of night to rescue the boat's crew, their stark white and orange helicopter the only splotch of color in a canvas of nothingness.

The Jayhawk was a standard flight vehicle for U.S. Coast Guard search and rescue missions. It had a range of 300 nautical miles and could hold their aircrew of four, plus an additional six people, more if they pushed it. And they'd have to push it; the boat's registered crew numbered eight, including the captain.

Rescue swimmer gear triple-checked—helmet, mask, snorkel, fins, and safety harness—Reid threaded his fingers over the collar of his orange dry suit, overlain with silver reflective tape, ready to go at a moment's notice. He'd trained hard for this job, and surviving the grueling Coast Guard Aviation Technical Training program and its high attrition rate was step one. Serving out of Cape Cod and handling its high case volume, step two. That he'd been tapped for the brand-new aircrew detachment out of Haven Cove Airport was no small thing, and the brass were watching. They had a reputation to build.

Potential mermaid complications aside, everything tonight was normal.

Maybe not a piece of cake, but at least familiar.

"Kruetz," said Alejandra Perez, their pilot, over the radio. "Get ready to drop."

Activating the strobe light attached to his dry suit, Reid nodded to the dropmaster, who opened the door, salty sea wind buffeting them both. The strobe light blinked on and off in a steady rhythm, the only piece of equipment that'd keep him visible if he swam beyond the helicopter's spotlight and into the dark.

Hatcher, the dropmaster, crowded the open doorway and peered over the edge, instead of skirting to the side so Reid could get through. It was like the man had forgotten how to do his damn job. "You gotta get them out of there."

That was the whole point.

"Get back." Reid roughly pulled him out of the way, not waiting for compliance. Not when every second mattered. "Get your head on straight."

Below, the helicopter's spotlight illuminated five out of the eight fishermen, each frantically waving up at them. He hoped the other three were somewhere nearby, clinging to debris, and not trapped inside the sinking boat. There was nothing he could do for them then.

With a quick assessment of the water, Reid stepped over the edge, fifteen feet down into the choppy waves. A basket lift would be lowered next to hoist survivors.

As the dark ocean rose to meet him, the worst of its icy temperatures were warded off by the dry suit he wore. Bobbing to the surface, Reid swam for the nearest fisherman, who was already doggy paddling toward him. Shouts rang out, some muffled by the beating helicopter blades, others as clear as day. Most were a variation of *help!* and *get me out of here!*

Hoisting one survivor at a time was the best they could do, given their equipment's limitations, but patience was hard won when fear was involved.

As Reid cut through the water in quick, measured strokes, he hoped no one climbed on top of him in a panic. While he never enjoyed knocking folks out, he wouldn't be rescuing anyone if they accidentally drowned him first, and necessity and survival sometimes demanded the harsh tactics drilled into him from "A" school.

"Coast Guard rescue swimmer, I'm here to help!" he yelled, reaching for the first fisherman, but before he could make contact, the man suddenly vanished, body jerked violently beneath the waves. There one moment, gone the next.

Reid lurched back, hand going to his diver's knife.

Screams coming from behind had him whisking around.

Another fisherman blinked from sight, then another. Lithe, streamlined creatures darted beneath the water at startling speeds, illuminated only by their blue, green, and amber bioluminescence, glittering like fireflies. If it weren't for this distinctly dire situation, they'd be pretty. But Reid had seen the news, had read the papers and scientific articles published over the last three years. Only one thing could be snatching these men so swiftly.

Radio crackling, Alejandra's voice barked, "Kruetz, what's happening down there?"

"Something's yanking them under, fast."

"Hatcher, drop the winch," she ordered. "We're getting him out of there."

"Winch descending."

A fourth fisherman vanished into the abyss; his startled cry sharply cut off.

"Fuck." The word was out before Reid could censor himself for radio, but given the situation, a stern reprimand from his commanding officer was the least of his worries. "There's only one left that I can see."

Hatcher's panicked voice cut in. "Reid, you have to save him!"

"Hatcher," Perez barked. "Keep the radio clear." In a calmer voice, she added, "Kruetz, do what you can, then get ready to clip in."

Pumping his arms and legs as fast as they'd go, Reid booked it for the man. Even if he saved only one, it was worth it. It had to be. He'd punched a shark once. If tonight was the night he punched a mermaid, so be it.

Overhead, the helicopter followed, a cable swaying back and forth beneath. His lifeline.

"Help me!" The last fisherman flailed, eyes wide with panic. An old scar gouged the man's upper lip, running from the right-side corner of his mouth up the length of his cheek. This one would attempt to climb him, for sure, but Reid was ready.

"Please, I don't want to die!" The other man launched at him, grasping, pulling, his weight shoving him under. Reid tried pushing him away, but the fisherman continued clambering, an errant knee connecting with his gut and knocking precious air right out of him. Just as Reid aimed for a pressure point—he was not drowning tonight, dammit—amber lights streaked through the water below, the heft of the last survivor suddenly wrenched away.

Reid surfaced with a hard kick, sucking in deep breaths. *Shit, fuck, damn.*

Several yards ahead, an amber-eyed woman popped above the surface, her mouth filled with razor-sharp teeth and lips red with blood. "Get back into your sky boat."

It sounded more like a command than a threat, yet ice ran down his spine, chilling him to the marrow. *It's really a...*

She inhaled deep. Naked, pale white shoulders rose from the water, her eyes fluttering a moment before flaring and pinning him with a hard look. Three horizontal slits flanked each side of her neck, rippling slightly as if disturbed by the moderate sea wind. He couldn't make out any more of her form in the dark, murky water, but from the clusters of lights he'd seen—the bioluminescence—there was no doubt as to what she was.

The Coast Guard officially recognized their existence, and yet no one in the service had encountered one directly.

"Kruetz, talk to us," Alejandra radioed in. "What's going on down there?"

"He's gone." The failure weighed heavily on his chest, but there'd be plenty of time to berate himself later if he made it out alive. "What about the other three?"

"Don't got eyes. We'll start a grid once you're back up."

"No, no, no, no," Hatcher whimpered. "This can't be happening."

This time, Perez didn't berate the dropmaster for clogging the radio, allowing him a moment before gently, but firmly saying, "Hatcher, I need you to focus and operate the hoist. Kruetz is depending on us, okay?"

A hard, wet sniff followed, but Hatcher's voice steadied. "Yes, Ma'am."

Reid should've mentioned his unwelcome visitor, but the words clammed up in his throat, his sanity hanging on by a thread. He couldn't afford to lose his shit now too.

In a flash of silver scales and orange fins, the creature darted forward, closing the distance between them to roughly grab his chin, wicked claws pinching, but notably not piercing his skin. "Now, Surface Dweller," she demanded. "You don't want to be down here with that."

"With what?" he sputtered, baffled, terrified, and waffling between being certain and uncertain of his imminent death. Between instinct and training, he should have punched her already and slashed his way to freedom with his diver's knife, but the fact that he wasn't currently fighting for his life stayed his hand. They wouldn't be chatting right now if she meant to kill him.

Her lambent eyes dipped down, staring at something on his person.

With a shuddering inhale, he wrestled his fear under control, taking a mental assessment of his body. She was staring somewhere below center mass, so it couldn't be the diver's knife on his hip. Other than the slight lactic acid burn in his muscles from hard swimming, some residual terror, and...

Oh, for fuck's sakes. He was stiff as a board.

He'd read about panic boners but never had the misfortune of having one himself, until now of all times—on a case and face-to-face with a creature that should've stayed a myth.

Finally looking up from his crotch, she said, "There are some here who'd take that as an invitation." Disgust flickered across her features.

Fuck, was he getting harder? Shit, shit, shit, what was wrong with him? Shriveling up toward his body would've been far better for self-preservation, but before he could say or do anything to account for his unfortunate pants situation, she leaned in, wicked mouth inches from the column of his throat.

He swallowed thickly, unable to move.

Weeks of arduous training, years of hands-on experience, and he gulped, fucking *gulped*, when he should be swimming away, putting as much distance between himself and the unknown. What would his instructors say if they could see him now? In his defense, they hadn't exactly prepared him for this kind of encounter. Sharks bit first, chatted never.

"I can only hold them off for so long."

It was only when he heard a faint click that he realized she hadn't bitten a chunk out of his neck but had instead clipped him into the winch. And it was then that her words sunk in. *I can only hold them off for so long.* Was this creature protecting him from her kin?

"The fishermen are hunting us, you know," she said, almost too quietly to be heard. "There's a whole fleet of them. Don't know what they do with our bodies once they've killed us. My companions think you're one of them."

His mind whirred at the claim. There was a foolish part of him that wanted to believe her, but he'd just watched five grown men get pulled under, never to resurface.

He had to get out of here.

Muscle memory kicking back in, he signaled to the aircrew, and the slack cable connecting him to the hovering helicopter above pulled tight, lifting him away from the water. *Away from her.*

With eerie, glimmering eyes, she watched his ascent, her body's amber bioluminescence winking back at him, revealing a long, finned tail swaying languorously beneath black water. Hints of her skeletal structure glowed from within, an odd translucent quality to her skin and muscles.

He couldn't tear his eyes from her, as strangely beautiful as she was lethal.

It wasn't until Hatcher roughly shook his shoulders, repeating his name for probably the millionth time, that it registered he was flat on his ass inside the Jayhawk. Head a bit fuzzy, he blinked slowly, pushing off his mask with shaky, freckled white hands.

"Was that what I think it was?" Their aircrew's dropmaster looked about as shocked as he felt.

Reid sat heavily in his seat and strapped in. It was one thing to know such creatures existed, another entirely to meet one face-to-face and tread the razor-thin edge between life and death. "That was a goddamned mermaid."

CHAPTER

TWO

NIREED PLUCKED AT A PIECE OF NETTING, ALMOST INVISIBLE to the eye, when an approaching pod of whales, including two calves, let out a volley of distressed clicks. Any closer and they'd get tangled.

She flashed her luminescent lights in rapid succession, issuing a warning, then indicated where they'd need to swim to get out.

The biggest whale, likely the matriarch, dipped her great big head and, with a series of whistles and pulsed calls, redirected her pod away from danger.

If only Nireed could swim away with them and forget this mess.

What in the deepest, foulest murk was she supposed to do about all this loose, drifting netting? It was miles wide and hundreds of feet deep, and she couldn't even attempt to reel it back up, not when the fishing vessel that towed it was now a groaning, sinking hunk of metal below them. Soon, it would drag this mass of netting into the deep, entangling any number of unsuspecting creatures in its descent.

All because of one young, hot-headed merman.

Cyrus.

The net had been encircling them, yes, gradually drawing up from below and threatening to trap them all inside, but there'd still been a clear, direct path overhead to the boat. They could've scaled over the side.

Instead, Cyrus had flown into a fit of rage and slashed open the boat's haul before she or anyone else in their hunting party could stop him and prevent this exact outcome. The boat took on water fast, its crew leaping into the ocean. Naturally, everyone wanted to attack right then and there, but Nireed slapped her fins hard and signed that they needed to guide the creatures trapped inside the net to safety first.

It was long, hard work. Miles of netting, hundreds, probably thousands of individual creatures, and only five of them to make it happen. But they did it.

"Why'd you let him go?" The younger male snapped his tail. "The orange one with weird fins."

Anger prickled along her scales. As if he'd any reason to be frustrated. He'd just eaten his fill of choice cuts from the boat crew.

Under normal circumstances, their waters were teeming with fish. Hunting should've been easy, and yet, fewer and fewer of their hunters returned each day, disappearing right alongside whole schools of fish and whatever other ocean denizens happened to be in the wrong place at the wrong time. In the last few weeks, their people had learned the hard way not to fall for the lure of potted meat, a recently introduced delicacy to their diet. But even knowing that now, with how large these walls of nets were, by the time they smelled it in the water it was sometimes too late.

As it had almost been tonight.

Merfolk were being baited, then captured or killed, and each of the boats—hard to say just how many—reported back to a larger ship that reeked of dead fish and diesel-run heavy machinery. *A factory ship.* A shore-bound friend had once explained to her what that was—a beast of a vessel that processed and packaged fish at sea in large quantities, sometimes more than 200 tons per day, and prepared it for Surface Dweller markets.

The floating factory was nearly 400 feet long and greedily gobbling up her pod's main food sources. Her people too.

"You should've killed him," Cyrus pressed, his challenge fiery and fierce.

She glared, gesturing to the netting with a hard slash of her hand. They had bigger problems to deal with, and he was wasting energy trying to undercut her authority as hunt leader. "He wasn't one of the others. He didn't do this." While the orange-clad human in question had tried to save the fishermen who'd attempted to catch and kill them, and maybe that made it unwise to let him go, his scent was curiously familiar, teasing at the edges of recollection. And she followed that instinct to protect him, to make sure he was able to get away.

"Far better uses for that one," Serpenra signed, a sly, suggestive smirk twisting her thin lips, bloodred from feasting. While her magenta scales were muted with age, she was one of their most clever hunters, and Nireed wouldn't leave her alone with a Surface Dweller male for anything. "He seemed quite taken with you. A shame you didn't make use of…"

"Leave it." Nireed slapped her hands together. There'd only been fear, nothing more to explain his body's reaction. "He's gone, and we've food to tow home."

Serpenra pouted. "You're no fun."

"Still don't understand why we let him go."

Grabbing the mouthy male by the scruff of his hair, Nireed yanked him toward the column of fuel and refuse belching from the sinking boat, shoving his face near its noxious plume. "You see that?" She held firm as Cyrus wriggled, using one hand to sign. "This is why we don't sink Surface Dweller vessels. When you have enough forethought to consider that and are not ruled by blind vengeance, I'll listen to your opinions. Until then, keep your mouth shut and don't presume I care whether you understand my decisions or not."

Pushing him away, Nireed took two of the eight rope leads they'd tethered around the lifeless fishermen. While their kind didn't actively hunt Surface Dwellers anymore, these men had tried to kill them, and meat was meat. To waste it was a grave offense, especially after so much destruction.

Casting one last helpless glance toward the mass of netting, Nireed pulled her catch into the deep, the others following behind with theirs. Her friends on shore would shudder at the sight, would beg her to find some other way to feed the pod.

But something good had to come out of this night.

Their people were hungry. And the flesh of their enemies would fill their bellies for now.

CHAPTER

THREE

H OURS OF COMBING DARK WATER AND THEY NEVER FOUND
the other three fishermen, alive or dead.

Pulling cruelly at the short, dark auburn curls on top of his head,
Reid stared at his computer screen and the case report he'd been trying
and failing to fill out for the last hour. It should've been easy. Just write
down the facts.

No bodies recovered. All eight fishermen were presumed dead, and
their boat lost at sea.

But he'd only typed three words.

Engaged a mermaid.

His cursor blinked back at him tauntingly.

What was he supposed to say about that? That while she'd
annihilated the fishermen, she'd not only allowed him to leave
unscathed, but had literally clipped him back into the hoist and sent him
on his merry way?

Then there was her claim, if it could be believed, that the deceased
fishermen were hunting and killing her kind. And for what—food,
trophies, or some black market thing? What was he supposed to do
about that?

This wasn't exactly a fisheries problem, although the National

Oceanic and Atmospheric Administration probably had something to say about it. The mermaids evidently had language and sapience, and that technically made them people. Just not entirely human.

According to the scientific articles he'd read, interspecies breeding made them biologically part human, but what did you call the part that wasn't? Pelagic? Extraterrestrial? With how much ocean remained unexplored—more than eighty percent was the last number he'd read—the ocean and its creatures might as well be as alien as space. So, what in the deep-sea hell had mermaids looked like before getting with humans? Did those creatures even still exist? The scientist who'd discovered the species seemed to think they probably did, although one had never been sighted.

He shuddered. God help them if one ever was.

Whatever degree of "humanness" the Gulf of Maine mermaids had, people were people, which brought him to one needling question: was this an international incident? Did a legal, political framework even exist yet for how to handle something like this? To his knowledge, merfolk were a recognized community but not a nation.

Oversimplify this report and the mermaids might be painted as hostile. Go into too much detail and supposition and the mermaids might not only be painted as hostile but also as a threat to national security.

This was leagues above his pay grade.

"Case report giving you trouble?" Perez plopped down in the chair next to him, crossing a black-booted foot over her knee, and lacing her hands over her stomach, skin a bronzy brown. She'd swapped over from an olive drab flight suit to utility blues, her dark brown hair pulled back into a tight, low bun. Two years ago, NPR had done a feature on her as one of the Coast Guard's few Latina pilots.

"I'm probably overthinking it." He pushed back from the desk with a huff, folding his arms behind his head.

"It's not every day you meet a mermaid."

"Yeah, well, I'm getting a real bad feeling this is going to be a repeat thing."

Perez cocked her head. "Why's that?"

"Because why stop at one boat?" He hesitated to say more. Would admitting to talking to the creature make him sound crazy?

"Spit it out. I can see your wheels turning."

"She told me the fishermen were hunting her kind."

The pilot let out a long, low whistle. "You actually talked to her?"

"A little."

The Merry Mariner, the boat that went down, was one of fifteen registered purse seine boats in the corporate fishing company Nautic Select Seafood's fleet, all of which supplied its factory ship in the Gulf of Maine. "Purse seine" was the type of net these boats used—a giant, miles long and hundreds of feet deep contraption that scooped everything in that radius out of the water, drawing up like a purse string. A bycatch nightmare.

If the mermaids were ticked off about competing over food sources, they wouldn't stop at just one of Nautic's boats, and the company would kick up a fuss, lobbying the federal government for swift and decisive action.

But...

If *The Merry Mariner*'s fishermen were targeting mermaids, that stood to reason the rest of the fleet was as well. And that kind of concerted, coordinated effort wouldn't happen without Nautic Select Seafood's blessing.

If, if, if.

When Reid voiced these possibilities, Perez's expression grew solemn. "You've thought a lot about this."

"Don't know why. I should just write the report and be done with it. This shit's for command to figure out anyway."

"Not wrong there, but I think you ought to share these thoughts with Lieutenant Commander Griffin. Either way it shakes out, CGIS might get involved, and the more they know, the better."

If he could put these pieces together, surely his superior officer and the Coast Guard Investigative Service didn't need him to reach similar conclusions.

But as if reading his mind, she continued, "You're the first person in the whole service to make contact with a real, live mermaid, and I doubt any of those guys come close to being the secret duck-scrubbing, science nerd you are."

He snorted.

"Duck scrubber" was the playful nickname they gave to the Coast Guard's Marine Science Technicians on account of cleaning up oil spills, and the wildlife caught in the middle, and once Reid's Plan B if he couldn't cut it as an Aviation Survival Technician. But Perez had a point. He was naturally curious about these things, and maybe the way he saw things wasn't the default.

"So..." The pilot's voice dropped into a conspiratorial tone. Curiosity twinkled in her dark brown eyes as she leaned forward, forearms draped across her knees. "What was she like? Did she say anything else?"

Reid ran a hand over his jaw. The flesh was tender, but despite the mermaid's powerful, claw-tipped grip, fifteen minutes spent searching in a mirror hadn't revealed any bruises or nicks.

Every time he shut his eyes, he saw her.

Amber eyes, so alien and otherworldly, stared at him from the dark of night, inky black waves bobbing between them. And with a single smile he was rendered immobile, unable to look away from rows of wicked, sharp teeth, so white they gleamed, as blood dripped from her cruel lips. This devastating amalgamation of beautiful woman and creature of the deep had come to wreak destruction. And he'd been at her mercy.

But she'd let him go. Protected him from her murderous kin.

Why?

"She was goddamn terrifying," he said finally. "Just told me to get back into my sky boat."

"Sky boat?" Perez laughed. "Oh, I love that. Pure gold. Anything else?"

The rest of that encounter was need-to-know, and Perez did not need to know about his panic boner.

"Was she pretty, at least? They're supposed to be really pretty."

"Tell that to the fishermen she ate."

"Didn't eat you though, which makes me think they might've provoked her."

"So you believe her."

Perez shrugged. "They were coming into her turf—or should I say surf? Anyways, if I had a quarter for every time a man's taken something that doesn't belong to him, and blamed a woman for his actions, I'd be eating well too."

There was no disputing that, but people were dying, and if his gut was correct, there'd be more.

When he didn't respond, she asked, "Well, what do you think? You were there."

Scrubbing his hands through his hair, he groaned. "I don't know what to think. Just that it's our job to save people." Not root for their demise, even if they'd brought it upon themselves. "Whether or not I believe her doesn't matter."

"It does matter." Something about her clipped tone made him think he'd just stuck his foot in his mouth. Or missed an important point. "Get the facts down. That's step one."

Perez left without a parting glance.

Sighing, Reid began to type. What was he missing?

CHAPTER

FOUR

THE OCEAN WAS NIREED'S HOME, AND SHE'D ALMOST LOST IT.

She had put her unearned trust into the hands of a Shorewalker, a mermaid born and raised on land. And she had put her life into the hands of a marine biologist, subjecting herself to scientific study and a year trapped in a tank, on the slim chance it might save her people from the ravenous hunger that controlled their minds and made them sick.

A shot at a cure.

A chance to restore her people's ability to choose.

The Surface Dweller scientists poked and prodded her. Studied and watched, sets of cold, indifferent eyes staring at her from all angles, not a moment left unobserved.

But not from the Shorewalker. And not from the marine biologist who became Cure Creator. They kept their promises and freed her when it became clear the other Surface Dwellers had no intention of ever letting her go.

Nireed stroked her wrists nervously, squeezing her eyes shut, a memory resurfacing.

Dank water encased her, fouled oxygen drawn in through her gills. Nowhere to go. No way to escape it. And the ocean called and called and called, a mother crying for its lost child. Always there. Always in sight. And yet, so far beyond reach.

She pounded against the thick, aquarium glass, bubbles concealing her view as she screamed.

Nireed stiffened, eyes shooting open. Some days her time in the lab felt like a lifetime ago, others only yesterday. She'd been so scared of failing, so scared of never returning home. In the end, those fears hadn't come true.

But now, because of these fishermen and their gigantic nets and murderous designs, her home was becoming its own cage, its own death sentence, and not just for her people but all the creatures of the sea.

The Land Above the Water was not a world she wanted any part of, but sometimes circumstances required that she walk it and undergo the metamorphosis that made it possible. For her scales and fins to retreat into her body, deep beneath the dermis, one tail exchanged for two legs. For gills to flatten and seal against her neck, traded for seldom-used lungs. The webbing between her fingers, withdrawn. Claws shrunk and fangs retracted, a row of square flat-edged teeth lying underneath. All the pieces that made Nireed a daughter of the sea tucked away and hidden from view so that she could blend in among the Surface Dwellers.

Like now.

The transformation wasn't painful, but it left behind an ache in her muscles and in her gums and nail beds. But none of that compared to the ever-present longing that weighed anchor in her chest, calling her home to the deep.

A throat cleared beside her. "What was the name of the boat again?"

"The Merry Mariner." It was the first name the pod had been able to get without being caught by fishing nets.

Shorewalker typed the name into her phone. "Just sent it to Jackie. She'll be able to look up who owns it."

Damp hair twisted into a loose, unraveling braid, Nireed sat on a park bench next to Lorelei Roth in the town green overlooking Haven Cove harbor. Behind them was a bustling thoroughfare lined with shops and various eating establishments, that was as much an assault on the senses as it was an intriguing display of behavior and daily life. Waves of Surface Dwellers dipped in and out of buildings, many toting bags of wares and fragrant food that might've been pleasant if it weren't for the offensive odors accompanying them from trash and fuel, the sea breeze only bringing a short-lived reprieve. And while Nireed was used to the constant ambient sounds in the ocean, on land, the relentless stream of machinery, things Lorelei had to identify for her and explain their purpose, things like air conditioning and cars, were so much closer and louder in her ears. Only wearing squishy, orange ear sponges made it bearable.

In front of them was a gently sloped green space and an ocean walk that twisted along the coastline, meant for leisurely strolling along and observing the sea. For all the harm the Surface Dwellers did to the ocean, they also admired it.

More and more, Nireed was acclimating herself to the surface world. Not because she meant to stay, but because the humans passing by were so interesting to watch and study.

That was, when it wasn't through a wall of aquarium glass.

The more she knew—how they moved, how they spoke, what they thought—the better she could blend in, and the better she could defend her people from the ones who meant them harm.

"I'm sorry this is happening. The pod doesn't deserve this."

"Just when we started to rebuild," Nireed grumbled. "Surface Dwellers."

Even though she'd said the last bit like a curse, Lorelei smiled. "Surface Dwellers, is it now?"

Not so long ago, the pod called humans "Two-Leggers," but with how often her kin had been using their shifting abilities to take a more human form on land, it was time for a new name.

"Why the change?"

"Sometimes I have two." Nireed gestured to her legs, all traces of her silvery tail hidden. "And sometimes you don't have two. Undine agreed it's not the distinction it once was." And what the leader of their pod said or did, the rest followed suit.

"I like it."

Lorelei's smile reminded Nireed of brightening bioluminescence, or when the sun hits the water's surface, making it glitter. While her friend's life on shore often kept her away from the pod, it also made her feel like she didn't fully belong, which was the furthest from the truth, not after everything she'd done to help their community. She never seemed to like the name "Two-Leggers," probably because it was once said in the same breath as "food," so if this small change made her at least feel thought of and considered, it was a change well made.

"Killian's next offshore run is at the end of this week." Lorelei tucked a windblown strand of auburn hair behind her ear. "Anything he can bring?"

"We need food, but the usual has been used as bait."

While *The Lovely Lorelei* was a safe vessel to approach, under the current circumstances, they couldn't get close enough to tell their friends and foes apart, not when the latter was using purse seine nets.

"If I came along, I could swim down and guide you," Lorelei suggested.

"It'd be risky, but if you come, I'll follow."

A Surface Dweller might've protested the offer, something Nireed had observed among Lorelei and her friends, but that was not the merfolk way. If you said you could do something, you'd have every right to try. Insinuating someone couldn't handle the danger was an insult.

"You've risked so much for me. It's the least I can do."

"That debt has been long paid." Bracing the back of the bench, Nireed rose to her feet. While her walking had gotten better, getting up and down still left her wobbly. "If you do this, do it because you're my friend."

"Fine then. I want to help, because you're my friend, and I'm overdue for a visit."

Nireed nodded approvingly. "That's much better, Shorewalker."

"Such a stickler for phrasing."

"I don't know what that means, but I'm going to guess and say you're a stickler for guilt."

"Ouch." Lorelei grabbed her neck. "Went right for my jugular with that one."

"Someone needs to keep you honest and guilt-free."

"Yeah, yeah, yeah. I know."

The wind shifted, carrying with it a strangely familiar scent. Surprised, Nireed glanced back, but Lorelei was busy rooting for something in her purse and didn't seem to notice. Nireed had only come across it once before, and recently, in the open ocean.

The Coast Warrior.

Surprise turned to panic but she took a deep, steadying breath, this form's lungs filling with air. She was more vulnerable on land when she traded a graceful tail for wobbly legs, but she was still a mermaid and a siren, no matter what form she took. She could rip out a man's throat with a single swipe. And she could sing him into submission before he could even think to draw a weapon or shout a warning.

Tension eased.

Maybe he wouldn't recognize her out of context. But she had to know for sure.

Nireed followed the scent down the grassy slope to the ocean walk, where she found a man with dark auburn hair leaning against a railing, staring out over the harbor. She'd made allies before from little—first with Shorewalker, then with Cure Creator. If she played this right, maybe she could do so again.

A Coast Warrior ally could be useful. Someone with ties to Surface Dweller leadership and its laws. Someone with jurisdiction over the fishermen killing her people. Someone who might be able to sway his leader's decisions based on what he reported back after each mission.

It was a risk to approach the Coast Warrior in his domain, but she was used to taking those.

"Mind if I join you?"

A woman sidled up to him. Her unsteady gait, and the fact that he'd never seen her before, made him think she'd had a drink too many and might be part of the latest batch of cruise ship tourists. She wore a simple, sleeveless dress—no bra—and a messy braid fell to pieces over her shoulder, some of the dark brown strands wet and clinging.

And yet, despite the disheveled appearance, her peculiar, golden eyes were sharp and keen, chips of amber reflecting sunlight. He'd never seen irises that shade before.

"Don't see why not." Reid swept a hand toward the harbor, royal blue water dotted with all manner of fishing and recreational boats. "The view's meant to be shared."

"How generous." The smile she threw his way was fleeting, but warm, as she folded her arms across the railing. "But that wasn't a yes or no."

Literal, this one, and despite appearances, lucid. "No, I don't mind."

"Better." The corner of her mouth lifted, a teasing twinkle illuminating her strange eyes. "You come here often?"

He shrugged. "It's close to where I work. This your first time visiting?"

To his surprise, she shook her head and said, "No. I come here quite often."

Not a tourist then. "I didn't peg you for a local."

"I'm not." She drummed long, pointed nails against the railing. "Not exactly. More…regional. You?"

"Nah. Just stationed here for a few years. I'm a rescue swimmer for the Coast Guard."

There was a curious pause before her reply. "Guarding coasts? What's that about?"

A small twinge of impatience sparked, but it didn't linger. Not everyone remembered that the Coast Guard was one of the military branches, or knew it even existed, but that just wasn't something worth getting hung up on. Recognition wasn't why he joined. "It's a lifesaving service," he replied. "When people are in trouble at sea, I'm there to help."

"Is it dangerous?"

Remembering the last case, and the fishermen devoured by flesh-eating mermaids, he swallowed thickly, careful to keep his tone light as he said, "It can be, especially when there's heavy weather."

Her brow pinched as she considered this. "You risk your life for people you don't know."

"All the time."

"That's honorable." The way she said it made it sound like he'd both surprised and impressed her with a rare trait, but other first responders —firefighters, EMTs—did it every day. He wasn't special. *"You're honorable, aren't you?"*

"Just trying to keep folks alive and bring them home to their families." Reid always felt weird about accepting compliments for doing his job, but coming from this attractive woman, he felt like he'd earned something important. "What do you do?"

"Many things." She stared out over the harbor, tensing as a NOAA research vessel puttered by. Strange how she tracked its course, not once looking away until it passed them. "Usually, it's what others don't have the stomach for, the hard things that need to be done, but are worth it because it can make a real difference."

Mysterious. She sounded like either a public servant or a vigilante. Leaning a little closer, Reid considered asking if she'd like to get a cup of coffee with him and keep this conversation going. "How come I've never seen you around before?"

It was an innocent question, he thought, but her demeanor shifted, a switch flipped. Pinning him with an unblinking stare, her smile darkened, a sinister, predatory thing. "What makes you think you haven't?"

"Do I know you?" Reid didn't do flings, and if it weren't for the distinctive golden eyes flecked with amber, he might've guessed an old classmate or some other passing acquaintance. But no, he'd never seen this woman before in his life. He'd remember those eyes—eerie and mesmerizing at the same time. Impossible to look away from.

"You don't remember?" Her smile was too wide, too wicked, too knowing, and unease settled cold and heavy in his stomach. It made him want to run in the opposite direction or square up and fight, which was a hell of a way to feel about a random woman he'd just been about to ask out on a coffee date. But his animal brain demanded alertness. *Don't turn your back. Or look away.*

"You sure you've got the right guy?"

She considered this for a moment, then inhaled deeply. "Positive."

Had he met her before? He tried picturing her with different eyes.

Maybe she was wearing colored contact lenses, and that's what was throwing him off. But when he tried imagining her with brown eyes or blue, he still drew a blank.

"I'm sorry." He rubbed a hand behind his neck, offering a sheepish half smile. "Remind me. Where'd we meet?"

Her smile grew impossibly wider, showing too many teeth.

And then her eyes flashed from gold to full-blown amber.

He jerked back, cursing.

For just a second, they'd been glowing, really glowing. Like fireflies on a summer night. Or...

Bioluminescence in the deep, dark ocean.

Good god. He bit hard on his inner cheek to hold back a scream, accidentally drawing blood. He *had* seen her before. Just not here. Not on land. And not anywhere close to shore.

Fishermen screamed around him, each yanked under, one by one. Not even the best swimming training could save him. He'd never move fast enough. Never be strong enough.

Bloodred lips curled over cruel, sharp teeth made for slicing and tearing, and in her unrelenting amber stare, lay the promise of death.

Her nostrils flared, breathing in deep, smelling *him*. And on some harebrained instinct, he pressed his tongue to the cut in his mouth, as if that would stem the bleeding or throw the monster off its scent.

How was she here? And where was her tail? He'd gotten an aerial view of it glittering beneath dark water, swaying back and forth with a long, sinuous grace.

"Remember now?"

Anger flared. She knew damn well that he did.

Land was his domain, and yet, she had the upper-hand here—that, he felt in the marrow in his bones and in the cacophony of alarm bells firing off in his brain. Was this a game to her? Was he a toy to toss around and discard at whim? Did his life, and the lives of the men she killed, mean nothing? "You murdered those men."

The mermaid frowned, the wicked gleam vanishing from her gaze. "Did I? Or was it self-defense? I thought Surface Dwellers respected that."

"You sank their ship." Fear receded as his anger spiked higher, and although he lowered his voice so he couldn't be overheard by casual passersby, his words were hard. "They were vulnerable out there, barely staying afloat. They weren't a threat."

Leaning in until her face was mere inches from his, she fired back in a tone equally low and hard, "Tell that to my kin taken by their nets."

She was so close he could count the gold and brown flecks in her odd, amber eyes, and it tripped his danger sense again, now firing on all cylinders, but he dared not pull away. When sharks smelled fear and blood, they bit. A mermaid wouldn't be any different.

Firming his stance, he replied, "And why should I believe you? I don't know you."

"You didn't know them."

"I know even less about flesh-eating mermaids."

"And flesh-eating fishermen are all the same?" she snapped.

"What the hell are you talking about? Flesh-eating fishermen..."

"Do Surface Dwellers not eat meat? Why else are you out there with your boats and giant nets? Is it not to hunt the flesh of creatures?"

"Not the same thing."

"Isn't it? Your kind doesn't have exclusive rights to mind and soul. If it breathes, it feels."

No point arguing with a half-fish woman if fish had feelings. Evidently, they did.

"I see your point," he muttered begrudgingly.

She relaxed a fraction, and in that split second, something vulnerable flickered across her face. Something that looked a lot like worry, exhaustion, and fear. That wasn't the face of a senseless killer, but of someone with loved ones on the line. He'd seen such trepidation before on the faces of families living in dread of the moment a search and rescue mission became a search and recovery. "I'm not lying. We are being hunted. I'd give you proof if I had it."

"You think they're eating your kind?" The prospect made his stomach turn just as much as remembering their last search and rescue case. He'd read the research, seen the blood on her lips. The woman before him had likely helped eat those fishermen, and yet he hated that humans might be eating mermaids like her just as much.

"I don't know," she said, wrapping her arms around herself, more protective than guarded. "If they did, I'd at least understand."

A chill ran down his spine. "Why would you prefer that?"

"We're not like you, Surface Dweller. When we kill, we kill for food. Nothing gets wasted. To think that they may have died for nothing? Left to rot in some fish hold?" She shook her head. "No, that's not a comfort."

When put like that, it did sound senseless.

"Life has value and so should death." She flipped her messy, nearly non-existent braid over her shoulder, and through the dark brown strands of hair Reid glimpsed something orange stuffed inside the mermaid's ears. It took him a second to realize they were earplugs. She was hearing sensitive. "Think about that first before you judge something you don't understand."

She'd carved a sizable chip out of his skepticism, that was for sure, but he couldn't shake the feeling she might be playing him. Just saying things that he might sympathize with and sprinkling in enough honesty to make it believable. Why would a mermaid leave her home to come here, walking among people she considered her enemy? It stank of something nefarious.

"Why are you here? And how?"

She rolled her eyes. "Not that it's any of your business, but I swam here to see a friend."

Head on a swivel, he glanced all around, trying to find this so called 'friend.' Were there more mermaids here walking among unsuspecting humans? The back of his neck prickled with the uncanny feeling of being watched. He turned.

There was a woman sitting on a park bench behind them, staring intently. That, or the dark sunglasses and ball cap she wore made it seem like it. For all he knew, she could be watching the boats sail by in the harbor, but something about her posture seemed too...alert.

Whirling back on the woman beside him, he demanded, "Are there other mermaids here?"

"So suspicious." Amusement twinkled in her eyes as she cocked her head to the side, staring at him with a catlike gaze. "But as highly as you may think of your Land Above the Water, it is dry, and smelly, and I feel gross just standing here." She plucked out the front of her dress, wrinkling her nose to emphasize the discomfort of clinging, sweat-damp fabric. "So no, we don't exactly swarm your shores."

This strange creature dished out more shade than a tree. "All right, fine. So I guess you're not staying long?"

"Patrolling your coasts, Coast Warrior?"

A snort of laughter burst out of him. If he'd been drinking something, he'd have sprayed it down the front of her dress. "Coast, what?"

She narrowed her eyes.

"Are you trying to say Coast Guard?"

"Don't be rude." She sneered. "Coast Warrior, Coast Guard, how would I magically remember everything about Surface Dweller World? I don't live here."

He bit his lower lip, trying not laugh.

She glared. "My people are dying, and I'm here because I need help. Does that satisfy you?"

That sobered him. No matter how deep the well of distrust between them spanned, there was honesty in her anger and a ring of truth to her fears. He'd be a massive dick to ignore this.

"I want to help you, but to do that, I need to trust you. Can you promise you're not lying to me?"

Frustration steamed out with a sharp exhale. "I'm not."

"I'm serious. This only works if there's honesty between us."

"I know what 'don't lie' means."

"Then promise me."

"Fine," she growled, heel bouncing irritably. "I promise I won't lie to you."

"Then, I'll help you." He was probably going to regret this, but what the hell. Sitting back and doing nothing wasn't in his DNA. If that was the case, he'd have chosen a different career. "Can't promise results, but if you want, I'll look into it. See if there's anything that can be done."

She held his gaze, unblinking.

He'd been dead wrong to mistake her for a tourist.

What he'd dismissed as an ungainly, drunken gait was, in truth, an impressive feat in traversing unfamiliar terrain on seldom-used limbs, and what he'd considered dishevelment was a wildness that couldn't, no, *wouldn't* be tamed.

And the fact that she'd acquired clothing and earplugs without drawing unwanted attention to herself suggested resourcefulness, even if it was with the help of a landside ally.

It was a while before she inclined her head and said, "That'll be more than I have now." And with that, she turned and walked away, heading toward a quiet footpath that led to the sea.

The mermaid had accepted his offer.

And now he had to deliver.

God help him whatever the consequences might be if he didn't.

CHAPTER

FIVE

"You can't be serious." Nireed's older sister, Aersila, set aside the whalebone dagger she was sharpening to pin her with an eviscerating glare. They were in Aersila's workshop, lined wall to wall with all manner of tools and weaponry, and one of many rooms their pod's foreparents carved out when they'd tunneled into a great underwater sea cliff to build their city. When Aersila wasn't out hunting, or visiting her son Ryn, this was where she spent her time. Creating. "Why would you talk to the strange Surface Dweller?"

Why indeed. Nireed flicked a jar on a nearby shelf, salvaged from a shipwreck, and the motion-sensitive plankton inside that Aersila used to illuminate her space twinkled all around them, alerted by the perceived "threat."

Nireed had identified the Surface Dweller's scent almost immediately. She didn't need to speak to him, but she'd wanted to know what kind of man he was, if he was someone who might help those in need beyond the scope of his job, and the impulse to see if he'd recognize her out of context overtook all good sense. And he hadn't recognized her. Not until she'd flashed her luminescent eyes and the kind of smile even Lorelei found disquieting.

It was wicked, cruel even, toying with him like that, but it had been a test, a self-assurance.

Masking the parts of herself that made her distinctly siren, she'd walked through a crowd of humans, mirroring the way they moved and talked. Claws sheathed, eyes dimmed, teeth and scales retracted, none were the wiser.

Look how well I blend in.

Each of the sea's creatures adapted to their surroundings, evolving over time to optimize their species' survival. And as the tuna's white belly rendered it nearly invisible against the backdrop of the surface's bright light, obscuring it from the predators lurking in the depths below, so too was Nireed, evolving her ability to hide in plain sight.

Blending in meant safety and not going back into that dreaded tank.

"I thought he'd be able to help us."

"I don't see why you'd think that." Folding her arms, Aersila twitched her fins irritably.

"He's a Coast...Warrior." Now was not the time to explain how he'd corrected her. "His duty is to save people from danger."

"Surface Dwellers, maybe. Not us."

If Nireed could convince him they weren't the mindless monsters he imagined, and appeal to his built-in sense of duty, they'd have another valuable Surface-Dweller ally on their side. Time and time again, working with humans, the *right* humans, at least, greatly benefited the pod.

This was an opportunity.

"He has resources our friends don't. A sky boat for one. And if there's any group of Surface Dwellers that can stop the fishermen hunting us, it's the one he belongs to. That's what Shorewalker said."

"Shorewalker said." Aersila hissed out an angry stream of bubbles. "She's the reason you were in that tank to begin with, but at least she has ties to the ocean and our people. He doesn't."

Going with Lorelei to shore had been Nireed's choice. Staying...not so much. But her friend rectified that situation and repaid the debt tenfold. So why was Aersila so upset? "I'm here. I'm fine."

"This time. But what if he'd taken you instead? You don't know where his allegiances lay."

"I can take care of myself."

"You were gone for over a year!" Aersila slapped her palm down so hard her workbench—solid stone—cracked down the center in a hairline fissure. "I thought I'd lost you."

"You didn't, and it paid off. We're not sick anymore. And you've reunited with your son. That wouldn't have been possible otherwise."

"You're so quick to take risks, diving in with little to no information and hoping for the best. This is no different. You've no reason to trust him. Those fishermen were his own kind, and he was there to save them. He's their ally. Not yours. Not ours."

That's what Aersila thought of her efforts? That she just flitted around the Surface Dwellers, not a single thought in mind, recklessly hoping everything would work out? It was one thing for Aersila to fear for her safety and the possibility that she might disappear and never return—either taken in captivity or outright killed—but another to treat her like a helpless child.

"Give me more credit than that, sister." She signed the words with harsh, cutting motions.

Their kind dove into the deep, dark unknown every single day. How they handled its dangers, especially the ones that surprised them, was the truest test of strength and mettle. But it never kept them from diving in the first place.

"I wish you'd just leave Undine to handle this."

Nireed clenched her teeth, and with a hard slap of her tail, zipped out of Aersila's workshop, and away from her people's underwater cliffside city. There were small clusters of merfolk swimming about, but she was too angry to talk or even attempt pleasantries, and the others gave her a wide berth. Sour moods were easily detected, the scent rippling out through the water in pungent waves. It was as good as a spoken warning.

With short, quick flicks of her tail, Nireed ascended to the kelp forest above the city, its towering green stalks standing sentry, swaying gently in the current.

This was where she came to think when she wanted to be alone.

"I wish you'd just leave Undine to handle this."

If she'd stayed any longer, she just *might've* listened. All her life, she'd looked up to her fiercer, braver older sister, let her take care of them, make all the decisions, shoulder all the worry, and risk her life again and again so that the pod could survive.

But while it was once easier to let Aersila, Undine, and all the older merfolk handle things, those days were done and gone. Not only was Nireed older now, but she'd also grown into full maturity, and it was well past time they treated her like it, especially when she could, and *had*, made a difference. Hanging back, doing nothing, grated against her instincts to serve and protect their own.

How could her sister not see that? And what right did she have to lecture her on risk-taking?

Aersila was the most daring of them all. She'd solo hunted sharks, and had even taken on a trespassing giant squid, hacking at its tentacles until it decided she was too much trouble and descended further into the deep where it belonged.

And when Nireed had been in captivity for over a year, Aersila scaled a Surface Dweller vessel, the first time their kind had done so in over a century, not since wood and sails had been traded for fuel-powered engines and propellers. The noise they made was horrendous, a constant, discordant grinding that left the ears ringing for days after. Approaching just wasn't worth the agony, and yet, Aersila had endured it for her, to demand Lorelei's mate that they give Nireed back.

But her sister's most daring mission of all left her with scars deeper than skin and scale. When the pod was still brainsick and divided—the mermen controlled by violence—she risked encounter after encounter just to get pregnant, desperately trying to bolster their rapidly dwindling numbers.

Her son Ryn was the result of such efforts. And because of the sickness, and the way it affected the male children, she had to give him up to the mermen to keep the pod safe, all without hope of ever seeing him again.

So, if Aersila thought Nireed's visits to the surface and interactions with a Coast Warrior were too risky, it must be so. She didn't fault Aersila for wanting to keep her safe. Nireed, herself, had felt that way about her sister time and time again, but the difference was she'd believed in her. When someone said they could do something, they had every right to try. That was the merfolk way.

"You're so quick to take risks." Aersila's words echoed back to her. *"Leave Undine to handle this."*

Nireed slapped her tail with extra force.

Hypocrite. And what did Undine know about the Land Above the Water? Or the Surface Dwellers' customs? Nothing. Nireed could count on one hand the number of times Undine had walked dry sand and stone, and she only spoke with Shorewalker when she had to.

Besides, their leader was needed here to watch over and guide the pod, especially as more and more of their own disappeared in the fishermen's nets. Not to mention, Undine now had a little one that she couldn't be away from for long.

No. There was only one mermaid for this task.

Drifting to the edge where the open ocean and kelp forest met, Nireed stared at the wall of green before her, then at the water above, a blue so deep and dark weaker eyes might call it black.

Nireed may have been trapped in a tank for over a year, but she'd learned a lot in that time, including the Surface Dwellers' language.

They needed her to do this.

And she *would* do this. It didn't matter what Aersila said. Nireed knew her own mind, her own capabilities, and not even her once-daring sister's reticence could stop her from doing what she knew was right.

It had been only a day since Nireed had last seen Shorewalker, but her reporter friend worked quickly and should have an answer by now about who owned *The Merry Mariner*, and why they were hunting merfolk.

Nireed swam for shore.

JUST UNDER A MILE OFFSHORE, REID AND HIS AIRCREW practiced emergency scenarios. When there wasn't maintenance to do or cases to run, they were training, because in this line of work, in this service, "Semper Paratus" were the words they lived by. Drills after drills after drills until knowing what to do became second nature, so that they could keep on going even when fear and exhaustion took hold.

Overhead, the helicopter hovered, its propeller beating a wide circumference onto the ocean's surface, spraying up water.

Perez's voice crackled over the radio. "Great day for a picnic."

Blue skies, calm water, and not a cloud in sight. The perfect sunny day in coastal Maine. Cold as fuck, though. It might've been summer, but the initial shock of jumping straight into fifty-degree water never went away, no matter how many times he did this.

"Too bad we're on duty for the next twenty-four hours." That was when the unit's second aircrew team would relieve them for a few days of liberty.

"Kruetz, where's your imagination? I was gonna lay out a blanket in the breakroom, pop a couple bottles of soda..."

"Do you two want some alone time?" A glance up and Reid saw Hatcher miming stepping off the edge, boot hovering in midair. "Should I leave?"

"You wanna swim back to shore?"

"Whatever the lovebirds need."

"Shut up and get in here." Reid could practically hear the eyeroll in Perez's voice.

Tuning out their banter, he swam to where they'd dropped Oscar the training dummy, now floating helplessly several meters away in an orange Type-5 PFD. Coming up from behind and hooking him under his floppy, plastic arms, Reid kicked back and towed him toward the pickup point.

Once Oscar was loaded into the basket lift, he gave the signal, and Hatcher got the hoist going. Water dripped from the metal basket as it rose, climbing steadily toward the helicopter above.

Even though Perez was joking about the picnic, his stomach rumbled with a vengeance at the thought of food. Swimming always made him ravenous, but there'd be several more drill evolutions to run through before they could call it a day and head back to shore. Several more hours until dinner.

A bright bit of orange caught the corner of his eye, something rippling just along the surface about a hundred feet away.

Had they lost a bit of equipment?

He kicked out with his fins, swimming toward the floating object, following its path through the rolling waves, taking him further and further away from the helicopter.

"Kruetz, where are you going?" Hatcher called.

"There's something in the water."

"Leave it."

But Reid couldn't. Something of theirs or not, it wouldn't do to leave shit around, polluting the ocean. He cut a straight line toward it, propelling himself forward with smooth, efficient strokes, and watched it rise with the swell of a wave, then dip down, disappearing from sight. He waited for the next swell to bring it back into view.

It never did.

Already icy water grew colder, some glacial current making him shiver, and the back of his neck prickled, each of the little hairs standing on end. He scanned the surface, looking for the lost object when something bumped his leg. Shark, seal, harbor porpoise, he couldn't tell, but fear dug in its claws when Perez began shouting over the radio, "Kruetz, abort, abort! There's a..."

Something grabbed onto his ankles with a punishing grip and yanked him under, the rest of the radio transmission lost to garbled static. Water rushed up around him, a pair of glowing amber eyes meeting his, maybe two feet from his face. *Jesus, fuck!* He lurched away, kicking hard, but the creature had already let him go.

He burst above the waterline, coughing and sputtering.

The mermaid.

She popped to the surface next to him, thrusting something orange and cylindrical against his chest. "I found this," she said brightly, strangely both proud and mischievous. "Thought it might be yours."

He caught it—a water rescue throw bag, something he used all the time when working swift water rescue in Michigan. But this one belonged to the Haven Cove fire department, judging by the emblem printed on its side. It wouldn't have taken much for a current to carry it out here, only a mile from shore.

It wouldn't have taken much for the mermaid to drown him either. "Why the hell did you yank me under like that?"

She cocked her head to the side, blinking slowly. "I had to get your attention."

"You could've drowned me!"

"Could've. But I didn't."

He slapped the water. "Dammit. That's not funny!"

Confusion, then concern pinched her brow. "I'm not laughing. And I wasn't trying to drown you either."

"Then if you wanted my attention, you could've just popped above the surface and waved. You didn't need to grab me."

"I'm sorry." She dipped her head, but more in acquiescence than shame. "That wasn't my intent. I wanted to prove a point."

"And what point was that?" This was her domain, that much was terrifyingly clear. It didn't need to be proved over and over again.

"That if I was a mindless creature driven to murder, you'd be dead twice over. But I've no reason to protect my own from you, do I?" The question was casual, but there was an unmistakable wary pointedness to it that struck him. It sounded a lot like uncertainty. Like *he* might be the threat in this situation and leaving him alive a risk she might one day come to regret.

That zapped his anger. "Are you...afraid of me?"

"Should I be?" It wasn't mockery he heard, but more of that wariness. She *was* afraid. Maybe not of him specifically, but of what he could do, and that disarmed him further.

"I don't know," he admitted quietly.

She nodded once, dimming. "I guess that's fair. You've your own to protect, too."

She sounded so resigned, he'd the odd desire to reassure her. They weren't enemies per se, but they weren't allies either. And yet, some weird, disturbing part of him missed her smile now that it was gone—

wicked thing though it was—and he missed, too, the mischief illuminating her eyes.

"You think I'm a monster," she continued, holding his gaze captive. "And I am. But not without reason."

"I don't want to be your enemy." The words just spilled out of him. No thought, no consideration, just plain, unvarnished truth, even though it didn't make a lick of sense. He should still be pissed at her for yanking him under, but when a small, half smile lifted the corner of her lips, all he felt was relief.

"Then don't be."

The radio crackled. "Kruetz, you good down there?" It was Perez.

"Yes, fine. Just give me a minute."

"Make it a quick one."

"Kruetz," the mermaid repeated. "Is that your name?"

He shook his head. "That's my family name. My name's Reid."

Her smile grew, some of that mischievousness returned, along with a healthy dose of amusement, and it was damnably infectious. It wrestled a smile out of him too.

"What?"

"Nothing."

"Don't hold out on me now. My name means something ridiculous in mermaid, doesn't it?"

"Not at all." Her smile softened, almost warm. "My name's Nireed."

*Well, I'll be...*He was just a couple letters off from sharing a name with a mythological creature. "That's pretty," he trailed, and immediately wanted to punch himself. There was no way of paying that kind of compliment without sounding conceited or trite. "I mean, it's..."

Prettier than mine? For fuck's sake, he was hopeless.

With a playful flick of her tail, she splashed water at his face. "See you around, *Reid*." And then she was gone, disappearing beneath the waves.

He kicked his legs faster, half expecting her to yank him under again, but she didn't. It was just him out here now.

A barrage of teasing awaited him inside the helicopter.

"Get her number while you were down there?" He could practically hear the smirk in Perez's voice.

"What? No."

"She was totally flirting with you."

"Shut up. No, she wasn't."

"Oh yes, she was."

"You're delusional."

Perez snickered, adding an evil lilt at the end, but otherwise let it drop.

They were halfway back to shore when Hatcher clasped his shoulder. "You good, man?"

Unlike their pilot, the dropmaster looked shaken. Gray even. "Yeah, just freezing my balls off."

"When she yanked you under, I thought we'd lost you. Just like those fishermen."

And he had, too, for one heart-stopping second. "She was messing with me. Didn't mean anything by it." He wasn't sure if he was defending her to reassure Hatcher or to soften the man's view of mermaids. "We're not a threat to her."

"What do you mean?" Hatcher's pale, blond brows furrowed. "'We' this crew? Or 'we' the Coast Guard?"

"Both."

"Kruetz's new friend just wants Nautic's fishermen to stop killing her family."

"She's not my…"

Hatcher's cheeks flamed red. "She could've killed him!"

One hundred percent true, but she didn't. "It's all right," Reid said, trying to reassure Hatcher. "She didn't hurt me."

"It's not all right! Eight people were killed by mermaids this week, and you easily could've been the ninth. How are y'all so calm about that?"

Reid lifted his hands for the dropmaster to see, both trembling, and not from cold. "Do I look all right to you?"

Hatcher buried his face in his hands, groaning. "Perez, you freaking out too?"

"Nope," she said a little too cheerfully, emphasizing the 'p' with a pop. "I'm great."

"What's wrong with you?"

"Forgive me if I'm more suspicious of a corporate fishing company than I am of the woman who lives in the sea."

"Yeah, well, the corporate company hasn't killed anybody," Hatcher shot back. "And the people they hire are just doing their jobs."

"You so sure about that? Kruetz's mermaid says they have killed people. *Her* people."

"If they're just following orders…"

This needed gentle correcting. "Following orders doesn't excuse someone of wrongdoing."

"That," Perez agreed.

Slumping in his seat with an aggravated sigh, Hatcher stared at the cabin ceiling. "We saw people die. But fuck me for being concerned, I guess." He drummed his fingers in an erratic, impatient rhythm along his knee. "Let's, for argument's sake, say I believe mermaid's telling the truth. That doesn't mean I trust her with my life." He pinned Reid with a hard look. "Or yours."

CHAPTER

SIX

THE COAST WARRIOR'S NAME WAS REID.

And an incredibly strong swimmer for a human. While he'd never match the sheer speed or grace the merfolk had, Nireed could appreciate the brute strength and willpower of his movements—arms knifing through the water in quick, efficient strokes, legs kicking out behind him, the strange black fins he wore on his feet propelling him faster while also conserving energy.

For all intents and purposes, his body wasn't designed for the sea. In fact, it was locked in a constant battle not to drown, and yet, he looked so at home among the waves. Almost at home with them as she.

An odd feeling washed over her. It was true she'd meant to prove a point, but watching his legs sway back and forth, muscles clenching, then unclenching, his dual fins waving at her from above, she wanted to touch him. To bring him into the water with her so she could look into his eyes without having to squint against the sun's too bright light. Eyes a shade of brown like the land he walked. Such a color didn't exist in the ocean, among her kind.

"I don't want to be your enemy."

Hope ticked in her chest. He'd said it so softly, and his shocked expression afterward told her his words were genuine. He hadn't meant to say them and that made them more believable.

Aersila doubted her judgment, and that stung more than salt in an open wound, but this affirmed what Nireed felt in her gut—that he could be won over. They needed answers. They needed proof. And they needed Surface Dweller leadership to act.

Reid was their way in.

Nireed squeezed the water from her hair, then shrugged into the dress she kept wedged between two rocks on shore. It felt weird and itchy and constricting, but blending in was more important than comfort, so she'd hidden several such dresses, scattering them along the coast. It was good to have options, multiple entry points to the Land Above the Water.

But this one was the safest.

Nakedness concealed, she hiked up the private cove's sandy beach to the abode her friend shared with her mate and knocked on the front door. Heavy footsteps approached. A moment later, the door opened, a tall man with wavy, silver-flecked brown hair standing on the other side.

"Nireed," he said, the corners of his eyes crinkling as he smiled. "Come in. She's just upstairs."

After quickly brushing sand from the soles of her feet outside, Nireed ducked in.

"Lorelei!" Killian called up a spiraling set of stairs. "You've got a visitor." Then to Nireed, he said, "Hungry?"

Her stomach growled on cue.

"One can of Spam coming right up."

Nireed sat down at their kitchen table while Killian rooted around the pantry. *The Merry Mariner's* fishermen had been enough to feed the whole pod for a day. Now she was hungry enough to take on a whole haunch of thigh meat all by herself, but her friends didn't need to know that.

Lorelei bounded down the steps. "I just got off the phone with Jackie."

"What did she find?"

"*The Merry Mariner*, and the factory ship it supplies, is owned by a company called Nautic Select Seafoods."

Killian retreated from the pantry, cracking open a can. "Those assholes?" He slid the delicacy across the table into Nireed's awaiting hands and offered her a fork. She accepted it and promptly dug in. It wasn't her preferred manner of eating, but it was good practice for her more public outings among the Surface Dwellers.

"You've run into them?" Lorelei asked, taking a chair across from Nireed.

"No one's been able to prove it, but they pull some shady shit. They blaze in and out of the harbor, plowing over lobster pots, cutting the lines, and the owner loses all that equipment. That's $500 to $600 a pop inshore, figuring traps, buoy, line, and the catch. But offshore, when there's twenty-five traps to a trawl line, it's easily $6,000, and there's plenty of those stories." Killian slipped into the seat next to his mate, joints creaking as he sat. "A captain I know swears they bribe the fisheries official too. He's a bit of a government conspiracy theorist, so I'd take what he says with a grain of salt, but if it's true, that means they're catching things they shouldn't, or in quantities above regulation. Either way it shakes out, Nautic's pushing out what's left of the small, independent fishing companies."

Nireed narrowed her eyes. "Have they hurt you?"

"We don't fish in the same area. At least, not anymore. But they do have a foot in lobster, and another in everything else."

Killian's trawling boat, *The Lovely Lorelei*, fell into the "everything else" category.

Lorelei nodded along. "Jackie got a hold of the registry and says they moved their purse seiners into your old zone about a few months back."

"Yeah." He rubbed a hand behind his neck. "It's a great fishing area. Never went home without a full hold, but ever since Lila began lobbying to have mermaid territory declared a marine sanctuary, we backed out of there."

"We were willing to share," Nireed interjected, fork hovering in front of her mouth. "But appreciate your support nonetheless."

"Nautic wouldn't have those moral reservations, which leads to

Jackie's theory." Lorelei met Nireed's eyes, expression grim. "She thinks they're hunting merfolk, because without you, there's no reason to have the area declared a marine sanctuary. And without a marine sanctuary, they can keep fishing where it's most lucrative."

Rage bubbled within. So her people were being killed for wasteful greed. It didn't surprise her, but she'd still hoped for another reason.

Lorelei cleared her throat, staring pointedly at her hand.

Nireed looked down and found that she'd bent the fork in half. "Sorry." She blushed, setting the ruined utensil aside.

"It's a theory." Lorelei blinked, continuing, "A very strong theory. But what we need is proof. That's the only way we can take them down."

"Enough to take down a corporation?" Killian shook his head. "That's going to be hard to get. And even with evidence, guys like those have deep pockets and the best lawyers."

Nireed rubbed her forehead. She recognized most of those words, but their meaning was lost. Still, there was something she could contribute to this conversation. "I might have someone who'll help."

Both Lorelei and Killian looked her way, but it was Lorelei who asked, "The man you were talking to the other day?"

Nireed nodded. "He's Coast Guard. If they get involved..."

Lorelei lit up. They'd spoken about this in theory before—that if anyone could ride out a lengthy Surface Dweller rules battle, it was their leadership. Or "government" as Lorelei called it. "If they've got a thumb on the pulse of this..."

Killian met Nireed's eyes. "How'd you meet him?" She couldn't tell if he sounded impressed or worried.

"*The Merry Mariner*," was all she said, and his expression darkened, the meaning conveyed more than well enough.

"Has he agreed to help us?" Lorelei hedged the question. And really, Nireed couldn't blame her for being uncertain. That shoreside conversation had gotten tense at several points, especially the part when Reid had called her a murderer.

"He seems open to it," she answered truthfully. While he said he'd look into the matter, and Nireed believed he would follow through, because of his sense of honor and drive to help people, it was too soon to know for sure, and she didn't want to give Shorewalker false hope.

Or herself.

"We'll do what we can in the meantime." Lorelei took Killian's hand, threading their fingers together. When their eyes met, time seemed to slow, and something eased between them as they appeared to find strength and comfort in one another.

Nireed marveled at their open affection, all the little ways they sought each other out, always in each other's orbit. A brief look, a touch, a smile. She'd never really paid much attention to such things before, but seeing how the two pledged their lives to each other in every moment of every day, it showed that real, romantic love was possible for their kind. And this was what it could look like. Something more than just two bodies colliding together again and again until a mutual end was achieved.

A deep ache split open her chest, swallowing her thoughts. It was her duty to the pod to find a mate and bolster their numbers, she knew that, and she genuinely wanted both of those things, but there weren't many unattached merfolk left who could give her a baby. There had been someone a year ago, not long after she'd been freed from the tank, but it was a brief arrangement that hadn't resulted in children, and now he was mated to another.

So many of the dedicated mating pairs in their pod, or groups in a couple of cases, began as short, task-oriented affairs, it was true, but that wasn't the case now. Partners shuffled around, eventually finding their one true mate, or the original arrangements evolved into permanence. And yet even then, something was missing from these pairings. More of a rote process than a relationship.

Fuck. Impregnate. Carry to term. Give birth and raise. Repeat.

There was respect, yes. Kind courting gestures. Dedication and help rearing the little ones. But love? Affection? Not like this. At least, not that she'd seen in her lifetime.

And she wanted more.

"What's your acquaintance's name?"

Nireed snapped to attention. "Reid Kruetz."

Surprise rolled off Shorewalker, flooding Nireed's senses. "Kruetz?" She repeated shakily.

"What is it?" Killian leaned in, draping an arm across the top of Lorelei's chair, all worry and protection.

"Nothing, never mind. Just not a name you hear every day."

While Killian didn't press any further, Nireed could smell the lie. What secrets was Shorewalker keeping?

REID SPENT HIS SPARE DOWNTIME BETWEEN CASES COMBING through Nautic's incident reports and witness statements accusing them of sabotaging their fishing competition—as well as news articles and blogs about the corporation.

He had to dig for it, but he eventually found dirt buried underneath all the latest news headlines about *The Merry Mariner*. The Coast Guard had released that merfolk were involved, and it was being called a massacre at sea by national media.

As Reid sifted through the files, making himself a tally of the reported incidents, a recording of a recent press conference played on his computer. The video was just getting started, a spokeswoman for Nautic Select Seafoods addressing the gathered crowd of reporters. But when she began introducing Nautic's CEO, Hugh Fairfield, Reid looked up, watching as a middle-aged, silver-haired white man entered the camera frame with practiced ease.

Fairfield wore beige slacks, a white-collared shirt, no tie, and an off-the-rack navy blazer. Its one-size-fits-most cut was the opposite of the CEO's usual polished, well-tailored styles. If Fairfield was going for a salt of the earth look to appeal to a working-class audience, mission accomplished.

"Eight hardworking fishermen were ruthlessly murdered this week." The man gripped the edges of the podium, bowing his head for dramatic effect. But Reid saw past the somber expression, had already caught the cold, calculated glint in his eyes. It could easily be mistaken for empathetic outrage, but high-powered men like this cared more about their company's bottom line than the people at the bottom of the corporate food chain. As vicious and lethal as the mermaids were, this man was a *shark*.

"Their families are devastated," Fairfield continued, voice rising in fervor as he lifted his eyes to the cameras. "No one wants to say that these sea people are hostile and pose a threat to national security. So, I'll say it. This was a massacre, not the equivalent of a 'shark attack.' And to try comparing it to one is a gross misrepresentation of what happened. Animals aren't malicious, people are, and these are people we're dealing with here."

Fairfield spewed more venomous rhetoric, but after about a minute, Reid swapped to a different video, unable to listen to that man's shit a second longer.

The incident had garnered enough attention that the State Governor made a public address, "mourning the loss of Maine fishermen" and promising to "investigate the incident." Behind-the-scenes, the administration asked the Coast Guard to increase their patrols in the Gulf of Maine.

Word on the Coast Guard grapevine, stations up and down the East Coast were being flooded by calls from scared, jumpy people reporting "mermaid sightings," none of which could be verified. All incensed and on edge from the news.

Reid returned to his reading.

There was speculation by some that Nautic's CEO had a toe in protected species trafficking and other unseemly underground activities. But "rumors" were where they stopped, and nothing concrete had ever surfaced that would lead anyone to take real action.

With the amount of time Nautic had spent fishing in merfolk territory these last few months, he bet they didn't like that it was going to be declared a marine sanctuary. Were they milking the area for all that it was worth before that happened? And merfolk had become the unfortunate bycatch?

Or was there something more going on? Something intentional and sinister. It wasn't much of a stretch to assume that someone like

Fairfield would take one look at a beautiful, mythical creature and see dollar signs.

Hatcher entered the room with a newspaper and thermos of coffee in hand. He paused to peer over Reid's shoulder before plopping down at a desk beside him, concern etched onto his face. "Those Nautic's files?"

"Yeah." Reid rubbed his eyes, aching from screen strain. He really wasn't a desk job kind of guy.

"You know that's CGIS's job, right?"

"Something's just not sitting right." He clicked over to a web browser. "It's bugging me."

"Is it bugging you because it's actually bugging you, or because *she* asked you to look into it?" No doubt who Hatcher meant. The biting way he said "she" said all.

"Can't it be both?"

Hatcher sighed. "I guess. Are you finding anything interesting?"

"Nothing concrete, but Nautic's definitely not squeaky clean."

"What corporation is?" Hatcher sipped his coffee, then leaned forward, squinting at the blog post Reid had pulled up on screen. "A rumored illegal aquarium fish market seller," Hatcher read out loud. "A mermaid would be quite the prize."

"That's what I was thinking."

Perez swept into the room. "What are we gossiping about?"

"Nautic." Both Reid and Hatcher answered simultaneously.

"That they're probably into illegal market stuff," Reid clarified. "And would see mermaids as an enticing business venture."

Perez rolled her eyes. "Well, duh."

Ignoring the jab, Reid jerked his head toward the newspaper in Hatcher's hand. "That today's paper? Can I see it?"

The dropmaster drew it closer to his person, grip tightening. "It is. Why?"

"I just want to see if they did a follow up on *The Merry Mariner* story."

Hatcher wheeled his desk chair back a pace. "It's probably online too."

"I'll give it back." When Hatcher didn't so much as twitch, Reid added, "What's up with you?"

"Nothing."

"Squirrelly much?" Perez reached for the paper, presumably to take it by force, but Hatcher skirted around her and handed it over, grumbling that he wanted it right back.

On the front page of the *Haven Cove Daily*, above the fold, was a special interest piece written by Jackie Gaten on the fishing crew who died. All eight of their pictures were laid out in a grid and cropped into headshots, either taken from family photos or social media profile pictures. Reid's eyes snagged on the first photo and the over-tan man smiling up at him with salt-and-pepper hair and a prominent scar that sliced up from the right-side corner of his upper lip to his cheek. The last man Reid had failed to save.

He checked the caption below. *Flick Rockland, Captain.*

The duty phone rang. Perez snatched it up. "Lieutenant Perez speaking." She paused, listening to the person speaking on the other end. "Yes, sir." More speaking. "Yes, sir. I'll get the helicopter ready." Then she hung up.

To the rest of them, she said, "We've got another case."

Hatcher noticeably perked up. "What is it?"

"I'll tell you on the way."

Reid left the newspaper behind. Reading the tribute piece would have to wait.

CHAPTER
SEVEN

"It came out of nowhere."

On the helicopter floor, the captain of the *Savvy Rose* huddled under emergency thermal blankets with his wet and shivering crew. One by one, Reid had plucked them from frigid water, where they'd bobbed among their fishing vessel's wreckage, and now his team was racing the borderline hypothermic men back to shore.

"It pinged on radar, but all we saw was darkness." Lips blue, the captain's teeth chattered as he spoke. "Just getting closer and closer. It wasn't until she was right on top of us that we finally saw her. No radios, no lights, and the transponder was off. Ran us right over."

Illegal, every bit of it. No lives lost this time, thank God, but the boat was gone, and the livelihood of these small, independent fishermen sunk right along with it.

"Anything you can tell me about the ship? Any identifying information?"

"About two-hundred feet long. Was hard to see in the dark, and it happened wicked fast, but it looked like the name on the hull was *The Seriphus*." Several of the other men nodded in agreement.

Surprise stole his next breath.

Nautic's factory ship and crew were getting their hands dirty.

The Coast Guard had several incident reports on file naming other boats in Nautic's fleet suspected of either sabotaging, or outright destroying, other fishermen's equipment. But the factory ship wreaking havoc itself—that was a first.

"Those greedy sonsofbitches have been going after us," one of the crew members said, volume rising.

But why? To push out smaller, local competition like these guys and monopolize the region's fishing industry? It was just the sort of shady shit Reid was coming to suspect wasn't mere conspiracy.

"How much more are they going to get away with before somebody does something about it? Is it when one of us is killed?" He didn't namedrop the Coast Guard, or "the government" at large, but it was clear as day that was what he meant.

"We're building a case." It wasn't much of an assurance, but it was all he could say. A handful of incidents weren't nearly enough to go to court. They needed dozens more, and a crushing amount of evidence, when filing a lawsuit against a corporation. It was time consuming and tedious, and a whole lot more shit had to go wrong to ultimately stop it.

Infuriating as hell and of no comfort to those affected by Nautic's shady activities.

The captain snorted. "Building a case, my ass. Tell Big Brother I want my tax money back so I can buy myself a new boat."

If only.

Back on shore, emergency responders awaited dockside to take the fishing crew to the hospital. Once they were squared away, Reid and his team returned to Haven Cove Airport for debriefing, some log entry, and sleep. As far as missions go, this one went well—a textbook SAR case where everyone made it home. But really anything that wasn't losing an entire crew to people-eating mermaids, categorically speaking, was a shining success.

At daybreak, Reid saw Hatcher coming out of the head, tucking a flip phone into his pants pocket.

"What's with the dinosaur tech?" Reid teased, going to the sink to brush his teeth.

Hatcher took the sink beside him, washing his hands. "Dropped my smartphone in a puddle."

"Shit luck, fumble fingers."

"Shut up."

After morning quarters, they were released from duty for the next few days, the unit's second aircrew coming in to take the next shift.

And Reid was more than ready for the break.

In a short period of time, he had to come to terms with critical mission failure and a mermaid situation that was far from cut and dry. Everything would've been so much easier to get straight in his head if their motives had been purely vicious. But as much as he was a simple man who liked simple answers, he hated convenient ones more.

Sliding a full-face black helmet over his head, he mounted his motorcycle, the engine roaring to life beneath him. Its steady rumbling drowned out all other sounds, right along with the turmoil fogging his mind. In minutes, he was shooting down the coastal highway, dense pine forests on either side, occasionally opening to reveal glimpses of the ocean and mountains beyond.

He drove to a shaded, empty picnic grove, someplace quiet by the water, but that still had cell service, and dialed his therapist. He'd scheduled the call while on duty. It wasn't for everyone, but Reid just couldn't imagine doing the work he did without one.

He'd found the little seaside grove shortly after moving to Haven Cove. Any time he had a tough case, he'd come here, hash things out for about forty-five minutes, and either go for a hike or swim afterward to further process and decompress, then return home with a six-pack of beer.

Maybe that made him frighteningly well-adjusted, but he just didn't fuck around when it came to his headspace. His only uncle was an alcoholic, so he never felt comfortable beelining it to booze to make himself feel better.

The line connected, a low, easy voice answering on the other side. "Hello, Reid. How are you?"

Alan, his therapist, was retired Air Force, which made talking to him so much simpler. All the rote military things he didn't have to explain—

the culture, the expectations, the rigorous demands, and command structure—allowed them to get to the meat of his troubles sooner.

"I've been better."

"Want to tell me what happened?"

Exhaustion fell over him in a way it hadn't even when they got *Savvy Rose*'s distress call, after hours of research and computer work. Between debriefing command, the reports, and filling in gaps for his team, he was sick of explaining everything again and again. If only he could just offload the memories, dump them in a big file folder, and hand them over to be picked apart and assessed while he lay on this picnic table bench and took a nap. But that wasn't how this shit worked and retelling it for the umpteenth time was all a part of the process.

"We had two cases." He sighed heavily, feeling his body sag. "The second was textbook, everybody made it home. But the first…"

Alan waited patiently, allowing him to get it out at his own pace.

"We lost them. Every single one."

"Didn't get there in time?"

"No. We did." Now for the spectacularly weird icing on the cake. "But we had company." Reid explained that he'd been in the water with flesh-eating mermaids, had been there when they devoured the crew, right beneath him.

When he finished, Alan drew in a deep breath. "That must've been hard watching them go under like that."

"I felt helpless. All that training, all those hours spent doing PT, and what good did any of it do?"

"Seeing people die is one of the hardest things a service member can experience. But your training wasn't for nothing. It kept you alive."

"Wasn't training that did that. She let me live."

"Okay, well, let's think about it this way. Elite training makes you damn good at what you do, but it doesn't make you a superhero. Did you feel like you did everything you could under these unique circumstances?"

"No." Reid rubbed the back of his neck. He hated sounding difficult, but it was the truth. "I feel like I should've been able to do more."

"Run me through standard procedure and what you would've done differently."

And that was why he liked this guy. Every time they ran through this exercise, Reid either realized there was nothing he could've changed, or if there was, he came out of it knowing what to fix and how to manage the boatload of guilt and self-loathing for fucking it up the first time. It was a painful process, but it worked.

No pain, no gain.

And this time wasn't any different.

"What you do under normal circumstances is hard. Facing a supernatural force? No use comparing apples to oranges. You're not a superhero, Reid. Don't try to be one."

"There's more." Piece by thorny piece, he unspooled complex truth after complex truth, a bigger picture so massive, he could barely wrap his head around it.

"That's a lot to unpack, and we'll work through it, but my most immediate concern—do you feel like your life is in danger? You said you've seen the mermaid twice since the incident."

"No." The answer whooshed out so fast it surprised him. She was scary as fuck, yes, and had him completely outmatched, but she'd never tried to kill him. And she'd been vulnerable, too, in her own way. Misunderstood, afraid, taking huge risks for the greater good. Trying to save...trying to save her own people. "She's just like…"

Just like me.

"You've had a lightbulb moment—I can hear it in your voice. What've you realized?"

"Our responsibilities, our goals, they're the same."

Fresh off the case, he'd been wary of giving Nireed his sympathy, but all that was different were their methods, and even those weren't completely unfamiliar when he thought about the other military branches. Nireed was one of the ocean's denizens, forced to play the part of a soldier, and the fishermen hunting her people were the invaders. No wonder Perez seemed pissed when he couldn't put that together. When he was so stuck on seeing Nireed as the monster.

It had been shocking, traumatizing even, witnessing that

annihilation, but of course it was. He didn't see that kind of action. He didn't take lives, he saved them, and he'd effectively dropped into a war zone that night. And that, he could wrap his head around.

"We're more similar than I realized."

He could hear the smile in his therapist's voice when he said, "You came to that conclusion sooner than I thought you would. Good work."

Reid let out a shaky laugh, feeling fizzy and punch-drunk. "Damn. Well, I'm glad I'm not delusional for thinking that."

"Not at all."

When the call ended, hiking felt like a better escape than a swim, so he marched off into the trees, allowing the wilderness to swallow him whole for a day. Steady ground beneath his feet and a quiet path, broken only by birdsong and the scuff of his boots against rock and root, had a way of absorbing his cares.

That evening, Reid went home feeling lighter, better. Maybe not one hundred percent, but well enough he'd probably get some sleep tonight.

He stared out at the orange-cast horizon from the stern of his houseboat, legs dangling over the diving platform. He pulled a long swig from the neck of his beer bottle, some local brew he picked up at the grocery store on the way home.

He was anchored with several others in a quiet inlet, but between his odd schedule and theirs, he rarely saw his neighbors. One was a charge nurse who often picked up overtime shifts, and the other was a retired fisherman who spent more time at the bars than was strictly healthy.

"Is this your boat?"

Nireed popped from the water, a disturbingly beautiful jack-in-the-box. He nearly jumped out of his skin, scrambling back from the ledge, and spilling his beer in the process. Not so much as a stray ripple or subtle flash of silver scales. The effortless stealth was as impressive as it was terrifying, but damn, why'd she always have to scare him shitless? Some warning would be nice.

She stared at him unblinkingly, her eerie, lambent eyes made liquid amber in the light of the setting sun. Such dangerous promise in those eyes. But of what, he didn't know anymore, not when she'd no intention of killing him.

If not his life, then what?

He growled, probably a little more harshly than was necessary, but his fear was talking. "Where the fuck did you come from?"

She arched a brow, gesturing to the wide expanse of the ocean.

He huffed, wiping a beer-drenched hand dry on his shorts. *Smartass.* "How'd you find me?"

"I was around." She shrugged. "Picked up your scent. Is this your boat? It's very small."

It was small—smaller than he would've liked long-term—but he suddenly felt rather defensive of it. "I don't need a lot of space."

She eyed the narrow doorway warily, like it might bite her. "You don't?" The crease along her brow deepened, and if Reid wasn't mistaken, it looked a lot like concern. "Sky boat's small too." Glancing between him in his home, she began to wring her hands.

And that was when it hit him. She wasn't criticizing his home. Tight spaces freaked her out, and compared to a wide, open ocean, he could see how a compact space might feel claustrophobic.

His reply was gentle. "We call that a helicopter."

The mermaid repeated the word flawlessly.

"That's where I work. This"—he patted the deck fondly— "is my home."

"Does it have a name?"

The question took him off guard. It was tradition to name boats, but he hadn't named this one. Couldn't come up with something that fit.

She folded her arms across the diving platform, right next to where he sat. "I didn't get my name until my fifth year. Sometimes these things take time."

Was she trying to reassure him? It was unexpectedly touching. "What were you called before Nireed?"

"Starfish."

Shit, that was adorable. He set down his drink, stretching his arms wide open. "Well, you found me, Starfish."

She rested her cheek on top of her arms, watching him intently. "Do you want me to go?"

Something loosened deep inside his chest. Even with her sharp edges

—the claws and teeth made for ripping and tearing—there was something soft and sweet about how she laid in repose against his boat, orange and silver tailfin fanning out behind her. A girl next door kind of vibe. He shouldn't be comforted by that, knowing what he did of her, but he found himself saying anyway, "You can stay."

Her answering smile was warm, pointed teeth and all.

"You come this way often?" he asked, remembering she'd mentioned a friend in one of their previous encounters.

"Every few days. What with everything that's going on."

He whistled long and low. It was about sixty nautical miles from here to mermaid territory. "That's a long way."

She shrugged again. "I move fast."

It was in line with what other sea creatures could do. Dolphins could migrate up to eighty miles a day, whales one hundred. Still, her range was damn impressive.

"Is it hard, being away from home so often?"

Maine took his breath away, and there was no denying he lucked out being stationed here, but he missed Michigan and his mom and dad. Doing what he did, it was hard to go home, and he often missed holidays and birthdays and other life events. While he didn't regret his career choice for a second and had made plenty of new friends along the way, it hurt sometimes living far away from the place and people that raised him.

"It is, and it isn't." She sighed. "Sometimes I don't want to be needed, and here, no one needs me." A dark look crossed her face. "That is, when they don't know what I am."

"What do you mean?"

"Surface Dwellers like knowing things, and I'm an unknown. But if I blend in, I'm free."

It was a cryptic response, but one thing was clear: Nireed was risking everything to be here, to save her people. Her life, her freedom. Nautic's fishermen likely wanted to poach creatures like her, and the science community wanted to study another live mermaid. And yet, she was still here, trying to make a difference.

He stared at her in awe.

He had the forest, and its towering pines, when he needed to carve out space for himself, but what did Nireed have? Was there some place she could go when she needed to be alone with her thoughts, when the responsibility of saving her kind weighed heaviest? Or did she live her life raw and exposed, always on the lookout for danger, always fighting for survival, never afforded the luxury of having peace of mind?

He imagined taking her to his favorite spot and leading her down the path that wove in and out between the trees. To see her take in the forest for the first time, moving about his world on unsteady, but determined legs. The terrain, knotted with rocks and roots, could be treacherous to the inexperienced, but if she tripped, caught onto his arm, he wouldn't let her fall.

She fidgeted, eyes narrowing. "Why are you staring at me like that?"

He blinked, then shook his head. Shit, how'd he go from sheer terror to wanting to take a mermaid on a hike? He quickly changed the subject, waving a hand in front of his face, and teased, "Thought you said it was gross and smelly here."

"And dry." She shuddered, then splashed water onto herself using her fins. "I don't know how you live like this."

"I like the water, but I wasn't made for it."

"I was made for water but can adapt to land." She shrugged. "And besides, it's like home to you."

"That's perceptive."

She smirked. "Why else would you choose to fall out of a Hel i cop ter and live on a tiny boat?"

"I don't fall, I jump. There's a difference."

"If you say so, Coast Warrior." She winked, flicking a bit of water his way.

Hot damn. He hadn't wanted to believe it, but Perez was right. This was flirting. A man-eating mermaid was flirting with him. "I'm a Coast *Guard*." God dammit. What a spectacular time for his brain to short circuit. "I mean, a Coast Guardsman."

"I know," she said, looking pleased as punch. "But I like Coast Warrior better."

When she said it like that, like something that impressed her, maybe it didn't sound so silly after all. Maybe he even liked it. "That something you're into, a man in uniform?"

She appraised him openly, thoughtfully, and as her eyes tracked their way along his body, he felt his cheeks warm. From previous encounters, he should've remembered that she usually took what he said literally, and this had been as good as an invitation to check him out.

He was just wearing basic Coast Guard PT gear—a light gray T-shirt and blue gym shorts—nothing particularly flattering. It occurred to him then that she might not know the distinction, that "uniform" and "clothes" weren't quite the same thing, because the way her gaze lingered covetously on each stretch of exposed muscle, one would think he was decked out in dress blues.

"Merfolk don't wear clothes," she said, continuing her slow perusal, and it took all his willpower not to let his gaze dip. "We don't hide ourselves. That's not our way."

While she was mostly hidden by the boat, he had an unhampered view of her sleek, bare back, its ripped muscle, and glistening, sea-kissed skin. *God help me. Don't spring a boner two feet away from her face.*

"And yet," she said, tugging lightly on the hem of his shorts. "Not everything needs to be knowable. It makes me wonder." The curve of her claws grazed his thigh, sending an unexpected thrill up his spine. Was she saying what he thought she was saying? That she thought about what he looked like under his clothes?

Nope. None of that. His dick wasn't going to so much as twitch at the possibility. Leaning forward, he used an arm to block her view as he subtly pressed the heel of his hand into his crotch. Coming off an extremely stressful duty period, blowing off some steam made for a nice fantasy, but he wasn't going to complicate an already complicated situation by getting horny for the mermaid at the center of it all. He had better self-control than that.

"Not missing anything." He plucked out the front of his shirt, trying to get some fresh air on his skin. "Once you've seen one, you've seen them all."

Withdrawing her hand, Nireed returned to her repose. "There's nothing in the ocean like you." She said it so softly, he almost hadn't heard her.

That he might be as much of a wonder to her as she was to him was such an unexpected thought. But it made sense too. They were creatures from two different worlds, as foreign and alien to one another as the universe around them. While their species shared some anatomy similarities, when considering all their other differences, he might as well be from outer space.

"I guess we have a lot to learn about each other, don't we?"

"This has been a good start."

A start. So much promise and possibility in that word. Much more than "let's not be enemies" or even "can we be allies." She didn't just want his help, she wanted to get to know him, and that meant there was something here that could be nurtured, if he just made the leap.

He studied her open, hopeful expression, from the sparkle in her eyes to her round cheeks and soft lips. Such sweetness layered over sharp edges, a curious and mesmerizing contradiction. Seeing this side of Nireed almost made him wonder how he'd ever feared her, but the truth still resonated deep in his wary bones, and in muscles primed to flee. Seeing her like this was a gift, a privilege, and one not to be taken advantage of or squandered.

And for the first time, he allowed himself to look with eyes not shadowed by fear.

Her skin was pale, almost translucent in places, no doubt due in part to living hundreds of feet down from the surface, but there was a sort of plushness to it, too, that tempted touch. When she moved, a generous display of muscle rippled beneath, every inch of her a testament to a hard-fought life at sea and regular long-distance swims to the shore. And yet, such strength wasn't without beauty, each motion flowing from one into the next with a sinuous grace.

Then, the most striking non-human thing about her: the long tail.

It swayed languidly beneath the water, silver scales reflecting the warm tones of the setting sun, a gentle gradient of pinks and oranges, but there was no forgetting it was a powerhouse of strength, one that propelled her hundreds of miles every week.

If he touched her tail, ran his hand along the scales, would she be smooth one direction, rough the other? He continued drinking in the wonders of this mystifying creature, not quite daring.

A small smile curved her lips. She seemed so content resting against his boat, like it pleased her to watch him look his fill.

Most of her hair was wet and slicked back, save for one stray, drying bit, frizzing wildly out of control. He didn't know what compelled him, but he dipped his hand in the water and swiped down the wayward piece.

He should've pulled away then, but his fingers stayed put, lingering on the outer shell of her ear. Her eyes widened, searching his for several long beats, as she touched the piece he'd wetted down, her clawed fingers brushing his. She opened her mouth, then closed it, rendered utterly speechless.

Shit, she was cute, even as she gaped like a fish out of water.

He tapped his finger to the tip of her nose. "You don't like being dry, Starfish."

Her cheeks pinkened, and goddamn, he'd somehow managed to make this devastatingly and dangerously beautiful man-eating mermaid bashful.

"I have to go," she said suddenly, tearing her eyes away. "I'm sorry."

She pushed off from the boat, and in a flash of silver scales, disappeared beneath the surface.

The abruptness of it shocked him. He thought they were having a moment...

What had he done wrong?

CHAPTER

EIGHT

DEEPEST, MURKIEST DEPTHS, HER SCALES HAD PARTED.

Right along the front, revealing tender, secret parts that should only come out for a mating frenzy. And all he'd done was touch her.

"You don't like being dry, Starfish."

The nickname fell from his lips like an endearment, a little teasing, but entirely sweet.

And not just that.

Wetting down her hair had been a gesture. A ridiculously small, why-was-she-even-fixating-on-it kind of gesture, but a gesture, nonetheless. He knew she hated being dry—she'd apparently complained about it enough and how itchy, uncomfortable, and all around awful it was. What Reid did was sweet and thoughtful, and just the sort of thing Killian would do for Lorelei. Just the sort of thing Nireed always wanted from her own mate…

Not your mate. He barely even likes you.

Nireed slapped her tail hard, propelling herself through the water at breakneck speeds, tricking her body into thinking it was in flight-mode. Because even it knew better than to be primed for a potential mate when "danger" lurked. It didn't need to know that all that had been threatened was her pride.

Knowing how terrified and repulsed he'd been when they'd met, and still opening for him after a single touch? Mortifying. Reid would never want someone like her. Not when he knew she and her kin sometimes ate other Surface Dwellers.

Cold water caressed her scales, not something that discouraged arousal among her kind, but the urgency in her swimming demanded they close, shielding the vulnerable flesh beneath. That, at least, made the trip home less awkward.

On the dive to the city, she caught up with a returning hunting party and was relieved to see her friends Melusina and Delphine among the group. If anyone might offer her sympathy, it was those two. But apparently not Aersila, who wouldn't even look at her.

Her heart twinged, hating that they were fighting. They never fought.

What happened with Reid, and all the weird, confusing feelings that accompanied it, was exactly the sort of thing she'd want to talk with Aersila about. Everything from sharing the pangs of an ill-timed, unrequited mating frenzy to confessing the type of thoughtful, loving mate she wanted but would never have.

Melusina and Delphine flashed a cheerful greeting, their respective topaz and red lights winking back at her.

Melusina had dark brown skin, due largely to her Black Surface Dweller-ancestry, but she also spent a lot of time near the surface, hunting in the light of the sun. She wore her hair in long locs that fell to her hips, ornamented with shiny bits of metal scavenged and painstakingly polished from old, sunken ships.

Delphine, on the other hand, was white from head to fin, even her scales. She rarely ventured near the surface, the sun too bright for her pale, light blue eyes and too harsh for her even paler skin. But her inner luminescence was red, rendering her virtually invisible to the other creatures of the deep, making her an especially lethal deepwater hunter.

"Can we talk?" Nireed signed, her amber glow illuminating her hands.

Aersila stiffened, but still didn't look her way. And that cut deep.

No matter the risk, Nireed had always been there for her sister. Whether she agreed with her or not didn't matter. She never turned her back, never refused to talk. Why couldn't Aersila afford her the same respect and support?

Hurt turned to simmering anger.

Just because she was the younger, least experienced of the two didn't make her an incapable fool. She wasn't a child anymore and hadn't been for a long time.

If Aersila wanted to ignore her, fine.

Delphine glared at the older mermaid, blue eyes flaring red, then signed to Nireed. "Come on. Let's get out of here." Melusina nodded in agreement, snapping her tail with extra force.

Nireed didn't spare a single glance for her sister as she followed her friends. Why waste energy? Aersila had made her feelings perfectly clear.

They swam for the kelp forest, Delphine grabbing the old bit of rope they used to mark out pathways—a navigational network branching out through the towering stalks. This particular piece led to a series of others, each knotting around a barnacle-covered anchor, and spiraling out. One of them led to their old hangout, the place they'd been meeting since they were deemed old enough to swim away from the city unsupervised.

All those years ago, they cleared out a little grove for themselves, filling it with sunken "treasure"—pretty, but useless, trinkets scavenged from wrecks—and built a fort from old, rusted out ship parts. They'd play "Sirens and Sailors," a game that went exactly how one might expect. Two of them would pretend to be oblivious sailors, chugging across the sea in a roaring hunk of metal. They'd take turns being the third character, a powerful, shipwrecking siren who'd hunt them down despite the awful noise, quieting the ocean and feeding the pod in one fell swoop—a heroine to her people.

Other times, they'd just play with one sailor, and the spare would pretend to be Lady Leviathan, the mighty kraken goddess of the sea. There was a makeshift skirt around here somewhere, made from twenty strands of old rope, one for each of the goddess's tentacled arms.

Settling among their old treasures and childhood memories,

Delphine lightly touched Nireed's shoulder, getting her attention. "Are you okay?"

"Not really."

"What happened? Are you two fighting over a Surface Dweller?"

Nireed wavered her hand. "Not in the way you mean. Aersila only has eyes for Aquilus."

Melusina snorted. "Not that she does anything about it."

"She's been through a lot." Her sister pined for Ryn's adopted father from afar, too hurt and scared by the past to take a chance on something new. It didn't matter that he only had eyes for her in return, turning down all other mating offers, waiting on a slim maybe.

"What's the fight about then?" Delphine pressed.

"She thinks he'll side with the fishermen and hurt me, but that's not what my instincts tell me. He has a protective nature. He cares deeply about his people, but he's also sympathetic to the danger our pod is in." With a sigh, Nireed explained the circumstances around meeting Reid, and every encounter since, sparing no details. "A part of me fears Aersila is seeing something I don't."

"Or she's wrong." Lounging against their old fort, Melusina flicked off a barnacle. "Seems more to me like she's misplacing her fear for herself onto you. She's never met him, so how would she know?"

"He does sound like he could be a worthy ally." Picking up one of their treasures from the silt—a crown made from twisted cutlery—Delphine shook it clear of debris, then placed it on her head.

Nireed wrung her hands a moment before confessing, "My scales parted for him."

"Oh." Delphine's brows ticked up a fraction, but a slow, wicked grin spread across her lips. "How exciting."

"You should go for it." Melusina crudely thrusted her tail upward. Both friends fell into a fit of bubbling giggles.

When the water cleared from their laughter, Nireed said, her cheeks hot, "He didn't see, he doesn't know. He *can't* know."

Both friends frowned, replying with a simultaneous, "Why not?"

"Because I've eaten men like him, and he knows it. He'll never accept me."

"You don't know that…" Delphine began, but Nireed wasn't done.

"What if this kicks off a mating frenzy? I don't want to just accept whoever will have me." It was a heat, a lust, that overtook the senses and drove one wild with need to fuck. *To propagate.* And because her people were sensitive to each other's emotions and scents, it was a catching predicament. When one of them began feeling its effects, the rest were sure to follow.

Melusina and Delphine exchanged looks.

A mating frenzy was how Undine had gotten pregnant last year. Many in the pod for that matter. And while that was perfectly fine for them, Nireed wanted so much more. She wanted someone to look at her like Killian looked at Lorelei, or Aquilus stared longingly after Aersila, never knowing if she'd ever reciprocate his feelings.

She wanted to be loved. And she felt nothing for any of the pod's three remaining unattached males. One of which was Aquilus, so he didn't count. The second was Cyrus, the reckless, barely old enough male who challenged her authority anytime she was hunt leader. And the third, while willing to do the rounds with multiple partners, was so notoriously terrible at mating, Undine was trying to convince attached males to loan out their services from time to time. A battle she was badly losing.

The ratio had always been low, but it was even lower now with Nautic's killings.

"It's not so bad," Delphine said. "It starts as a convenience, but it gets good quite quickly. Zavier didn't stop until well after I started showing."

"Never stopped is more like it." Melusina smirked. "He visited you right up until Celia was born. And is *still* coming around."

Delphine giggled.

Both had dedicated mates and little ones at home, but as far as their pod went, Nireed wasn't the exception. Many others who could carry babies were unpaired—Aersila and Undine being other notables. While the latter had a baby, it was the result of a temporary arrangement early on in their community's reunification, before the father entered into a dedicated pairing with another.

"Is there a way to stop a frenzy?"

Now her friends looked startled. Had anyone ever tried? The need for numbers was at the forefront of all their minds in their pod's never-ending fight for survival.

"He's agreed to help us stop the fishermen killing our kind," Nireed continued. "I won't jeopardize that alliance by making a fool of myself."

"What if he's not opposed?" Melusina's hands moved with passionate poignance. "You say he'll never accept you, but hasn't he already begun to? Surface Dwellers don't touch us unless they want us —otherwise, they're too scared they'll get their hand bit off. That's why your scales parted. Your body knows it even if you don't."

"Nireed, do you want him to accept you?" Delphine signed slowly, brow pinched with concern.

"I don't know." Nireed rubbed her chest before continuing. "There's this pull. Every time, I could've let him be, just kept on swimming or walked away, but I keep going back."

Delphine smiled, taking the cutlery crown from her head and placing it on Nireed's. "Worth exploring, I say. But if you don't want to, self-pleasure takes the edge off. You can get through a frenzy without mating."

Melusina nodded. "But if you do want to, don't be like Aersila and let fear deny you your mate. You deserve to be happy, Nireed. You've given so much to this pod. Now it's time you take something for yourself."

"If Reid is your mate, and he makes you happy, Aersila will come around."

CHAPTER

NINE

For nearly his whole life, Reid had no idea mermaids existed, and now, he couldn't go anywhere without bumping into one. Water, land, it didn't matter, because here he was, down at the docks, looking to buy lobster from one of the local, independent fishermen, and there was Nireed across the pier, slinking between outbuildings, dripping wet in an ill-fitted dress.

He cast a look around, a light rain pelting his rain jacket.

The docks were bustling with afternoon activity—fishermen offloading their catch and getting it ready for market—all too wrapped up in their routine to notice the siren sneaking around. Nireed weaved between stacks of lobster pots and other equipment, pausing occasionally to read a building sign before shaking her head and continuing onward.

What are you up to, Starfish? It looked more like searching than hunting, but there was only one way to be sure.

Abandoning his place in line, Reid tailed after her, fully preparing to talk her out of trouble. He ducked behind a bit of equipment and whisper-yelled, "Nireed, wait up!"

Body tensing, she spun into a crouched position, poised to lunge.

Throwing up his hands, he quickly added, "It's just me."

"Coast Warrior." She relaxed, a smile softening her face. She seemed more pleased to see him than he expected. "What a pleasant surprise."

The last time he saw her, he'd scared her away with his touch. No matter how well intentioned—wetting a drying bit of hair, playfully tapping her nose—he hadn't asked if it was all right, and that wasn't cool. His mother had taught him better than that.

He crouched beside Nireed, their bodies hidden behind a cluster of barrels. This brought them closer together, but she didn't move away, and he hoped that was a good sign.

"About the other night," he began, pretending to be fascinated by a callous on his thumb. Apologies were hard to get right, but that didn't mean he wouldn't try. "I made you uncomfortable, and I'm sorry."

"Reid." She tilted his chin, bringing his eyes to hers. Chips of amber glinted back at him, so bold and unflinching. What horrors and wonders those eyes must've seen. What truths. "Look at me when you have something important to say."

Respect. Honesty. That's what she was demanding. No matter their differences, what uncertainties remained between them, he owed her that, and for the simple reason that she was a person. He stared into those eyes, both eerie and beautiful, and said, "I shouldn't have touched you." No matter how much he'd wanted to.

A flush rose to the mermaid's cheeks, but she kept her eyes trained on his. "I wasn't expecting it, but I'm not mad that you did."

"No? You swam away pretty fast."

"That wasn't because I didn't like it." Her fingers slid away, scraping his stubble as they went, before dropping to her side. "I liked it a little too much."

An unexpected thrill curled up his spine at what those words implied. This had nothing to do with the circumstances that brought them together. His voice was a little hoarse when he finally replied, "How much?"

"Enough to hope you'll do it again."

Swallowing thickly, he edged closer, daring to take a drenched lock of hair between his fingers. "Don't know that I need to. The rain's got you soaked."

"A shame that it has." She sighed. "Another time, then." The siren took his hand, pulling him up with her as she stood, their little moment passed. "Come. You might as well help me while you're here."

"Help you with what?"

"Looking."

For what, for whom, she didn't elaborate, and yet, he allowed himself to be towed along, their hands still linked. At every twist and turn, they took care to stay out of sight. Whatever had brought Nireed to the docks, whatever her goal, required secrecy, that much was clear, and he hoped that whatever it was, he'd be able to keep her out of trouble.

Together, they peeked around a corner.

A white warehouse loomed ahead, larger than the ones surrounding it, with Nautic's navy blue logo emblazoned across the side in giant letters. Two eighteen-wheelers with the same branding were parked outside, backed up to loading bays. All was quiet, for now. Nautic's crews were likely still offloading at the docks.

Goddammit. There was no way what came next would be legal. She was hunting for proof and staking out the place didn't seem like her style.

She started for the warehouse, but Reid pulled her back. "What are you doing?"

"Going to have a look inside."

Breaking and entering was more like it. And it was a bad idea, but she probably didn't care much about legality when she thought her people were intentionally being killed, so he tried a different tactic. "What're we going to do if we get caught in there? You're not going to knock them out and eat them, are you?" He was only half joking.

"Too full," she deadpanned, patting her belly. "Already ate today."

Good Lord. "I can't tell if you're joking."

"About being too full?"

"No, about tactically eating someone."

"Too inefficient. Was planning to sing."

"Uh, weird but charming. How's that help us?"

"Our song has compulsion qualities."

"For weak-minded folks, maybe."

She snorted.

There wasn't much research on siren singing. What little was known about it was either conjecture or anecdotal, and while Reid could see there being a kernel of truth to the latter, it was likely exaggerated to suit the myth. And he'd admit that the merfolk's ability to shift from one form to the other seemed more fantastical than biological, but at least metamorphosis had a precedent in nature: caterpillars to butterflies, tadpoles to frogs.

Merfolk just did it at will, and he looked forward to the day when science caught up and could explain that biological process.

"Oh, you're serious. You don't think it works?"

"I believe in the power of suggestion. But outright controlling someone with supernatural abilities? Nah."

A slow smirk crept up her face. "Think you can resist me?"

"Sure, why not?" He shrugged. "Weak minds don't become Aviation Survival Technicians."

Her expression turned feral. "We shall see, Coast Warrior."

He should've known this creature would enjoy a challenge.

Whisking the hood of his rain jacket over his head, Reid grumbled, "Just keep your head down. There's a security camera above the door." Around here, security cameras were often just for show, and sure, sometimes corporate companies cheapened out and cut corners, too, but he didn't like the odds of that being the case.

Nireed swiped strands of hair in front of her face, and it made her look like *The Ring* girl, which was terrifying, but at least it obscured her features.

With their heads bowed, they approached the warehouse's side entrance. The mermaid beside him appeared perfectly calm, while his stomach knotted with nerves as he watched her test the door handle. It was locked.

"Going to have to break it," she muttered, undeterred.

Stilling her hand, he quickly searched for a key code panel. If there was one, it might mean that busting in would trigger an alarm.

This was such a terrible idea.

Although Reid didn't find a panel, he swiped a hand over his face. He could get into a lot of trouble for this if they got caught. Lose his job. Get slapped with criminal charges. Possibly go to jail. But if Nireed was right about Nautic, the stakes would be even higher for her. If they truly were mermaid-killers, and they realized what she was, this could get her killed.

"Are you sure about this?" he asked. "If they realize what you are…"

"I know, but I face that danger every day. I need to do this. Are *you* sure?"

"Not even a little bit."

Her expression softened. "You don't have to come in. I can do this on my own."

The thought of leaving Nireed to face whatever lay ahead alone made him uneasy. He withdrew his hand. "No, where you go, I go."

She pushed down hard on the handle, and a crunching sound followed as she broke its locking mechanism. With a good shove from her shoulder, the door opened. He was no slouch when it came to strength and endurance, but Nireed had him outmatched ten times over.

Peeking in, she murmured, "It's clear," and slipped inside.

Everything about this situation was a gamble. The risks far outweighed any chance of reward, but reminding himself that literal lives were on the line, Reid followed.

It was cool inside the warehouse, intended to keep the inventory fresh. Some of it would be distributed locally, but most would be trucked out to grocery stores and restaurants across New England.

Reid spotted a pair of discarded work gloves sitting on a nearby shelf and donned them. Leaving his fingerprints everywhere would be peak idiocy, especially since all federal employees like him were fingerprinted as a part of their pre-employment background checks. He was an absolute idiot for breaking in to begin with, but hopefully, a smart idiot.

Together, they crept down the rows of shelving units, him one side, her the other, peeking into bins, reading labels, on the hunt for anything that might suggest Nautic was harvesting mermaid parts.

Fish, fish, lobster, fish.

The labeling was all rather straightforward—pollock, bluefish, haddock, tuna, flounder—nothing vague that might be code for "merperson." But he kept looking. Maybe there was something to find in the figurative "fine print."

"Any luck over there?" he asked on the loud end of a whisper.

She shook her head curtly.

Row by row, bin by bin, they searched, carefully combing through Nautic's products. Not even a hint that there might be nefarious underpinnings to the company's business. Disappointment and frustration radiated from the tense set of Nireed's shoulders, far too palpable to be disingenuous. She'd been counting on finding something damning.

An unexpected desire to offer the vicious mermaid comfort settled over him.

"There's nothing here," she hissed, yanking roughly on her hair roots. Angry tears sprung from her eyes.

The can of premade lobster bisque held in his hands was quickly abandoned on the nearest shelf. "Hey," he soothed, crossing the aisle. He entwined her fingers with his, gently prying them away from her hair. "This place is probably checked regularly by a fisheries inspector. Nautic wouldn't dare keep anything suspicious here." He'd no idea if that was true, but Nireed seemed crushed by the lack of evidence, and he hated seeing her so distraught. "Looking here was a good hunch."

She huffed out a frustrated breath, eyes shining with tears as she gazed up at him. "I need to stop them before more of my people die, and I'd hoped to find something here that proves we're not lying." She gestured limply to the shelving around them. "But nothing I do brings me any closer to securing my people's safety."

For all her strength and confidence on the docks, this Nireed seemed on the verge of a breakdown. It was the most vulnerable Reid had ever seen her. There was no thinking involved, he just tugged her into his chest, arms enfolding her body, comforting, shielding, being a rock to lean on, even if only just for a moment.

This sense of helplessness, of not being enough for the people counting on you, was a feeling he knew all too well. No matter how long he did his job, it would never be easy coming to terms with the fact that he couldn't save everyone. Didn't matter how strong, how fast, how smart a person was, no one was a miracle worker, not even supernatural creatures like Nireed.

He rested his cheek on top of her head, unfazed by the touch of cold, damp hair.

The mermaid had helped slaughter at least eight fishermen, and yet, it was getting harder and harder to distrust her.

"Hey, Carl!" A voice called out. "You see this? Door's busted."

They both froze, clinging to each other for one tense moment, before instinct, or acute dread, finally kicked in. Reid yanked Nireed into a tight, shadowy nook between shelving units, neither daring to breathe as their bodies pressed together.

They had to get out of here. There was another door toward the front of the warehouse, maybe one hundred or so feet away. Should they sneak out? Make a run for it?

Reid was making mental calculations when a second person shouted back. "Someone break in?"

"It sure looks like it. Better call the cops."

The heavy plod of booted feet approaching made them both shrink back, Nireed's claws curling into his jacket, but one look at her face, at the tightness in her jaw, and the ferocity in her eyes, said it was more restraint than fear.

Two grown adults squeezed into a small space, there wasn't a part of him that wasn't touching her, and if it weren't for the utter dread of getting caught, he might've appreciated that more.

"Carl, get your ass back here! We drive forklifts and load freight. Neither of us get paid enough to fuck around with thieves."

Reid whispered against Nireed's ear. "Can you tell how far away he is?"

She nodded faintly. "About one whale length."

If Reid wasn't such a nerd, that information wouldn't have meant anything to him, but he was, and the whale species found in the Gulf of Maine—humpback and right whales, namely—were approximately fifty feet in length. "Same aisle?"

She carefully peered around him, hands laid flat against his chest. "Yes."

"Feel like running? Or singing?" The last option he said as a joke, and she shot him a dirty look.

"Hey! Whoever's in here, if you're thinking of stealing anything, make my day and stick around. Otherwise, get the fuck out!"

"*Caaarl*, why would you taunt them like that?" Whoever this second Nautic employee was, he was well and truly over Carl's bravado.

Nireed's eyes met Reid's as she leaned into him, reaching for something above his head, bringing them so close he felt her breath tickle his cheek, her mouth mere inches from his.

He swallowed thickly.

A small smirk teased her lips as she leaned back, a can of tuna fish in hand. He was about to joke that now was not the time for a snack, but she'd already whisked out of their hiding place, winding up her arm like a professional baseball player, and hurled the can down the aisle.

A meaty thud, followed by a shocked, "Ow! What the fuck?" was his only indication she'd hit her target.

"Come on." Nireed snatched Reid's hand, and they both ran.

There was shouting behind them. He glanced back only once—one of the men, Carl presumably, clutched his head, a dented tuna can at his feet, while his coworker tried to get a look at the injury.

"Assholes!" one of them yelled.

They burst out of the warehouse's front door. It didn't seem like they were being pursued, but neither of them stopped running until they'd left the docks and reached the edge of Haven Cove's town proper. About a mile by his estimation.

He stopped first, and Nireed, who had fallen behind the farther they ran, collided into his back with a winded "oof." He didn't think he'd stopped abruptly, but with the desperate way she clung to his jacket, using him for balance, maybe she didn't know how to stop on her own. Like a toddler, she just launched herself from one point to the next, relying on objects at rest to break her inertia.

Letting him go, Nireed bent over her knees, wheezing, then gradually straightened as she sucked in air, folding her arms above her head. The fact that she knew such a breathing technique meant she'd done this before, but not often enough that this getaway wouldn't leave her out of breath. Still, he was impressed. He'd gotten the distinct impression that walking and running were things this mermaid had only recently learned how to do.

"You run good," he blurted, groaning internally. Regressing into caveman vocabulary was quickly becoming a bad habit around Nireed.

She flashed him a brief, cheeky smile as she continued to gulp down air. For a moment, he quietly observed, absorbing the details. *Rosy cheeks. Wet dress. Heaving chest.*

No bra...

Startled, he tore his eyes away, pretending the cracked sidewalk at his feet had suddenly become extremely interesting. It wasn't subtle, but if Nireed noticed, she mercifully didn't comment.

Rain pelted his jacket, droplets rolling down the water-repellant fabric. He considered offering it to Nireed, but while this was crappy weather by human standards, he had a hunch she preferred it.

A hurt sounding "now what?" broke the silence, and he couldn't avoid looking at her anymore.

Standing there in the rain, soaking wet from head to toe, Nireed looked so forlorn, the weight of today's failure sinking in and weighing heavy on her shoulders. More like a kicked puppy than a terrifying, flesh-eating mermaid, and Reid just wasn't going to abide that. "Let's get a drink," he said, waving for her to follow. "Come on, Starfish."

He led the way toward Main Street, wondering if the mermaid would like the taste of beer.

NIREED FOLLOWED THE COAST WARRIOR DOWN A MOSTLY empty street. A few Surface Dwellers were milling about, some wearing water-repellant clothing like Reid, others holding a bizarre, half-dome shaped contraption above their heads.

With every step, the sandals on her feet made an annoying squelching sound. More than one Surface Dweller who passed them by openly stared at her, some mix of surprise and judgment in their expressions, which she didn't like. It gave her the distinct impression that she wasn't blending in very well, but the rain felt nice, so she held her head high and glared at anyone who stared too long.

Reid chuckled lightly. "You look like an angry, disheveled cat."

She'd seen pictures of the creatures, including ones where they'd been given unwanted baths, their tiny bodies tensed in quiet rage as they stared at the camera with yellow, unamused eyes. Apparently, many of her mannerisms reminded Lorelei of them, and if Reid thought so, too, it must be true.

"They keep staring." She dropped her voice to a whisper. "Do you think they know what I am?"

His gaze fell on her, soft and thoughtful. "Nah. I don't think that's why they're staring."

"Why, then?"

A blush pinkened his cheeks. Whatever it was, he seemed reluctant to say it.

"Reid, just say it."

"You've noticed that humans hide their bodies behind clothing," he began, cutting sharply to the left, then opening the door to a public Surface Dweller establishment.

"Yes," she affirmed, following him inside. "Am I not also?"

There were seating arrangements lining the wall to the left, a wall of bottled liquids to the right. Reid led them to a table near the front, sliding into a chair, away from a small group of Surface Dwellers who were singing and playing instruments. Given how loud they were, she appreciated the distance.

When she slid into the chair opposite him, he leaned forward, keeping his volume discreet as he said, "The way that dress is clinging to you..." He paused, rolling his lips. "Well, it's almost like you're not wearing clothes at all."

Looking down at herself, she noted how the wet cloth stuck to her skin, the shape of her breasts and nipples visible. A quick survey of the room revealed that this was not the case with any of the Surface Dwellers. "Does that bother you?"

"No." He sat back, drumming his fingers along the tabletop. "If they don't like what they see, they should look away."

That made her smirk. "What's not to like?"

He just rolled his eyes. "You're a shameless flirt, you know that?"

"I don't know what 'flirt' means, but I am shameless."

The Coast Warrior snorted.

A strange Surface Dweller abruptly approached their table. "What can I get you?" she asked cheerfully, hands perched confidently on her hips.

Nireed reared back. What was happening? Why was this woman talking to them? Should they run? Fight?

Beneath the table, Reid's hand settled over her knee, giving it a reassuring squeeze as he turned to address the person. He didn't falter for a second and asked for something called an "An Acadia Lager."

Taking a deep breath, Nireed attempted to match his easygoing posture.

"And for you?" The woman turned her smile on her. This one met her eye and in a way that denoted respect.

Nireed inclined her head. "The same, please."

"You got it." And then she was gone, off to fetch whatever Acadia Lagers were.

"Smooth," Reid commented, studying her thoughtfully. "For a second there, I thought the claws were going to come out, but you handled that quite well."

"What just happened?"

"She works here as a server. It's her job to come ask what we want. She gets paid to bring visitors food and drinks."

"Oh." Nireed watched with fascination as the woman approached other tables, repeating the gesture. "I see."

"I take it merfolk don't have bars and restaurants?" When she quirked an eyebrow, he rephrased the unfamiliar words for her, "Public eating and drinking establishments."

Nodding her understanding, she replied, "Not like this. We hunt together and feast together, but nothing so"—she waved a hand—"I don't know the word."

"Formal?" he offered.

"Maybe? There's no 'serving.' Everyone just dives in."

The next time the Surface Dweller server approached their table, Nireed didn't flinch.

"Here you go," the woman said, sliding two tall glasses of amber liquid onto the table, one in front of each of them. Both were topped with sea foam. After a polite thank you from Reid, the woman replied, "Sure thing. Just let me know if you need anything else."

When Reid picked up the glass and took a sip, Nireed followed suit, curious about this Surface Dweller delicacy. As the frothy, bitter liquid hit her tongue, confusion turned to utter disgust, and she spit it right back into the cup, Surface Dweller manners be damned.

Such betrayal.

That was *not* sea foam.

"Don't like it?" Reid's mouth twisted with barely contained laughter.

How could a people who created something as delicious as potted meat also make and regularly imbibe this atrocity? She pushed the glass away, cringing. "That is vile."

"You know the word 'vile' but not 'flirt'?"

She shrugged. "I pick things up as I go."

Reid continued drinking his beverage perfectly content, much to her bafflement. "How do you know our language so well?"

The tank flashed across her mind, but she batted away the memory. While she'd learned a lot by listening to the Surface Dweller scientists beyond the glass, fueled by survival and need, that wasn't the whole of it. And certainly not the piece that deserved the most credit. "A friend taught me. She's like you but also like me. A Shorewalker."

"A Shorewalker," he repeated. "So half-human, half-merperson?"

"Half isn't quite right. There's Surface Dweller in my blood too. It's more that she lives on shore while the rest of us live in the sea. That, and she was raised human."

"How often do Surface Dwellers and merfolk get it on together? Is that a regular thing?"

While the phrasing was weird, she understood the implication. "My foreparents sometimes mated with Surface Dwellers. It's what gives us our ability to shift between forms. Our deep-sea ancestors can't do it."

Curiosity flickered in Reid's eyes. "Have you ever seen one? Do they still exist?"

"I haven't. None of us have in recent memory. But we think they're still out there somewhere, deeper than even we dare to go."

This bit of information seemed to disturb him.

"Reid?"

"Yeah, Starfish?"

Her cheeks warmed. That endearment falling from his lips was so soft and sweet. "Even if we had seen them, I'd never let one near you. The night we met, some of my kin couldn't tell the difference between you and the fishermen. And the fisherman who pushed you under..." Nireed was so used to saying exactly what she meant, but for once, she just couldn't bring herself to admit to Reid that she'd killed that man. "I just wanted to keep you safe."

Surprise rolled off his scent as her meaning sunk in. "You're the one who pulled him off me?"

"Yes."

"Did you kill him too?"

Goddess, she didn't want to answer, but she'd previously promised him nothing but honesty. "I think you already know," she said quietly.

A grim expression fell over his features. "Yeah, I guess I did. I wish you hadn't done that. The way he climbed on top of me—it happens during rescues all the time. It's nothing malicious. Just a scared man trying to keep his head above water. I've had a lot of training getting out of those situations. He didn't need to die."

"I didn't know. I truly thought he was drowning you." Not that it would've made a difference. They were hunting the hunters that night, and Nireed would never regret protecting and feeding her people, but that was probably more truth than the Coast Warrior could handle.

"I believe you." He downed his drink. When he was done, a tired expression had fallen over his features. "Thank you for being honest with me."

She wanted to say more. Something to heal the rift this topic had ripped open. Something to bring laughing, smiling Reid back, but she didn't know how to take away the sting of her honesty. Surface Dwellers were so hard to understand sometimes, asking for things they didn't truly want, but maybe there was such a thing as too much honesty and revealing this had been a mistake.

And maybe Reid was reacting more calmly than she deserved.

Turning her attention to the room around them, Nireed studied the other Surface Dwellers sharing the space. As time wore on, a few got up from their chairs to sway their arms and bodies in front of the music-makers, some in time to the beat, some not.

She observed them closely. The touching, the tension in the not touching, the meaningful eye contact, the sensual bump and grind of bodies. Happiness. Bliss. Aroused energy. It radiated from them all.

"What are they doing?"

Reid looked over his shoulder, then back at her, some of the light returning to his eyes. "Dancing."

"What's dancing? Is it a mating ritual?"

He sputtered, spraying his drink across the table. "Jesus, Starfish. You always just say the first thing that pops into your head?" Grabbing small square sheets from a box on the table, he began wiping up the mess.

"Are you always so easily embarrassed?"

"You got me there." Balling up the soaked sheets, Reid shoved them to the side. "I guess I hadn't ever thought of it that way, but yeah, sometimes it's like that."

"Bolder than I expected from your clothes-loving kin."

Amusement sparkled in his eyes. Any evidence of the dismal conversation they'd had was gone without a trace. "It's also just for fun. Wanna try?"

A funny floating sensation seized her stomach, but rather than alarm her, it made her smile. "Show me."

He held out his hand, and she took it, letting him pull her to her feet.

Out on what Reid called "the dance floor," he placed her arms around his neck. Excitement and nerves knotted her stomach in equal measure. "Just relax." His hands fell to her hips, warm and reassuring. "Move to the music."

As he began to sway, he guided her hips in time to him and to the music pulsing in her ears, fluid like seagrass in a gentle ocean current. There was a pattern to it, a beat, and she gave herself to the push and pull, luxuriating in the weight of Reid's hands. No thinking, just moving.

Moving because it felt good, not because purpose or survival dictated it.

When her hips brushed his, a delicious thrill raced up her spine. It was a familiar sensation in an unfamiliar body, and for once Nireed was grateful for the discretion her Surface Dweller form granted. In siren form, her scales would have surely parted.

"Am I doing this right?" She sounded a little breathless, even to her own ears.

Reid's eyes darkened, rich brown swallowed by black. "Yeah." There was a harsh quality to his voice, and like his eyes, it was penetrating and all-consuming. Every nerve ending in her body alighted to that sound and silently begged for more. "You're good at this."

Delighted in the praise, she leaned in close, mouth at his ear. "If I sang right now, do you think you could resist me?"

So many senses fired off at once. His breath hitched, and his heart raced. Beneath her hands, warm skin heated, and something tantalizing spiked in his scent. Something that edged dangerously close to arousal.

Their hips brushed again, and this time, it felt less like an accident. Dancing was a language of itself, and Nireed liked how Reid's body was speaking to her.

"No, Starfish," he admitted quietly. "And I don't think I'd want to."

And yet, with a gentle push, he put a modicum of space between them, the meaning of their dance changing as inches became an ocean.

CHAPTER

TEN

INVITING NIREED TO DANCE HAD BEEN A MISTAKE. THERE shouldn't've been any harm in demonstrating a simple two-step, just some innocent fun, but the weight of her arms around his neck, and the slow, sinuous grace of her hips beneath his hands, so responsive to him and the music's rhythm, had fogged his brain.

Dancing had a way of lowering inhibitions, and he should have anticipated that, but this bordered dangerously close to a full-blown, lust-drunk haze. Off one beer, he didn't even have a decent buzz going to blame it on. This was all him.

Was he attracted to the mermaid? Did he want her?

He wasn't sure how he felt about that possibility, not when he didn't know if he'd moved past the fact that she'd helped kill and devour eight fishermen. Or that she'd personally taken out Captain Flick Rockland just because she thought the guy was attacking him.

So Reid put stiff middle school dance distance between them.

It was effective. He'd dumped a bucket of cold water on the moment, and she quickly lost interest, disengaging, and returning to their table.

It was also confusing. Losing her heat and the feel of her curves beneath his palms hollowed out a hole in his chest, like he'd given up something he shouldn't have.

Back at the table, he ordered another beer and asked the server to take away the one they'd left unattended, all the while struggling with what to say. He was afraid to ask Nireed what she thought of dancing after he'd made it spectacularly awkward.

A wave of humid air rushed in as the bar door opened, followed by a surprised, but cheery, "Kruetz?"

Well, shit.

Perez and Hatcher headed their way. Neither had seen Nireed up close before, so maybe the mermaid could pass as a townie, but would that be fucked up to ask her to lie about who and what she was?

Nireed tensed, leaning across the table. "What is it?"

"Friends. Fellow, uh, Coast Warriors. They don't know you can walk on land."

"Do they know what I look like?"

"Don't think so. Not from the helicopter. It's too far away."

Rather than match his panic, she perked up, seemingly interested, but offered no helpful ideas on how to play this off. *Great.* He was up shit creek without a paddle.

"Hey, guys," he trailed awkwardly, standing up to give Perez a quick one-armed hug. "It's like we live in a small town or something."

"So much for work-life balance," Hatcher joked, clapping him on the shoulder. "Mind if we join you? Or is this a date or something?"

Reid looked to Nireed for help, but she was too busy observing his friends with rapt fascination. Had he told them the mermaid's name? They'd put two and two together right away, if he had. "No, um, I was just showing...her...around."

"Her?" Perez pinned him with an unimpressed, did-you-just-fucking-dare glare. Even Hatcher gave him a funny look. Great, now they thought he was a player.

"Sorry." He swiped a hand over his face and weakly said, "This is Nireed. Nireed this is Alejandra Perez and Jake Hatcher. Both are friends and coworkers of mine."

Then he braced himself.

But their expressions softened, no hint of recognition or outrage. He hadn't told them the mermaid's name, then. They had no idea this was her.

The relief was only temporary. Hiding the truth from them felt like shit, but he couldn't out her, especially not in public. That was a recipe for disaster. Perez might take it well, but Hatcher was more of a wild card.

"Nice to meet you, Nireed." Perez extended her hand.

The mermaid must have observed enough human behavior because she didn't miss a beat taking Perez's hand and shaking it. Hatcher's too.

Both pulled out chairs and sat down. "How'd you two meet?" Perez asked.

When Nireed met his eyes, he noticed a subtle shift in her demeanor. Curiosity had morphed into uncertainty. "Swimming," she trailed, and he nodded eagerly, like it was exactly what he'd just been about to say.

Perez began to ask another question, but Hatcher flagged down the waitress, bringing conversation to a pause. As a new round of drink orders was placed, Reid noticed Nireed staring at something over his shoulder, her complexion paling.

She stood slowly. The movement was so careful, so measured, neither of his friends batted an eye. It easily could've been mistaken for getting up to go to the bathroom, but Reid sensed something was wrong. Bending down, she whispered into his ear, "I need to go. Now. And maybe you should too."

Before he could ask why, she strode out of the bar without another word. No hurried goodbye or even a glance back. He looked over his shoulder, trying to figure out what had spooked her. It couldn't be the dancers, the live band, or the waitstaff slinging drinks.

And then he saw it.

On one of the overhead TVs was a local breaking news report.

Break-in at Nautic warehouse.

B-roll of the docks switched over to a blurry photo of him and Nireed loitering outside the warehouse side entrance. Neither of their faces were visible, but their clothing was certainly identifiable. Nondescript, but identifiable.

Reid quickly shucked off his rain jacket. It was a dime-a-dozen charcoal gray color, but he didn't need anyone making associations, and the green T-shirt he wore underneath felt comfortingly dissimilar.

Next, an interview clip played, featuring the two forklift operators. One had a nasty purple bump on his head, but otherwise appeared fine —eager for his fifteen seconds of limelight even. Reid couldn't hear what he was saying over the bar's live music, but there was closed captioning:

Carl: She must've been a softball player or something. Hit me square in the head with a can of tuna.

Reporter: Did you feel like your life was in danger at any point?

Carl: Nuh. They just ran out of there. Didn't even look like they took anything.

Paul: Maybe they were investigative journalists?

Reporter: ...

Carl: ...

Paul: ...

Reporter: What would they have been investigating?

Paul: Uh.

They had no fucking clue. Thank Christ.

Relieved, Reid turned back to his friends, but they were both staring at him hard.

Hatcher pointed at the TV. "What the fuck's going on? Who was that woman we just met, and why are you both on the evening news?"

"Keep your voice down," Reid hissed. "Nireed's a..."

"Journalist? Environmental activist?" Perez supplied. Her tone was light, but she didn't look happy.

"No. She's the mermaid I've been running into."

"Jesus Fuck, man!" Hatcher whisper-yelled. "What are you thinking? You trying to get masted? Kicked out of the Coast Guard?"

"For once, I agree with him." Perez jutted her thumb at Hatcher. "If they can kick us out for smoking weed, they'd sure as shit kick you out for breaking and entering."

"She's desperate. Her people are dying, and she's trying to prove it before more are killed."

Hatcher folded his arms. "Okay, but why are you mixed up in this?"

Great fucking question. "I don't know." He shoved his hands into his hair. "I guess I thought I could keep her out of trouble. And I genuinely want to help, just don't know how. I'm not CGIS. I'm not command. Just a rescue swimmer."

Perez sighed, pinching her brow. "You're an idiot. But a noble idiot. I hope it goes without saying, but you can't do something like this again. You're going to have to be way more subtle going forward."

"Going forward? Don't you mean 'drop this altogether' before he makes it worse?" Hatcher side-eyed Perez. To Reid, he added, "Nireed's not your responsibility. Even if she's telling the truth. Or thinks she is."

"I wouldn't go that far." Perez waggled a finger. "A corporate company murdering people is not something to turn a blind eye to."

"*Allegedly* murdering."

"God, you're insufferable. Yes, fine. Allegedly. But my point remains."

"Look, I'd say that about anyone who convinced a friend to commit a crime. It's not just because of what she is, although that freaks me out too. Also, are we not going to talk about how mermaids can just sprout legs and walk on land?"

"How obvious is it?" Reid interjected. All things considered, his friends seemed to be handling the news relatively well, but he wouldn't get that kind of grace elsewhere. "Will command put two and two together?"

His friends shared a look, then shook their heads.

"You kept your head down and hood up," Hatcher grumbled. "I only noticed because I saw you two sitting here together and the clothes matched. Plus, the Nautic context."

"That, and your guilty body language," Perez added. "You yanked off your jacket like it was on fire. Also lucky for you, those eyewitnesses were terrible. Painfully untrained in talking to media."

"I'm sorry, you guys. I obviously didn't think this through very well."

"Or at all," Hatcher snarked. Ouch, but mostly fair. "Did you find anything useful?"

"Nope. It was a complete bust."

When the waitress brought their next round of beers, they collectively took one big, long drink.

"IT'S NOT GREAT, BUT I THINK IT'LL BLOW OVER." LORELEI switched off the moving picture box. *A television.* "They got nothing to tie you or him to this. And no one's going to put together that you were the research center's captive mermaid. Not from looking at the back of your head."

Nireed sighed with relief, as much for Reid's sake as hers. After fleeing the Surface Dweller establishment, Nireed swam straight to Lorelei's, frantically sending her pleas on the currents to the Twenty-Armed Goddess, begging the mighty kraken to spare her from the tank.

Can't go back. Can't go back. Can't go back.

Quick escape. Blend in. Hide. Survive. She didn't think, she just did.

And now that she was safe, guilt ate at her insides. She should've waited for Reid. Should've made sure he got out okay. But she'd left him behind.

"I would recommend laying low for a while." Lorelei curled up on the couch, tucking her legs beneath her. "Avoid the docks. You don't want to be seen down there and jog somebody's memory."

"I won't." There was no reason to go back. But even if there was, Nireed wouldn't be any good to her people or herself if she got caught. A willingness to do anything, and risk everything for her people didn't mean it came without calculations.

I'm not that bad, Aersila.

"Do you want to talk about what happened?"

Nireed sighed. "Not really. Was trying to find proof and failed."

"The process of elimination has its values, too. At least now you know."

"True." Nireed picked at the hem of her dress. "I just wish I knew what to do next."

That was a lie. She did have an idea. One that entailed sneaking onboard Nautic's boats one by one, but she wasn't about to tell Shorewalker that. Not when she wasn't even sure herself.

Swimming close enough to find one was risky. She'd just as soon as get caught in a net herself as succeed, and the repeated proximity to loud, discordant boat engines would damage her hearing. And that was something she hadn't yet worked up the courage to risk. Not when there weren't any guarantees she'd even locate a Nautic vessel or that the one she chose had evidence onboard.

"I wish I knew, too." Lorelei pulled a blanket onto her lap, hugging it more for its comfort than its warmth. "But we're not giving up. And Nautic's bound to get sloppy."

"Thank you, Shorewalker. And I hope you're right."

"Is something else bothering you?"

There were several things, but Reid was one she couldn't talk to Aersila about. Melusina and Delphine would listen if they were here, but they were miles and miles away. "When I asked the Coast Warrior for his help, I hadn't considered that I might get him into trouble. I just assumed he'd be safe from other Surface Dwellers."

Lorelei's bright green eyes were searching. "You're worried about him."

"I don't want anything to happen to him—to any of you—but I also know it's your choice to help us, and it's not our way to dissuade you. But I feel…"

"Guilty?"

"Yes. It's a new feeling for me."

"I think that's because the stakes have changed. Guilt goes hand in hand with fear. I should know." They shared a half-hearted smile. "You're afraid in a way you haven't been before because the risk was always to yourself, and yourself alone. But now the people you care about are on the line and your choices have the potential to affect the outcome."

She had a point.

"Insightful, Shorewalker." Nireed smirked. "Must've gotten that from me."

Lorelei playfully chucked a decorative pillow at her. "You should talk to him about it. Maybe he's changed his mind, maybe he hasn't. Let him decide."

"More wise words."

Never able to accept a compliment, Lorelei shrugged dismissively, mouth lifting into a bashful smile. One day, Nireed would get the stubborn woman to own her merits. "What's he like, this Reid?"

"Never hesitates to argue," Nireed scoffed. Then, a little more softly, "Speaks his mind, even when he's afraid."

"Keeping you humble."

Nireed rolled her eyes.

"Go on."

"He's strong in the water. Not as strong as us, but he far surpasses any Surface Dweller I've ever seen. Wears some funny thing over his eyes." Nireed framed the outside of hers with her hands, demonstrating the shape.

"Goggles." Lorelei laughed.

"Goggles." The word felt as weird to say as the contraption looked. "Keep going?"

Lorelei nodded eagerly, tucking a bit of blanket under her cheek.

If Nireed didn't know any better, she'd say Shorewalker was hanging onto every word, but why would she be so interested in the Coast Warrior? "He's purpose driven. Believes in helping people, even those such as me. Seems patient and sweet when he lets his guard down. And even when he disagrees, I think he really listens."

"Sounds like someone worth knowing." Her friend sounded so wistful, Nireed had to wonder if there was something more to her interest. Something Shorewalker wasn't telling her.

CHAPTER

ELEVEN

TOO TIRED TO SWIM HOME, NIREED SPENT THE NIGHT IN Shorewalker's cove, snugly wedged between two rocks, hugging a ball of seaweed to her chest. Not so snug that she'd get stuck, or be unable to move water past her gills, but secure enough that a current wouldn't carry her away while she slept.

Shorewalker had offered the spare bedroom inside the house, but the sea was familiar.

The swim to Reid's houseboat the next morning was easy, just three inlets to the north, which saw significantly less fishing and shipping traffic than the main Haven Cove harbor. Staying close to the murky seafloor to avoid detection, Nireed dodged the occasional anchor and lobster pot.

Please be home and safe.

If he wasn't, she'd search the town from top to bottom, and if he wasn't there either, she'd return to the docks despite her promise to Lorelei and scour that place down to its last barnacle-encrusted plank.

She couldn't return home without knowing whether she'd doomed him.

As she approached the houseboat, she took care to stay well beneath the surface until she was right up against the stern, using the vessel to shield her from sight. To her relief, she could smell him inside, hear his quiet, even breathing.

He was asleep.

But how to get his attention? Rock the boat? Yell out his name? Sing? The first option would likely scare him, and she'd done that more than enough times. The second two might draw attention from his neighbors, and that was undesirable, especially after the events of yesterday.

She could shift and walk in, but the thought of entering such a small, enclosed space made her shudder. Even her tank had been bigger than this glorified tin can.

Another idea hit her.

Diving to the seafloor, Nireed scooped up a handful of pebbles. One by one, she tossed them at the backdoor. *Tink. Tink. Tink.* Then listened.

A sharp, sleepy inhale, followed by a groggy, "What?"

She threw a few more pebbles.

An exasperated sigh precipitated creaking bedsprings and approaching footsteps. The door was wrenched open, framing a tired, but alert Coast Warrior on the other side. Reid's hair was mussed, dark auburn curls sticking up at odd angles, and his clothes a bit rumpled, but otherwise seemed fine. "Starfish? What are you doing here?"

"I had to make sure you were okay."

A faint smile graced his lips. "You were worried about me?"

"Yes."

"Oh." His brows ticked up, genuinely surprised, like he hadn't been expecting her to admit it. Sitting down, he dangled his legs over the edge. "Yeah, I'm okay, other than staying up late obsessively checking the news for updates."

"Did they find anything?"

"No. We'll see what the next few days bring, of course, but I'm thinking we got lucky. Helps too that the public seems to have latched onto the idea that it was investigative journalists or environmental activists who broke in. People tend to believe the most plausible explanation, and I don't think a mermaid and a Coast Guard rescue swimmer even qualifies as one."

Shorewalker had been of the same opinion, but it felt better to hear it echoed by him. This put her at ease about his continued safety. "I shouldn't have left you behind last night. That's not what a good podmate does, and you deserve the same courtesy. I didn't even think, just fled."

"It wasn't as bad as you're making it sound. You warned me. I could've followed."

"This is true. But I am the one who brought you into all this, and I never thought it could get you in trouble with other Surface Dwellers. For that I'm sorry."

"It was my decision. I knew what I was risking, and you offered me an out, but I appreciate you acknowledging it all the same."

She dipped her head, accepting this, but promised herself to be more careful about the kind of help she asked from him in the future.

"But thanks for coming to check on me. That was thoughtful."

Nireed pushed off the stern, preparing to dive. Now that she knew Reid was safe, and probably would remain so for the near future, she needed to return home. It wasn't unusual for her to visit Shorewalker for a few days at a time, but with Nautic being a constant threat, Aersila would be worried. "I know I can be vicious. But I'm not heartless."

He watched her, quiet and thoughtful. "No. I don't think you are."

THE SWIM HOME WAS A LONG ONE. AND NOT JUST BECAUSE of the distance. Recent failure and the Coast Warrior's quiet rejection the night before weighed heavily on Nireed's mind.

She wasn't any closer to proving Nautic's murderous designs and, until she did, more and more of her people would die. Though the fault lay entirely with Nautic, it felt more like her own. Because she had an idea. She just hadn't worked up the courage to attempt it. Yet, the longer she dawdled, the more time Nautic had to exact their ruthless slaughter.

And Reid. Dancing with him had muddied her feelings. This was supposed to be an alliance, and yet, the easy way they moved together made her consider more seriously the possibility she might desire something more from him. Something he seemed to also want but couldn't, or wouldn't, give.

Or maybe this was just the beginning of a mating frenzy, and she was confusing it with real feelings. But at least that problem had the luxury of time to resolve. The other did not.

At home, Nireed found both her sister and Undine waiting for her, grimly serious expressions on their faces. She'd expected the former, but their pod leader being there as well could only mean one thing: an intervention. All her shoreside efforts would be questioned, maybe even stopped. All because her own sister didn't believe she could make a difference.

Her heart sunk to the pit of her stomach.

"Where were you?" Aersila signed. "You were gone for two days."

"I was with Shorewalker. That's nothing new. I regularly see her for days at a time."

Her sister narrowed her eyes. "I smell more than just Shorewalker on you."

Had his scent rubbed off on her that much? "And?"

"And you need to stop seeing that Surface Dweller."

"His name is Reid."

"Fine, this Reid. And Shorewalker too." Such vehemence, such authority in those demands, and she had no right.

Anger flared hotter than the water near a hydrothermal vent. "Why?" She smacked out the word with her hands, tail twitching irritably.

"It's too dangerous, not worth the risk," Undine signed, finally deigning to join the conversation.

"And sending me to shore to be a Surface Dweller experiment was?"

"We were sick, desperate."

"Are we not desperate now?"

"It's not the same. We can rely on our own now." Undine shifted the bundle wrapped around her chest. Her baby was swaddled in a woven seaweed blanket, nursing at their leader's breast, pudgy little hands holding on.

Longing panged low in Nireed's belly, her heart, her arms. The desire to cradle and nuzzle a little one of her own swept over her like a tidal wave. She wanted to be a mother someday and not just because the pod expected her to.

Baby reoriented, Undine continued, "Two more of our own have gone missing. It's not that I don't trust Shorewalker or Cure Creator—I'll always be grateful for what they've done for this pod—but you stray to shore too often, Nireed. It's going to get you captured again or killed."

"That only happened because you asked me to go. And I went willingly to help the pod, so it won't happen again unless I mean it to." Undine didn't need to know that Nireed had doubts at points about her ability to blend in and not get caught.

"If you want to help the pod, boost our numbers." Undine paused to press a kiss to the top of her baby's head. "We can smell the beginnings of mating frenzy on you. Make use of it. Find a mate."

"One of the mermen," Aersila added pointedly. "Not the Surface Dweller."

This was ridiculous. Her scales parted just once, and everyone had an opinion about it. "Who, Aquilus?" Nireed slapped the words out, and Aersila flinched. "Cyrus, who's barely old enough, or the one who's just as overenthusiastic as he is lackluster? I don't see why I need to bother. Our kind have mated with Surface Dwellers plenty in the past."

"Out of necessity." Undine's expression was stern, but motherly, which only made Nireed angrier. Their pod leader had ten years on her, that was it. "Now we can mate with our own. Few options are still options. Your Surface Dweller can give you babies, yes, but he can't be here to help you raise them."

"When the mating frenzy takes hold, you'll be insatiable," Undine continued. "It'll trickle over to the rest of the pod, so you might be able to find a few attached males willing to see you through it. If you'd like, I can help arrange…"

Nireed scoffed. As if that made it any better. They were discussing her life as if she had no choice. Shorewalker had always given her a choice. Cure Creator too. And when that had been taken away from them all, they fought for her.

And Reid? What if she didn't want to mate with him? While she had felt a spark of something, some unexplored potential, she barely even had the time to think about it, much less make any sort of decision. Wanting a baby soon didn't mean right now. It was worth waiting for a connection. For love.

"Why is she here?" Nireed signed to Aersila in sharp, cutting motions. "Are you going to make me mate someone I don't want to? Are you going to chain me here? Because that's what it'll take."

Her sister reared back as if she'd been slapped.

"Of course not, but if you don't mate…"

"What? My tail will fall off? I'll perish from unfulfilled lust?"

"Well, no…"

"Then what, Aersila? What will happen? I'll hurt my wrist taking care of myself for a few weeks? My frenzy will spread to you, and you'll finally work up the courage to tangle tails with Aquilus?"

"It makes you rash, stupidly fearless." Aersila slammed her hands together, harshly punctuating each word. But her face had crumpled, anguish and defeat etched into every line. Nireed didn't need to see the tears to know they were there. "You'll go against your instincts and take risks you shouldn't. You'll make mistakes."

Tender feelings for her sister displaced the anger. While Aersila had been wrong to bring Undine into a private, personal matter, it had come from a deep well of hurts. Of experience she did not want Nireed to repeat.

The motions of Nireed's hands softened as she signed, "Do you regret yours?"

"Not Ryn, but yes, sometimes." Aersila's body slumped. "Don't follow in my wake, Nireed. Be smarter than me."

Taking her sister's face in her hands, Nireed pressed their foreheads together for a long moment. Aersila stilled, waiting. This quiet acquiescence meant she'd listen to what Nireed had to say next.

Nireed pulled back to sign, "I have been following my instincts. Haven't gone against them once. Believe I'm capable. Believe in *me*, sister."

"But a Surface Dweller, Nireed? He's so far away. If you have a baby together…"

Frustration leeched in. "I haven't decided if I even want to try, much less with him."

"Just let me finish." Her sister's gaze was pleading. "It needs to be said."

Whatever her sister needed to say, even if it pissed her off, she'd hear it out this once, and then no more. The conversation about what Nireed did with her body, and who she did or didn't give her tail to, ended after that.

"He's so far away. If you want to be with him, raise your children together, he can't come to you. You'd have to go to him, away from the city, away from the pod, away from me. You'd be a Shallows Dweller. Your babies too. And you might be clever enough to avoid detection, to skirt a fisherman's net, but what about them? What will you do if they take your children?"

Understanding harpooned through her. Here, she'd been thinking short-term, but Aersila had her eye on the horizon.

Undine, who'd gone quiet throughout the exchange, held her baby closer.

They were good points, every one of them, but they didn't have the effect her sister intended. What Aersila saw as reasons to divert course, Nireed saw as a need to steer steady.

She would make these waters safer. For Aersila, for Ryn, for the baby in Undine's arms, and for all the babies she'd one day hold in hers.

And Reid was going to help her.

Before she could say as much, a wave of panic flooded the water, erratic topaz light filling the space as Melusina darted into her and her sister's shared abode.

"What is it?" Undine straightened.

"Celia's missing." Melusina looked sick. "Delphine and Zavier have already gone out to look for her."

Dread trickled its glacial current down Nireed's spine, and the collective spike of emotion in the water meant she wasn't alone.

Celia was only a year old, but siren children were born able to swim on their own. Look away for just a moment, and they've darted off, getting their fins in things they shouldn't. That Undine swaddled hers to her breast for nursing was more about motherly connection than need.

"Gather the others." Each one of Undine's movements held fierce command, her electric blue luminescence blinking steadily, and Nireed admired her assuredness and strength. This was why she was their leader, even though many of their elders had thought her too young. Undine did not falter in the face of adversity. "Whatever it takes, we'll find her."

The pod took to the open water as one, their chorus of desperate, searching song flowing on the currents, pleading to the Twenty-Armed Goddess for intercession, pleading to Celia to follow the sound of their song. To come back to them. To safety.

A weak, but unalarmed note answered.

Through a game of call and response, Nireed and the others found Celia, spotted her at a distance, close to the surface, happily twirling around in the water, giggles bubbling from her mouth. Oblivious to the danger rapidly closing in.

By natural law, there should be safety in numbers. But how had Nireed forgotten? There was no such thing when a net hundreds of feet wide and deep could swallow entire pods whole. But for now, they were on the outside looking in. Watching in horror as the unthinkable happened.

Their song died.

They only saw the net because it was already cinching, pulling everything inside it closer and closer together. Everything including Celia, who'd swum unknowingly right into its snare.

Delphine let out a heart wrenching screech as she raced toward the net. Toward the rapidly shrinking opening at its bottom. Toward her baby.

"Delphine!" Nireed screamed.

But the ocean swallowed her name.

CHAPTER
TWELVE

Two cases in one night, that was the only reason Reid and his team were recalled from liberty. Annoying, but it came with emergency-responder territory.

"I see it," Perez said over the radio. "Kruetz, get ready to be lowered on deck."

For the last fifteen minutes, they'd flown a grid with a spotlight on the water, looking for *Gale's Promise*, another one of Nautic's boats. The captain's distress call had given them an approximate location, but for the last few hours, that line of communication had been dead.

Either something had happened to their radios, or the crew was gone.

Seeing it now, Reid suspected the latter. The boat should've been lit up like a sports field for nighttime visibility, but the boat was completely dark save for a few dim auxiliary lights. Unpiloted and unmoored, *Gale's Promise* drifted aimlessly, the waves gently rocking it from side to side.

Clipping in, Reid clapped Hatcher on the upper arm, his crewmate unusually quiet. "I'll be okay. She won't hurt me."

He firmly believed that now.

"Yeah, but what about her friends?"

A reasonable concern, but if Nireed could fend off her kin during a feeding frenzy when he was a stranger, she could do the same now when he was not. It was a lot of faith to put in a person he barely knew, but Reid prided himself on having strong instincts, and right now his were telling him he could trust her.

"She might not be down there," Hatcher warned.

"They're just protecting their own. And I'm going to prove it."

"Man, I sure hope you're right."

The helicopter hovered over the purse seiner, its spotlight illuminating the boat as Reid was lowered onto it. It was too quiet, too still. Even amid power failure, there should've been more activity on deck—the crew attempting maintenance, shooting distress flares into the sky, anything. But there was none of that. Only cables and ropes knocking against metal in the helicopter's downdraft.

When Reid's feet hit the deck, he unclipped, head on a swivel as he made his way to the pilothouse. Loud as the Jayhawk was, he didn't need to call out and announce his presence, the boat crew should be able to hear it, but he did so anyway.

No one called back.

A veritable ghost ship.

As he reached for the pilothouse door, his foot skidded on something slick, and his heart lurched in that uncertain moment between thinking his ass might hit the deck and catching himself. Boat decks were supposed to be covered in anti-slip tape. He shouldn't have...

Blood, it was blood.

And a lot of it too. But not just that, the deck beneath his feet was littered with bullet holes. Unless the crew had lost their minds and started shooting each other, this blood belonged to a mermaid, not a fisherman.

Dread laced around his spine in a wicked vise grip.

Nireed.

Flashes of memory consumed him. Her wicked smile and biting tongue. The feeling of her body crammed next to his, hiding in Nautic's warehouse. Her stunning aim. The way she danced.

The fiery determination in which she demanded his help and fought for her people every single day.

Fear froze him, but the desperate need to find Nireed thawed his limbs. He whisked open the door, not missing the blood smeared on both sides. The sticky mass of it. If she was here, if she'd been shot, she'd either be fighting for her life or...

Dead.

God no, please no.

The bodies of two fishermen lay on the floor, their entrails spilling from gaping gut wounds, and he clapped a hand over his nose and mouth, trying not to hurl at the sight and sewer stench of perforated offal. Given their location, this was probably the captain and the helmsman. Each held a weapon in their hands—one a gun, the other a knife. Little good they did either of them.

Reid searched the remainder of the room in a half-blind panic.

Radio static, then Perez's voice filled his ears. "Kruetz, talk to us."

"Two deceased fishermen in the pilothouse," he answered, brain and body on autopilot. "Going to check the rest of the boat."

"Negative." This was Hatcher. "Get back on deck. We gotta get you out of there."

"There might be survivors."

"A fat load of good that'll do anybody if you're dead!"

Reid ignored his crewmate and finished checking the pilothouse. No mermaids. But that didn't ease the fear-fueled adrenaline pumping through his veins. When he didn't find any more bodies in the pilothouse, he continued his search outside.

There was another dead fisherman, this one tucked behind a deck box, which he'd missed during his initial pass. He turned away quickly, feeling queasy. Most of the guy's head was missing, ripped away at the jaw, and he didn't need to see that in any close detail. The gun still clenched in the corpse's hand had him thinking the man ducked behind here for cover while shooting at the mermaid storming the pilothouse.

"Found a third on deck," he said into the radio, sounding calmer than he felt.

"Let us know if you find the rest of the crew." Just Perez this time.

"Roger that. Heading below."

"Be careful. If you prove Hatcher right, I'll have to come down there myself and start punching mermaids."

If he wasn't so goddamn terrified for Nireed's well-being, he might've laughed.

He found the stairs and began his descent.

The first thing he noticed was the stench. The bowels of the boat reeked of fish, something coppery, and worse. The second was the pitch-black darkness. Not even the auxiliary lights still worked down here. Reid briefly nudged aside his headset, but the only thing he could hear was the muffled sound of waves lapping against the hull outside. Not the engine. Not even the refrigerated fish hold.

Flicking on his headlamp, Reid discovered where the rest of the crew had gone and stifled another heave, bile burning the back of his throat.

They were...all over the place, body parts strewn along the hall, blood splattered, and viscera smeared.

But still no mermaids.

Maybe they'd gotten off the boat. Injured, but alive.

Shaky relief whooshed out of him for one glorious moment, until something caught his eye—a severed, booted foot propping open the fish hold door.

Something Nireed said came to him in a rush, something that made his blood run cold.

"The fishermen are hunting us, you know. There's a whole fleet of them. Don't know what they do with our bodies once they've killed us."

He wove around the gore, avoiding it wherever he could, but where he couldn't, he didn't think too deeply about whatever squished beneath his neoprene booties. Reid yanked open the fish hold door and kicked aside the severed foot, a wall of cold air slamming into him. When he looked down...

Horror and anguish hit him like a tidal wave, a silent scream clawing up his throat before shock killed it on his tongue.

Mermaids. Two of them.

He tripped over a dismembered fisherman to get to the one with silver scales, collapsing to his knees beside her and gathering her up into his arms. After several shaky, panicked swipes, he freed her face of the stiff, frozen hair plastered to it.

"Kruetz, what's going on? You're breathing hard."

"It's not her," he croaked, dizzy with mind-numbing relief. *Oh, thank God, it's not you, Starfish.*

And neither was the mermaid next to her. The deep burgundy scales tipped him off right away in the seconds it had taken him to assess the scene.

The mermaid in his arms was stone cold and rigid, sightless eyes a milky white. Her body was badly broken and bruised, but that was not what killed her. There was a bullet hole in the dead center of her forehead.

She'd been dead awhile. Days, not hours.

This happened before the attack, not during.

And given her other extensive injuries, either the fishermen had beaten her before they killed her, or she'd gotten them when they hauled her from the water. Trapped inside a purse seine net with other sea creatures, that massive crush of bodies, the sheer weight, easily could've killed her. But she'd held on, only to be done in by a bullet to the head.

"Kruetz, who's not her? Give me an update."

"There are two frozen mermaids in the fish hold, each with a gunshot wound to the head. Forensics will have to confirm it, but I'm certain they were dead well before the attack began. Still need to check the galley and the living quarters, but I feel confident the crew's all dead." And he'd seen more to them than he'd ever cared to.

"Hatcher will lower a camera down to you. Get as many photographs as you can and collect anything that looks too important to lose if bad weather hits the area."

Reid dimly registered the instruction. "I gotta find her." Make sure she wasn't bleeding out on this goddamned boat.

"Great, just great. He's worried about his flesh-eating gal pal."

"She's not my..."

"Yeah, whatever man. I'll believe it when you get your ass back up here."

"Hatcher! You're not helping. Just get him that camera and let him search."

Gently, Reid laid the mermaid on the freezer hold floor. He tried folding her arms across her middle, some quiet gesture of respect, but rigor mortis had set in, or maybe it was deep freeze. In either case, he wasn't going to fight it.

As he clambered to his feet, he saw that one of the two severed hands in the room still gripped something. A peculiar looking gun. Its sleek, rounded design looked more like something out of a sci-fi movie than something a fisherman would carry.

Without touching it, he crouched down to get a closer look. No magazine. No slide or sight either. A trigger, but no guard. Then he followed the oddly rounded barrel down to its muzzle.

Dual sensations hit his limbs in waves. First numbing cold, then prickling heat.

"Perez." He swallowed past the lump forming in his throat. "I found something."

"Keep talking to me. What did you find?"

"It wasn't bullets that killed them."

"What do you mean?"

"I just found a cattle gun."

All along, Nireed had been telling the truth. Not only were her people being murdered, Nautic's fishermen were slaughtering them like animals.

Turning away from the evidence, Reid finally lost the contents of his stomach.

HUNDREDS OF PHOTOS LATER, REID SECURED THE CAMERA and the other evidence he found onboard *Gale's Promise* in a zip-top plastic bag and sent the bundle up to the helicopter in the basket lift. They'd pushed the limit of their fuel reserves collecting evidence, but there was an oncoming storm pinging on radar, and they couldn't risk losing what he'd found, namely the ship's log and security camera system's memory card.

There hadn't been time to truly read through the log, but Reid had spotted at least one damning entry a few months back.

No mermaids, no sanctuary. $10,000/lb.

It was so alarming he'd taken a photo of it.

The merfolk had exacted their vengeance in a horrifying show of blood and carnage, there was no doubt about that, but he couldn't find it within himself to pass judgment. And maybe that made him a monster, but after seeing the mermaids in the freezer, both executed with a cattle gun, then commoditized, he couldn't bring himself to feel ashamed.

Reid stood on deck awaiting his turn, sucking in lungfuls of fresh sea air, trying to purge the scent of death. He wanted off this graveyard of a ship stat, but taking care meant taking time, and he'd rather Hatcher move slow and sure than jeopardize the evidence. This was the first serious proof they had and could turn the tide of the investigation in the merfolk's favor. Not only was Nautic involved in black market trade, its fishermen were committing murder.

Worry for Nireed gnawed at his gut. She could be hurt and in need of medical attention, but with no way to find her, there was nothing he could do. Beyond getting this evidence safely into the hands of his commanding officer and CGIS, he was completely and dismally useless.

A strong gust of wind rocked Reid on his feet, and he braced the starboard-side railing for balance. The temperature was dropping, the waves kicking up, too, all signs that the storm that pinged on their radar was nearly here.

"Oh shit, incoming!"

It was the panic in Hatcher's voice that had Reid jerking away from the side, half expecting a pissed off mermaid to launch out of the water.

"What's going on back there? What do you see?"

A blur of motion caught the corner of his eye. Something falling, then hitting the railing with a solid crack, before toppling over into the ocean. In that split second, Reid saw it.

The evidence bag.

Camera. Ship's log. All of it.

"Reid, leave it!" Hatcher yelled. "It's not worth it."

Reid didn't think. He just leapt.

CELIA WAS SAFE. THEY'D GOTTEN HER BACK, THANK THE Twenty-Armed Goddess. Now, Nireed just had to get to shore, had to explain what happened to Reid. If he thought the bloodbath had been without just cause, he and his people might retaliate. And hers would be utterly decimated.

Groaning, Nireed clutched her bleeding side. One of the fishermen's bullets had raked across her flesh, leaving behind a gaping gash.

In the chaos that followed the fight, Nireed separated from the rest of the pod, but not before telling Melusina that she needed to make things right with Reid. Someone had to know she was on a mission, and not missing, which her friend acknowledged with a nod, but she was also so preoccupied with safely towing Fortuna, a badly injured podmate, that she didn't argue with Nireed about her injuries.

Fortuna was the only reason Celia was still alive.

As the pod raced toward the little one, caught inside the rapidly cinching net, Fortuna, one of their fastest swimmers, ascended the depths at a dangerous rate. She darted up inside and took Celia into their arms as it closed, shielding her with their body from the mass of trapped fish pressing in.

Nireed would never forget seeing Delphine slam against the net from the outside, would never forget hearing her friend's anguished screeching as she tried clawing her way in. But with the net squeezing in tight, it was a wall of fish-flesh she was fighting her way through, not just the net itself. The whole pod joined in on the frantic effort until Undine redirected them to the boat above.

They scaled the side, braving Surface Dweller guns when their singing did not work against the crew's ear-protection. Not that it saved them in the end. Rage, necessity, and a desire to protect and to kill had launched Nireed into motion.

She'd lunged for the fisherman who was shooting her kin from behind a deck box, ripping the upper portion of his head clean off, but also took a bullet to her side for the trouble.

Everything after that happened so fast. Screaming. More gunshots. Screaming. Then silence. Someone had even shut off the engine. Or smashed it to bits, more like. It had been a rescue, then aggressive self-defense. Some retribution, too, and a show of strength, but Reid had to understand that. He had to.

Nireed swam on, each mile passing slower than the next. Her strength was flagging. But she had to keep pushing. If she stopped, if she passed out, she was shark food.

And one had been tailing her since the fight.

CHAPTER

FOURTEEN

THE EVIDENCE THEY HAD AGAINST NAUTIC WAS GONE.
Destroyed. Reid leapt off *Gale's Promise*, dove into the rising waves, and
grabbed the evidence bag. He'd moved so fast it hadn't the time, nor the
weight, to sink very deep. But water had gotten inside and damaged the
contents, despite his quadruple checks on the seal before putting it into
the basket lift.

CGIS was going to try recovering the digital files, but it was more a
formality than any real hope of success.

After a few hours of shitty sleep at the station, Reid stumbled his
way to the head, tired, cranky, his guts a tangled mass of knots and
stress. Someone was talking within, the voice too muffled to make out
words, just harsh, clipped tones beyond the door. Reid went in, the
hinges creaking, and beelined for the sink. Morning quarters was in
fifteen minutes, and he could stand to look a little less like death
warmed over in front of command.

"Gotta go." A second later, Hatcher pushed out of one of the stalls,
shoving his relic of a flip phone into his pocket.

Reid splashed water on his face. "Who were you talking to?"

"My mom."

"While you were taking a shit?" Reid wrenched the faucet shut and straightened, roughly swiping water from his face.

"Man, mind your own business. Can't even talk on the damn phone around here without someone butting in." Hatcher grumbled the last bit as he tried brushing past, but Reid stood in the way, a wall of muscle and zero fucks.

"Don't get pissy with me, fumble fingers."

"Now who's getting pissy?"

Dropping the evidence bag wasn't some minor fuck up. Not only did Hatcher's clumsiness derail an active CGIS investigation, but there were lives at stake, both human and merfolk. This setback put them all at risk. "What happened last night?

"The wind picked up. I lost my grip. You know the rest." Once more Hatcher tried to skirt around him, but Reid blocked the door, the two of them teetering on a very, very fine line. One that bordered on shoving.

"The basket was right there. What were you doing, juggling the evidence bag?"

"No! God, it was an accident. Stress, maybe. I'm sorry. Is that what you want to hear?"

"I'm not looking for an apology. I need to know if I can count on you. After last night, I'm not so sure."

Hatcher reeled back, offended, pissed. "What exactly are you accusing me of?"

"Being sloppy."

"You know what? Fuck you." Hatcher jabbed a finger toward Reid's chest, though never quite touching. What little restraint remained between them would snap if he did. "Ever since that mermaid chic got into your head, you've been insufferable. Yeah, I dropped the evidence bag, but if you want to point fingers, maybe consider that I'm not the one who let eight fishermen die."

The fight emotionally gut-punched out of him, Reid stood aside. Hatcher left without another word.

That night, the failure with *The Merry Mariner's* crew cut deep. It wasn't Reid's fault, he knew that, but next to the loss of evidence, the loss of lives didn't compare. Maybe sleep deprivation, stress, and fear had muddled his mind. Maybe he was being too hard on Hatcher, and if he took a moment to breathe, he'd realize last night wasn't the guy's fault either.

Some things really were just beyond their control.

After a long morning debriefing, in which Hatcher thoroughly ignored him, they were dismissed. A half hour drive later, Reid was finally home. He shoved off his work boots and was about to fall into bed when he heard a weak voice call out his name.

And just like that, he snapped to attention, sleep forgotten. *Nireed.*

She sounded hurt. Scared.

The question "how bad?" looped on repeat as he crossed the length of his houseboat. He was out his back door in seconds, heart in his throat.

Nireed was draped across the diving platform off the stern, bleeding from a gash in her side. While she'd managed to pull herself out of the water, her complexion was ghostly pale, a little too gray, even for her. She swam injured all this way in a night. But why would she do that? What was so important that she'd risk her life to get here?

Was she in trouble? The pod...gone? He hadn't seen more than the two in the freezer hold, but that didn't mean the rest survived the journey home.

Shoving all his questions aside, he crouched down to assess Nireed for other injuries—broken bones, internal bleeding—before attempting to move her. Her pretty orange and silver tailfin was ripped, a piece possibly even missing, but otherwise, the gash along her side seemed to be the worst of it.

Gently, he scooped her into his arms. "Hang on, Starfish. I got you."

Carefully navigating the narrow doorway, he carried her inside and laid her on his bed, propping her tail and lower back with rolled-up army surplus blankets, something he didn't mind getting blood on while keeping her lower half elevated. "This will help me stop the bleeding," he explained when she stared at him with wide, watering eyes.

After washing and drying his hands, he whisked his EMS kit out of a cupboard and beelined it for a pair of latex gloves, quickly donning them. His stash of clean cloths came out next, and he folded one into a thick wad.

"Don't hate me." Tears rolled down her cheeks, and when she lifted a hand to pry away a strand of salt-stiff hair from her cheek, he saw there was dried blood caked to her claws. Not only had Nireed been on *Gale's Promise* last night, it seemed she'd also taken part in the carnage. "They stole my friend's baby. We had to get her back."

Good God. He hadn't seen a baby mermaid among the corpses, but maybe in all the chaos, he'd missed her. "Is the baby..." He swallowed and began again. "Is she all right?" He almost couldn't bear to ask.

"We saved her. Many of us were wounded, but we got her back."

Relief was a cool glass of water. "And your friend?"

"Her hands got cut up clawing her baby free, and a bullet grazed her shoulder, but mostly just shaken."

He didn't have any kids of his own, but he couldn't imagine a worse nightmare.

"I saw the bodies in the freezer hold," he said, leaning over her to press the wad to her wound. She winced but kept still. "I'm sorry about your..." Who had they been to her? Friends? Family? Neighbors?

"Podmates," she finished, face crumpling. "Leaving them like that." She clapped a hand over her mouth, but the choked sob still came. A gush of warmth seeped through the cloth beneath his hands. He reached for another and applied more pressure.

"Stay still for me, Starfish. I need to stop this bleeding."

She inhaled wetly.

"That's it. Deep breaths. In and out."

Her chest rose and fell in time to his instructions, calming bit by bit. Although tears still streamed down her cheeks, she was no longer convulsing and jarring her wound. "We wanted to take them back into the deep with us," she sniffled. "Bring them home, give them the funerary rites they deserve, but with so many of us injured, and all the blood and sharks..."

"Shh," he soothed, pausing to smooth back the hair from her forehead with the heel of his hand, the only part not yet stained with blood. "You don't have to explain. The living take priority. I would've done the same."

"You would have?"

"Yeah." He met her gaze, maintaining pressure on the wound. "What's got you so worried about what I think?"

"We killed those fishermen, ripped them all to pieces, and I helped. I know that looks bad."

"Do you regret it?"

Her luminescent eyes flashed. "No." Though her voice cracked, she didn't look away. It wasn't pride he saw there, shame neither, just the truth.

Maybe he was turning into a psycho, but he was glad she had no regrets. Anything nearing that seemed like a betrayal of her true nature, of the creature she was. Nireed was ruthless, but she was fair, too, and maybe the murderous, baby-stealing fishermen deserved what they got. "Which one was yours?"

"My what? My kill?" When he nodded, her expression darkened. "Are you sure you want to know that?"

It made for morbid bedside conversation, but yeah, he wanted to know which baby-stealing fucker met his doom at the end of Nireed's claws. When he said as much, she replied, "The one behind the deck box."

So the one who made a mother rescue her baby under gunfire. While Reid had been collecting evidence and taking pictures, he had found more bullet holes over by the net. It didn't take a forensic scientist to put two and two together. "Damn. You ripped his head right off. I almost puked. He the one who hurt you?"

"Yes."

"Guess there's a lesson to be learned here, huh? Don't fuck with merfolk." What he didn't say was he was damn glad that ass wipe hadn't killed her. Just a little to the left and she would've suffered the slow, agonizing death of a gut wound.

Nireed quieted, sinking back into his pillows, an arm draped above her head. Her chest was bare, but he continued working with detached, clinical precision. Attraction didn't factor in when his body was running on the kind of adrenaline that cared more about keeping her alive.

Once he got the bleeding to stop, he rinsed and cleaned the wound until Nireed said it no longer stung. Then, he applied antibiotic ointment to help prevent infection and gave her a non-NSAID for the pain while he got the sutures ready, threading a curved needle.

She eyed it warily. "That's not a fishing hook, is it?"

It did sort of look like one. "It's a surgical needle. We use it for sewing wounds." He demonstrated on top of his skin without puncturing it. "What does the pod use?"

Surprise flickered across her face. "Whale bone. Part of the rib, so it does curve a little. Just not that much."

"Nice. What's with the surprise though?"

"Didn't think you'd be interested in our methods."

"Why wouldn't I be?

She opened her mouth to say something, then closed it. "I don't know," she said after a time. "I guess with the fishermen hunting us, I sometimes forget not all Surface Dwellers think we're animals."

"I get that, but with any luck, it will all be over soon. Gathered a lot of evidence last night." Hope illuminated her features, so bright not even the threaded needle he held up dimmed it. "Ready to get started?"

"Ready."

"Take deep breaths. I'm pretty quick, but it's a long injury, so just tell me if you need a break."

She nodded, taking slow, deep breaths.

"All right. Here we go."

He could feel her eyes on him, watching him while he worked. She felt her flinch from time to time but was all around handling the stitching process exceptionally well. The irritable way she twitched her tail was the only other sign she was in pain.

Before joining the Coast Guard, he'd done river rescue in Michigan, which was where he'd gotten his first round of EMS training, but it also came with the territory of being an Aviation Survival Technician, so his skills had remained sharp.

Halfway through, her breathing came out in heavy, rasping pants.

"Need a break?"

She shook her head, inhaling deeply.

"That's it," he said, admiring her strength. "Keep breathing."

A few more stitches. "I always knew you were tough, but damn, I'm impressed. Best patient I've ever had."

In, out, in, out. "You're so good at sitting still."

Her breath stuttered, then resumed, deeper than before.

"There you go. Deep breaths."

In, out, in, out.

"Good girl."

She clutched his forearm, her grip surprisingly gentle, but firm. "Reid?"

"Yeah, Starfish?" He stilled, thinking she needed a break, but when he looked up, he saw her cheeks were flaming red.

"I'm going to need you to stop doing that."

That wasn't pain talking. She sounded too embarrassed. "Doing what? Stitching?"

"No, not that." Her voice was strained, pleading.

Confused, he drew back to assess the situation.

Oh.

Some of her silver scales at the base of her pelvis had retreated to reveal a pink, glistening slit beneath. Swallowing thickly, he met her eyes once more. He had wondered. And now he knew. "Praise kink, huh?" he joked nervously, reaching for a sheet to pull over her waist for privacy.

Her nostrils flared.

"I guess we're even now."

"Even?"

"First night we met." He sprung his finger in demonstration. It hadn't been arousal that did it, but she'd seen what he'd been packing, and that counted.

A slow smile broke out across her lips. "I remember."

She relaxed after that, and Reid finished stitching her side in comfortable silence.

He moved on to her tailfin, which she told him had been mauled by a shark attracted to her blood. The flowy membrane was thicker than it looked, and piscine in texture, but took to the sutures well enough. And Nireed said she didn't have much feeling there, so sewing it was a cakewalk by comparison.

Once she was cleaned up and bandaged, he peeled his gloves off and stood. The cabin of his boat looked every bit like the makeshift emergency room it became, so he set to straighten the place up, clearing away bloodied blankets and biohazardous trash.

When it came time to change his sheets, she stiffly scooted off the bed and into a nearby chair. He moved quickly to get the bed remade.

"You're really brave," he said, tucking in the corners of the new set. Then, threading his arms under hers, helped her back in. "You know that, right?"

She watched him intently but didn't reply.

He sat next to her, taking her hand, and marveled at the smooth webbing between each finger, the texture so much like her fins. "For the record, I don't hate you. Not even close. When I saw the bullet holes on deck, I was afraid something had happened to you." He swallowed, clasping her hand between both of his. "I thought they'd killed you, Starfish."

She cupped his cheek, turning him to her. Her amber eyes were a warm place to get lost in, glowing soft as lantern light, and her smile was sweet, and a little unsure. "You were afraid for me?"

"Terrified."

He stared at her mouth, drawn to it. He knew what lurked behind those sensuous lips. He'd heard the screams, seen the blood that had coated her lips. *And yet.* He wanted to devour that mouth. Throw caution to the wind and capture and plunder it until the world fell away and he forgot all sense and reason. Until he forgot his name and why he shouldn't fall for this in the first place.

Wasn't that how all the tales went? Sailors lured in by beauty, lonely and wanting, only to find death at the other end of a pretty smile.

"Reid?" Her gaze flicked down, just a moment, before meeting his eyes once more, searching.

She almost died saving a friend and her baby. And she almost died again getting here, all while thinking that he hated her, when he felt anything but.

Nireed was a monster. There was no denying that. She'd ripped off a man's head with her bare hands and sometimes consumed human flesh. But she was also the bravest, most selfless person he knew.

Perez and Hatcher were right, damn them.

He wanted her. So damn bad.

But kissing her right now was out of the question. She was hurt, and she didn't need him complicating things when she'd just survived some harrowing shit. "We should get some sleep." He slapped his hands to his thighs, abruptly standing, before desire got the better of him. "You can have my bed. I'll take the couch."

Her smile fell. Was that disappointment he saw?

"I don't know," she said, rubbing her upper arms. "I think I should go."

A surge of protectiveness rose inside him. "Not with that injury." It came out harsher, more demanding than he meant it to, and she rightly glared at him.

Dammit. He'd regressed to the communicative range of a caveman.

"I'm sorry." He knelt in front of her, his hands framing but not quite touching her tail. "Please stay. Don't go back out there. Not yet."

Her expression softened.

"It's a long way," he continued. "You're exhausted, and you've been through a lot. Please rest here."

Nireed stared at the horizon through a nearby window. He couldn't know what she was thinking, but if he had to guess, several things weighed heavily there. Mental calculations about energy reserves and the long miles ahead. Worry for her friends and podmates. Grief for those who never made it home. A whole community counting on her. The burden of responsibility. Rage.

She lay on his bed, arms folding across her middle. Not quite fitting, her tail hung over the edge, fins draping across the floor. "Okay," she said quietly. "I'll stay."

CHAPTER
FIFTEEN

REID HAD BEEN RIGHT. SHE WAS EXHAUSTED. EXHAUSTED enough to find even this dry Surface Dweller bed comfortable. But he'd confused her too.

One moment, she thought he was about to kiss her. The next, he jumped away so fast one would think she was about to bite him.

Oh. Maybe he did think that.

Disappointment sank to the pit of her stomach like a rock. He said he didn't hate her, and she believed him when he said he was afraid she'd been killed, but she barely had the energy to think a coherent thought, let alone untangle the meaning behind Reid's mixed signals.

That was a problem for tomorrow.

Right now, she needed to ask a favor from Shorewalker before she let sleep claim her. Reid jumped at the opportunity to help—maybe he felt bad—and together they looked up Lorelei's work phone number. Some instructing and a lot of pointing later, she had Reid's cell phone in her hand, a strange noise she couldn't even begin to describe repeating at regular intervals.

A click. "Lorelei Roth, Director of the Haven Cove Museum of Oceanic Discovery."

"Shorewalker, it's Nireed."

"Nireed?" Lorelei's voice quieted on the other end. "How'd you get a hold of a phone?"

"Borrowed from the, uh, Coast Warrior friend I told you about. He looked up your number on the Inter-Net."

The line went quiet on the other end.

Nireed handed the phone to Reid. "I think it stopped working."

"Ms. Roth? Are you still there?"

A throat cleared on the other end. "Um, yes, still here. You can put Nireed back on."

Nireed accepted the phone, and continued, dimly noting how Reid went into the boat's tiny kitchen section to give her privacy. "I need a favor."

"Anything. What can I do?"

"Nautic's fishermen took Delphine's baby. We got her back, but there was a fight, and I got hurt. I'm staying with the Coast Warrior while I heal, but I need someone to let the pod know I'm okay and bring food and healing supplies. Can you do that, Shorewalker?"

With so many members of the pod hurt during the attack, hunting would be hard, maybe impossible. Their kind healed fast, but with meager food stores it would be a difficult few days.

"Killian's going out first thing tomorrow morning. I'll stowaway and get him to divert course."

"I appreciate his sense of honor but tell him to fish in our waters. It's the least we can do for his troubles."

"I will, Nireed. Thanks. If I need to get a hold of you again, is this the number I should reach you on?"

Nireed paused to ask Reid, then brought the thin, shiny brick back toward her mouth. "Coast Warrior says yes."

"Okay, great. Writing it down now. Are you okay? You said you got hurt."

"I will be fine, Shorewalker. Don't worry. Just need to rest."

"Do you want me to come get you? You can stay with Killian and me."

They had a lot more room and a private cove she could swim in while she regained her strength. But Reid wouldn't be there. She studied him from across the room, where he leaned over the counter, cutting up raw filets of fish, his expression focused and thoughtful. "He's taking good care of me."

"Is he now?" There was a teasing, rhetorical lilt to the question, but Reid didn't want her in the way Lorelei's tone implied.

Putting down his knife, Reid beckoned to the phone with his hand. "Can I talk to her a sec before you hang up?"

Nireed nodded. "Coast Warrior would like to speak with you."

"He does?" If Nireed didn't know any better, she'd say Shorewalker sounded nervous, but there was no reason for her to be.

"Yes. Here he is."

He took the phone and talked to Lorelei for several minutes—giving her his address and work schedule in case she wanted to visit Nireed. When he hung up, he turned to Nireed. "She's got a little bit of a Yooper accent. Kinda like my mom's."

"Mm." Nireed didn't know what that meant, only that the way Shorewalker spoke to him was different from how she spoke to her. Some Surface Dweller thing? She hadn't meant to eavesdrop on the conversation, but her sensitive siren hearing couldn't be helped.

He shrugged, as if it was an inconsequential thought he'd just had and pocketed his phone. "Hungry?" Reid retreated into the kitchen, returning with cuts of raw fish neatly arranged on a plate.

She took it, sniffing it tentatively. It was fresh enough. "Thank you, Coast Warrior. For everything."

The air between them was awkward and tense as she ate his offering in silence, but Nireed didn't have the energy left to try to fix this. When she finished, she laid the plate on the floor and got situated for sleep.

Maybe it was rude not to say anything more, not to thank him again for all his help. After all, the Surface Dwellers loved their platitudes and niceties. But surely, after everything that had happened, she was allowed to skip them just this once.

Hugging herself, Nireed closed her eyes and willed sleep to carry her away. A little rest and she'd be strong enough to make the journey home. Update Undine. Get back to Aersila. Check on Delphine and Celia. Then figure out…

Figure out…

CHAPTER
SIXTEEN

N<small>IREED</small> <small>DRIFTED</small> <small>LISTLESSLY</small> <small>IN</small> <small>FOUL</small>, <small>DANK</small> <small>WATER</small>. H<small>ER</small> <small>TAIL</small> <small>TWITCHED</small> *occasionally, just enough to push water past her gills and keep her breathing. This was her life now. Day after day. Week after week. She never used to mind spending time in her head, but her thoughts had become grim company.*

Change only came when the Surface Dweller scientists wanted something. More tests. More poking. More prodding. Then back into the tank, its glass squeezing in on all sides. An unbreakable net. A never-ending cycle.

Cold, curious eyes stared and stared and stared. And what did they learn? Was it how easily they could break her?

Didn't they know? They couldn't get answers from her when she was dead.

But no. That wasn't true. Surface Dweller scientists liked cutting into things.

"Dissections," they called it.

"Nireed."

She never told Shorewalker that.

That they'd wanted to cut her open to study what was inside.

"Nireed."

A hand fell to her shoulder, shaking.

Something was in the tank with her.

"Nireed!"

She shot up, eyes flying open. She was walled in on all sides, the air close in the small, cramped space. Trapped. She was trapped. A horrible shriek ripped out of her mouth, dry and rasping and parched. *No, no, no, no, no. Not again.*

"Nireed?"

Ignoring the panicked voice beside her, she scanned her surroundings for a means of escape. Wall, window, wall. Door! She lunged forward, crashing into a chair, before slamming to the floor, sharp pain shooting up her side. Black spots dotted her vision, but she wouldn't, couldn't stop.

Hand over hand, she dragged herself toward freedom.

Almost there. Almost there.

It struck her that this was too easy. Something should jump out and stop her—a security guard, a scientist—but nothing did.

Reaching up, she grabbed the door handle and wrenched it open—cool, salty sea air embracing her. And the ocean. There was the ocean, beckoning her to safety.

She dove in.

REID DARTED AFTER NIREED, SHUCKING OFF HIS SHIRT along the way, the water rippling from where she dove in. Maybe she'd be okay with those injuries. But maybe not. And that just wasn't something he could leave to chance.

Something had spooked her badly.

Something from her past. He'd seen it before in seasoned Aviation Survival Technicians, haunted by nightmares and memory in equal measure.

It was risky.

It was stupid.

It was the furthest thing from self-preservation that had him following a man-eating mermaid with PTSD into the water.

But he dove in after her.

NIREED DOUBLED OVER IN PAIN, HER SIDE SPASMING something fierce before cramping and locking up tight. She couldn't move, couldn't breathe. Oh Goddess, why couldn't she move? If she didn't move, water wouldn't flow past her gills, and she'd drown.

Twisted fate for a mermaid.

Something plunged into the water behind her.

She flinched, bracing for an attack she couldn't defend against. Whatever it was flutter kicked hard, getting closer and closer. It was coming straight for her. *I'm sorry, Aersila. I'm so, so sorry.*

A familiar scent filled her senses, cutting through her fear.

Reid?

His strong arms threaded underneath hers, and he pulled her back against his chest, kicking up hard. Back and forth, back and forth, until their heads burst above the surface.

Nireed gasped for air as sharp, shooting pains lanced up her side.

"I got you." He towed her backward, but the pain worsened.

It was unbearable. "Stop, stop, stop, stop, stop."

He stopped, kicking only enough to keep them afloat. "Talk to me. Is it your side? Is it cramping?"

"Yes," she said through gritted teeth.

"We're going to need to stretch it out and loosen up the muscles, okay? It's going to hurt like a sonofabitch, but I need you to trust me."

Nireed didn't know what a sonofabitch was, but it sounded awful.

"Lean back on me." Her side twinged as she gave him her full weight, but she could endure it.

"That's it. Now, lean to the right."

She whimpered as she pushed through it, tight, aching muscles screaming in pain.

"You got this, sweetheart. Keep going. Keep going. Stop. Hold it right there."

"Reid," she cried. This was too much.

"I know. Now let's ease it back."

It got harder before it got easier, but it did get easier, and he patiently supported her through every stretch. They paused from time to time, so he could knead at her knotted muscles, coaxing them to release and relax, all the while taking care not to come too close to her wound.

By the time he was done, she was exhausted and sore, but she could move again.

Still, he bid her to lie back and let him tow her in.

Boarding the boat was tricky, but she managed it on her own, using her arms and a little artless wriggling to get up onto the diving platform. Reid got out with a lot more grace, water sluicing off his body as he spun around to sit beside her.

Nireed swallowed, her tail waving nervously in the water.

She'd never seen him with so few clothes on before. She knew he was strong, but she never knew a Surface Dweller could look so...built.

No judgment to their kind, but they lived softer, kinder lives, and yet, Reid's physique wasn't that much different from his oceanic counterparts. Broad, chiseled chest that tapered down to a trim waist. Forearms twice the size of hers and the biceps to match. And he wore these black, short things that clung to his thick upper thighs and bottom but nothing else.

There was an interesting bulge at the apex, too, and as she eyed it curiously, it twitched.

Cheeks burning, she averted her eyes. Mighty Twenty-Armed Goddess, Surface Dwellers wore their genitalia on the outside of their bodies, even when they weren't aroused. If he noticed her staring, he didn't mention it.

They were silent a long time before Nireed spoke. "Bad memories find me in my dreams sometimes. Sometimes when I'm awake too."

"What happened?"

"Have you heard about the Haven Cove mermaid lab?"

He rocked forward, the muscles in his arms flexing. "Yeah, it was notorious for keeping a mermaid captive. There was an exposé about it last year."

She dipped her tailfin in and out of the sea, just to watch the water roll off. "That was me."

He tensed beside her.

"Small spaces make me feel trapped." She hadn't talked about it with anyone, not even Melusina or Delphine. They had their families and their own slew of cares to worry about, and she wasn't going to heap her burdens on them.

Her first few days back home after Shorewalker and Cure Creator freed her from the tank had been about celebration and healing. And then all her focus went back into the pod: getting the cure to her people, reunifying their community, maintaining relationships with their Surface Dweller allies.

From the outside looking in, she was fine. Nothing had changed. There just wasn't a reason to let anyone think otherwise.

Nireed nodded behind them. "I was okay in there until I woke up from a bad dream. I forgot where I was."

"They kept you in that tank for a whole year." She always knew it was bad, but to hear the shock in his voice, from someone who didn't know her then, was validating in a way she didn't know she needed. What had happened to her wasn't acceptable Surface Dweller behavior even to other Surface Dwellers.

"Lorelei, the friend we called earlier, got me out. She's also the reason I was there in the first place." Weariness weighed down her shoulders. The thought of trying to explain the whole situation drained what little energy she had left. "It's a really, really long story."

And not all of it was hers to tell.

"You don't have to tell it. Whatever happened, she must be a good friend now to have your trust."

"She is."

"You look like you're about to fall over. You good?"

"Can I..." Nireed faltered. Twenty-Armed Goddess, she was so tired.

"What do you need?" He gently nudged her tail with his foot.

"Can I go back inside and sleep?"

Worry pinched his brow. "Won't you feel trapped in there?"

That was a concern, but what choice did she have? "I'm exposed out here."

"Right. What if I open the windows and prop open the door? Would that feel better?"

She nodded. Not just spaces she could "escape" through, but

smelling and hearing the ocean might keep her from feeling trapped in the first place.

She waited outside while he worked on opening his home.

When he came back, he crouched beside her, holding out his arms. "Come on. I'm not going to make you crawl."

That made her smile. He was so thoughtful, so attentive, and each time he said or did something that showed he valued her despite their differences was another little hook in her heart, pulling her to him.

He carried her back to his bed, and when he sat her down, she grabbed his forearm. "Stay."

It had been a while since she'd slept curled up against another—her sister, her friends. There was a simple comfort to it that she missed, a promise of peaceful sleep, and a reminder that no matter how hard things got, there was still always this. There was always each other.

Nireed needed some of that now.

Reid hesitated, his gaze darting between himself, her, and the bed.

"Please." She pulled gently.

And then he nodded. Either to himself, or her, she couldn't be sure, but he slid in next to her, and she draped an arm across his bare chest, propping her wounded side against him for support. He flinched a little, his heart rate speeding up, but he wrapped an arm around her and snuggled in.

"Thank you for helping me."

"Anytime, Starfish." He rubbed her shoulder, the motion pressing her closer. "Whatever you need."

She nuzzled into his body's warmth and promptly fell asleep.

CHAPTER
SEVENTEEN

THERE WAS A NAKED WOMAN IN HIS BED.

There was a naked woman in his bed draped across his body, and yes, that was her bare breast smooshed between them, touching his bare skin.

What had Reid gotten himself into?

His mind and body were in complete opposition.

She was fierce, lethal, but vulnerable too. She'd just shared some seriously fucked up shit about her past, and here he was mentally begging his ill-timed erection to go down. This was not an appropriate time to quietly lust.

He'd seen the photos. The exposé had included graphic pictures of Nireed in captivity.

Now that he knew it was her, knew what to look for, there were traces of her in that mermaid. Things like the color of her hair and scales and fins, but apart from that, they were hardly recognizable. And it was a damn good thing. That version of Nireed had been dying. Her complexion was gray, her scales dull and flaking off. Her body was too thin, and her eyes dim.

There was none of her current vibrance and luster in those photos.

Now, here she was in his arms, risking everything to help her people.

It was bravery in the truest sense of the word. She knew the consequences of getting caught. She knew exactly what would happen to her. *Because she'd lived it.*

And it haunted her.

Last night's nightmare had begun with a whimper. He was so used to living alone in this quiet space beside the sea, and so used to living on the edge of the next emergency, that even that soft sound had woken him. When he'd looked over at her sleeping form, her tail was twitching, and her shoulders occasionally gave a slight jerk, but when those little, hypnic movements turned into thrashing, the word "No" cried out on repeat, he'd launched from the couch to her side.

He shouldn't have tried to wake her. It was PTSD 101, and he'd remembered that too late. She'd already woken up in a blind panic, scrambling for safety, only to nearly drown when her injured muscles locked tight. "I'm sorry, Starfish," he murmured, pressing his cheek to the top of her head. "I won't make that mistake again."

Until she healed from her injuries, being around while she slept was going to be a repeat thing. It made his insides all weird and fluttery, like the moment before his stomach dropped on a rollercoaster ride.

He let out a heavy sigh, Nireed rising and falling with his chest. No hesitation, no shyness, she just latched onto him. Just like a...

Just like a little starfish. Fuck. She'd no right being this damn cute. He held her a little closer, and a little tighter, feeling like he'd just learned something deeply intimate. A vicious creature of the deep she may be, but she was also an indomitable snuggler, and he'd bet money she'd been that way her whole life.

Shrugging down into a more relaxed position, he closed his eyes, tuning in to the boat's gentle rocking motion and the waves lapping in steady rhythm against its hull. The sea breeze brought coolness and the ocean's signature, pungent salt and algae scent. The strip of forest on shore nearby was a chorus of crickets and tree frogs. And Nireed. She'd nuzzled her face into the groove where arm met pectoral, a fist bunched loosely on his chest, her soft breaths fanning out across his skin.

The ocean's soothing lullaby and Nireed's reassuring warmth lulled him into a deep sleep.

The next time Reid opened his eyes, night had fallen, and Nireed was right where he'd left her. Amber bioluminescence winked faintly in the dark, like clusters of fireflies had come to rest on her skin. Her tailfin flexed up, then down, twinkling.

They'd evidently slept through the entire day. And if they slept through his next two liberty days, it wouldn't be a bad thing. They sorely needed it.

A soft, hitched gasp escaped Nireed as she shifted her weight, her hips rolling into his thigh at the exact moment her hand slid dangerously close to his junk. Which was fantastically bad timing. He fell asleep hard but woke up even harder.

He tried to angle his hips away, but her hand was curled firmly at the juncture between hip and thigh, claws curving inward, and she held him in place, sighing contently. It didn't hurt, but he wasn't going anywhere, anytime soon.

While he tried to discreetly readjust himself without jostling her, she chose that moment of all moments to roll on top of him, blinking down at him sleepily with glowing amber eyes. Her body settled in the cradle of his hips, very much pinning his dick between them. Save for the tight, compression boxers he wore, there wasn't a stitch of clothing between them. And yet, his hands fell to her hips, his knees instinctively bent to brace her, framing her tail with his legs.

Like he was getting ready to start bucking up into her.

Oh fucking no.

She rubbed her throat, her voice harsh and rasping. "It's dry in here."

Oh, is that all? God help him.

"Want a glass of water?" The question came out sounding a little bit strangled even to his own ears.

She shook her head. "Need to swim." She pushed off him, his breath whooshing out in a quiet "oof" as she slunk to the floor. "Come with me. Make sure I don't almost drown again."

Either she somehow hadn't noticed his hard-on, or she was politely ignoring it.

Tucking his dick into the waistband of his boxers, he swung his legs off the bed. He should see how her wound was healing, make sure infection wasn't setting in. "Let me swap out your bandages first."

First responder mode would get his body back under control.

Huffing impatiently, Nireed rolled onto her back, propping herself up on her elbows.

He swallowed thickly, reaching for his EMS kit with a shaky hand.

Her long, dark brown hair had fallen back, giving him an eyeful, as she splayed out along his floor, not a stitch of clothing on her, looking like a goddamn feast.

Using the kit to hide himself, he knelt on the floor next to her. But the cramped quarters meant he couldn't do so without some part of him touching some part of her. He desperately tried not to think about how his thigh pressed snugly against her cool scales and warm skin as he worked a corner loose on the old bandage. "How's it feel?"

"A little sore. Kind of itchy."

He peeled back the bandage and sucked in a surprised breath.

"What?" She looked down. "It looks fine."

That was just it. Not only did the injury look fine, it looked mostly healed. What had been a gaping wound less than twelve hours ago was now a deep pink scar. He'd used dissolvable sutures, and in most places, they were gone. At this stage in healing, there wasn't any reason to rebandage it.

"You heal fast," he marveled, running a thumb beneath the spot.

"Have to. Blood attracts sharks."

Shuffling back, he examined her tailfin, taking the flowing, piscine material into his hands. It shimmered as he sifted through the folds, checking on the sutures he'd stitched. The healing was patchier here. In some places, the membrane had fused back together; in others, it was still red and raw, but even those spots didn't look inflamed. Her fin was healing well, just not as rapidly as her flesh.

"Does it hurt?" He applied antiseptic ointment to the reddest areas. Even if it all washed off in five minutes during her swim, with how fast her body healed, maybe it would absorb this quickly, too. Anything, even if just a little, to help the process along couldn't hurt.

"Not much. Not a lot of feeling there, remember?"

He did remember, but it was a part of his training to ask, and he was going through the motions in a feeble attempt to keep his lust in check.

When he finished up her tail, he returned to her side, applying scar cream this time.

"Thank you, Reid," she said softly. "For taking care of me."

"Always." He looked up into her awaiting eyes. "I'm really glad you're healing this well. I don't like seeing you hurt."

It wasn't until she rested her hand on top of his that he realized two things. One, he hadn't stopped touching her. And two, not only was he still touching her, he'd gone and laid his hand across her belly.

"Come swim with me?" Something that looked a lot like hope sparked in her eyes. How could he say no to that? Especially not after stealing that light with an almost kiss he'd been too chicken to follow through with.

He nodded. "Go on. Just need to put this away first."

Reid waited for her to clear the door before readjusting himself and following her.

The air was cool when he stepped out onto the diving platform, a thick tapestry of stars overhead. He placed his hands on his hips, gazing up. He never tired of that view.

"It's beautiful, isn't it?" Nireed was looking up, too, from the water, her tail fanning beneath in long, easy strokes. The mystifying translucent quality of her skin and muscles had returned, hints of her skeletal structure glowing from within, and she twinkled like starlight, a mini universe under her skin.

Reid wanted nothing more than to be in her orbit. "It's breathtaking."

She smiled up at the sky, and despite that smile's sharp edges, it didn't look malicious. Just serene.

Not wanting to ruin this tranquility, he lowered himself into the water—which was fucking cold—but he wasn't going to undercut the moment by complaining. He swam beside her.

When she turned that smile on him, his breath caught in his throat.

How cold it was no longer mattered. How scared and unsure he'd been, a distant memory. When she smiled at him like that, looked at him like he brought her peace, he knew.

Something big had changed in the time between the night they met and now, something cataclysmic. And he had a choice to make. Nireed was a bright, shining beacon in a fathomless sea, and he was standing on the continental shelf, peering down into the deep, dark unknown. Once he dove in, he could never turn back.

Beneath the water, he slid his hand into hers, her fins swaying, and his legs fluttering to the same easy beat. Warmth radiated from her body, chasing away the ocean's cold caress.

"I made a mistake earlier today," he said, holding her gaze. Nodes of light dotted her face in biologically strategic clusters—at her temples, down the bridge of her nose, and one singular dot below her chin—illuminating just enough of her face in the dark that he could see expression. "And I'd like to make up for it, if you'll let me."

Her gaze dipped to his lips before meeting his eyes once more, uncertainty writ in the pinch of her brows. "What was your mistake?" She clutched his hand a little tighter, waiting for his response. For all she knew, whatever he said next could break her heart, and yet, she still sought him for comfort.

He pulled her closer, pressing his forehead to hers.

Ever so carefully, she threaded her claws through his hair. "Among my people, this," she gently bumped her forehead to his, "means listen closely. I'm listening, Reid."

"I should have kissed you." He threaded an arm around her waist, pulling their bodies flush.

Her bioluminescence pulsed. "Why didn't you?"

"You were hurt." That was part of it, but if he was honest, it wasn't the only reason. "And I was scared, too, of what I'm feeling for you."

"What I am, where I come from, it won't be easy."

Leagues of ocean stood between them. His demanding work schedule, too, and her obligations to her people. But a strange sort of certainty aligned within him. Something about swimming beneath the stars made the impossible feel possible. Or maybe it was her, and some unspoken, unknowable thing between them, telling him they could make this work.

"Maybe not, but I think it'll be worth it. Can I kiss you, Starfish?"

A bright, pretty smile ticked up the corners of her mouth, and she nodded, angling in.

Slotting his lips over hers, Reid captured their softness and laid claim to that joy. The thought of razor-sharp teeth pricking his lip crossed his mind, but it was that smile he leaned into. They went slowly, carefully. Her taking as much, if not more, care than him. This kiss was aware of the danger, but not hindered by it.

Lifting their hands, he brought hers to his hip, then cupped her cheek, seeking, searching, molding his mouth to the shape of hers. The taste of salt gave way to sweet, and a surprised gasp escaped her when he deepened the kiss, delving past parted lips and sharp teeth to caress his tongue to hers, an intrepid explorer boldly diving into the unknown.

Reid embraced Nireed like he had the ocean, fully and without fear.

NIREED ARCHED INTO HIM, HOLDING BACK A TEMPEST, wanting to possess his mouth, part his lips further and pour in her desire, but if she took too much too soon, he would flee. He liked her well enough to initiate a kiss, but how much would he like her if she accidentally bit him? Drew blood?

A guilty thrill raced up her spine, wondering how he'd taste.

"I can take it," he broke away to say, stroking a thumb across her cheek. "Can feel you holding back. Don't."

"Reid, I need you to listen to me." She bowed her forehead to his. "If I cut you, if you bleed, I'm going to like the taste. Will you be all right with that?"

He paused. "Does the thought of tasting me turn you on?" There was a little trepidation in his voice, but his cock twitched, too, the press of her body keeping him warm. But this was different from the night they first met. Tonight, the scent of his interest was stronger than his fear.

"It does," she answered truthfully. "But how you feel is more important."

"I think I'd like to try."

An idea struck. This didn't have to be one-sided.

"Taste me first. It's only fair." She lifted a claw to her lower lip, nicking it down the center. Blood welled, then beaded.

His heartbeat sped up, but he took her chin between his thumb and forefinger, and leaned in. She thought he'd give a quick lick and be done with it, but no. He dragged his tongue across her lower lip, lingering and laving, before sucking it into his mouth and savoring her taste like one might a rare delicacy.

A soft moan escaped her, her scales beginning to part. Reid seized her hips with both hands, pressing her to his rock-hard length.

He tugged at her lip before releasing it, and the self-assured grin that followed wrecked her insides. "You liked that?"

"Yeah," she said, a little breathless. "You?"

"Mhm." He ensnared her mouth in another kiss, more forceful and searching than the last, urging her to finally give him her all. It was a frenzy of entangled lips, and hungry, lashing tongues. A fearless kiss that consumed them both, and when he inevitably cut himself on her teeth, rather than pull away, he slid his hands up her bare back, tangling them in her hair, utterly unyielding.

And he tasted good. So blissfully good, her head spun. This wasn't just acceptance of what she was. This was craving it, and the possibilities that came with that made her dizzy.

Brushing her hair over her shoulders, Reid broke their kiss, drinking her in with a heavy-lidded gaze. When she invited him to touch her, he filled his hand with her breast, pushing and tenderly squeezing the soft flesh. When she begged for more, he bent, sucking a nipple into his mouth, pulling pleasure straight up from her core.

A shared moan filled the quiet night, harmonized by the lapping waves.

Reaching between them, his fingers ghosted along her tail. "Part your pretty scales for me."

Her heart thudded wildly against her chest.

She knew he wanted her the moment she woke up and rolled over to find his erection pressing insistently between them. That, and the air had been ripe with his need. But as much as she'd wanted to answer that call right then and there, she wanted him to be sure more.

And he was plenty sure now.

Taking his hand, she guided him in stroking her front, along the section of scales not yet parted—down, but not up. She was smooth in one direction, abrasive the other, and she didn't want him cutting himself. He was an attentive student, and soon she opened wide for him, presenting the flesh of her seam, dewy and luminescent.

Reid sucked in a breath. He met her eyes a moment before looking between them, running the pad of his finger lightly along her swell. "Is this okay?"

"Yes," she breathed, threading her arms around his neck. "Touch me."

She watched as he dipped two fingers into her glowing amber seam, wetting himself on her moisture. One by one, he eased them in with gentle, measured strokes. Taking his hand again, she guided him where her sensitive pearl hid, just on the upper-inside lip of her seam.

"Right here?" He rubbed circles around the spot with his thumb.

"Right there." She gasped, clutching him.

Wrapping his arm around her waist for support, he pumped his fingers in and out, sending pleasure rippling throughout her body, her luminescence winking in time to his ministrations.

"God, that's beautiful," he murmured against the corner of her mouth. "You're iridescent."

She rocked her tail into his hand, craving the release he could give. "You're good at this."

But it was more than that. This felt *right*. This was what she'd held out for. What she longed for.

When arguing with Aersila and Undine about duties to the pod, and who she should or shouldn't mate with, she hadn't known yet if Reid and she had a future together. But locked here with him in this intimate embrace, she knew. This was her mate. Her one and only. And nothing, not her sister, not Undine, and not the distance between them, would keep her from him.

He bumped his nose affectionately to hers. "Getting feedback in real-time is encouraging."

"You like praise too?"

"Yeah, Starfish. I do." He increased his pace, fingers hitting up to the knuckle. "You gonna tell me I'm a good boy?"

From the top of her head to her tingling tailfins, her body tremored, a wave of slick coating his fingers. "A very good boy."

A curse fell from his lips, and he bowed his head, burying his face in her neck. "This water's damn cold, but I don't feel it. I'm burning up inside."

Maybe he was made for these waters, after all.

Carefully, oh so carefully, she dragged a claw down the center of his chest to the flat of his stomach, pausing only to tease the fabric that covered him.

"I think you can make me come without touching me," he began to say, but she nipped delicately at his lower lip, easing the fabric down his hips, his length springing free.

"But I want to touch you," she said, gliding a hand over him, loving the feel of him in her palm. Back and forth, back and forth. "So very much."

He let out a ragged breath, his gaze meeting hers. In the dark, his brown eyes were two shining pools as black as the abyss. "Nireed, I need…"

She squeezed him lightly, drawing out a groan.

A song as old as the oceans thrummed through her veins. A need for what he gave and what more he could give tumbled from her lips in a breathless plea, "Mate with me."

CHAPTER
EIGHTEEN

HIS DICK JERKED LIKE THE EAGER FUCKER IT WAS, BUT Nireed's plea had his mind racing at a million miles an hour. Mating wasn't a flippant word choice. Wasn't synonymous with good old fun sex. It came with connotations, and given how close the merfolk lived to nature, to the harsh realities of survival, to life and death, he wouldn't be surprised if they readily answered their biological drives. This would be deeply important to them. And to Nireed.

The last thing he wanted to do was offend her.

"Well," he began, collecting himself. "It's not just about fucking, right? It's about making a baby." He linked his arms around her waist. Catching on to his serious tone, she released him, her hands coming up to rest on his chest.

His eyes dipped down, and he allowed himself to picture, just for a second, her belly round. Maybe even with his kid. It was a terrifying, and yet surprisingly thrilling prospect. "Do you want a baby, Nireed?"

Her brow furrowed. "Is that strange?"

"Just different." He chose his next words carefully. "Humans don't lead right out of the gate with that. We date first. It's like a practice run. We spend lots of time getting to know one another to make sure we're compatible."

"Oh." Not only did her face fall, but her bioluminescence also flickered out, leaving them in complete darkness.

"Hey," he soothed, lifting her chin. "I'm not telling you no. Just not yet."

A faint glow returned.

"I still want you. Just let me get a condom, okay?"

She tilted her head with a curious, catlike expression. "Okay."

He felt her eyes on him as he swam back to the boat. His boxers had been swallowed by the sea, so she had a full view of his backside as he pulled himself out.

A few months after moving to Maine, he'd made a dating profile and had bought a box of condoms to go along with it. There'd been plenty of interest, but only a few made it to drinks, and only one to dinner. If only Reid-then could see Reid-now, about to go all the way with a mystical creature of the sea.

Nireed was waiting for him by the diving platform when he sat down, a foil packet in hand.

"How's your side? Any cramping?" As enthusiastic as he was to get inside her, he wasn't going to jeopardize her health to do it.

She crinkled her nose in thought, seriously considering the question, which he appreciated. "Forgot about it until you asked. Still sore, but not bad."

"Have you ever done this before?" He tore open the packet, watching her study him as he rolled it down his length. Either way it went, he was going to be careful, but it helped to know.

"For a short time." She spread her hands up his bare thighs, claws mindfully angled up. "About a year ago. But he's mated to another now. No babies."

He swallowed thickly. Never thought to ask her if she had kids.

Even if it wasn't *the* first time for either of them, it was theirs together, which was just as, if not more special, because they were choosing each other after all that had come before.

He was going to savor this with her.

Palming his shaft and giving it a deliberate stroke, he asked one more question. "Still want this with me?"

Her inner amber light flickered to life. "Reid, I want whatever you're willing to give."

Slipping into the water, he pulled her in for a slow, drugging kiss. Even if he couldn't give her everything right now, there was a whole lot he could. A world of possibility lay before them—they had time—and starting here, with their bodies doing all the talking, saying the things words couldn't, wasn't a bad way to begin.

His fingers found the sensitive round pearl of flesh she'd shown him and didn't stop lavishing it with attention until she was trembling and gushing over his fingers, her bioluminescence pulsing in time with clenching muscles. He noticed that she produced more of it, too, than human women did, no doubt accounting for the need to have more lubrication in the water.

Nature rising to the occasion.

Their heads were bowed together when he lined himself up, his dick a dark silhouette against her pretty, luminescent pussy. "So damn gorgeous." His voice was gruff. Holding her hip as he fed himself into her depths, he watched her part around him, then envelop him whole, that inner flesh ridiculously plush and smooth as it suctioned onto him in a dizzying, watertight seal.

It was fucking hot. She was fucking hot.

"Mm," she purred, bumping her nose to his. "Feels good?"

"Unbelievably." Using her hips as anchor points, he eased in and out in slow, measured thrusts. She grasped the hair at the top of his head, on the cusp of too long for regulations, and his hip, too, to help with leverage. "You?"

Her eyes had fluttered closed, her lips slightly parted. "So good."

God, he was burying himself in her, and it wasn't enough. He wanted that beautiful, dangerous mouth on his. Wanted to feel every hitched breath, every gasp, every moan. He wanted to taste her pleasure, her joy, the moment she broke and came, waves upon waves crashing on his shores.

"Can't get enough of you," he murmured, recapturing her lips, feeling her hold on tighter and clench. As their bodies sought each other again and again, he kissed her slowly, loosely, just enough to keep his lips on the pulse of her desire.

This was a little more than just fucking. He knew that in the way his heart beat an ecstatic, relieved staccato in his chest, and in the way his stomach swooped even as the tingling at the base of his spine grew and grew.

"Reid." She gasped against his lips, her brows pinched so fucking beautifully. Concentrating on him, on her pleasure, on the sensations they built together.

"Getting close, sweetheart?" He rolled his hips, intentionally delivering pressure on her inner clit. He loved its placement, so easy to pay devotion to with every stroke.

She nodded, her forehead still pressed to his. "You?"

"Oh, yeah." He nipped at her lower lip. "But I'm going to try to get you off first."

Her eyes met his with a heavy-lidded gaze. "You make this feel so good. I don't want it to end."

His heart stuttered, an unfathomably warm feeling building in his chest. "It doesn't have to be just this once. I've got a whole box in there."

"First of many," she agreed, matching his rolling rhythm. "You'll have to get more boxes."

God, he loved the sound of that. He never wanted to stop. "I will, Starfish. I promise."

Clutching each other, they sped their efforts, gasping and panting through their need, racing toward the finish line. She was so swollen and sensitive around him, her channel getting all at once slicker and tighter. He did navigational calculations in his head just so he wouldn't blow before she did.

"Come for me," he pleaded, seeking her lips.

With a sharp inhale, she arched in his arms, her muscles contracting around him, sucking him in, and keeping their hips pinned. It was such a tight, delicious squeeze, he almost blacked out from the pleasure of it.

"That's it," he groaned against her mouth. Licking against the parted opening, he intentionally nicked his tongue against her teeth, sharing the coppery taste of his blood. She pressed into the kiss, worrying her tongue over that spot with soothing strokes.

He came hard, her channel fluttering in time to her pulsing bioluminescence as she fell over the edge with him.

Breathing heavily, they clung to each other under the stars, lost in the fog of their release.

CHAPTER

NINETEEN

REID WOKE HER WITH A SLOW, DROWSY KISS.

Last night, he'd carried her back to his bed, where they'd coupled for the second time, his legs bracketing her tail and weight pressing her into the mattress with every punching thrust of his hips. And she'd loved every second of it. Their first time had been marvelous, perfect even, in the way their bodies relied on each other for stability, as well as pleasure. But this, this had let all other cares fall away. No worries about keeping his head above the surface or maintaining the right leverage. They could just fall into each other and get lost.

"Need to get some supplies." He pressed another kiss to her cheek, then her neck. Inhaling deeply, he said with a little growl in his voice, "But God, you make me feral."

"We call it a mating frenzy." He hadn't even touched her scales, but they were already parting for him. So, so eager. "Must affect Surface Dwellers too."

"How long's it last?" He sucked on the flesh just beneath her jaw, a sensation she felt all the way down her core.

"At least a week. Sometimes more." Nireed rolled him onto his back, reaching for the box of condoms peeking out from under his pillow.

"Once more before you go?" She lightly shook out a sleeve of the sheaths he covered himself in every time they mated, not trusting her claws to handle them without piercing one. They seemed like such flimsy, fragile things, but their purpose clicked in her head when he'd pulled out, his spend pooling at the tip, captured in a watertight net of sorts.

"Yes, Ma'am." He grinned, peeling one off. She scooted back, watching his fingers pinch the tip while his palm glided down his shaft, rolling it into place. He held himself upright at the base. "Come up here and take what you need."

She crawled forward, bracing herself on either side of his body, a fine display of his strength laid out before her. His skin was smooth and deeply shadowed where his muscles dipped, cut and carved from a life dedicated to saving others.

This was a man who cared deeply about his purpose, highlighted more so by the fact that the people he saved were strangers. Everything she did was for the pod, people she knew and swam with every day. She admired this selflessness about him, this drive to help those who needed him.

Looking down at the space between them, they worked in tandem to get themselves properly aligned. When she finally sank down onto his length, he groaned, knees drawing up to frame her tail. "I fantasized about this last night," he said, holding her gaze. "When you rolled on top of me. I wanted to bury myself in you."

This close, with the light of day reflecting in his eyes, she noticed hints of gold hidden among the deep, warm brown. And what a treasure that was, to be close enough to learn this secret thing about him.

Rolling her hips, she seated him to the brim. "I'm yours. Then, now." Forever. But saying that was too much, too soon. Reid wanted to take this slow, make sure they were compatible, and she'd respect that wish, for as long as it took, even though she knew it deep in her bones.

They were just too good together, just too right, not to be.

Another roll of her hips and her eager channel sucked him in and clamped down, creating a merciless seal. A curse hissed out of him, part pain, but largely overwhelming pleasure, as the heady scent of his arousal flooded between them.

They weren't submerged. This sealing wasn't needed, but her body's natural drive wanted him locked down tight. "Okay?" She paused, nuzzling his nose.

"More than." His voice was hoarse and raw. Grasping her hips, he bucked up into her, each thrust sending pleasure spiraling outward.

She matched her rhythm to his, letting him dictate the pace. This was his fantasy unfolding, and in the stories her foreparents told, sirens sometimes granted sailors wishes, and Reid made her want to fulfill every one of his.

But ever the conscientious mate, he angled his strokes in a manner that hit her sensitive pearl every time, making her tail tingle from the base of her spine to the very tips of her fins.

Deepest, darkest depths, what had she ever done to deserve this man?

When his hips began to stutter, their rhythm faltering, she knew he was getting close and took over control. Claws tucked into her palms, she slid her hands beneath his shoulders, then held him as she undulated, churning. He enfolded her in his arms, one wrapped around her waist, the other braced along her spine, fingers bunching in her hair.

Lightly pinching the lobe of his ear between her teeth, she tugged, drawing another moan from his lips. "My turn to take care of you." She increased their pace, remembering he liked praise. "What does my good boy need?"

His arms squeezed around her, lips seeking hers. Her Coast Warrior loved kisses she was quickly learning. Giving him full reign of her mouth, she focused on bringing them over the edge, relishing the feel of his legs tangling around her tail, holding her close.

When he broke the kiss, hips jerking upward, she opened her eyes, watching the way his handsome face slackened as he came. Her channel clenched around him in a vise grip, catching every single relieved throb.

For several long, delicious moments, their bodies tensed, shared release pulsing through them in a repeating loop of pleasure. Then they relaxed, easing into a loose embrace, utterly spent.

Reid was breathing heavily when he said, "Damn. Don't know how I'm ever leaving this bed."

"I believe in you. You'll find a way."

He snorted, folding his hands comfortably across her lower back. "Did you just make a joke, vicious siren of mine?"

The word 'mine' thrilled her, but she kept an even tone. "I'm serious. I've watched you swim. You've incredible strength and willpower."

"Wow. I think that's the best compliment anyone's ever given me."

"Own your merits, Reid. It's true."

"Yes, Ma'am."

She threaded her claws through his dark auburn hair, playing with the waves as she waited for her body to relax. It took a few minutes for the watertight seal to release, her pleasure coating his thighs in a warm, sticky tide.

As she began to lift off him, he encircled his fingers around the base of his shaft, holding the condom in place. Even though her channel had loosened its hold, it still tried to unsheathe him, something they'd learned last night when the condom was nearly yanked off.

Parted, they studied the mess they made together, his sheets covered in her glittering, shimmering silver scales.

"Does that hurt?"

She shook her head, combing a hand through her hair, a few stray strands coming away in her claws. "No more than this."

"Okay, good. How's your tail feeling?"

She smirked, her parted scales closing. "Asking if you've made me sore?"

The look he shot her as he got up from bed to discard the condom was heated. "Was asking about your stitches, but you can tell me that too."

Drawing up her tail, she bent to examine her fins, spreading them out over her hands. "Good as new." She smiled, willing the transformation. "And it's the best kind of sore. It'll keep me thinking about you awhile." Seamlessly, fins and scales retracted, giving way to two sturdy legs. Now, she could move about his boat without crawling.

When she stood shakily, Reid's gruff voice had her looking up. "You're trying my willpower."

Lifting her arms above her head in a stretch that elongated her body, she shook back her hair. His eyes darkened as he greedily drank her in, a fist clenching at his side. She smirked. "Any clothes I can borrow?"

SITTING ON THE DIVE PLATFORM, HER FEET SWINGING BACK and forth through the water, Nireed carefully leafed through a stack of photography books. She cradled and examined each page, every single one a precious, breathtaking treasure. Reid had said that the photos were taken in National Parks and scenic places around the world. She hadn't realized the Land Above the Water could be so beautiful. So otherworldly.

Reid left her to run errands—something about grocery shopping and hitting the laundry mat because they'd fucked their way through all his clean sheets. She smiled to herself, flipping a page. He had good stamina.

She heard a car roll into the small parking lot adjoining the pier and kept flipping. It was too soon for Reid to be back, but she'd already met one of his neighbors, a healer lady with a kind smile. She was on her way to work, so they didn't talk long, but Nireed thought she did pretty well pretending to be a Surface Dweller.

Maybe his other neighbor had returned.

Crunching, then thudding footsteps approached the boat.

"Nireed?" A familiar voice called out.

Setting the books aside, Nireed shot to her feet, teetering a bit, before clambering onto the docks and racing down the wooden planks, momentum keeping her stable.

She threw her arms around a tall Black woman, whose hair was braided back today, nearly barreling her over in a hug. "Cure Creator! What are you doing here?"

"Lorelei sent me." Dr. Lila Branson chuckled, giving her a firm squeeze around all the tote bags she was carrying. "It's good to see you too."

"Let me help." Nireed reached for some of the bags and led the way.

Lila was the world's leading marine biologist in mermaid research.

When she studied Nireed, she'd done it thoughtfully and with dignity and care. That was the environment of the Haven Cove Marine Research Center's mermaid lab when Nireed joined the study. It was hard being away from the ocean, away from her sister and the pod, but finding a cure for her people's uncontrollable hunger was a worthy cause.

It only got truly bad when Lila was demoted and shut out from large parts of the project. But she never gave up on Nireed. She plotted, planned, and with the help of friends and family, broke Nireed out of the lab and returned her home.

"Cozy." Lila nodded with approval as she stepped inside. "Actually clean."

"Are Surface Dweller males dirty?"

"Dirty, messy. Kind of a pain in the ass." Setting down her bags, Lila brushed off her hands, then winked. "There are a few exceptions though."

"What did you bring?" Nireed peeked into one of the bags, brightening. She pulled out a collection of potted meat, but one in particular caught her eye. Holding up an orange can, she slowly read the words. "Limited. Edition. Pumpkin. Spice. Spam." She quirked a brow. "What is pumpkin spice?"

"Don't question it, just try it."

The wicked glint in Cure Creator's eyes was so positively evil, Nireed wasn't sure she would. Wordlessly, she added the can to the back of the neat arrangement she'd made on Reid's kitchen counter.

"Also brought a few sets of clothes for you. Thought you might need…" Lila trailed off. She'd gone to set the rest of the bags on the bed, but paused, slowly turning back, her wicked smile growing even wider. "Girl, you banging the man who lives here?"

"Banging?"

Only when Lila began making crude hand gestures and pointed to the condom box left out on the bed did Nireed understand.

"Oh! Yes." She gave a firm nod, coming over to peruse the clothes Lila brought. All had soft fabrics and textures, thoughtfully chosen to make wearing them less terrible. "Lots of times."

"I love how straightforward you are. Never change." Gesturing to the clothes, Lila added, "Thought you'd need these, but maybe not, if you're not planning on leaving the love shack."

Nireed got the distinct impression that Lila was making a joke, but the reference was lost on her. "It's good to have options. Thank you for bringing these and the food."

"Of course. Lorelei mentioned you got hurt, but I'm guessing with you engaging in all these extracurricular activities that you're healing fine?"

Lifting the side of her borrowed shirt, Nireed showed her the deep pink scar. "I think I'm feeling well enough to return." She frowned. "But I don't want to leave without saying goodbye to Reid."

Lila's warm hand squeezed her shoulder. "Lorelei has gone to check on everyone and will call with an update tomorrow morning. Rushing home isn't going to change what already is. Give yourself, and him, some more time. After everything you've done for your pod, you've more than earned a break at least ten times over."

Melusina and Delphine had said the same thing. If three of her friends thought this, it must be true, and Nireed wasn't going to insult them by ignoring their wisdom.

"One more day," Nireed agreed. "Maybe two."

"That's the spirit."

CHAPTER
TWENTY

Reid found Nireed right where he'd left her, only now there was a stack of potted meat on his counter and a pile of women's clothing on his bed.

"Friend stopped by?" He set down a sack of clean laundry along with groceries and supplies.

Nodding, Nireed splashed her face and neck with water before coming inside. "One of them. Dr. Lila Branson."

*Dr. Lila...*whoa.

Even he, a casual science lover, knew that name. Dr. Branson was huge in the scientific community as both the discoverer of, and the world's leading researcher of mermaids. And she'd just seen the inside of his tiny houseboat. Thank fuck, he'd tidied before leaving.

"Hungry?" He spread out an assortment of freshly caught fish he'd picked up from the pier in town. A thrill of pride swelled in his chest when he saw Nireed bend over to sniff and nod her head approvingly. Extracting a knife from the knife block, she quickly began filleting each one, her hands moving quickly and dexterously, like one might expect to see with a professional chef. Occasionally, she'd pause to eat a piece.

Glancing sidelong at him, she said, "My sister Aersila makes these."

"Your sister is a knife smith?"

Nireed nodded. "And other tools. She doesn't like that I'm here."

That was a non sequitur if he ever heard one. "On shore or with me?"

Her face fell, her eyes sad when they found his. "Both. I've tried to make her understand, but I don't think she ever will unless she sees for herself."

Settling behind her, he smoothed his hands over her shoulders, then rubbed the tight muscles in her neck with his thumbs. She leaned into the touch, a soft, pretty hum rumbling from her throat. "That's a lot of unknowns. I imagine my mom would be really freaked out if I came to live with you in Under Water Mermaid Land."

Nireed looked over her shoulder, pinning him with an unamused glare. "Under Water Mermaid Land?"

"Land Above the Water, Under Water Mermaid Land. I think we're matching energy here."

She snorted. Setting the knife down, she turned around in his arms, a small, wry smile creeping across her lips. "Perhaps you're right, Coast Warrior."

"It happens sometimes." He tapped her on the nose. "Got a present for you."

Her eyes lit up. "Show me."

Pulling a box from one of the bags, he began unpacking the device inside. She watched him curiously as he filled the basin with water and plugged it in. A quiet rumbling, then mist spouted out the top, making her jump back with a surprised little shriek. She glared at him when he began to laugh.

"Sorry, Starfish," he said, hiding his smile behind his hand. "Should've warned you."

She crouched beside him, peering at it with interest, irritation forgotten. "What is it?"

"A humidifier. Puts moisture in the air. Was hoping it might help you feel less dry."

"Oh." It was a quiet, breathless 'oh,' and when he twisted to look at her, to gauge her reaction, he saw that her eyes were shining. Then, without warning, she pounced, hugging him fiercely. "Thank you," she said into his shirt.

"I hope it helps." He enveloped her in his arms. "Now, what do you say? You up for a little bit of adventure?"

She lifted her head. "I'm listening."

Fifteen minutes later, she was dressed for hiking and eyeing his motorcycle warily. "You should know I don't do car rides well."

"You've been in a car?" He zipped up his black leather riding jacket.

"A few times. Friends gave me something called Drama…" Her brow pinched as she struggled to recall the name. "Drama…"

"Dramamine?"

"Yes!"

"I've got some of that right here." He opened the storage box and plucked out a container of pills. "I usually swallow this with water…"

"I will just suffer." She waved a hand dismissively, before popping open her mouth and sticking out her tongue rather cutely.

Chuckling, he shook out a pill and dropped it on her tongue. She reared back, her face scrunching in comical displeasure, before she swallowed and shuddered.

"You good?"

"Alive. If that evil medicine didn't work so well…"

No exaggeration there. It was nasty stuff, but it did work like a charm.

Beckoning her closer, he slid his spare helmet, a sporty, black piece that matched his own, over her head. "We gotta wait for that medicine to kick in, but I want to make sure this fits. How's that feel? Any pinching?"

Her amber eyes flashed behind the black tint visor. It was positively spooky. "Strange, but fine."

While they waited, he explained the different parts of the motorcycle, how it worked, and what to expect. When he got to the part about the loud engine, she expressed concern about her hearing sensitivity, so he went and got her earplugs.

"Come up here, Starfish." He patted the bit of seat behind him.

Tentatively, she came forward, holding onto his shoulders as she threw her leg over the bike, placing her feet where he'd told her to. "Hold me tight," he said, turning the key, the engine rumbling to life beneath them.

She crushed him in a bruising grip, the air whooshing out of him. He patted her arm urgently, and she loosened her hold, relaxing against his back. *Good girl.*

He gave her knee a reassuring squeeze, then eased on the throttle. He took it easy down the access road, but once they hit the coastal highway, he brought them up in speed, zipping down the blacktop. Trees and stretches of coast whipped by, Nireed holding on firm and doing a happy little wiggle behind him.

He grinned.

When they were going over safety, they came up with a simple code so she could tell him without words whether she was having a good time. Two squeezes to slow down, three to stop, and anything else meant keep going.

He brought them to the seaside picnic grove where he liked to hike. The moment the engine quieted, Nireed slid off the back of the bike and pulled the helmet off her head. Her smile was as bright as her eyes. "That was fun!"

Such wonder and awe filled those luminescent eyes. Here was a creature who had seen the deep unknowns of the ocean, and yet a simple motorcycle ride, an experience he was able to provide her, brought her this unfettered joy.

He kicked out the kickstand and swung off, peeling his own helmet away.

Hooking his fingers in the waistband of her leggings, he yanked her to him and kissed her fiercely, tasting that excitement for himself. Not only did he love that she had a good time trying this new thing with him, he loved her thrill for the ride.

Just seeing her like that made him hot all over. And maybe it was the mating frenzy talking, but he was pretty sure tons of new couples went through a period of insatiable horniness early on in a relationship. As much as he wanted to continue that trend right now, he had an adventure to deliver.

Her cheeks were flushed when he pulled away. "What was that for?"

"Turns out I really like seeing you happy."

She smiled bashfully, the rosy tinge to her cheeks brightening.

After trading their helmets for a water bottle, he took her hand, leading her toward the trailhead. They hit the trail at a slow, easy pace, both so that Nireed could take her time over the tricky terrain and enjoy the new surroundings.

As far as summer days went, it was a good one for hiking. Low eighties, the sun bright and shining, but under the shadowy canopy of pine and birch, the air was almost chill, undercut even further by a crisp sea breeze threading through the trees. The trail hugged the coastline, never leaving the ocean far from sight. Beneath their feet, the ground was at times a soft blanket of fallen needles and moss. Others, a rugged obstacle course of boulders and roots.

"How do you know the way?" Nireed asked, holding onto his arm as they traversed a gnarly patch of roots.

Slowing to a stop, he pointed to a nearby tree trunk. "You see that blue stripe?"

She leaned against him, resting her temple to his shoulder, making his heart squeeze at her casual affection. "That marks the way?"

"Yup. They're painted at regular intervals."

"It reminds me of our kelp forest." She looked up. "The stalks are spaced closer unless we weed them out. But some of them are just as tall as this." She let go of his arm, carefully picking her way over to the birch tree next to them. She studied its white peeling bark with a gentle touch and drew a finger along the dark trunk beneath.

"How do you find your way?"

"We use rope scavenged from shipwrecks." She looked at him over her shoulder, expression thoughtful. "There's a lot we reuse that Surface Dwellers have lost at the sea."

He'd sometimes wondered at the sheer amount of trash and wreckage at the bottom of the ocean. Graveyard. Junkyard. Landfill. So many things all at once. He wasn't sure if a community of sea people reclaiming and giving new life to those things made him feel better or worse.

"What's your greatest treasure?"

She brushed her hand lightly down the trunk, curls of bark catching on her palm. "Food. Family. Safety." She paused. "But that's not what you mean. My favorite piece of salvage...it's, um, something that shows you who you are. What you look like."

A mirror.

"It shocked me. Jumped and everything. I thought there was another siren in the hull with me. But then I noticed she was moving exactly as I was." She turned around, pressing her back to the tree. "It was me."

"Did you keep it?"

"I did. A small piece for myself and Aersila. The rest is mounted on a wall in the city, so others can see and know too."

"Nireed, that's really..." Sweet. Meaningful. Selfless. "I wish I could see it. The kelp forest and the city you live in. But I can't dive that far." His heart, his stomach, everything plummeted at the thought. Here he was, sharing his world with her, but she might not ever get to do the same. Not because he wasn't willing, but without the proper training and a work schedule that would allow it, he'd never survive the journey.

In recreational scuba diving, advanced divers could descend to a recommended maximum of 130 feet—a certification he had and jumped through a lot of schedule hoops to maintain every year. Technical divers, with specialized training and equipment, could hit the 170 to 350 feet range, and according to Dr. Lila Branson's research, the merfolk lived within the topmost portion of that range now, but they'd had also been known to live deep, deep down on the edge of the Mesopelagic Zone. At the shallowest, that was 650 feet from the surface.

"I may never see it," he whispered, but she heard him regardless, and came over to cup his face in her hands. It was the one-sidedness of it that troubled him the most. Her people, her world, were important. She should get to share what she loved too.

"Lila has told me of cameras that can go deep down. If she has one,

I'll ask if I can take it. If there's a way for me to show you, I will. I promise."

That shit had to be wicked expensive. "Maybe you can tell me about it?"

She smiled, hands falling to take his hands. "I'll tell you whatever you want to know."

They continued onward and along the way Reid learned that their city was carved into the face of an underwater cliff. In the days of old, when ships were made of wood, not metal, the Gulf of Maine merfolk would host other pods around the world for a festival honoring their goddess. It was as much a time for feasting and competitions as it was for trade and diplomacy.

The oceans were quieter and less hazardous then. Oil spills, plastics, and floating trash islands didn't exist yet, but the modern age made all those things, and lengthy migrations became especially dangerous. Someone always got hurt, or worse, and no festival was worth that risk.

It left whole pods segmented and isolated from each other, including Nireed and Aersila from their mother. "The last time I saw her," Nireed said, clutching his hand as she navigated a gnarly cluster of roots. "'Starfish' was my only name. My memories of her are fuzzy and scarce. But Aersila told me, when I was old enough, that our mother swam to southern waters to visit our aging grandmother and just never made it back. It's easier to believe she's stuck out there somewhere with another pod than to admit she might not have survived the journey."

The sort of open-ended question that might never be answered. "I'm sorry. Not knowing must be hard."

"It's harder for Aersila." Nireed shrugged her shoulder, but her tone was wistful. "She was thirteen when our mother disappeared. She lost the one who raised her. I didn't. My sister was all I knew."

"You can still miss someone you've never met."

She thought about this for a moment, then nodded. "That's true. I would've liked to have known her, but when I sing my pleas to the Twenty-Armed Goddess for her return, it's more for Aersila's benefit than my own."

"The Twenty-Armed Goddess?"

"We believe she hears all things in time, as sound is carried to her on the currents." Letting go of his hand, Nireed crouched to pick up a stick, drawing in the dirt. It was a rudimentary picture, but he got the message loud and clear.

A leviathan. A kraken. Something in between.

A true horror of the deep.

"You're a friend of the ocean." Rising to her feet, Nireed took his hand again, no doubt sensing his fear. "You need not fear her return."

He shuddered. "Her return?"

"A creature as old as her must sleep a long, long time between risings."

"And the next rising is when exactly?"

Nireed just shrugged, completely unperturbed, but his next ten minutes were spent mentally scrubbing that whole conversation from his brain, followed by a giant heap of denial. If he didn't make peace with the ocean before his next duty period, he could kiss his career as a Coast Guard rescue swimmer goodbye.

Reid helped Nireed down steep slopes and over rock scrambles, offering a hand whenever she needed it. They took regular breaks so she could rest and catch her breath because being in swimming shape wasn't the same as being in hiking shape. But she quickly adapted. Her situational awareness was great to begin with, but in the space of a single hike, her balance improved, and she held onto him less and less. And while a part of him felt bereft of her touch, he was damn proud.

Spotting a low shrub dotted with light blue, Reid stopped them. He felt Nireed's eyes on him as he crouched, picking a handful of berries. "All right. This is my redemption." He stood, a single, fat blueberry pinched between his forefinger and thumb.

Without so much as a command, or moment's hesitation, Nireed opened her mouth and stuck out her tongue.

A thrill ran up his spine. So eager and willing and trusting.

He dropped it onto her tongue, watching as she chewed thoughtfully. Her brows ticked up in surprise, a smile breaking.

"Good?"

She promptly bent to pick more to eat. "Mhm."

Human flesh and blueberries. Who could've guessed?

At the summit, he led her to his favorite overlook, and they sat down together, their legs dangling over the ledge. It was so quiet up here. Just the wind and creak of trees. Neither of them spoke for a while, some inherent understanding passing between them about the sanctity of this moment.

They stared out over the landscape at the mountains and trees and dark blue bay beyond, enjoying the view and the silence. The world seemed so untouched.

"I didn't expect it to be so beautiful," Nireed said after a time.

"Not too smelly?" Reid teased. "Or dry?"

"Oh, it's far too dry, but the smells here are good. And I like the quiet. It's strange, but nice."

One would think the ocean was quiet, but between sound traveling faster in water and all the shipping traffic, there was always ambient noise. Some time ago, he'd read an article about the effects noise pollution had on whales and the constant stress it put on them. That had stuck with him ever since.

It would be Nireed's reality too.

"This is where I go when I need to think."

Nireed smiled. "You grew up here?"

He shook his head, pulling out his phone to show her pictures of home and hikes in Michigan's own brand of wilderness.

"What's it like to live away from home?"

There was more to the question than surface level curiosity. It was in the halting way she asked the question as well as the hesitance in her eyes. Was she contemplating a life near the shore, a life *near him*?

Sooner rather than later they'd have to figure out the answers to some big questions. They'd begun something yesterday. It was bright and shiny and new, but it also had the feeling of permanence. He'd no idea how they'd make it work, or whether there was a way to evenly split the time and distance and effort, but goddammit, he wanted to try. Even if they could only take it day by day.

"It's hard," he answered truthfully. If he one day captured Nireed's heart, it wasn't going to be through half-truths and artifice. "I miss my family. I miss my friends. You meet new people, make new friends, but you still miss the ones you have back home. And you miss the familiar feeling of the place you left behind." He paused to rub the back of his neck. "It's not like I don't go back to visit. I do. Just maybe not as often as I'd like."

She gently took his hand, threading their fingers together. It was weird seeing them tipped with rounded nails rather than claws or without webbing in between, but he couldn't deny how good it felt to have their hands fit so snugly together. "Is it only your purpose that keeps you here?"

"Not at all." A grin fought its way to the surface. "I've got a strong streak of wanderlust in me. This?" He gestured around them. "This is an adventure. A way to see and do more in the world. It's so easy to fall into a comfortable routine, which there's nothing wrong with, but I like exploring and getting to live in new places."

"We have a lot to think about, don't we?"

"We do. But I like this." He caressed her thumb with his. "And I like you, Nireed."

"I like you too." She stretched out her hand to the expansive wilderness, just as he had a moment ago. "And I like this. I feel how you do—missing my home and my pod but wanting adventure. I loved riding on the back of your motorcycle, and I loved the pictures you showed me on your phone and in those books. I think I want to see those places."

"And I'll take you to every single one of them. But when you're ready to go home, you'll go home." Then, bumping their shoulders together, he teased, "I'll just have to get you a squirt bottle to carry around."

He had to explain what that was, but once it clicked, Nireed was cutely serious and excited. "Yes! I want a squirt bottle!"

Dropping her hand, he uncapped his canteen. They'd make do for now.

As he flicked water at her—which had her grinning like the Cheshire cat—he said softly, "I think we're allowed to have both things."

He wanted to show her the world above the sea, as much as she would let him, but he also didn't want a one-sided relationship where he just took and took and took.

Took her time. Her energy. Her home beneath the sea.

Took her away from pod and family.

Took her wildness.

But maybe, just maybe, he could give her adventure. A chance to explore this world and feel safe doing it.

Excitement shone in Nireed's eyes as she turned to him and said, "I think so too."

"Ever have sex in human form?"

The question might've been abrupt and forward to a Surface Dweller, but Nireed had scented Reid's quiet, persistent need all afternoon. And on the hike down the mountain, as day fell into dusk, his lingering touches and longing sidelong glances had increased to near maddening frequency.

As far as she was concerned, it was about damn time he asked.

Peering up at him, and into teasing eyes hiding hunger in their depths, a slow grin spread across her face. "Is there a reason you're asking?"

The corner of his mouth ticked up. "Wanna give it a go?"

She took his hand, slowly walking backward toward his motorcycle. "Show me."

His scent spiked, something feral flashing in his eyes. "Hands on the seat."

Currents of heat swept through her. That growly command weakened her already unsteady legs and made her tremble with an intolerable aching desperation. She thought he'd take her back to his houseboat, but no, he wanted her right here. Right now. In the place that brought him peace.

She needed this man like she needed the ocean. Only if she let her guard down with Reid, let herself fall into blissful abandon, he'd keep her safe. Where the ocean doled out harsh lessons in vigilance, Reid gave her the courage to let go.

"Are you asking me to submit to you?" She flashed him a sharp smile, claws extending from her fingertips. In this quiet, empty place, there was no one to see her partial transformation, or the wicked things they were about to do together.

The fading sunlight caught fire in his dark auburn hair as he approached her with a slow, easy swagger, crowding her in, demanding she take notice of his strength and virility. And oh, did she notice. He was an unbreachable wall of primal heat, and it ensnared her mind, body, and soul.

Capturing her chin, he stared down at her with eyes as dark as the abyss, and though a crooked smile teased his lips, each word was a hard, reassertion of dominance. "Did it sound like a question?"

"No," she said in a breathless whisper.

"Hands on the seat. Won't tell you again."

She turned around then, her bottom brushing the generous bulge straining the front of his pants, and though it made her wild with need, she obediently braced herself, feverishly curious to learn how Surface Dwellers mated. This was already vastly different from how merfolk did things, their tails dictating a front-facing approach every single time.

Reid smoothed a hand up the length of her spine, then gently, but firmly, pushed her down, splaying her across the seat. "That's it, sweetheart," he praised. "Get those hips up."

She arched for him, backside on display. Exposed. Vulnerable. No scales to shield her most tender flesh, just thin, flimsy fabric. It was an utterly terrible position to fend off an attack, but with Reid, she didn't need to fear. "Like this?"

"Just like that." He knelt behind her, inching her pants and panties down her legs, kissing her bare flesh along the way, before leaving them in a pool around her ankles. "Glorious."

"What is?" She couldn't see him, but he was there, a steady presence behind her.

"Pussy's as pretty as your tail." His palms charted a slow course up her legs. The newness, the anticipation, his hot breath on her seam, were doing disastrous things to her insides. "I think you've done something to me," he continued, half accusation, half awe. "Seeing you wet and gleaming like this gives me the most wicked thoughts."

"Tell me." She pleaded. Every wicked one.

"I want to consume you." She sucked in a sharp breath as he swiped his tongue up her center. "Just like this. Like fucking ice cream." He licked her again, slower this time. "What do you think of that?"

Shivers ran up her spine. She knew enough about Surface Dwellers to know it was a sweet treat they adored very, very much. "You like how I taste."

"Mm." He kissed and licked her tender folds, pausing only to curl his tongue into her channel. "So goddamn much."

She mewled with pleasure. He nipped her ass, her inner thighs, her folds, not stopping until her thighs were wet and dripping, and she was quaking so hard she could barely stand. He held her up when an orgasm ripped through her sudden and fierce, buckling her knees. "I got you."

Fists clenching, she cried out, eyes squeezed tight, but the screech of bowing metal snapped her from her lust-filled fog. There was a twin set of dents on either side of Reid's motorcycle seat. "Reid, I'm…"

His fond chuckling cut off her apology. "Made you come that hard, did I? Give me a little something to always remember you by?" He pressed a kiss to the base of her spine, his voice lowering. "Worth it. Fucking worth it."

She heard him stand behind her and every sound that followed after was more tantalizing than the last. The clink of belt, a lowered zipper, a condom being rolled onto hardened flesh. He stepped closer, the outside of his boots slotting next to the inside of hers, nudging out her stance as he wet his tip in her sodden slit.

"All right, sweetheart. I'm going to take this nice and easy. But you let me know if it gets to be too much."

She nodded.

He worked himself in gently, rocking in and out in short, shallow thrusts, his fingers paying homage to her sensitive pearl. Even when he was seated in her fully, he kept a restrained pace. Not too hard, not too fast, and she appreciated the care. From this angle, she felt him so much more, filling her to the brim and pressing on her belly from the inside out, almost too much to take.

When she began to hold herself, trying to apply some pressure to ease the discomfort, he reangled her hips, tilting them at a steeper slant so that when he rocked in, he hit her pearl every time. The unwanted pressure immediately disappeared, a pleasant tingling sensation building in its place. "Better?" he asked.

"Much." She exhaled, relieved.

"Always tell me if you're uncomfortable."

It felt so good now, her delayed "yes" tumbled from her lips in a gasping moan.

He smoothed his hands over her. Up her back, down her curves, over the round of her backside. "What do you think?"

"I like this." Really liked this.

"Would you like it more if I went faster?"

"Please."

Speed was a delicious blessing. Each collision delivered another wave of pleasure spiraling out to every corner of her body, a repeating rhythm of "yes," "yes," "yes" harmonized by "more." It left her breathless and spellbound.

"Fuck, I love your tail, but I can't have you from behind with it."

"This is...how...Surface...Dwellers...mate?" It came out in halting clusters. There was something so viscerally raw and primal about it. She couldn't explain why or how. But she reveled in it as if it were the answer to all her baser instincts.

"Sometimes." His voice was a harsh rasp against her ear.

"There's other ways?"

Reid's grip around her hips tightened, his rhythm growing fierce and urgent, and she loved that she drove him to such frenzied need. One that matched hers. This angle, this wonderful, demanding angle, was taking to her higher highs, and when she fell, she would shatter into oblivion, her pieces as innumerable as the stars.

Together they climbed higher and higher until she was wound so taut, she thought she might snap. "How many?" she ground out through clenched teeth.

His hips punched forward and with a sharply hissed curse, he came apart. Her body responded in kind, her channel fluttering and squeezing all around him. Even in this form, it did not want to let him go, not for anything.

"So many." Two simple words shouldn't sound so filthy, but falling from Reid's lips it was an indecent promise.

CHAPTER

TWENTY-TWO

"I GOT THIS FOR YOU." REID HELD A SMALL WATERPROOF notebook in his hand, a pen hooked to the front flap.

"Another present?" Nireed had returned to her mermaid form, arms folded across the diving platform as she looked up at him, silvery tail waving languidly behind her.

"It's for if you come, and I'm not here. My schedule's unpredictable sometimes with work and errands, but this way you can leave me a note. And I can write back. I'll keep it in here." He patted the red pouch he'd adhered to the side of the boat.

She took the notebook from his hand and clicked open the pen. "I have been practicing my writing." Flipping the book open to the first page, she began to write something, slow and careful. "Shorewalker and Cure Creator have been teaching me, and I'm a quick learner."

Odd nicknames she gave her friends, but they seemed to hold social significance, particularly the last one, which he'd figured out was what she called Dr. Lila Branson. The marine biologist published papers on the virophages she'd had a hand in creating to treat morbillivirus in merfolk.

Shorewalker...he wasn't sure what that meant or why she called her friend that. Was it categorically different from Surface Dweller or just a polite synonym?

When Nireed finished writing, she tucked the notebook and pen into the red pouch, grinning proudly.

Crouching down low, he leaned forward to kiss her.

He missed her already. Too soon Nireed had to return home. But he was due back at the station, and she needed to see her family and friends. The last time she'd seen them, they'd all been fighting for their lives.

Pulling back, he playfully flicked water at her. "See you around, Starfish. Try not to scare the shit out of me next time?"

Her amber eyes flashed, positively mischievous. "No promises, Coast Warrior."

And then, in a flash of scales, and a circle of rippling water, she was gone. Just like that.

The past few days felt like a wild fever dream, all at once too terrifying and blissful to be real. Needing a dose of reality, Reid reached for the red pouch and the notebook inside, half expecting the first page to be empty. But he had to know, had to confirm that this wasn't all an elaborate figment of his imagination.

Taking a deep breath, he flipped open to the first page.

And there it was, scratched out in the kind of perfect, uniform letters one would expect to see in early grade school primers. He couldn't help but smile to himself. Not just a quick learner, but an overachiever too.

Until the next adventure.
Or revenge against bad fishermen. Whatever comes first.
-Nireed

He smirked. True to form, vicious mermaid. True to form.

His vicious mermaid.

Putting the notebook back where he found it, he grabbed his overnight work bag and left for work. There, Perez cornered him in the break room, a tumbler of iced coffee in hand. "How are you holding up? Any word from Nireed?"

It took him a moment longer than it should have to put together that she was talking about their last case and the butchery they'd found onboard *Gale's Promise*. The last three days with Nireed had kept his mind off it and the evidence they had lost.

"Yeah, actually. She found me at home. Helped her patch up some flesh wounds and let her stay and heal for a few days. She swam home this morning." He stuffed his hands in his pockets. "Nautic caught a baby mermaid in their net. That's what started this. It was a rescue mission."

Horror and rage darkened Perez's expression, and while Reid hurried to assure her that the kid was okay, it did nothing to stem the long string of curses that erupted in both Spanish and English.

A throat cleared behind them.

In unison, they spun to attention, saluting their commanding officer as he entered the room, Hatcher on his heels.

"At ease." Lieutenant Commander Griffin barely came up to Reid's shoulder, but what he lacked in height, he more than made up for with a commandeering presence. "Good news. CGIS was able to recover most of the digital footage and wants us to continue turning over any evidence and witness statements to them. We've got a long road ahead, but every bit helps them build a case against Nautic."

Surprised relief quickly became disappointment. A long road ahead? Didn't they already have a clear picture? "Sir, is the security footage not enough? And the photos?"

"They're solid, but CGIS still needs to prove that what happened the other night wasn't just *Gale's Promise* being a sole actor. They can't take this to court until they can prove that the command came from corporate."

Anger surged, but he kept it tightly locked down.

It wasn't his commanding officer's fault. It wasn't CGIS's either. You didn't yank a weed without getting all its roots too. But how many more members of Nireed's pod would have to die until they finally had enough to nail Nautic to the wall?

In as even a tone as he could muster, Reid asked, "Is there anything preventative we can do in the meantime?"

Griffin's grim expression said it all. "Stay the course. It's all we can do for now."

For the rest of the morning briefing, Reid kept his mouth shut but this inability to do anything grated his nerves something fierce. He was a part of a lifesaving service. His instincts screamed at him to spring into action and save lives. No room for hesitation. Sitting back and knowing that people would continue to get hurt made him so mad he could barely see straight.

Nautic might not ultimately get away with this, but no amount of punishment and reparations would bring back all the merfolk they had and would continue to murder.

When the commander left, Perez laid a firm hand on his shoulder. "Deep breaths, you look like you're about to explode."

And he thought he'd done so well keeping his cool. Reid exhaled heavily, staring up at the ceiling. "It's not right."

"It really sucks," Perez agreed.

"I don't have a 'do nothing' bone in my body." There had to be something. Fines, assets patrolling the territory, something to deter Nautic.

"We do the job," Hatcher said firmly, but not unkindly. "I know that's not what you want to hear right now, but we have to keep our heads in the game and be ready for the people we can help."

The guy wasn't wrong, though it grated his nerves something fierce to hear it from him. If they got called out on a case in the next few minutes, and Reid didn't have his head on straight, mistakes would be made. And mistakes meant putting his life, the life of his aircrew, and the lives of the people he was meant to save at risk.

"I'm sorry about what I said the other day." Hatcher stuffed his hands into his pockets, staring down at his boots. "I didn't mean it. I was tired, and frustrated, and I lashed out. You didn't fuck up *The Merry Mariner* case."

"You told him he fucked up the case?" Perez sounded outraged.

"Yeah, but I don't really believe that." Finally looking Reid in the eye, Hatcher added, "And neither should you."

"I don't."

"Good."

"Reid, is there something else going on?" Perez almost never used his first name. Or a gentling tone. "With Nireed, I mean?"

It was a fair question, but it rankled his already prickly mood. "I care about her if that's what you're asking. I hate seeing her hurt."

Perez hesitated. There was clearly more she wanted to say.

"Just ask."

"What is she to you? A friend? Something more?"

Reid heaved a sigh. He really didn't want to talk about this right now, but it was going to come out sooner or later, and he was a rip the Band-Aid off kind of guy. "Something more."

A tense, awkward silence followed.

"Are you sure that's a good idea?" Perez winced as she said it. And dammit, that stung. Out of all his friends, he thought she'd at least be on his side with this. "I know I've teased you about her before, but that's a complicated relationship at best." She ticked several examples off her fingers. "Distance. Different species. Different moral code."

"Different moral code is a real nice way of saying she's killed and eaten people," Hatcher muttered. "Can you really be with someone who's done either of those things?"

"That." Perez jutted her thumb in Hatcher's direction. "I have nothing against Nireed, but that's some heavy shit to know about a partner."

"You let me worry about that."

"We're worried about *you*. Whatever you want from this, I don't see how it would work in the long term. What happens when you get new orders and need to move? Would you ask her to move with you? Can she live on land? And even if that answer is 'yes,' would it be fair to ask her to leave behind her truest self? To lie about who she really is? How would your parents react if they knew?"

Perez wasn't wrong, but man, she sure picked a hell of a time to say it. In as calm a voice as Reid could muster, he said, "I hear you. I've thought about a lot of this stuff myself. But I'm gonna need a minute. Bringing this up while I was already pissed off was not the move."

"That's fair. I'm sorry."

Hatcher nodded toward the door and Perez followed him out, giving him room to get his shit together.

Stressing out about relationship challenges and disapproving friends would have to wait. The still unresolved Nautic situation was a much bigger concern.

Not having answers now didn't mean they wouldn't come. But fuck, what was he going to tell Nireed? After everything—witnessing her friend claw her baby out of a fishing net, getting shot protecting them, finding the frozen bodies of her kin in a fishing hold— Lieutenant Commander Griffin's lackluster news would be a slap in the face. Even though there was a strategy and a process, it still reeked of inaction.

Reid's phone vibrated against his leg. There was only one of two people who regularly called him, and sure enough, *Mom* illuminated the screen. She knew his work schedule, so for her to be calling now probably meant it was important. "Hi Mom. Everything okay?"

"Reid." He heard her fraught sigh of relief. "Sorry to bother you at work. I just needed to hear your voice."

"Mom, what's going on?"

"Nothing. The Mom alarm bells were going off. You are okay, right?"

"A lot going on at work, but yeah, I'm good." It wasn't technically a lie, but in the space of what could only be a five-minute phone call while he was on duty, he wasn't about to say something that might make her spiral out in a panic.

This was the woman who didn't even want him to be a lifeguard, let alone join a river rescue team. And when he announced that he wanted to enlist in the Coast Guard, they'd gotten into several heated arguments. It wasn't until he got sent off to basic that she'd finally laid off, but man, he'd never known someone so terrified of water.

But nothing quite beat the time he shared the news about his reassignment to Haven Cove. She'd gone deathly pale, found the nearest chair and sat down, claiming a dizzy spell. A strange and alarming reaction considering she'd already been making trips out to the area. Something for work.

He'd tried asking her about her reaction but each time she'd brush him off. "It's the thalassophobia," she'd say. There was more she wasn't telling him, he was certain, but what could he do?

"How about I call you as soon as I'm off duty, and we catch up?"

"Actually, I'll be in Haven Cove tomorrow for a work trip. I know it's last minute, but I'll get a room at a local inn, so don't you worry about hosting. Maybe we could meet for brunch or something on your day off? Catch up in person?"

Worry curdled his stomach. Did she book this flight because of the thalassophobia? Or just because she missed him? Keeping his voice steady, he replied, "That sounds great. Send me your flight and lodging details?"

"As soon as we hang up. I won't keep you any longer. Just happy to hear your voice. I love you and can't wait to see you soon."

"Love you, too, Mom."

Why did he get the feeling there was more she wasn't saying?

CHAPTER
TWENTY-THREE

A POD-WIDE MATING FRENZY WAS IN FULL SWING, JUST AS Aersila predicted.

Nireed could scent it in the water, not to mention she'd already passed three pairs brazenly mating out in the open, wherever the mood struck. Either this was a chain reaction from the onset of Nireed's own mating frenzy during her last trip home, or everyone was just thrilled to be alive after the fight on *Gale's Promise*. No more lives were lost, thank the Twenty-Armed Goddess.

The pod appeared to be mostly healed. Or at least, their injuries weren't impeding their "expansion" efforts. Which was just as well. Some joy and bliss were needed after all they had endured.

And when she'd stopped by to check on Delphine and Melusina, both had been relieved to see her but distracted. While Nireed hadn't technically interrupted anything, they longed for their mates, and really it was only a small matter of time before they were all at it again.

She was glad to see their injuries had healed, and that Celia was happily playing in a corner, blowing bubbles, and swatting them with pudgy, clawed hands. If the little one remembered being trapped in a net, she didn't show it. With any luck, she'd be too young for any such terrible memories to stick.

All that was left to do was go home. Nireed wasn't keen to get to the moment when Aersila scented Reid on her again, even after swimming sixty miles, but there was nothing for it. She couldn't avoid her older sister forever.

Nireed took several centering passes outside their shared abode, getting air through her gills, before entering.

What she saw took her breath away.

Aquilus held her sister's hands, his forehead pressed to hers. The way he held her gaze was so patient and tender and loving, but it was desire that rolled off him in waves. And her sister looked so tempted, but unsure. This was a fragile moment.

Dimming her own bioluminescence, Nireed very, very carefully twitched her fins, disturbing the water as little as possible to make a quiet exit.

Nireed was nearly out the door when Aersila's eyes snapped to her. She lurched back, yanking her hands away. "Nireed," she signed shakily, turning away from her should-be mate. Giving him the cold shoulder.

No. Don't push him away.

Her heart hurt to see the way Aquilus's face fell a split second before his light dimmed, obscuring it from sight. He'd been so close to breaking through to her sister's heart. And Nireed had ruined it with her poor timing. If only she'd been less determined to face her sister and address the growing chasm between them.

"I'm sorry. I'll just go." Nireed signed to them both, but her final look fell on Aquilus. A mistake. Aersila stiffened, the water around them made bitter with her darkening mood.

To Aquilus, Aersila signed in curt motions, "Please leave."

He bowed his head, hurt and disappointed. "As you wish." Looking at neither of them, he swam out without another word.

The moment he was gone, Nireed whirled on Aersila, the movement of her hands punctuated by angry flashes of bioluminescent light. "Why do you do that?"

"Do what?" Aersila huffed, swimming past her. Swiping a knife off a shelf, she ascended to their food preparation table, a large circular slab of stone suspended from the ceiling with thick chains. Nireed followed, watching her sister furiously slice and chop the hunks of potted meat left out to brine.

"Push him away."

"He's too young for me." Aquilus was two years older than Nireed, putting him at eight years younger than Aersila. It wasn't that big of a difference. And he was one of the most mature males in the pod. He'd effectively raised Ryn after all.

"That's not why."

Aersila cut through the malleable meat with more force than necessary, then paused to say, "Forget about it, Nireed. The reason doesn't matter."

"Do you not like him?"

"Sister, I think we have something more important to discuss." Aersila pinned her with a hard glare. "Why do you smell like Reid?"

"I think you know why."

"Does nothing I've said matter to you? You saw what happened to Celia in our own waters, and the risk the pod took to get her back. After everything, how can you be so careless?"

Rows of sharp teeth slotted together as Nireed clenched her jaw. "The answer is to make the waters safer to swim in, not to avoid them."

"And how's that going?" Aersila's hands slapped together.

Slow. Far slower than Nireed would like, there was no denying that, but this kind of change didn't happen overnight unless they said screw it to diplomacy and slew Nautic's whole fishing fleet. A temptation to be sure, but without the general Surface Dweller public knowing the truth, without their sympathies, the blowback would be devastating. They'd just see them as murdering sea creatures and react with outrage and fear.

More merfolk would die.

"It's a delicate process," Nireed finally answered. "Their leadership needs proof, but now, after *Gale's Promise*, they should have more than plenty. We're making progress."

"I've yet to see it."

As much as Nireed wanted to keep arguing, she couldn't begrudge her sister this skepticism. She had her own doubts, a sinking feeling, that despite everything, all the death and destruction, there would never be enough proof. But if she let those doubts take hold and stopped believing in a chance for a better future, she'd stop fighting. None of them could afford that.

"I'm trying, Aersila. I'm really trying, and it's hard enough facing all these unknowns without my own sister telling me I can't do it. That I won't succeed. Do you know how much it hurts to see again and again how little confidence you have in me?"

Aersila drew back, startled. "It's not you I doubt." The motions of her hands were much softer now. "It's the Surface Dwellers. Despite your best intentions, and your very best efforts, they'll disappoint you. Or worse, take advantage. You're alone and vulnerable every time you go to shore."

"I know that better than you do," Nireed signed gently. "And I'm not alone. Whatever happens between Reid and I, I still have a pod of my own there—Shorewalker, Cure Creator, and all their friends and family. I know you blame them for what happened to me, but it was beyond any of our control, and yet, I would do it all again without question if it meant a chance at securing a better future for us. You've risked your life for this pod time and time again. It's my turn now."

"But…"

Nireed cut her off. "I'm aware of the consequences. I lived them. And even still, this is my choice. I need you to understand and respect that. You, Ryn, this pod, are all worth the risk."

Aersila swallowed, her hands motionless.

"Despite what you may think," Nireed continued, "I've thought a lot about this. And meeting Reid hasn't been all fun and fucking, which by the way, is a type of mating that doesn't produce children."

A flash of something illuminated Aersila's eyes. Interest, perhaps? "There's no such thing," she replied, but her movements were halting. Unsure.

"There is. The Surface Dwellers use these protective sheaths." Nireed paused to hold up two fingers and mimed rolling a condom down the length. "It catches everything."

"Oh." Aersila's brow pinched thoughtfully. "And it works underwater?"

"I don't know, but I can ask." Maybe all this time her sister's hesitation with Aquilus was not because she feared a relationship, but because she didn't want more children. This knowledge could be freeing. "And if they do, I can bring some home next time I visit the shore."

"I don't know." Aersila looked so torn. "I don't want to complicate things with Ryn. He sees Aquilus as his father. If it doesn't work out…"

"Me bringing them back doesn't mean you have to use them. They'll just be here in case you change your mind."

"I suppose it couldn't hurt."

Her sister deserved to be happy. And she deserved to have a mate who loved and adored her. A mate like Aquilus. "You've accused me of taking too many risks. But I think you've been taking too few of late."

Aersila rubbed her forehead, a heavy sigh billowing out in a cloud of bubbles.

"Where is my nephew anyway?"

"Napping." Aersila gestured toward their sleeping quarters. "But stop changing the subject. We were discussing your fling with the Surface Dweller."

If anyone was guilty of subject changing, it was Aersila, but Nireed would let it slide for now. "It's not a fling. We've a lot to figure out, yes, but it's not temporary."

"But he's so far away," Aersila signed halfheartedly, as if already knowing she'd lost this battle.

"It's worth it. He's good to me. Really, really good to me."

"He makes you happy." It wasn't a question, but a statement of fact.

"He does."

Aersila sighed again, a common response lately. "I don't like the distance, but it's better than Caspian." The pod's overeager, and yet abysmally lackluster, stand-in mate.

"I'm glad you agree. I wasn't sure."

Aersila scrunched her nose with displeasure. "I've higher standards for you than that."

"That's not comforting. There's only two others and one of them is sea sludge."

"If I asked Aquilus, I think he might've…"

Alarmed, Nireed stilled her sister's hands. Then signed, "Don't you ever ask something like that of him. He'd do anything for you, and it'd be wrong to take advantage."

Her sister bowed her head. "I'm not proud of it, but I thought that maybe you could've made him happy where I couldn't. And he you."

"I don't understand. Why would you think that?" Nireed paused to cup Aersila's cheeks.

"Because I don't have enough of me left to give." Her shoulders began to shake. The ocean might swallow her tears, but Nireed knew they were there.

"You're enough. You're more than enough." Nireed pulled her into a fierce hug.

TWENTY-FOUR

REID HUGGED HIS MOM, AND WAVES OF WHITE-FROSTED, auburn hair pressed against his cheek. Her light, floral perfume filled his nose and reminded him of days past. "This was a pleasant surprise."

She patted his back. "Missed my boy."

The hostess showed them to a booth near the back of the restaurant, but Reid wasn't complaining. Between the regular tourist bustle and local, noontime lunch crowd, the place was crowded, but it was quieter back here. "So, what's new?" his mom asked, unrolling a linen napkin and laying it across her lap.

Reid followed suit. "I'm not really sure where to begin."

"Bad news first. Save the best for last."

A waiter stopped by to introduce himself and fill their water glasses, but he was gone as soon as he'd arrived. Too many tables to serve to linger any longer. And yet, it gave Reid just enough time to think through what he wanted to say.

This was a short trip. Telling his water-fearing mom about interacting with people-eating mermaids was not on the table. So instead, he said, "There's no bad news to share. Just a heavy caseload is all. Should ease up once summer's done." While there was no guarantee of that, he didn't want his mother to worry.

She studied his face a moment before putting on her glasses and picking up a menu. "Do you want to talk about any of the cases?" She asked it casually, but he noted the concern.

"Standard stuff stacking, really." Another lie. "I think I'm just ready to take some leave."

"Any good news then?"

He rubbed a hand behind his neck. "Yeah, actually."

His mother peered at him from above the rim of her glasses, a smile forming. "That's a special someone sort of blushing." She smacked his arm playfully with the menu. "Don't leave me in suspense. Tell me."

Annaliese Kruetz, daughter of longtime Marquette County judge Greta Roth, did not leave such things up for debate.

Despite his best efforts to keep it cool, a shit-eating grin fought its way to the forefront. "It's brand new, but I'm seeing someone. She's no one like I've ever met before." There. That was one truth at least.

"Tell me about her."

"I don't know. She's playful. A little mischievous. Could easily kick my ass." He sipped his water, giving himself time to think. "She's observant. Misses nothing and is probably the most literal person I've ever met, but it makes her sweet and thoughtful too. Feels like she can stare straight into me sometimes, you know?"

His mother's smile grew. "She sounds delightful. A local?"

"Sort of. More...regional."

"I'd love to meet her, you know, once it feels right." She was trying to play it so cool, but he could tell she was chomping at the bit for more information. "What's her name?"

"Nireed."

"That's..." she trailed before her expression darkened, every bit of her body language tensing. "A strange name."

The waiter chose that time to return to take their orders. Reid picked at random, and his mom seemed to do the same, before handing over both their menus with a tight smile.

"What is it?"

"Nothing. It's just I've heard that name before. Read it in an article, I think."

Shit. Was his mom putting two and two together? She read articles from scientific community publications sometimes. It wasn't beyond reason she'd have read the ones coming out of this area, what with all her business trips here. And the pieces about merfolk and Nireed's captivity would be the most notable ones.

But if that were the case, why would she be so cagey about it?

Conversation for the duration of lunch was amiable but stilted, and he got the distinct sense that they were both trying too hard to keep it going, much of it either small talk or things they'd already spoken about over the phone in the last few months.

Over and over, he wondered whether he should tell her the truth, but if his mom had already linked Nireed-his-maybe-girlfriend to the mermaid studies and science journal articles, then why wasn't she asking the obvious? It was alarming to think that this might be the sort of something not even his mother could bear.

When lunch was done and the bill paid, Reid asked, "Would you like to meet for dinner?"

Distractedly, his mom waved a hand before typing something into her phone. Odd. She was normally more attentive. Either work was particularly strenuous or something else was going on here. "I would, if I didn't already have plans," she said in a clipped, brusque tone. "Breakfast tomorrow?"

"Sure. Seven early enough?"

She nodded curtly, finishing a text before locking her screen and shoving her phone in her purse. "Give me a hug."

He did, but it was awkward.

Why was his mother acting all squirrelly?

TAILING HIS OWN MOTHER LIKE A GODDAMN PRIVATE investigator was not how he'd wanted to spend his afternoon, but with how weird she was acting, he had to make sure she was all right. If she'd connected the dots about Nireed, maybe this odd behavior was some kind of manifestation of her thalassophobia, and if it was, he wanted to be there if things took a turn for the worst.

From afar, he watched her stop at an ATM, then duck into a coffee shop, where a person sitting at a window seat inside stood up and hugged her. He couldn't see what the person looked like through the sun's glare on the shopfront window, but it couldn't be the business acquaintance she was here to see, could it? He certainly didn't hug anyone at work. But maybe in the civilian world hugging clients and colleagues wasn't weird.

She was probably fine, but curiosity got the best of him, and he plopped down on a park bench that gave him direct line of sight to the front door while also remaining tucked out of view from the folks inside. The tree and trash can next to him helped.

When an hour passed, he started feeling like an idiot. What the hell was he doing stalking his mother and staking out her business meeting? She was a capable, responsible adult who could call her therapist if she had an episode. She didn't need her son lurking around, checking up on her.

Reid was just about to get up and walk away when his mom stood, exiting the coffee shop with her acquaintance in tow.

He immediately sat his ass back down, floored by what he saw.

The younger woman she was with had dark auburn hair just like his. It wasn't a rare color, but it wasn't common either, and more to the point, this woman was the spitting image of his mom when she was in her early thirties, minus the perm and flashy eighties clothing.

Who was she? And why did she look like they could be related?

He only had an uncle on his dad's side, no kids. His mom didn't have any siblings and neither did his late maternal grandmother, so cousin was out of the question.

"Would you like to stop by the house for dinner tomorrow?" His mother's lookalike asked. "Killian's making lobster mac 'n' cheese."

"I'd love to. When should I come by?"

"Any time after six is fine." The woman shifted awkwardly, looking mildly uncomfortable. "So, um, have you told Reid about me yet?"

He leaned forward, pretending to play a game on his phone, all while straining to hear.

His mom sighed. "Not yet."

"Mom, you really need to."

Mom? His vision narrowed down to a single point, at some weed sprouting up from a crack in the sidewalk, his surroundings blurring at the edges. He gripped the edge of the bench for support, feeling wobbly even as he was sitting.

Did this strange woman just call his mother *mom*?

"It's not fair to him or to me," the woman continued. "And I really hate keeping this secret from Nireed. It feels like lying. She's seeing him, you know, and I think she really likes him. That makes it harder."

Wait, this woman knew Nireed? And his mom had a secret child? What the fuck was going on here? An affair? Was his mom living a double life?

"I want to meet my brother," the woman added gently.

"I know, I know. But the truth is so difficult. You know that."

The woman rubbed his—*their*—mother's arm. "I do, but he deserves to know he has a sister. And really, that's all. I don't see why you'd have to tell him the how of it—not unless you wanted to. The sooner you get it off your chest, the sooner you'll be able to move on."

The *how* of it?

"I need to think about it some more."

"Okay."

"I'll see you soon, Lorelei."

Lorelei. He knew that name. Had heard it recently, in fact.

Was this the same woman Nireed called from his cellphone several days ago, whose number he looked up online? Racing to the internet app on his phone, he looked up the Haven Cove Museum of Oceanic Discovery's webpage, beelining to the contact page and the staff directory he'd pulled up before. Emails, phone numbers, just no headshots.

But after a little tapping around, he found a Meet the Staff page he hadn't noticed before, and there she was, smiling at the very top of the page. *Lorelei Roth, Museum Director.*

Lorelei *Roth*.

Not only did she look like his mother's younger twin, she shared a surname with his maternal grandmother, Greta Roth. How hadn't he put this together sooner? The past few days had been a whirlwind of opposites, starting with horrifically traumatic and ending on wildly orgasmic, but still. He should've thought more of it.

And the Yooper accent she'd slipped into over the phone...

Lorelei hugged his mom one more time, whispering something he couldn't hear, before leaving. His mom lingered outside the coffee shop, watching her go with a wistful smile.

Fuck. He had a sister. A goddamn sister!

His mother kept it from him his whole life. And what was worse, if that conversation was any indication, she hadn't ever planned on telling him. Launching off the bench, he approached his mom. Her back was turned to him, so she never saw him coming. "Does Dad know?"

She jumped, whirling around with her eyes as round as saucers. "Reid!"

Before she could even think of making up excuses, he snapped, "Don't deny it. I heard everything."

"What? How? Were you...spying on me?" She sounded angry.

"The way we left things at lunch, I thought you were having an episode. I wanted to make sure you were okay."

"It's been an hour!"

"Not the most important thing at the moment. I have a sister?"

His mom looked skyward, taking a deep, frustrated breath. "Yes."

He folded his arms across his chest and repeated. "Does Dad know?"

"Yes. I had her before I met him."

No cheating then, that was a fucking relief. "Why was she saying, 'how doesn't matter?' And what's Nireed got to do with any of this?"

"Keep your voice down." His mom hissed, glancing all around them. People were staring. "Let's go back to my rental to talk."

"Fine." He gestured curtly for her to lead the way and followed her a block up the road. She unlocked an unfamiliar sleek, silver sedan with Maine plates and slipped into the driver's seat.

Taking the passenger's side, Reid slammed the door behind him a little more harshly than he should've, making his mom jump again, and in that split second, she looked too much like a frightened deer. He hated that he'd done that. The thought that he might scare her, his mom, made him sick to his stomach.

"I'm sorry," he murmured, forcing calm into his words. It was one thing to be upset about her lies, another to be aggressive.

"I'm only going to say this once, so listen closely." She'd gone ghostly pale.

The sick feeling in his stomach deepened. Whatever she was about to say was bad, but he nodded to her to continue.

She squeezed the steering wheel in a white-knuckled grip, a hard set to her jaw. "I was assaulted. Here, in Haven Cove." Each short, clipped sentence was a sucker punch. "Lorelei was the result, and Nireed knows your sister, because she's not human. Not completely."

He barely choked the words out. "My sister's a...mermaid?"

His mom nodded, eyes growing distant. "I was out for a night swim. My then-boyfriend was on shore when I got yanked under. I thought it was a shark at first. Until I didn't." Her grip tightened. "It dragged me behind some rocks on shore. By the time my date found me, it was done. And that's all I'm going to say about it."

He wanted to yell, scream, punch the dashboard. He wanted to hug his mom, too, but she was so stiff and tense, he didn't think she'd appreciate being touched right now. If that fucker was still alive...

"Grandma Greta took Lorelei in after she was born and raised her." Her leg began to bounce. "I couldn't keep her, and not just because of what happened, but also because I sincerely thought she was a monster. I'll never forget those eyes. Such a terrifying shade of green. And the teeth and claws...Your grandmother believed me when I said I'd been assaulted, but not what by. Same with your father, until, well, the merfolk studies were released. My therapist hadn't believed me until then either."

Angry tears stung his eyes. Anger for his mom. Anger at his mom.

All these years, he thought he never saw Grandma Greta, even over the holidays, because of her demanding job and a strained mother-daughter relationship. But in truth, it was because she was busy raising his secret older sister. His secret mermaid, possibly flesh-craving, older sister.

"Why didn't you tell me?" His voice was weak, strained.

"Because it's my business. Mine." Tears rolled down her cheeks as she slapped her palm against the steering wheel. "I'm more than just your mother. I'm my own damn person and rehashing what happened is extremely painful, especially when no one else believed me when I said a freaking merman did it. And you're my child. *My son*. When and why would you ever have to know your mother was raped unless it happened to you too?"

Another wave of hot tears wet his cheeks, rage curling tight in his gut. "Is he alive?" He'd find that vile, oversized fish and kill him.

"No." His mom exhaled heavily, her hands falling to her lap. She looked so drained, the lines around her eyes and mouth deepening. "Lorelei talked to Undine and the other merfolk about it. Lorelei's got distinct tail and fin coloring, so they were able to piece together who her…father…was, and he's been long gone, it turns out. Undine's and Nireed's mothers tore him apart."

He let that sink in. The anger, the relief. As much as he would've liked to kill the fucker himself, it was better that monster wasn't still in this world, hurting people for the last thirty-something years. "Mom?"

"Yeah?"

"Can I hug you?"

She began to sob, shoulders quaking as she nodded, reaching for him. He enveloped her in his arms and hugged her tight, not caring a fucking whit that the car's gear shift was digging into his leg.

"I love you, Mom."

"I love you too." She squeezed him fiercely, protectively. "So, so much."

They remained like that for a long while.

Sniffing loudly, she eventually pulled away, wiping her eyes. "I could've made something up, but try to understand I wasn't in Lorelei's life, and I never planned to be. I was hurt and scared, and when you were born, that feeling increased a hundred-fold." She took his hand, cradling it in both of hers. "All I wanted to do was protect you. I'd have nightmares of you two swimming in the lake together or at a pool party. And every time, they ended with her transforming into a monster and killing you."

His gut twisted in sympathy for his mother, so desperate to put the past behind her, but it never allowed her to forget, did it? These nightmares, the thalassophobia, now her son demanding answers. One way or another, circumstances dredged up the truth time and time again, and for most of her adult life, the people she loved and trusted most never believed her.

That must have been maddening.

He was still angry and upset. If he hadn't been eavesdropping, he might've gone his entire life never knowing he had a sister. In a family as small as his, that shit mattered. One day, when his parents were gone, he'd have no one left. There was his dad's alcoholic brother, but with the self-destructive lifestyle he lived, he would probably be gone too.

Maybe Lorelei would've defied their mom's wishes and tracked him down. Her wanting to meet him certainly sounded earnest and genuine, and the thought brought some comfort.

"I'm sorry I kept her from you." His mom stared at their clasped hands. "If it makes you feel any better, I only told her recently."

It didn't, but that wasn't something he wanted to argue about. He'd much rather move forward and give her the comfort she needed. The apology would have to be enough. "It hurts," he said, squeezing her hand. "But I get it."

"Thank you for understanding. I know none of this was easy to hear."

Silence fell between them.

There were so many things Reid wanted to ask her. Why are you back in Lorelei's life if you thought she was a monster? What changed? How long have you two been meeting up? And why would you tell her about me, but not me about her? But it all sounded too aggressive and accusatory, especially with how prickly he still felt.

"You seem close," he said finally, hoping it would get her talking.

"Trying to be. I've a lot of time to make up for."

"So not a monster after all, huh?"

"No more than your Nireed." She smiled. "Definitely someone worth knowing."

Your Nireed.

Longing rolled in like high tide after a storm. It had only been days, but he missed her, and while they hadn't put a label on anything, she did feel like she could be his. He certainly was hers. The little Starfish had suckered herself onto his heart.

There was nothing he wanted more right now than to hold her. To share the secret that was burning a hole in his mind.

That he had a sister.

A mermaid just like Nireed, and possibly her best friend.

TWENTY-FIVE

"RYN!" NIREED LAUGHED, DUCKING AS HER NEPHEW SWUNG A wooden, child-sized trident. "Slow down. You're better at this than I."

Ryn pouted, pausing to sign one-handed. "You're supposed to block."

Nireed had the other toy trident in the pair Aersila had crafted for her son. The wood, already slick and worn by algae and time, wouldn't hold up for more than a few more years. But by then, Ryn would be ready for the real thing, a project Aersila was already working on, traveling past the continental shelf and thousands of feet down to forge it in deep sea volcanic vents.

"I panicked. You're a fierce warrior, you know."

Ryn beamed, mismatched rows of sharp teeth on display. He was losing his baby teeth, the adult fangs crowding in, fighting for dominance. It gave him an adorably shark-like appearance. Teeth aside, the youngster shared the features of the Emera-line: gold-flecked amber eyes, dark brown hair, a silver tail and fins slashed with orange. Just like his mother, his aunt, and grandmother before him.

"Come here, Ryn." Her sister signed, bioluminescence flashing to get her son's attention.

The boy swam to Aersila's side, an endearing mix of eager and shy—

eager, for his mother's affection. Shy, for the newness of that bond. They'd only just recently come back into each other's lives.

Aquilus was spectating, too, but at a notable distance from her sister. And yet, despite the tense chasm between them, he smiled as Aersila gently took Ryn's hands, bringing them closer together.

Once satisfied that his hands were where they needed to be, Aersila signed, "Remember, shoulders width apart. Increases stability and..."

"Lowers risk of injury," Ryn finished.

"Yes, very good." Aersila patted him on the shoulder. It was a little stiff, but not for a lack of affection—her sister was still acclimating to her mothering role—and Ryn ducked his head in response, hiding another smile. He didn't seem to mind his mother's well-intended but awkward gestures.

A tap on the shoulder brought Nireed's attention back to Aquilus. While she was watching her sister and nephew, he'd swum up beside her, his golden scales glinting with every ripple of movement. "May I?" he signed, pointing to the wooden trident in her hands.

Smiling, she nodded, handing it over.

It looked comical in his hands, but he swooped in proudly, tangling the toy's prongs with Ryn's, winning bubbling laughter from his adopted son. They clashed again and again, their unfettered joy suffusing the water around them.

"Aquilus!" Aersila scolded with the sharp slap of her hands. "You're holding your hands too close!"

Flashing a winsome smile, he signed one-handed, "Not trying to beat up *our* kid."

A golden, bioluminescent hue illuminated Aersila's cheeks, but she recovered quickly, her response adorably grumpy. "He won't learn if you hold back."

"Then come over here and show me." There was a hint of wicked edge to that request, almost a challenge, and Nireed couldn't help but smirk at Aersila's huffy expression.

"Show him! Show him!" Ryn pleaded. And if Nireed wasn't wrong, there was a little mischief in the boy's smile, too.

A stream of bubbles erupted from Aersila's mouth as she sighed and swam behind Aquilus, reaching around him to adjust his grip. Despite the irritable twitch to her fins, her touch was gentle, and dare Nireed say, lingering.

Ryn stared at the pair, thin arms wrapped around his trident in a hug —a child's longing for his blood mother and father-by-circumstance to get together and unite their family of three. It made Nireed's chest tighten. She hoped beyond hope that her nephew would get his wish.

Once trident lessons ended, Aquilus left with Ryn in tow, it being his turn to keep the boy overnight, leaving the sisters alone.

"I'm sorry," Aersila signed when it was just the two of them.

"For what?"

"For making you feel like I didn't believe in you. I do believe in you, but sometimes, despite our capabilities, we still get hurt. I mean, just look at me. I've a long history of bad consequences for my risk-taking."

"I know you don't want to see me hurt," Nireed conceded. "You wouldn't be much of a sister if you did."

"I want you to be happy. And if this Reid, the shallows, or even the Land Above the Water makes you happy, then I'm happy for you, and more than anything, I want you to live the life that keeps you happy. But you better come back to visit me at least several times a year, or I'll have to drag my old tail up the shore and get you."

Nireed threw her arms around her sister, hugging and rocking them both. "Parts of the Land Above the Water are more beautiful than I could've ever imagined, and I want to explore them all, but it will never be home. Not fully. Not like here. You're not going to lose me to it."

TWENTY-SIX

REID CAME HOME TO FIND A NEW NOTE IN THE WATERPROOF
journal. Already it was making itself useful.

> *Good news. Made up with my sister. We have her blessing
> now.*
>
> *Was hoping to see you. I'll visit Lorelei for a little while and
> return this evening. Hoping you'll be back by then.*
>
> *Miss you.*
>
> *-Nireed*

He traced a finger over Lorelei's name, then Nireed's. The shock
hadn't worn off and probably wouldn't for a long while. All these years,
he had a sister, and she was friends with his Starfish. What a strange
twist of fate.

In a roundabout way, Nireed had brought this heavy secret to light. If
he hadn't mentioned her name, if his mom hadn't gotten squirrelly, and
he hadn't followed her, he'd still be in the dark about all this.

Now was probably a good time to text his therapist, but he didn't
want a professional opinion just yet. He wanted to talk to Nireed first,

someone who knew his sister and could tell him what she was like without being dragged down by painful memories.

He uncapped a pen and committed the secret to waterproof paper. Just three simple words.

Lorelei's my sister.

There was so much more to say, but that was all he could manage.

His hands shook as he returned the journal to its pouch, installed on the side of his boat.

Evening was hours away, forever when the same obsessive thoughts cycled through. What he needed was a distraction, but he wasn't going to get it inside. Every spare inch of his home reminded him of Nireed. Her sweet, sea-salt-tinged scent lingered in each breath he took, and her silver scales still clung to his sheets like glitter.

God, he wanted to talk to her.

He stripped down and swam until his body and mind were numb.

Sometime later, someone was shaking his shoulder and calling his name. He swung his legs out and bolted upright with a start, ready to yank on his gear. It took him a second to register where he was—standing off the stern of his houseboat and not in the middle of a berthing area.

Nireed stared up at him from the water with wide, glowing eyes, clutching the waterproof journal in her hand. The last thing he remembered after his swim was sprawling across the diving platform, letting the sun rewarm his skin. He must've fallen asleep.

"Starfish," he said weakly. "You read it?"

She opened her mouth, then shut it, bowing her head to read the words again. They had rendered the siren speechless.

He began pulling on his clothes. "Kinda glad I'm not the only one surprised by this."

"I know what these words say, and yet, the more I try to read them, the less I understand."

"I know. I only found out today."

Dressed, he flopped back down onto the platform, crossing his legs.

"Shorewalker is your sister?"

"Half sister. Same mom, different..." He flexed his hands, trying not to ball them into fists. That was a conversation for another time.

Setting the journal down, Nireed tilted her head, studying him carefully. "You do have the same hair, but that's the only obvious feature."

"I take after my dad." He shrugged. "She's the spitting image of my mom."

Nireed leaned in, nostrils flaring as she sniffed him. She didn't even try to hide it.

A thoughtful look crossed her face. "There's a similarity in your scents. It's subtle. And I think I noticed it before, but I didn't realize what it meant. I just thought it was familiar because I recognized you from the night we met."

"You can smell that we're siblings?"

"It's not that specific. Just that you're family."

"Still, that's wild."

"It's in the blood." Nireed lightly traced a claw down a prominent vein in his forearm. "We can smell emotion too. Whether a person is angry or sad or scared. Any changes in the body really. When someone's aroused. Or pregnant."

He swallowed thickly. "I didn't realize it was that acute."

"It is."

"Why do you call her Shorewalker? What does it mean?"

Nireed's expression darkened. And he did not like it one bit.

"Tell me."

"Shorewalkers don't have happy origins," she forced out. "Not in the last two generations, anyway."

It wasn't like her to be indirect. "What are you saying?"

"The Surface Dwellers weren't willing."

As the meaning filtered in, he felt hot and cold all over. Extreme aggression had been noted repeatedly in the mermaid studies, caused by a mutated morbillivirus with rabies-like symptoms. It also said that the virus expressed itself differently between sexes but not to this extent.

The research said nothing about mermen attacking human women on shore.

What happened to his mom wasn't a onetime thing. In fact, it had happened often enough that the merfolk had a special word for it. A word they gave to his sister as a nickname, defining her by her dark history.

"Why would you call her that?" he bit out, unable to hide his anger. He'd never met the woman, but he was furious on her behalf.

Nireed reared back, surprised. "It wasn't always like that. And it isn't anymore."

"But it's real for her!"

She sunk down, her chin skimming the water's surface. "That's true," she admitted quietly. "I never thought of it like that. Don't think the others did either."

"How many other Shorewalkers are out there?"

"We don't know."

Anger boiled inside him. He tried to dial it down to a simmer, but the words that flew out of his mouth were brutal. "What do you mean, you don't know? Your kind just fucks then bolts? Doesn't bother keeping tabs on the kids they force on others?"

Nireed flinched. "Why are you yelling at me? I didn't do this."

"I'm sorry." He yanked his hair, staring up at the sky as he let out a feral growl. "But my mom was one of the people hurt, and she's carried those scars alone for years. No one believed her, not even my dad. Do you realize how fucked up that is? How angry that makes me?"

"As you should be. It made me angry too."

"Made?"

"Our pod dies out if we don't move forward." Her next words were said so quietly, he almost didn't hear them. "It wasn't just Surface Dwellers."

Dread lanced down his spine, a step away from rage. "Nireed, were you…"

Tears sprung to her eyes. "No," she whispered. "My sister. She carries such scars. And your sister—Lorelei and Cure Creator saved us by developing a special cure."

He'd about read that. The study implemented a little used, little researched treatment method—injecting a virophage into the body, essentially co-infecting a patient with another virus, weakening, and deactivating them both simultaneously. Neutralizing the excessive aggression in merfolk, the lack of control, that was the whole point of the study.

That's why...

All the things he knew about Nireed, and extant mermaid science, were finally coalescing in his brain. She'd told him that she was a part of the study, but never why. He'd assumed capture, but that wasn't it, was it? "They needed a test subject, and you gave them one."

A small, pained smile twisted Nireed's lips. "What happened to your mom, my sister, and the others like them, that is my people's greatest shame. It needed to stop, no matter the cost. I went into that tank willingly."

And left it on death's door.

"Nireed, I'm so sorry." When he reached for her, she rose from the water and embraced him. The hurt, the anger, and all the other emotions of the day were still there, sharp as ever, but in that Pandora's Box of dark feelings was another that squeezed his heart and made him hold on to Nireed tighter as he cried like a baby.

Reid buried his nose in her wet hair, not caring a smidge that she was soaking his clothes. And in return, she didn't comment on his tears, just gently stroked her claws through his hair.

"Your sister was angry too." Nireed's breath was warm and comforting against his neck. "She negotiated a deal with our pod leader, a mermaid to study in exchange for a cure. I didn't have to go, but she was right. Things had to change. To this day, Lorelei harbors a lot of guilt for what the study eventually came to, even though what happened to me wasn't her fault. I think it's because, at the start, a part of her wanted revenge. And not just for her origins, but because her entire crew had been devoured."

The Osprey. It wasn't just a storm.

Startled, he pulled back to meet Nireed's tear-filled eyes.

The world didn't know this.

"You might be thinking right now that what's happening to us with Nautic is deserved. That the world is righting itself of past wrongs. But we're trying to be better."

His voice broke. "I know you are. You've a right to defend yourself." But when he looked down at her mouth, all he saw was blood.

"Reid, why do you smell like fear?"

"I..." He stood on trembling legs, dimly aware that he'd unceremoniously dumped her off his lap.

Reid remembered that case. He was the rescue swimmer onboard the plane dispatched from the air station down in Cape Cod. The detachment in Haven Cove hadn't existed yet. They'd gotten the call in the middle of the night and booked it up the coast, racing against time and grim odds. They arrived on scene early in the morning, but by then it had been too late. The crew was gone, more than thirty people lost at sea.

All that was left of any of them was a bloody immersion suit and some debris.

Except his sister. Lorelei Roth's name had been plastered all over national news, the maritime mystery of the year, because she was the tragedy's sole survivor.

And now he knew why.

The storm couldn't kill her, and merfolk didn't eat their own kind.

"Did you eat my sister's crewmates?"

Nireed looked away from him then, hunching in on herself. She looked so small and lost sitting at the edge of the diving platform. It made her less threatening, but these dark truths, one after another after another, hung over them like a shroud.

And yet, none of it stopped him from wanting to reach out and hold her.

Like all those people's deaths didn't matter.

"I have to go." Reid stumbled onto the pier, his vision going blurry at the edges. "I'm sorry."

"Please don't run." She turned toward him, eyes panicked and pleading. But he couldn't stay.

He needed space. Some time to think.

Reid ran. Peeled off on his motorcycle, gravel shooting behind him. Out on the coastal highway he went heavy on the throttle, barreling down the blacktop with a ferocious mechanical roar.

He couldn't see them now, sitting astride, but beneath his legs were the dents Nireed made, a permanent reminder of how she trembled and quaked across his bike. Vulnerable, but entirely trusting herself to his care. Even while running from her, he missed her, wanted her, but he'd just been mentally and emotionally bulldozed.

Knowing that Nireed had eaten people? That was nothing new. The practice started somewhere. Whether it was *The Merry Mariner*, the sinking of *The Osprey*, or an earlier event didn't really make a difference.

Context mattered. He knew that. And yet, he passed the turnoff to his favorite seaside picnic grove, driving on and on, his motorcycle's roaring engine fueling his Pandora's Box of feelings and resolving none of them.

A more stable version of himself would've called his therapist, but he was too afraid to admit that maybe Perez and Hatcher were right to ask him if he could handle Nireed's past.

No matter how much he cared about her or admired her protective instincts or the sacrifices she made to atone for her people's gravest sins, her history horrified him. And yet, there was nothing more terrifying than the things he still felt for her despite it all.

Teeth and claws were wicked sharp, and yet none cut as deep as the truth.

NIREED WATCHED HELPLESSLY AS REID RACED AWAY ON HIS motorcycle, her stomach queasy from the smell of his fear. Of all the things that came to light during their conversation, she hadn't expected *The Osprey's* demise to be the part that drove him away. Or maybe it was simply one truth too many.

There was a Surface Dweller saying about it, something about straws and camels, but she couldn't for the life of her remember how it went. Not that it mattered. Reid was gone.

She waited an hour, then two, waiting to hear the motorcycle's horrendously loud engine once again. Never would've thought she'd long for such an ear-splitting sound, but it was preferable to the agony building in her chest.

The sun dipped below the horizon, leaving her in darkness. The truth sank with it.

Reid was not coming back.

Eyes burning, she withdrew the waterproof journal from the pouch Reid kept it in, staring at the last entry.

Lorelei's my sister.

Tears dripped onto the page.

It should've been happy news, a cause for celebration. Two people she cared about deeply were related, and had both gained a sibling in each other, but there was just so much ugliness wrapped up in it. Maybe if Reid hadn't run from her, she could've told him more about his sister and focused on the joy.

Or maybe she wasn't meant to have those things, and had been deluding herself all along, ensnared by her own desire to be loved.

Nireed began to write.

I'm sorry. For your mom. For the other people that were hurt and killed. For Lorelei's crewmates. I'm sorry for everything.

I've only ever wanted to protect you, but I've made you fearful instead. You deserve to feel safe, including from me.

There was more she wanted to say. Namely, that she wanted a future with him, but she didn't know if that was possible now, not while he feared her. Closing the journal, Nireed dropped it back inside its pouch. Maybe he'd read her message, maybe he wouldn't, but it still needed to be said.

With a hard slap of her tail, Nireed shot away from the houseboat, furiously eating up the distance between land and home. As tears burned her eyes, heartbreak anchored heavy in her chest. No one person made up her entire world, but she had wanted Reid to be a part of it.

What a fool she'd been to ever think he'd see her as more than a monster.

TWENTY-SEVEN

"What's going on, Reid? You're not looking so hot."

Perez sat across the booth, anxiously picking at a basket of French fries. She'd met him at a local diner chain, responding to his panicked text message, *I think I fucked up. Or maybe, I'm fucked up.*

"Don't feel it either." Shoving his hands into his hair, he tugged ruthlessly at the roots. "I've been thinking about what you and Hatcher said the other day. About Nireed."

"We didn't say those things to hurt you." Perez pulled his hands away, shooting them a disapproving look, as if they'd committed the offense all on their own. "Or judge you."

"From you? I believe that. Not so convinced that's the case with him."

"Hatcher cares about you. He's a distrustful asshole about it sometimes, especially when it comes to the merfolk. I'm not gonna lie, I'm side-eyeing him a bit for that, but I do believe it's ignorance, not outright maliciousness."

"Not much of a comfort though, is it?"

"Not really," she admitted. "But the mindset at the time was 'wow, yikes, our friend just did something,'" her voice dropped to a whisper, "'illegal.' And we just found out that you had feelings for Nireed and felt we needed to open your eyes to some things before you got too serious."

"It's already serious. And the thought that maybe this should be the end is eating me up inside, because I don't want it to be."

"Yeah?" she asked softly, far more forgiving than he'd expected. The last time they'd talked about personal shit, it had scraped his nerves like nails on a chalkboard, and he'd barely reigned in his temper. "Tell me why. Maybe it'll help."

"I think Nireed's the bravest, most selfless person I know." While Reid had waited for Perez to arrive, he reread the exposé about the mermaid lab on his phone twice over. Now, he showed it to his friend. "She volunteered for this because she wanted to make a real difference. And she's risking herself again now to keep her people safe from Nautic, knowing captivity or worse could be the consequence. That's who she really is." He lowered his voice. "The killing, and the rest, is a part of the picture, but it's not the whole picture. I think I'm supposed to feel more disgusted about that than I do."

"Is that why your text message said, 'maybe, I'm fucked up'?"

He nodded. "While I'm not exactly thrilled about all the things she's done, it doesn't change how I feel about her. And yeah, maybe that's messed up, but I can rationalize it with the context. Merfolk don't hunt humans, not since the culmination of the study, and while they do hunt their enemies, they believe that death has value. Leaving a body unconsumed is to waste it."

Perez looked up from his phone, surprised. "That's morbid, but it makes a grim sort of logic."

"With *The Merry Mariner*, they took out an enemy and fed their families. With *Gale's Promise*, they prioritized getting the injured home safely. I think most would find fault with their methods, but they're not human. They live by different rules."

"And you're at peace with that." It wasn't even a question. Or a judgment. "And with the fact that Nireed also lives by these rules."

"I think I am."

Perez smiled. "That's all I wanted to hear. I was never against Nireed. Just wanted you to really understand what you were signing up for, and most of all, to be happy. Because that's how something like this works in the long term for the both of you. You gotta be damn sure about it. Resentments and doubts will only fester."

"You don't think there's either of those things?"

"Nah, it sounds more to me like you're totally gone for her. Even Hatcher couldn't disagree with that. I mean, it'll probably take him a long ass time to come around to this, but I think he will once he hears the full story and has a chance to get to know your girl."

"You really think so?"

"Wouldn't have said it if I didn't." Perez handed back his phone and popped a French fry into her mouth. "So, how'd you 'fuck up'? Your text message said that too."

He groaned, and went to grab his hair again, but she swatted his hands away.

"Ah! None of that. What happened?"

Dropping his hands to the table, he began shredding a napkin into confetti instead. "We were talking about some dark, heavy shit. I got overwhelmed by it all and just left her, alone. I needed the space, but I didn't even take the time to explain why I was leaving."

"Yeah, you messed up, but it's fixable. If you manage to find her out there in that big, wide ocean, that is. She's not exactly reachable by phone."

"Don't I know it."

These past few weeks, Nireed had been everywhere he turned, but now, if she meant to avoid him? Mermaids had been elusive myths for centuries. She could easily disappear into the ocean if she wanted to and never see his sorry ass again.

Reid didn't go home until well past dark, all while wishing he might find Nireed right where he'd left her, but knowing she'd be gone.

And she was. But there was a new note in the journal, beads of tears trapped between its waxy pages. It broke his heart to see them and the apology she wrote. She didn't say it outright, but she thought what they'd started was over, that he thought she was an irredeemable monster.

He hadn't given her a reason to believe otherwise. He ran. And in fear. But it wasn't because he realized he loathed the monster. Quite the opposite, in fact.

THE NEXT MORNING, REID FOUND HIMSELF ONCE AGAIN searching the museum's website for his sister's work number. He paced the length of his houseboat six times before taking a deep breath and dialing.

She picked up on the fourth ring. "Lorelei Roth, Museum Director. What can I do for you?"

There it was, that slight Yooper accent. He'd dismissed it before, but it was a glaring beacon of proof now. "Hi, uh, it's Reid." He swallowed thickly. "Your brother."

The line was quiet on the other end.

Several long seconds ticked by, and he was just about to say 'hello?' when his sister responded, voice steeped in teary emotion, "You know?"

He exhaled, tears stinging his eyes. "Yeah, my—I mean—our mom told me yesterday. So, it's true?"

"Yeah," she said with a nervous laugh. "Apparently. Wild, right?"

"Wild, yeah." He rubbed his hand behind his neck. "You know, you kind of sound like her. Grandma Greta, I mean."

"Grandma Greta," she repeated softly. "I used to think of her as my mom."

"I mean she raised you, right? Did you know?"

"No, never. I thought she'd adopted me from the child welfare system."

"Damn." So, this had been a closely guarded secret from them both.

"Did Annaliese—I mean, Mom—tell you everything?"

Fuck. What a loaded question. That she was a child born out of sexual assault? A flesh-craving mermaid? Or was there even more to this story that hadn't been divulged to him yet? "I know about the 'how.' And that you and Nireed have more in common than meets the eye. Anything else I'm missing?"

"Nope." Lorelei chuckled darkly. "That about sums it up."

"Well, thank Jesus. I don't think I could take more earth-shattering news."

"No triple whammies here. Just hitting doubles."

A long pause fell between them.

"Do you, uh, maybe want to meet?" he ventured.

"Oh, fuck yes." She exhaled, sounding relieved. "You're more than welcome to come over, I promise I don't bite." Knowing what he did about her, it wasn't just a flippant joke, but his heart twinged at the thought that maybe his sister had gotten unkind responses to her oceanic heritage in the past. "Or we can meet somewhere public if you feel more comfortable with that."

He didn't know her. Really, there was no reason to trust her, but he did, implicitly. His mom did, after all, and they were family. That had to count for something. "We can meet at your place."

"I still have your number from when Nireed called. I'll text you my address."

Nireed.

Bitter regret weighed heavy in his chest. He'd really botched that up. When he demanded the truth from her, she gave it, and while it was a hard pill to swallow, he never should've run from her like he was fleeing a bloodthirsty monster. It would serve him right if she swam off into the proverbial sunset and never looked back, just as he realized how much she really meant to him.

"Reid?"

"Yeah, sorry. Text me your address. I'm off duty for the next two days."

Reid drove to Lorelei's house for brunch the next day after having an early breakfast with their mom.

He zipped down a long country road, stretching through a dense, forested corridor. It was slightly overcast, a light layer of fog spilling out from between the trees and onto the road. A touch spooky but at least it didn't impair visibility. He slowed down to make the turnoff, easing his bike up an access road and to a tall iron gate. The property's perimeter was walled off with high-stacked stone, cutting through the forest as far as his eye could see.

Noting a security camera and speaker system, he took off his helmet and punched the intercom with his finger. A few seconds ticked by before the speaker crackled, followed by a deep male-sounding voice on the other end. "Quinn-Roth residence."

A boyfriend? A partner? It struck him especially hard in that moment that he barely knew anything about his older sister.

Clearing his throat, he replied, "Hi. I'm Reid. Lorelei's long-lost half brother?"

A pause, then, "She told me you were coming. Come on up."

Gears and other mechanisms whirred to life as the gate slid back, clearing the way forward, and his heart climbed to his throat. It was now or nothing. After sliding the helmet back onto his head, Reid lightly eased the throttle forward, puttering up toward the house.

The trees opened to the ocean and a stunning, isolated inlet.

Given the state-of-the-art gate system, he'd expected to find a coastal mansion on the other end, but instead he pulled up to a charming, but modest, two-story stone cottage. He would've thought the thick wall of trees and long stretch of empty country road, would've provided enough privacy, but maybe one couldn't be too careful when they were a shore-dwelling mermaid.

Leaving his helmet and leather jacket with his bike, Reid approached the front door, gravel crunching beneath his boots. He paused, staring at its iron ring knocker a moment before taking a deep breath and using it. The door opened so suddenly she had to have been waiting for him on the other side.

A dark-haired redhead with striking green eyes stared back at him, her mouth slightly ajar. Lorelei. His sister.

His family.

She had mom's mismatched eyebrows and Grandma Greta's proud, stubborn chin. But aside from the unusual shade of green that contrasted with the rest of the family's dark browns, she didn't look like a mermaid.

And then she pounced, wrapping him in a fierce, too tight hug, the air whooshing out of him. Ah, there it was. The mermaid strength.

"Easy, sis." He wheezed, tapping her back, and she immediately loosened her arms without ending the hug.

"Sorry. I forget sometimes."

"It's all right." He hugged her back, the all-encompassing kind that only siblings can give moments before a headlock or wet willy. Not that he was going to do either, but the pesky, little brother urge was there, lurking somewhere in the background, waiting for the right moment. "Could've used you in grade school."

They both drew back at the same time.

"It's not too late." Her eyes flashed an eerie neon green as she waggled her fingers, the rounded tips extending into sharp claws, and he couldn't help but stare in wonder. There'd been no reason to doubt she was a mermaid, but here was the confirmation. "Can still beat up your bullies if you want."

"Great. I'll put you on speed-dial."

"Come on." She took his hand, tugging him inside. "Killian's got second breakfast on."

The open-concept interior was all handcrafted stone and reclaimed driftwood. Truly quintessential seaside cottage vibes. And in the kitchen was a tall guy with salt and pepper hair, pulling a steaming pie dish out of the oven. Quiche, by the looks and smells of it.

After setting the dish on the counter, the man turned around, shucking off an oven mitt and offering his hand.

Gesturing between the two of them, Lorelei beamed. "Husband, meet brother."

"Killian," the man supplied, clasping Reid's hand in a firm handshake. Short scruff lined his jaw and prominent crow's feet flanked grayish blue eyes. His sister's husband was significantly older than them both. Early forties if he had to guess, and no stranger to the sun. Fisherman, perhaps?

"How'd you two meet?"

The couple shared a wistful look.

"That's a long story," Lorelei replied.

"I've got time."

They sat around the dining room table, sharing the story over breakfast. Turned out, Killian was the captain of the fishing crew that found Lorelei among *The Osprey's* wreckage and had brought her back to shore for medical evaluation.

And Killian's first fishing boat, *Dawn Chaser*, had sunk just over a year later. Reid had been the rescue swimmer on that case, too, flown up from Cape Cod. But again, too late, and he later learned that the injured and hypothermic crew had been towed back to shore by merfolk and treated by landside EMS.

Those two incidents, and a general uptick in merfolk activity, were driving factors in installing a new Coast Guard aviation unit at Haven Cove Airport. Being closer meant getting on scene quicker and increasing their chances of saving lives.

But to think, he and his sister had come so close to crossing paths before, not just once, but twice. Maybe it had always been just a matter of time.

He'd tried to help with dishes once brunch was done, but the couple waved him off, so he wandered over to a pair of bookshelves in the living room. Picture frames were interspersed between the stacks of titles, one catching his eye in particular.

A wedding photo.

Lorelei and Killian stood off-center, hands clasped, with their bodies twisted to face the camera. To their right was Dr. Lila Branson with an older Black couple and a man giving jovial, short Thor energy. To their left was a dark-haired white woman wearing a bridesmaid's dress, and beside her, Nireed.

He brushed a finger along the frame, longing dropping anchor in his chest.

Nireed's hair had been loosely curled and braided, spilling over a bare shoulder in a waterfall of silky brown. Her Grecian-style dress was a deliberate nod to the sirens of old and in a light blue shade that reminded him of the periwinkle flowers his mom grew back home. The bouquet in her hands was a mix of blues, whites, and filler greens, and he didn't know enough about plants to identify any of them, but they had a distinctly wild, plucked from a field look.

At a glance, Nireed might be mistaken for human, but her eyes were just a little too luminescent, her nails a little too sharp, and along the smooth, ivory column of her neck, three faint horizontal slashes teased where her gills would be. That was, if you knew to look.

His sister drew up beside him, only the whisper of footsteps alerting him to her approach. "She's beautiful, isn't she?"

Ethereal. A sea goddess gracing the shore with her divinity.

"Takes my breath away every single time." Figuratively, sometimes literally.

Smiling, his sister bent, pulling a black photo album from the bottom shelf, and flipped it open to a page with individual shots of all the bridesmaids. Carefully, she removed the one of Nireed from its sleeve and handed it to him. "You can have this one."

He took it reverently, keeping his fingers at the edges so not to smudge the surface.

Fierce amber eyes stared straight into the camera; lips quirked mischievously. This one snapshot in time was so quintessentially Nireed his heart squeezed, and for one beautiful moment, it felt like she was looking right at him and smiling, and that they existed in a world where he hadn't run when she needed him to trust her. "Thank you."

Lorelei took him down to the beach to talk, just the two of them. They plopped on the sand, sitting side-by-side with their arms folded around their knees, wind whipping their dark auburn hair. Mirror images of one another.

"So, you and Nireed, huh?" Lorelei bumped her shoulder into his. "That's new."

He sighed heavily.

"Uh-oh. That's got 'complicated' written all over it."

Picking up a broken piece of mussel shell, Reid ran his thumb across its sharp edge before chucking it out into the ocean. "I fucked it up already."

Her smile dimmed. "Want to talk about it?"

"I didn't exactly handle my emotions well when I found out the truth behind *The Osprey* and the origins of Shorewalkers. She gave context, and I understood it, but I had also just found out that you were my sister and that Mom had been attacked. It all just dogpiled. I took off without explanation."

"It's a lot to take in. I'm sure she understands that."

He bowed his head. "She could smell fear on me. Since the day I met her, she's tried to prove to me that she's not some mindless, bloodthirsty monster. Leaving like I did? It's like I never listened."

"You had a lot to process." Lorelei's tone was even and judgment-free, which was rather gracious considering he'd hurt her friend. "It's okay to shut down for a little bit and make space to lick your wounds. I've done it plenty, in my own way. And yeah, it would've been better if you'd told her, but there's still time to do that."

He nodded along, unable to voice his fear that he'd irreparably broken Nireed's trust, as if saying it would make it come true.

"What were you afraid of?"

"Loving her."

"Oh," she breathed. "You love her?"

Practically heartsick with it.

When he didn't answer, she kept going. "This kind of stuff happens to couples all the time. Doesn't mean it's over. Not until one of you says it is."

A shred of hope was still hope, and he'd take it if it meant he'd a chance at earning Nireed's forgiveness and keeping her affection.

"I want to find her and apologize, but I don't know how."

Lorelei perked up. "Oh, I do!"

Launching to her feet, she reached for his hand and yanked him up with ease despite their significant height and weight difference. "Come on. We're calling Lila."

CHAPTER
TWENTY-EIGHT

Curled around an oversized ball of seaweed, something to cuddle while her heart ached and her eyes wouldn't stop stinging, Nireed occasionally twitched her fins to keep water passing through her gills. Thankfully by the time she'd gotten home and had swum to her room, her older sister was already out at the deep-sea vents and would be working on the trident project for Ryn over the next few days. Nireed wasn't ready to face her, or the "I told you so" that was sure to follow.

Delphine and Melusina had come to check on her at some point, bringing food and worried questions, but she'd waved them off, wanting to be left alone. She wasn't ready to admit to anyone that she had already lost her could-be mate, or worse yet, that she'd shared pod secrets with him that could be used to fuel ire against merfolk. Reid had asked for honesty, and she trusted him enough to give it, but he'd been so horrified by her and what the pod had done, she might've made an enemy out of him instead.

And yet, her traitorous, reckless heart, which apparently didn't have a shred of self-preservation left, couldn't bear the possibility that she might never see him again. Nireed didn't want to lose him. At least not the version of Reid who helped her break into a Nautic warehouse to look for evidence; or asked about merfolk medicine as he treated her wounds; or rescued her from drowning when she was too injured to move; or held her as she cried, because she didn't know how to keep her people from dying.

Maybe he just needed space, and once he'd had time to think, he'd come back. And then she could explain what she'd done to try to make amends.

Nireed shook her head, hurt, angry tears burning her eyes.

Her people just wanted to be left alone, and she was getting tired of trying to prove why they deserved to live.

IT HADN'T TAKEN REID LONG TO REALIZE HE'D A BUILT-IN best friend for life with his older sister. He'd gone over for brunch and a sibling heart-to-heart, but in just a few short hours, she'd helped him work out the logistics for a grand gesture that would hopefully salvage his relationship with Nireed. No questions asked. She'd just leapt to help him.

Because they were family. He'd been missing out on that kind of ride or die, big-sibling energy.

They embarked on a borrowed research vessel the next morning, catching sight of *The Lovely Lorelei* in the distance as they left the harbor. Not only was it a fishing day for Killian and his crew, but they were also planning to dip in and out of mermaid territory with a mission of their own. There was a local reporter onboard, a close friend of the family apparently, working on an investigative piece about Nautic's attempt to push out local independent fishermen and monopolize the Gulf of Maine. They were going to see if they could catch *The Seriphus* in action by using *The Lovely Lorelei* as bait.

Hands tucked beneath her armpits for warmth, Lorelei stared at the fishing trawler across the waterway, no doubt thinking about the family she had onboard. It wasn't just Killian out there, but Dr. Branson's husband and father, too, whom she was quite close with.

"Hey." He gently nudged her with his elbow. "What's up?"

"Just hoping it goes well."

"You good with your husband putting his neck on the line like this?"

She smiled wistfully. "He and the crew have skin in the game too. They're angry about what Nautic's doing to the industry and other local fishermen. Killian fights for what he believes in and wants to ensure his crew has a future continuing what they do, and I love that about him. Sure, I'm worried, and I'd hate to see him potentially lose another boat doing this, but considering the number of times I've done something risky, who am I to preach to him about doing the safe thing?"

"That's fair." Reid nodded, performing gear checks as he spoke. "Thank you both for doing this by the way." Both Lorelei and Dr. Lila Branson had dropped everything on their day off to cart his sorry ass out to merfolk territory so he could beg his people-eating mermaid girlfriend for forgiveness. This was an overwhelming gesture from people he barely knew.

"We all fuck up sometimes." Lila, occupied at the helm, shot a gracious smile his way. "Not that I'd quite qualify this as one. I'm sure she'll be relieved to see you." He hoped that was true. They would spend the better part of the morning powering through the ocean in one of her research boats, a little forty-footer. "And this is for Nireed too. That girl deserves to be happy."

The "after everything she's been through" part was left unspoken, but he heard it all the same. "She told me a little about her time in captivity."

"It was really bad." Lila nodded grimly. "We got her out in time, but..."

"Only just barely," Lorelei finished, readjusting her wet suit. It was uniquely designed to reconfigure between her human and mermaid forms. It also had a GPS device clipped to it that allowed Lila to track her location and depth, something they'd be monitoring closely on this trip. What came next had to be timed just right. "We're not sure how much she remembers, and we didn't have the heart to tell her in case she never knew, but in the months after, Lila found documentation that a few ex-colleagues of ours were planning to dissect her."

He sucked in a sharp breath.

"Doctorates in marine science and those idiots couldn't figure out how to properly wipe a hard drive." Lila huffed a bitter laugh. "Suppose I should thank them for giving the legal team even more damning evidence to serve up in court."

"She has nightmares," Reid said quietly. "Wakes up thinking she's back in the tank."

Neither of them seemed surprised.

"I have PTSD too." The way his sister said it was so matter of fact she could've been describing her hair color. No hesitation, no shame, just truth. "I'll talk to her."

A trained therapist was what Nireed needed, but who would see her? No medical records, no social security number, no insurance. Even if she was his...dependent...it would still be complicated. Talking with his sister wasn't the same as talking to a professional, but at least it was something.

"So, Reid," Lila said in a lighter tone, signaling a subject change. "You in the Coast Guard for the long haul?"

It was casually asked but far from a simple question with a simple answer.

That certainly had been his plan when he made it through basic, then aviation school. But now, with Nireed to consider?

If there's even a relationship left, dumb ass.

Optimistically speaking, if he made up with Nireed, he had a few more years left at his current assignment in Haven Cove. But after that, he could end up anywhere. The Great Lakes, deep down south, the West Coast. While he most certainly could put in for other stations in the New England region, that didn't guarantee he'd get them. And it didn't change the fact that any other unit would be farther away from Nireed and her home.

Could he really ask her to swim farther than she already did? He'd gladly use all his leave to fly back to Haven Cove and visit, but would it be enough?

A sinking feeling settled into the pit of his stomach.

That was a few weeks out of the year at most. Something was better than nothing, of course, but it would be hard.

"You know," Lila continued, keeping her tone casual. "Mermaid research is starting to bring in the kind of funding for ocean exploration that outer space has always gotten. We're going to have a large research ship out here soon once the area is officially declared a marine sanctuary. Think of it like a space station. We're going to need a rescue swimmer onboard, and there'll be research internship positions, too, for anyone with an interest in marine science. No experience necessary."

Lorelei smirked. "Are you offering him a job?"

"Wouldn't be the first time I got someone a job who needed it *for love*," Lila replied with a sly, knowing grin.

"And career dreams!" Lorelei playfully whacked her friend on the arm.

"The pay and *benefits* will be so good."

Reid snorted. That was an innuendo if he ever heard one.

"Lila, gross. That's my brother."

"We'll get you technical diver certified," Lila plowed on shamelessly, "so you can visit Nireed during your downtime. I guess it would still be a long-distance relationship, what with breathing limitations, but she's less than two hundred feet below us right now, so really, it's like you'd be living in the same neighborhood, same block even. Which is a lot better than being sixty miles away, or more, at any given time."

The wheels in his head were turning.

Stationed out here permanently as a civilian rescue swimmer and a duck scrubber? It was a good pitch. Great even. Something he might've considered regardless of the circumstances. It would be like living in a National Geographic documentary—always on the forefront of discovery. His casual love of science didn't have to be casual or vicarious. He could do actual field work in the Gulf of Maine and with a world-renowned marine biologist. *The* expert in mermaid science.

Who was also an unapologetic matchmaker.

And his sister lived here. Not to mention his mom already made regular trips out to see her. Why not for him, too?

Opportunities like this didn't come around often. And he didn't see why he shouldn't consider it.

Lorelei was the last person Nireed expected to see. But here she was, in the underwater abode Nireed shared with her sister, shaking her from a depressed stupor and dragging her out by the arm and into a fresh current of water.

"What's happening?" Nireed signed one-handed. "Is it Nautic?"

Lorelei shook her head, continuing to tow her along.

Scenting the water around them, Nireed tried to decipher Lorelei's mood, but it was annoyingly obscure. But what she did catch was a whiff of a familiar scent she'd been desperately trying to forget up until now. *Why did Lorelei smell like...*Panic spliced through her. Freeing her arm, she signed in a flurry of motion, "Is it Reid? Is he okay? What happened?"

Lorelei took her hands, gently stilling them. She touched their foreheads together a moment, a quiet demand that Nireed listen, before pulling back to sign, "Just trust me, okay? Everything will be all right."

Nireed swallowed thickly, then nodded, letting Lorelei lead the way. Whatever it was must have been big for her to come out all this way, and yet, she wasn't detecting panic, upset, or any number of alarming emotions. Lorelei was as cool as a clam.

Together, they ascended out of the city and toward the surface. But notably, not toward shore. There was a small boat drifting overhead, engine still and silent, and nothing else. No Coast Warrior Helicopter. No Reid.

Disappointment and fear ravaged her already frayed emotions.

Nireed tried flashing her bioluminescence to get Lorelei's attention. She wanted to sign "where are we going?" but the other mermaid either didn't notice or ignored her and kept on swimming.

I don't understand. What's happening?

Just as she was about to give Lorelei's tail fins a sharp tug, a splash overhead caught her attention, followed by the spike of a familiar scent. Not a stale, lingering scent leftover from past contact, but strong and penetrating her senses, shearing a deep pang of longing through her.

No. It couldn't be.

She drew up short, hands clutched to her chest, not daring to hope. She scented the water again, sure she'd imagined it.

There was a Surface Dweller here. In the water, with them, but not just any Surface Dweller.

Reid?

And then she saw him.

A sleek form diving down, his black and silver gear distinguishing him in an ocean of blue. It didn't look like him—the goggles, the suit, the fins, and the large, cylindrical contraption strapped to his back obscured his features—but she knew.

Down and down he swam—ten feet, twenty, thirty—gradually and carefully descending to seventy feet below the surface, pausing at regular intervals along the way. This was more than twice what humans could safely free dive, according to Cure Creator, and while Reid wasn't free diving, that he'd come this far into the deep for her, set her heart racing.

This was unknown territory for him.

Lorelei finally turned; a soft smile illuminated by her glowing green bioluminescence. "We'll give you two some privacy. Be back in an hour," she signed, before swimming straight for the shadowy silhouette of the boat above. Nireed watched as Lorelei slithered onboard, the engine rumbling to life. And then, Reid's only way home raced off, leaving them completely alone.

Reid was here. Underneath the water. With her. He'd come all this way. Found a way to breathe. These were not the actions of a man who feared her.

He lifted a hand, a closed fist rotating twice over his heart. "I'm sorry," the sign said. Slashes of silver outlined his gloves, some kind of reflective material to help her see his hands' motions. Pointing his index fingers toward the surface, he brushed his fists together up and down, then opened one palm to make a waving motion with his hand like a fish's tail.

Reid stilled his hands, waiting. He'd practiced the words with Lorelei again and again until his execution was flawless, and he didn't have to think about making the motions anymore. But Nireed wasn't moving, save for the barest of twitches from her tail to keep water flowing past her gills.

What if he'd gotten it wrong anyway? Messed up the words in his overconfidence? For all he knew, he may have just insulted her, and his only lifeline to shore had just driven off to collect research samples. Maybe he'd been hasty in agreeing to that.

It was so dark down here he saw nothing else but Nireed, more beautiful and terrifying than ever before. A hundred or so feet spanned between them, her human-piscine skeletal structure glowing faintly in the darkness and her skin a canvas of twinkling amber starlight. Otherworldly. Extraterrestrial. A creature in her domain.

And he was at her complete and utter mercy.

Drown him. Devour him. Smash him on some rocks. Whatever pleased her most. But not leave. At least, not until he had the chance to lay himself bare, as she had so many times before.

She didn't have to forgive him, or even stick around to see what more he had to say, but he silently begged her not to swim off. He didn't think he could take it if she turned her back on him and dove where he could not follow.

Something changed in her demeanor as he watched. Her tail swished and bioluminescence brightened to a near blinding degree, like an incandescent bulb moments before bursting.

And then, she sprung.

She darted so fast through the water his eyes could only track the movement as a flash of lightning.

Oh God. This was it.

This was the end.

She's actually going to eat me.

Those were his final thoughts before Nireed slammed into him.

HEAD OVER FIN THEY TUMBLED THROUGH THE WATER, HER momentum keeping them spinning round and round. Nireed's already tender eyes were awash in a fresh, searing wave of tears. He'd learned her name sign.

Starfish.

And not just that. He was here, actually here, underwater with her. At the heart of merfolk territory. Just a dozen feet down began the kelp forest's canopy, and about one hundred or so more began the cliff-side city where she and her people lived.

When they finally stopped, Reid was sucking in great gulps of air from the mouthpiece between his lips and clutching his middle, fear permeating the water. He'd begun to ascend, the influx of air into his lungs making him buoyant.

No, no, no, please don't be afraid!

Grabbing the center of his weighted diving belt, she pulled him back down and anchored him in place. In hindsight, tackling him hadn't been the best move, considering how they'd left things. For once, she wasn't even trying to scare him, but Reid must've mistaken excitement for an attack.

Twenty-Armed Goddess, she was glad to see him. All those grim, defeatist feelings she'd felt for the past day faded into the background, a spark of hope blooming in its stead. When he was by her side, they felt like a possibility again, and that what was damaged could be mended.

Down here, he was vulnerable and exposed, humbled by the open ocean. That meant something.

Still breathing heavy from being pounced on, Reid signed again, "I'm so sorry, Starfish. I shouldn't have run." The contrition was in his scent as much as his words, and scents didn't lie, but they could be misleading.

"You don't think I'm a monster?" she fingerspelled slowly, hoping he'd learned that much. Otherwise, they were going to have to surface for this conversation.

There was a glimmer of excitement in his scent, not because of what she'd said, but because he seemed to understand it. A lot of pausing and halting signing followed, but letter by letter he eventually replied, "I don't. Stay and read?"

She cocked her head to the right, curious. "Go on."

Dropping his hands, he withdrew something from the pouch strapped to his waist. The notebook. She watched as he flipped open to a page, fingers trembling. Carefully, she took it from him, smoothing a clawed hand over its waxy, water-resistant surface. Several pages were filled with his words.

Starfish,

You are the bravest, most selfless person I know. And by far, the most honorable. I asked for honesty, and you gave it, even though your history must have been painful and terrifying to share. It was hard to hear, I'll admit, but I never should have run from you, which I see now was probably the worst thing I could've done.

But I didn't run for the reasons you may think.

I needed some space to process, but not whether I felt unsafe around you. I don't fear your strength, I cherish it. The truth is, Nireed, I admire you, and want you, a terrifying amount. You fight to make a better, safer world each day. You're a protector. And I love that about you.

I'm so sorry for hurting you by letting you think otherwise.

I know we haven't known each other long, but there's not a night that goes by that I don't fall asleep to the thought of you. Not a morning either that I don't wake up wondering when I'll see you next. The days you stayed with me are my greatest treasure. I've replayed those memories over and over, cherishing every single one.

Staring up at the stars together. Watching you climb a mountain and ask to be flicked with bottled water because, of course you did. You're as fucking adorable as you are a terrifying wonder. It's the most mind-boggling combination, but it works for you, sweetheart.

I'd be remiss if I didn't also say that I think about tucking you inside my boat, in my bed...or spreading you across the seat of my bike...

A taste, that's all we've had, but I want the whole feast.

You've already gone great lengths to be with me. Now, this is me showing that I can come to you too. That I want to make this work. That I'm willing to fight for—and protect—us.

I want there to be an "us" if you'll have me.

Yours always,
Reid

By the time Nireed finished reading, her hands were trembling. This was how Reid saw her. Not as a monster, but as a hero, and he wanted her so bad it scared him. She'd been so afraid that what they'd shared in their few blissful days together meant more to her than it did to him, but this didn't sound like that at all.

Flipping back to the first pages, she began rereading, wanting to soak in every one of his words, when there was a light tap on her shoulder. She paused, looking up into the deep, dark abyss of Reid's eyes, her chest constricting at the grief she saw there.

"I don't want to lose you," he spelled out with his hands, a yawning ache stretching between them. He wanted to touch her—she could sense that—but he didn't dare.

Closing the notebook and tucking it safely inside the pouch he'd carried it in, she drew near, her luminescence soft as she cupped the nape of his neck, bringing her forehead to his. This was the version of Reid she wanted, the version that was worth fighting for, even when they argued. He didn't need to be perfect—she'd never expect that of him—but she needed him to try, and as long as he was trying, she'd have him, flaws and all.

"You won't," Nireed mouthed, as she signed one-handed. "But if you run again, I'll chase you."

Tension whooshed out of him, relief blooming in the water as his hands encircled her waist. He bumped his forehead to hers, nodding, a wordless promise. She kissed one cheek, then the other, all while lifting a hand to his mouthpiece. He gave another little nod, and she eased it from his mouth, claiming his lips for herself in a slow, drugging kiss.

There was a hunger in her heart. An ancient call pulsing through her veins.

Kraken Goddess, she wanted this man.

Lore warned sailors about kisses from sirens, a lovely but deadly temptation, and it was true. So many had been lured to their doom by her kind, only enjoying a few moments of bliss before the end. And right now, she held Reid's life in her hands, the very air he breathed.

Every press and pull from his mouth stoked a craving she needed to sate, the scales covering her needy flesh parting. His fingers bunched at her sides as he softly exhaled his last breath. A precious gift, given seventy feet beneath the surface.

For all that she would've loved to get lost in the heat of his mouth, she gave back his breathing apparatus. This wasn't an ending to their story, but a new beginning, and her greedy, hungry siren heart had room for forgiveness and affection too. She held him in place as he sucked in air, bubbles erupting between them on his exhale.

In and out. In and out.

When the water cleared, he threaded his fingers through her hair, his pupils blown wide, want hanging heavy between them.

"How much air?" she signed.

Lifting his wrist, he tapped the quietly ticking clock strapped there. "Seventy-five minutes." Left of ninety total.

There was enough time.

"Do you trust me?" Slipping her arms around his waist, Nireed hugged him close, his dual fins brushing against her tail.

He held her gaze. "Take me down."

CHAPTER
TWENTY-NINE

DOWN, DOWN, DOWN, THEY WENT. TO DOOM OR SALVATION, who could say? A dim voice whispered that this was madness, and it definitely was, but Reid clung to Nireed, tucked his face into her neck, bowing to her and the ocean's will.

Into the depths she pulled him, the surface's light a halo that became fainter and fainter, forsaking safety for the black void. Only her light showed the way.

Fronds of sea kelp brushed his back as they descended into the forest below, some of the stalks as tall as trees. This was where she came to think, where she went to find peace. That day she told him, and that mountain they'd climbed, seemed so far away now. A whole other world.

She laid him gently on a bed of silt, her hands sliding up his body to cup his face.

Every inch of her was alight with bioluminescence, a shining constellation in this place of darkness. *His Starfish.* A sense of wonder filled him as he brushed his fingers along her cheek, an amber blush answering his touch.

He loved her. More than anything. It wasn't lust that brought him here. Lust alone couldn't bear the risk, pushing the limits of even his advanced recreational diving abilities.

As she unzipped the front of his wetsuit, and loosened his belt, baring him to the ocean's caress, her amber light illuminated his skin, giving it its own otherworldly glow. A rush of glacial water should've followed, he was sure, but Nireed radiated heat that chased away the cold. With great care, she reached between them, enclosing his hard length in her webbing and claws, easing him out.

The place where her scales parted for him glowed, a swirling vortex at the center of the universe. Such unearthly beauty, a cosmos at his fingertips, never failed to leave him breathless and in awe.

He tapped the pouch at his side, and her answering grin was a fierce, ferocious thing in the dark of the deep—all sharp teeth, more grimace than smile—and yet, he only felt its warmth.

Here, at the bottom of the ocean, as he knew it, he was safe in her arms.

Carefully, Nireed withdrew a square foil packet from the pouch, tearing it open with the pads of her fingers. Mirroring what she'd seen him do before, she pinched the tip as she rolled it on, sheathing him completely. There was a cock ring in the pouch, too, and he had her slip it over him and down to the base to help keep the condom secure.

It was a gamble. This whole damn thing. He couldn't be certain it would hold up down here—the condom, his air supply—and yet, he wanted this with his siren. To wholly give himself to her in her place of peace.

And really, if one of those things had to give out, was it so bad if he gave her the baby she'd asked him for? There wouldn't be a more fitting place than here.

Maybe his emotions were running away from him. Or nitrogen narcosis talking.

Or maybe this was a confirmation of something he'd always felt but couldn't admit because the thought of being a parent was as terrifying as it was exhilarating. A grand adventure of its own, and if there was ever someone he'd embark on that journey with, it was her. He could do anything with her fearlessly by his side.

Lying together on the sea floor, everything felt right.

They pressed their foreheads together, aligning their bodies just so. She pressed a kiss to the corner of his mouth, taking care not to disturb the regulator, and his hands fell to her hips, steadying her as she sank down upon him.

Her lithe, undulating body delivered each stroke with sinuous grace.

Rapture of the deep, that felt like heaven and sin.

He rose to meet her, but she pinned his hips, bumping her nose to his in quiet admonishment. *Let me*, it said. A gentle reminder to conserve his energy and his breath.

If they were anywhere else, he'd protest. He couldn't take and not give at least as good as he got, but now was not the time for bravado. This was her domain, his life was in her hands, and she should reign supreme.

He lay back, opening himself up to ravishment. *Have your wicked way with me.*

And his siren smiled, holding his gaze as she delivered, deploying her whole body to the task. She rose and fell in time to the pulse of the ocean, measured out by the swaying fronds around them, her light growing ever brighter. She was glorious like this. A goddess of the deep.

So taken by the sight of her, by the pleasure she wrought, he barely registered her lifting his wrist to check the time on his watch. He'd a finite air supply, something that needed to be monitored. If they didn't budget enough time to safely ascend, he'd get decompression sickness. Or worse. He'd run out of air and drown.

That should alarm him, and the fact that he couldn't concentrate on anything else but the sensations her body doled, but his limbs felt heavy, blissfully lethargic.

Nireed pressed a kiss to his palm before laying it above his head, her unhurried movements soothing. "I've got you," she mouthed, before redoubling her efforts.

All he could do was stare up at her, enthralled by her intoxicating spell.

It wasn't long before his back arched off the seabed, euphoria stealing over him.

CHAPTER
THIRTY

AFTER ASCENDING AT A CAUTIOUS THIRTY FEET PER MINUTE, and taking a longer break during the last twenty feet, Nireed returned Reid to the surface with plenty of time to spare—thirty-six minutes to be exact. It was in the mermaid lab that she'd learned to tell time, the clock ticking above the door an agonizing reminder of its slow passage. But she'd felt none of that pain watching it for Reid. It was with loving attentiveness that she made sure he had enough air in his tank.

Pushing his goggles to the top of his head, Reid spat out his mouthpiece, grinning wide. A red outline of where his goggles had been cutely ringed around his eyes. Looping an arm around her shoulders, he pulled her in, kissing her fiercely.

"That was amazing." He laughed, water droplets dripping from his lashes and dotting his cheeks.

It was the stuff of dreams. She never could've hoped it might be a reality for them, what with the limitations of his biology. "Would you do it again?"

"In a heartbeat. Although, I think I might've experienced nitrogen narcosis."

"Is that bad or good?" It sounded bad, but he was still smiling.

"Not great, safety-wise. Could've been really bad, if I'm being honest, but you took care of me." He lightly tapped a finger to her nose. "It's an altered state of mind that impairs judgment. Causes fatigue. Sometimes hallucinations. Kicks in at around one hundred feet. If someone else isn't looking out for you when it happens, you may forget to surface, which is bad for obvious reasons."

Deepest murk, that did sound quite bad. Next time, they'd stick to shallower water. "I will always look out for you."

He tipped his forehead to hers. "I know. Thank you, Starfish."

Her tail waved back and forth beneath them, and because Reid liked to match her rhythm, she kept an easy, leisurely pace. It might be a little while before Lorelei and Lila returned for him, and he needed to conserve his strength.

"It's fitting, in a way. Would your first time in the deep even be right if I didn't blow your mind and endanger your life in the same forty minutes?"

"Did you just crack a siren joke?"

She smirked.

"Man, I'm lucky I'm cute."

She just smiled, showing more teeth than strictly necessary.

"I am too cute to eat, right?"

"Cute, yes." Playfully, she nipped at his earlobe. "But I do like the way you taste."

He swatted at her face, and she licked his hand.

But all playfulness died when she detected a shift in atmosphere.

She pulled Reid in close as a thick fog rolled in, a wall of smoky white even her siren eyes couldn't penetrate. It curled around them, enshrouding their surroundings. People got lost in this kind of fog, never to be found.

"That's not good," Reid murmured, arms looped around her waist. "They're not going to see us through that."

"Shh, let me listen." Her hearing wasn't as good above water as below, but it was still sensitive and engine sounds were easy to pick out. If she could get a sense of distance and location, they could start swimming in that direction. They'd have a better chance at finding Cure Creator's research vessel than the other way around.

Concentrating, she filtered out the sound of Reid's breathing, the beating of his heart, the waves, and the wind. She thought she caught snatches of a small engine, puttering somewhere in the distance, maybe three or so miles away. But there was something else. Something too big to be the research vessel, drowning out all other nearby sound.

They weren't alone out here.

She clutched Reid tighter.

"What is it?" he whispered.

"Bigger boat."

"Could be Killian and his crew. They're out here too."

She shook her head. *The Lovely Lorelei* was familiar, this wasn't. "Something bigger."

"One of Nautic's then." His voice was low. "They're the only other ones still fishing out here. Chased everybody else off."

She nodded, gently fitting his goggles back over his eyes. "It's getting closer. Be prepared to dive."

He complied wordlessly, adjusting the goggles, and fitted the breathing apparatus back into his mouth. With one hand on his diver's belt, keeping them anchored together, Nireed dipped down into the water, listening.

The engines were more distinct now, though one was significantly larger, louder, and quickly overtaking the other.

Her heart sped up, panic flaring.

They were too close together.

Five short horn blasts preceded horrendous crunching and screeching, tearing metal. The terrible sound cut across the distance. Jerking back, Nireed clapped a hand over her ear, pressed the other into her shoulder. It hurt, but she refused to let go of Reid. Not in this fog, not even for a second.

An urgent tap on her hand brought her back to the surface. Reid's eyes were wide with fear.

"You heard it too?"

He nodded, cheeks chalk white. "It's got to be *The Seraphis*. Nothing else is big enough to do that. They plowed into one of the local fishing boats just last week." A fishing boat was a whole lot bigger than Cure

Creator's little vessel; a factory ship would be massive by comparison. Reid swallowed thickly, clenching her hand. "I can't lose my sister. I only just met her."

If Lorelei and Lila had been crushed on impact...

No. Nireed couldn't think like that. Her friends were alive, and they needed her to hold it together. They needed her help. "Lorelei's fast. She would've grabbed Lila."

"She's strong like you?" His voice was quiet, uncertain.

"Yes. She's strong like me." And Nireed meant it, every word. Lorelei may not have been raised ocean-hard, but she was a capable siren and had overcome her fair share of trials and tribulations. Getting run over by a hulking Surface Dweller ship was not what was going to do her in. Taking Reid's hand, Nireed placed it on her shoulder. "Let's find them."

He nodded, determination fixed in the hard set of his jaw.

Nireed raced toward the collision site and the sound of *The Seriphus*'s engines. It went against everything she'd learned from birth, wisdom passed down from her foreparents. Stay away from the Surface Dweller ships and their deafening noise and ensnaring nets. But risking her hearing was nothing compared to the lives of her friends.

With each passing mile, the noise grew, quickly moving into uncomfortable territory. The factory ship's shadowy hull loomed ahead, propeller churning the water. They needed to dive. Flashing her bioluminescence, Nireed hoped it was enough warning, and Reid's responding squeeze on her shoulder made her think it was. She eased into the descent, putting five, ten, twenty feet between them and *The Seriphus*. A glance back to check on Reid was met with a thumbs up, the Surface Dweller sign for approval; her resilient mate was stalwartly flutter kicking along, and her heart squeezed to see it.

The water went dark as *The Seriphus* passed overhead, all 200 feet of its hulking form blocking out the sun. It chugged along, the discordant, metallic grinding grating on her ears, but she gritted her teeth and kept on swimming, because Lorelei and Cure Creator needed her.

When they cleared the ship's underbelly, the water suffused with surface light once more, she brought Reid back to the surface. The less they had to use his canned air supply the better. A horrid ringing plagued Nireed's ears, but she kept swimming, pushing on and on.

She knew they were getting close when she began to smell leaking fuel. It worsened the closer they got.

The surface was littered with broken bits of Dr. Branson's research boat. It hadn't sunk, not yet at least, but it was taking on water, and it was only a matter of time before it made its final plunge into the deep.

Yet, another Surface Dweller vessel destined for the sea floor, Nireed thought bitterly. But she didn't linger on it because the lives of those onboard were far more precious.

Reid let go of her shoulder, and they both fervently began searching the site, making shallow dives for their friends.

Nothing. No one.

Reid's eyes had a wild, desperate look to them Nireed didn't like.

"There's no blood." She assured him, sensing his growing panic. "And I don't smell death."

"Nautic took them. Nautic fucking took them!" He smacked the surface of the water, but anger quickly turned to fear. "Nireed, I don't know what to do. It's going to take the Coast Guard at least thirty minutes to get a helicopter here. If Nautic's crew finds out Lorelei's a mermaid, she's not going to have that long. And who knows what they'll do to Dr. Branson if they feel like they need to tie up loose ends."

Dread sank its ugly claws into her gut. He was right.

A grim sort of determination stole over her. "I need to go after them. You're certain the Coast Warriors will come?"

He nodded. "The boat has an emergency radio beacon that'll ping its location. As long as I stay with the wreckage, they'll be able to find me."

That settled it then.

"I'm going after them."

"Nireed..." He'd seen the bodies of her kin. He knew the risk, the danger, just as well as she did. A protest was forming, she could see it in his eyes.

But they had no other choice, and she couldn't just float here and do nothing. Not when she knew she'd a shot at saving them. He knew it, too, even if he didn't want to admit it. "This is what we do, Reid. We risk our lives to save others."

"I know." He caressed her cheek, each word pained and reluctant. "I know."

"I'm going to get your sister back. Lila too."

Grim acceptance fell over his features. "If only I'd the strength you do," he trailed, before pulling her in for a fierce kiss. "I'll be coming with help, okay? Stay alive, Starfish."

"They can't have me." Her claws framed his face as she pressed another kiss to his lips. "This ends today."

"Give 'em hell."

And then she dove. Tearing through the water at breakneck speeds. Chasing the sound of a rumbling engine and rotating propellers. Chasing *The Seriphus*'s giant wake. Trusting the Coast Warriors to come for her mate.

The mermaid-killers had Lorelei. She begged the Twenty-Armed Goddess they didn't find out what she was.

CHAPTER

THIRTY-ONE

THE FOG WAS CLEARING, BUT NOT BY MUCH. REID CLUNG TO the orange life ring that had been onboard Dr. Branson's research vessel, bobbing among its wreckage, conserving his energy, and waiting.

Those mermaid-murdering bastards had his sister and *the* marine biologist at the forefront of advocating for merfolk rights and protections.

Now the love of his life was hunting them down, and Godspeed to her. Nautic had fucked with the wrong siren, and he didn't care what she had to do to set things right. If at the end of the day only his Starfish, sister, and Dr. Branson made it off that ship alive, so be it. See if he cared.

One way or another, it would be Nautic's final mistake. He was sure of that.

The Seriphus crew kidnapped two civilians. No doubt they thought they'd get away with it. That the Coast Guard would arrive to find wreckage, but no bodies, and leave none the wiser, chalking it up to yet another tragedy at sea. Way out here, they didn't think there'd be witnesses.

But Reid had seen and soon he'd have access to a radio.

There'd be a manhunt for *The Seriphus*. It wasn't just the Coast Guard they had to contend with now. The consequence of kidnapping people in federal waters meant the FBI would get involved too.

Beating propellers overhead alerted Reid to an approaching Jayhawk. He activated the strobe light attached to his wetsuit, blinking on and off, and glanced down at his watch. Thirty minutes on the dot, just as he'd predicted.

There was no point in waving down the helicopter. Not in this fog and not when his black scuba gear wasn't visible on a good day against the ocean's backdrop. The silver reflective strips he'd tacked on had been for Nireed's benefit; they wouldn't be seen from the sky.

The helicopter passed him over but circled back around.

They'd seen the strobe light.

As the Jayhawk hovered overhead, a fellow AST dropped into the water. He began freestyling toward Reid the moment he surfaced.

"Coast Guard rescue swimmer..." his crewmate began to shout, but Reid waved him off.

"It's Petty Officer Reid Kruetz," he shouted back, whisking off his goggles. Even though they didn't stand duty together, they'd seen each other plenty on the mornings they swapped out.

The other AST—Petty Officer Jensen—slowed. "What are you doing out here?"

"Clip me in. I'll tell you about it on the way up."

Inside the helicopter, Jensen announced to the rest of the crew, "It's Petty Officer Kruetz."

"Reid?" Perez yelled back from the cockpit. "What are you doing out here?"

"What am I doing out here?" He began divesting his scuba gear, the crew onboard wordlessly jumping in to help. "What are you doing out here?"

"I'm covering a shift. What's your excuse?"

"I was getting diving hours in."

"Way out here? On whose boat?"

"One of the Marine Research Center's."

"Why were you diving in mermaid territory?" They'd covered some of the "what" on the ascent, but not this. Jensen looked at him like he was both the ballsiest motherfucker he ever laid eyes on and someone who might sniff markers for fun.

"Not mission critical." Snapping into work-mode, Reid braced his hands against the cockpit threshold. "Perez, *The Seraphis* crew kidnapped two civilians—Dr. Lila Branson, a marine biologist, and her colleague Lorelei Roth. I need you to call it in. Last I saw it, the ship was heading north."

"Sector, 60207, Fishing Vessel *Seraphis* has taken 02 civilians captive. Vessel's last known course bearing 015° from my last position, over." She paused, listening to orders. "Roger that."

"We're to begin the search," Perez reported back to aircrew. "Standing by for information on other assets in the area. If we find *The Seriphus*, we're not to engage, just tail."

To hell with that. If they found *The Seriphus*, he was going down, even if he had to jump out and swim. And yeah, it'd be reckless, and no, he didn't have a plan for getting his ass onboard. *Yet.*

Reid drummed his fingers, mind whirring.

The Jayhawk wasn't equipped to take on a potentially armed crew, and he wouldn't endanger Perez or others. They needed a white hull—one of the Coast Guard's cutter class boats—and a boarding team.

Or the Navy.

But those assets might be too far away, and limited fuel reserves might force this Jayhawk back to shore before anyone else arrived on scene.

What to do, what to do…

And then it dawned on him.

There *was* someone in the area with a vested interest in his sister's safety. Someone who didn't have to answer to the Coast Guard's chain of command.

"Perez, can you swap to channel 16? I know a fisherman who's out here today who can help us look."

The Coast Guard called on local fishermen to help with search and rescues all the time. Something like this wouldn't be outside normal operating procedure. And their sector command hadn't told them not to do it.

"Wanna come up here and do the honors?"

Ducking in, Reid took the radio headset from the junior pilot sitting next to Perez, pausing a moment to gather his thoughts. And then he spoke, "This is the Coast Guard calling on all offshore fishermen in the Haven Cove AOR to be on the lookout for *The Seriphus*. Two civilians have been kidnapped and are believed onboard. Last known location was in merfolk territory, heading north." He rattled off his best estimate of the coordinates. "We'll take all the help we can get tracking it down."

Several long seconds ticked by. The channel quiet.

And then a voice he recognized crackled on the other end. "This is *The Lovely Lorelei*. We're in the area and on the lookout. Will report back on this channel if we see *The Seriphus*."

It was like a dam release. Other voices began chiming in.

"This is the *Wind Catcher*. We're heading in that direction now."

"*Reel 'Em In*, coming to join the party."

"*Never Better*. We're with you."

And so many others.

These fishermen knew the gulf better than anyone. If anybody was going to find the elusive factory ship, it was them.

CHAPTER

THIRTY-TWO

HAND OVER HAND, NIREED SCALED THE SIDE OF *THE SERIPHUS*, its engines roaring in her ears. Deepest, murkiest depths, it was so loud. The moment she got onboard she'd stuff her ears. With what, she didn't know, but something. Anything.

Just several more feet and you're over the side.

Claws dug in the hull, gouging hand holds out of slick, barnacle encrusted metal. Up, up, and up she climbed, fueled by rage, spite, and the desperate need for this all to finally be over. She was so sick of these Surface Dwellers and their nets taking whatever they wanted—her podmates, her friends, the sanctity of her own home.

Slowly, she rose to the gunwale, peering over the edge. Much of the crew appeared to be working out on deck, ten or so men with their backs turned to her, guns holstered at their hips.

She'd have to be careful.

Slinking over the side, Nireed found her footing, each movement quietly taken. The last time she'd been on a Nautic-owned fishing vessel her people had been fighting for their lives. Her side twinged at the memory; the pain of a phantom gunshot wound only just recently healed. She quickly ducked behind a deck box, seeking shelter.

It was a long shot, but she tested her siren song, a low crooning hum.

Shut off the engines. Quiet the ship.

That was the intention, but it wasn't answered.

Another glance over the deck box confirmed what she'd feared—the crew wore protective ear coverings, the noise canceling kind that silenced siren song. And, begrudgingly, the kind she needed to block out this awful engine.

Hands clasped firmly over her ears, she sank back down, giving herself a moment to breathe, to think. All this racket made it hard to do either.

She scanned her surroundings for something she could plug her ears with and spotted a light gray hoodie abandoned on top a pile of line. Snatching it, she was just about to carve it up when she thought to check the pockets. Sometimes Killian's crew carried around little orange sponges that they stuck in their ears.

To her delight, there were a couple pairs shoved inside this garment. Tearing into the plastic, she rolled the orange bits with the pads of her fingers and stuffed them inside her ears like she'd seen the crew do.

She sighed quietly to herself. Instant relief.

While the engine was still loud, and she could hear everything going on around her, it took the edge off and didn't make her feel like her ears might bleed. She could think now.

Where would they hold Lorelei and Lila?

Below deck. Yes, that seemed right.

Making sure *The Seriphus* crew's backs were still turned, Nireed darted across deck and down the hatch.

The first room she snuck into appeared to be the crew's sleeping quarters. It was mostly empty. There was one man snoring obnoxiously in one of the bunks, a dreadful, sawing sound that could easily rival the ship's engines.

Quietly closing the door, she moved on to check other rooms.

Supplies. Eating area. But no Lorelei or Lila.

They were on this boat somewhere. Beneath the reek of burning diesel, she was picking up faint traces of their scents. Wringing her claws, she peeked around a corner to make sure the way was clear. Two men were coming up the stairs, so she scurried back, dipping inside the room that held all the supplies.

Their voices grew louder as they entered the narrow mid-deck hallway, their thick-soled boots plodding along. She shrunk back as tight as she could, begging the Twenty-Armed Goddess that they didn't open this door. She could easily take them, that wasn't the problem.

If they found her, sounded the alarm, well, this rescue would be a whole lot easier if she didn't have thirty-odd armed men breathing down her neck. Despite their crimes against her and her people, she was trying not to hurt any of them. For the sake of peace, and not feeding assumptions about her kind, she was going to let Surface Dweller leadership handle doling out their punishment.

They passed her door, opening the one next to it, and a horrid, garbled snoring sound peeled out into the hallway. The two men laughed, then the door clicked shut. Quiet followed.

Carefully and slowly, Nireed cracked open her door, peeking out. Empty.

She hurried down the hall and to the metal-grated steps.

Fear, then nausea, clenched her belly as she descended to the bottom-most deck. A noxious fog hung in the corridor, fouling the air with the stink of fish and slow decay. Holding her breath, only to later suck in greater gulps of air, made it worse. Death thrived here. There was nothing to do but power forward.

This level was where the engine room and fish hold would be. Nireed didn't want to think about why the crew might be holding Lorelei and Lila down here.

A large metal door loomed ahead.

Inside was where they allegedly processed and packaged fish, and made some egregious, breaded atrocity called "fish sticks," getting their catch shelf-ready for Surface Dweller markets.

Nireed's hand trembled as it closed over the door handle, icy cold to the touch.

Twenty-Armed Goddess, give me strength. Whatever lay beyond, she had to keep going. For Lorelei and Lila. For the pod.

Taking a deep, punishing breath, she opened the door.

At first, she wasn't sure what she was looking at.

Rows of people holding knives hovered over moving…shelves? Long, narrow tables? She wasn't sure what they were. Loud, whirring machinery that was for sure, and she was once again grateful for finding orange sponges for her ears.

The too bright florescent lights overhead and the room's oddly clean, rigid order resembled the mermaid lab, in a way. But where the lab had been designed for cold, calculated observation, its scientists dissecting her with their eyes, this place held people just as mechanical as the machines they worked alongside, taking apart creatures with their hands.

The workers wore thick rubber gloves, aprons, and some weird head covering that sort of looked like a net as they repeated the same tasks with rote efficiency. Slicing, chopping, discarding unwanted bits into troughs. She peeked into one of them—offal, body fluids, and shorn, colorful scales mixing to make a gruesome sludge.

So focused on their work, none of them noticed her as she crept over to a table filled with packaged fish. She rifled through a few of them. Diced. Chopped. Filleted cuts. Another table held canned goods, and something called "Pâté."

One of the workers looked up, starting.

Pressing a clawed finger to her lips, Nireed flashed her amber eyes, a low hum forming at the back of her throat, and the individual froze, lacing the air with their fear.

These Surface Dwellers weren't wearing noise cancellation headsets.

With all the noise this machinery was making, they probably couldn't hear anything beyond this room, siren song included.

Others began to look up, too, sharing equally frightened looks.

Don't move. Don't make a sound.

No one said anything, or so much as twitched a muscle, as she sniffed the air and checked the contents of a third table. Something was off. The reek of this room was overpowering, making it hard to pick out individual scents, but there was something else here, and it wasn't a normal fish smell.

She picked up one of the finished packages, nose wrinkling at the distinctive round shape. It looked like a...

Heart.

She dropped the package, looking around the table wildly.

Heart. Liver. Brain. Tongue. Eyes.

Twenty-Armed Goddess, the eyes.

Gold. Green. Blue. Topaz.

There was a section of the room cordoned off by a large, semi-opaque sheet of plastic. She whisked it aside with a rough yank.

Rows of mermaid tails, severed at the waist, hung from meat hooks, their tailfins dragging across the floor, and scales dim and dull, washed out of their usual vibrant color. On a table off to the side was the upper half of one of her podmates, tail cleaved and gone.

Two empty sockets where her eyes had been stared back at Nireed, her hand hanging limply off the table, claws and webbing sliced away. Her flesh was being cut into and divvied up; her organs harvested.

Packaged. Labeled.

It came from low in her belly. A piercing, shattering scream.

Every worker in the room dropped to their knees, covering their ears.

Nireed upended table after table, rage and anguish her only allies as she set upon destroying this evil. An avenging maelstrom. The ocean had been pillaged, her people slain and dismembered like animals, and there would be a reckoning.

Metal screeched as she ripped the processing hold's door off its hinges and hurled it at a wall, crumpling in on itself.

Shouting above. Running footsteps. Down the stairs, then in the hall outside.

Picking up a four pound can labeled Sea Maiden Pâté, Nireed threw it at the first crew member to darken the threshold, gun drawn. The can hit his head with a wet, meaty crack, and his hand jerked up, setting the gun off.

CHAPTER
THIRTY-THREE

OVERHEAD FLUORESCENTS SHATTERED, SHOWERING THE floor in broken glass, the lowermost deck doused in darkness. Surface Dwellers screamed, pathetic creatures flailing uselessly without their precious light, shoving, scratching, crawling over one other, trying to get somewhere, anywhere, away from her. It was so easy to wrench away their defenses, hard plastic crunching in her hands, gunmetal twisted beyond repair.

Some made it to the stairs.

One fisherman, braver and more foolish than the rest, covered their retreat, shooting wildly from the other end of the hallway. She let them have their glimpse of freedom.

Bang. Bang. Bang. Bang.

No conservation, just fear.

Bang. Bang. Bang. Click. Click. Click. Click.

Siren Song rose from her throat, filling the tight quarters, taking the crew into her thrall. Their fear spiked, a most delicious, pungent scent that made her mouth water and her stomach growl. She was agony and wrath incarnate. There would be no escape.

On all fours, she slunk from the fish processing hold, and into the hallway, ensuring the fishermen were truly helpless and well ensnared.

When no additional gunfire followed, she rose to her feet, her inner luminescence the only light in the dark.

They would see, as well as hear, her coming.

She stalked down the hallway with her arms outstretched, ripping deep gouges in the walls, the metal groaning and screeching as it tore. With each step she gritted her teeth, bare feet passing through shattered glass and metal shards; it was but a fraction of the pain clawing from her chest.

The bottlenecked crew froze in place, unable to move, their hammering hearts a symphony of fear and dread.

A flicker of movement to her left, and a familiar, friendly scent, drew her to a stop. Lorelei stood in the threshold of a doorway, a fisherman trembling in her grasp, and a puddle of urine pooling at his feet.

Good. They hadn't hurt her.

If they had…

Rage filled her anew, red and blindingly hot.

Striking fast, Nireed lunged at the last man to fire a gun at her, dropping the thrall she had on him. He tried taking a swing, but she grabbed his wrist and wrenched him around sharply, knocking his feet out from underneath him. He twisted and kicked and screamed as she dragged him across the floor toward the fish processing hold. She could've continued subduing him like she had the others, but she chose not to.

She *allowed* the struggle.

Lorelei stepped into the hallway behind them. "Nireed, wait! Don't do this."

She paused, turning to meet her fellow siren's pleading green gaze. Did such monstrous creatures even deserve mercy? Raw fury twisted her insides. Not at her friend, but at these fishermen, for what could've happened. For what had already happened. "Help me make an example of them."

With a rough jerk of her arm, she yanked the man into the hold, his screaming abruptly cut off.

The ship was finally quiet.

CHAPTER
THIRTY-FOUR

"This is *The Lovely Lorelei*. We have eyes on *The Seriphus*."

Killian and his crew. They found it.

Adrenaline coursed through Reid's veins. It had been two hours since the collision. A lot could happen in that amount of time, and it was making him downright antsy considering the possibilities, but he needed to stay calm and focused, or he wouldn't be any good to anyone.

The last they'd heard from sector, three FBI agents from the Boston field office were being flown out to a Coast Guard cutter patrolling off the coast of Portland, which would take them the rest of the way, but it would be at least ten more hours until they arrived on scene.

Perez checked the coordinates Killian gave against their current location. "Thank you, Captain. We'll be there soon. Hang tight."

Reid waited for a more explicit "do not engage" directive, but it never came. The corner of his mouth ticked up in a small, half smile. While he couldn't in good conscience professionally condone a bunch of local fishermen storming a fish factory, personally, he'd no problem with them sticking it to the Man, especially since they just might be Nireed, Lorelei, and Lila's best chances of getting out alive.

Be careful, Killian.

"Would you look at that?" Perez exhaled, her awe unmistakable.

Reid leaned forward.

Ahead, a ring of local fishermen had encircled *The Seriphus*, the whole lot of them boxing the factory ship in, rendering it immobile. While Perez began updating their sector command, Reid dug out a pair of binoculars. The *Lovely Lorelei* was there, *Wind Catcher, Reel 'Em In, Never Better,* and many, many others. It looked as if all of Haven Cove's offshore roster had joined the party.

On *The Seriphus*, ten or so crew members were sitting in a group on deck, their arms behind their backs. He'd no way of knowing for sure, but it looked as if they'd been bound. Odd. Had the fishermen boarded the ship and subdued the crew?

There hadn't been enough time for that unless they waited until after the action was already over to report *The Seriphus*'s whereabouts…

Reid scanned the length of the ship, catching a flash of red, before doubling back.

"Well, I'll be," he murmured, hardly believing his eyes.

"What are you seeing?" Perez asked.

That was his sister on deck, lowering a ladder over the side. Killian and several others used it to climb onboard.

"Would you believe me if I told you I recently found out I have a half sister?"

Perez glanced over, arching a brow. "Funny time to bring that up. Can't tell if you're pulling my leg or not."

"I'm not." He pointed to the deck of *The Seriphus*. "That's her, mid-deck. Lorelei Roth."

"One of the civilians we're out here looking for?"

"Yup." She'd as good as rescued herself. "She's got at least ten of the crew tied up on deck."

Perez's brow climbed higher. "What does she do for a living?"

"She's a museum director."

"What, she put them to sleep with history facts?"

Reid snorted, continuing to scan the deck. He didn't see either Nireed or Lila, which made his stomach clench, but no reason to panic yet. They might be below deck keeping an eye on the remaining crew. "I need to get down there."

"Thought you might say that." Perez called back to the dropmaster. "Get the hoist ready."

Reid geared up as Perez brought them in close. Clipping into the hoist, he was lowered on deck, where Lorelei was waiting.

"You get around." She grinned, as he touched down, pulling him in for a hug.

"You good?"

"Yeah. They sedated us, but mine wore off first." She gestured to the tied-up crew. "Figured I'd make myself useful waiting for the rescue to arrive." Her voice dropped to a whisper. "A little siren song goes a long way."

"Where's Dr. Branson?"

Lorelei waved for him to follow. "Had to carry her up."

A dirty-blond-haired white man and an older Black gentleman he recognized from his sister's wedding photos were crouched across the deck with Dr. Branson. She was conscious and sitting up on her own, but barely, her head lolling back and forth with a deeply dazed expression.

He began heading their way. "Is she okay?"

"Whatever tranquilizer they used is taking a while to wear off."

Crouching down, he quickly introduced himself to the men caring for Dr. Branson and learned they were her husband and father, both members of Killian's crew, while he checked her vital signs.

"She's going to be fine," he assured her family. "Just really groggy. But to play it safe, we're going to fly her back to shore and to a hospital, okay?"

"Can one of us go with her?" Dr. Branson's husband asked, cradling her head to keep it steady.

"Afraid not, but she's in good hands, I promise."

He updated the helicopter team and got Dr. Branson situated inside the basket lift, all while worry gnawed at his insides. Where was Nireed? Why wasn't she on deck with everyone else?

"Did Nireed make it onboard?"

Lorelei's face fell, unsettlingly grim. "She did."

"Why are you giving me that look? Is she all right?" If any one of those fishermen laid a hand on her…well, let's just say he was about to lose his job. And probably go to jail.

"As much as one can be. She saw some rough things below deck, black market kind of stuff. I was just about to take our friend Jackie down there to film some b-roll and document the operation Nautic had going on here." When he blinked at her blankly, she continued, "She's a reporter. Covers the local fishing industry for the *Haven Cove Daily*."

"What's her name again?"

"Jackie Gaten."

That rang a bell. He'd seen the name before, and recently. Filtering through the last few weeks' memories, he snagged on the elusive thread. Jackie Gaten was the reporter who wrote the special interest piece on *The Merry Mariner's* deceased crew.

"Legal cases take time, but there's plenty onboard she can use to eviscerate Nautic in the court of public opinion. We've got them, Reid."

They finally had enough to pin the corporation to the wall, but Reid only nodded dimly, distracted by his worry for Nireed. Whatever she'd seen must've been really bad. His gaze swept across the deck again, looking for his brave mermaid.

"She's up in the pilothouse, guarding the captain, but before you go up there"—Lorelei laid a hand on his arm— "I think you need to go below decks first. See it firsthand. So you can understand."

The radio crackled in his ear. "Your sister needs to come too," Perez said. "Protocol and all. But if you want to stay, I'm sure I can come up with a reasonable excuse."

"She's right." Lorelei sighed, hands on her hips. "It would look weird if I didn't go. Raise too many questions. But do consider what I said. And be careful. Nireed is angry and grieving."

And with that, his sister turned away, wasting no time in saying her goodbyes. Once she'd finished, he helped her get clipped into the hoist.

Watching Lorelei's ascent into the helicopter, he said to Perez, "I'm staying."

"Figured. Our second helicopter is on the way. Should be here to replace us in about ten minutes."

"Copy that."

It was Killian who ended up going down below decks with him—the reporter, too, a petite, fluffy white-haired woman with a camcorder. It took every bit of self-restraint Reid had to follow his sister's advice and not just beeline it to Nireed. She must've had a good reason.

He'd never forget what he saw onboard *Gale's Promise*. The broken bodies, the dismembered limbs, the fisherman missing the top part of his head, ripped away at the jaw. Nireed had contributed to that, but this time, whatever carnage they found would be all hers.

Jackie went down first. "It's like a horror movie down here," she whispered, gently panning the camcorder from left to right.

It was dead quiet like *Gale's Promise*.

The factory ship should've been loud, boisterous, its assembly line equipment a constant mechanical clamor, but it was so quiet Reid could hear the ocean on the other side of the hull, waves lapping against the side.

Busted florescent lights flickered in and out overhead. Claw marks slashed across the walls, leaving deep gouges. And bullet casings littered the floor. There were crushed headsets and guns with their barrels twisted too.

A force of nature had ripped through here, leaving destruction in her wake, but where was the blood? The bodies? The rest of the ship's crew and factory line workers? Aside from a single set of smeared, bloody footprints, there was nothing but a strange, unsettling stillness.

Reid's stomach clenched. The bloody footprints had to be Nireed's. And right now, she was alone in the pilothouse, hurt. Why hadn't Lorelei said anything?

Their footsteps echoed as they inched down the empty hallway, pausing every few steps so Jackie could take pictures. It got colder and colder the farther they went, the refrigeration unit quietly humming.

"I'll never get used to the fish hold smell." Jackie stepped around the bloody footprints, glass crunching beneath her shoes. "It'll be burned into my nose for the rest of the day. I don't know how you do it, Killian."

"It's better than the alternative. It's when you stop smelling it that there's a problem."

"Did a story on that some years back. A couple of greenhorn fishermen noticed a strange odor and went down into the hold. Lost consciousness. It was hydrogen sulfide buildup from all the dead fish."

"I remember that. The fire department had to go in and clear the space."

"Did they get the fishermen out?" Such cases weren't within the scope of his job, but Reid had heard about them.

"Had to be hospitalized, but yeah, they got lucky." Jackie stopped so abruptly, Reid almost bowled her over. "Damn. Would you look at that?" She pointed at the empty threshold before them.

Their motley trio hovered outside the fish processing hold, each staring at the thick metal door ripped clean off its hinges. The sheer strength that must've taken. Reid always knew Nireed was strong, but this was far greater than he ever could've imagined.

No one made a move to venture inside.

"Lorelei said it was safe to come down here." Killian's voice trailed, but even he sounded unsure.

"Says the woman with mermaid strength." Jackie huffed, snapping another round of photos.

So the reporter knew. And Killian didn't seem alarmed by it, so it must be all right.

"I'll go first." Reid was a rescue swimmer, not a boarding officer, so he didn't exactly know how to clear a room, but as the only service member present, he figured he ought to take on the most risk.

Neither of his companions protested, so he took the initiative and edged inside, mentally bracing himself for what he might see.

There was the missing crew.

Every single one of them hung from the ceiling in a net, staring down at him with pleading eyes, but apart from a few bumps and scrapes, they didn't appear to be hurt. Some looked more angry than fearful, many were crying, but none yelled or begged for help. They must've been compelled into complete and utter silence by either Nireed or his sister.

How in the hell had they gotten them up there? That was the first question.

How in the hell are we going to get them down? Was the second.

Jackie scooted past him to continue snapping photos farther in, but quickly turned away, a hand clasped over her mouth. She went very, very still and glassy-eyed.

Reid tore his attention from *The Seriphus's* crew.

On first look, the horror seemed to be the wreckage Nireed left behind, a classic tale of monster meets man, but there was a grislier truth beneath it all. The true horror wasn't Nireed, but what Nautic had done in greed.

For all the carnage Reid had seen onboard *Gale's Promise*, none of it could've prepared him for this. Beside him, Killian vomited.

Conveyor belts of packaged mermaid parts. Tails on meat hooks. Dissected, divvied up, and labeled. Lives reduced to corporate processing.

But worst of all was the humanoid torso laid out on a metal slab, bisected from the waist down. The siren's face was turned their way, her orbital sockets a black void where eyes should be.

How had Nireed seen this, and yet, spilled no blood in all her rage?

REID CLIMBED THE STAIRS TO THE PILOTHOUSE, FOLLOWING a trail of bloody footprints, softly calling Nireed's name. The last thing he wanted to do was startle her.

When she didn't answer, he lightly rapped on the door, cracking it open just enough to peek in. The navigation console had been smashed; charts were strewn all over the floor as if a maelstrom had torn through. There wasn't anyone in his direct line of sight, but he did hear sobbing.

Reid crept in, quietly closing the door behind him.

His Starfish was sitting on the floor in a sad, rageful puddle, knees hugged to her chest, a noise cancellation headset crushed in her hand. There was a small, bloody pile of glass fragments beside her, the cuts on her feet already closing. While he was grateful for her speedy, siren healing, it made Reid's stomach clench to see that she had to dig out every shard herself.

Across from her, *The Seriphus's* captain was bleeding from shallow cut on his forehead but sitting docilely with a logbook, stack of folders, and satellite phone resting on his lap. He'd have to treat that, but for the moment, taking care of Nireed was his top priority.

He crouched down, lightly smoothing a hand across her shoulder. "Hey, Starfish."

She sniffed, but didn't look up, just held herself tighter, body quaking as she cried.

"Rough couple of hours, huh?"

Sniffling, she looked up, eyes dim at first, but as they focused on him a spark of light returned. "I had him gather evidence." She gestured weakly to the captain.

"That was…rather cooperative of him."

The crushed headset fell from her hands, hitting the floor with a clatter. "I can be rather persuasive."

Her siren song. Today, she'd wielded it as one might a weapon, but was it ever used for joy? He hoped that it was, and that one day, under far better circumstances, he might be lucky enough to hear it. "You did good."

Pain rolled over her features. "Did I? I'm not so sure."

Her throat worked, thick tears rolling down her cheeks. Touching her fingers to one, a flicker of surprise crossed her features as she pulled them away, finding them wet. Tears rarely felt. The surprise quickly passed, settling into something that looked a lot like regret.

"Do you regret sparing them?"

"It's not that. Killing the crew would just confirm everything the Surface Dwellers think they know about us." She picked shards of metal from beneath her claws. "I was in that tank for a year. I thought it was worth it because my people were cured, and our territory was going to be protected, declared a 'marine sanctuary,' as Cure Creator calls it. But I read the words in that book. 'Restock galley, clear out mermaids, deliver shipment at $10,000 per pound, fix the bilge pump.' While I've known all along why my people were being killed—so that these Surface Dwellers could keep fishing in our waters—seeing it written down like that…"

Like just another line item on a long to-do list.

Nireed looked lost, shattered. "All my suffering and sacrifice was meant to save my people. Not put targets on their backs."

Reid yanked her into a fierce hug. "No, don't you dare blame yourself for their greed." He buried his nose in her hair, inhaling its sea salt smell. "That's not on you."

"Then why does it feel like it?" Her voice wavered, the sound heavy and wet.

"Because you're trying to make sense of something senseless. You're used to seeing the world in terms of survival—kill or be killed. But this…" He gestured to the boat around them. "What they're doing here? Is just evil, and evil has a way of coming for us no matter what we do."

"You really think so?" She sniffled.

"I know so." He touched his forehead to hers. "They've stolen so much already, don't let them steal your peace. You're not to blame, and they don't get to make you think otherwise, you hear me?"

A small smile lifted the corners of her mouth. "I hear you."

"Good." He pressed a kiss to her forehead. "Now, as much as I'd love to keep you right here with me, more Surface Dwellers are coming, and while they're going to see to it that Nautic is punished, it's probably better that you're not here when they arrive."

Who knew how the FBI would react to her, or Nireed to them, and that was not a gamble he cared to take.

"Okay."

Cupping her ankle, Reid asked, "Is it all right if I take a look?"

She nodded.

Lifting one foot, then the other, he examined the undersides, each smeared with dirt and dried blood. There were no more open wounds. Some parts looked newly sealed and a little raw, but thankfully not inflamed. Sirens must've also had ironclad immune systems, killing common infections with a vengeance.

"Does it hurt?"

"Not really."

"Think you can stand?" Knowing Nireed, she'd probably grin and bear it, even if she shouldn't, so he added, "Or maybe you better not?"

"If I can't stand, then I shouldn't shift, but I can't stay here either." She lifted her chin, the set of her jaw brave and determined. "I should try."

Taking her hands, he gently helped her to her feet. He watched her face carefully for signs of discomfort. Now that the adrenaline had worn off, the distance she covered with open wounds might be unbearable.

"Sore," she admitted, wriggling her toes. "But manageable."

"Good. That's really good, Starfish."

But she didn't move toward the door. "I suppose we can't bring them home, the ones we lost."

He brushed back her hair and cupped her cheek. "I'm sorry, love. But the world needs to see what was done here so that Nautic never sails again. There can't be any doubt."

"I don't like it, but I understand." Nireed hugged herself. "A part of me is glad their deaths weren't completely wasted, but it's not the comfort I thought it would be."

There was distance and safety in imagining what might've happened. Room for denial, the blunting of reality's sharp edges, but seeing the truth in the flesh afforded no such luxuries.

She continued, "I wish we could lay them to rest in the deep where they belong."

Remains were routinely returned to their families after cases closed. Why not for the merfolk too? "Can't promise anything, but maybe when the investigation is over, we can make arrangements to have their bones returned."

A glimmer of hope sparked in her teary eyes. "That would be best."

It was only right the merfolk got to properly mourn and bury their dead. He'd raise hell if he had to. His fellow Surface Dwellers owed them that dignity and respect, at the very least.

After collecting the pile of evidence from The Seriphus's captain, and putting Killian in charge of safeguarding it, Reid coaxed Nireed out of the pilothouse. He hated feeling like he was shooing her off, but he didn't want her anywhere near this ship when the FBI arrived; and despite what The Seriphus crew had done, he did need to find a way to get the rest of them down and tend to their wounds. It was his job. He'd have to temper his rage and do it as clinically and indiscriminately as possible.

Navigating the stairs down to the main deck, Nireed's tight grip on the railing made the metal groan and creak with every gray-faced, reluctant step she took. He slowed to thread a stabilizing arm around her waist. "You afraid of heights, love?"

She nodded, clutching his shoulders like a scared cat, claws pricking skin.

Wincing, he tapped her waist. "Ease up."

She relaxed her hold, claws retracting. "Sorry."

"Why didn't you tell me before? On the hike?" He'd marched her straight up that mountain, sat them at the edge of an overlook, legs dangling over the side.

"That was different." She toed the open metal grating, shuddering. "That felt solid. This is...exposing. Barely anything to hang onto."

Open backed steps, a flimsy—by siren standards—railing, the stomach drop feeling of falling. He'd never considered how alarming that must feel to a creature used to living in suspension, and he could see why good, solid earth would feel safer by comparison. Boulders and trees made good handholds.

He paused, heart swelling with affection and awe, as he drank her in —tangled dark brown hair, wild amber eyes, the clench of her sharp teeth and steel of her resolve.

Another fear faced to protect the ones she loved and stop Nautic's reign once and for all.

God, he loved this woman.

"Want me to carry you down?"

"Yes." She nodded firmly, already climbing onto his back, and burying her face in his neck.

Threading his arms under her legs, and readjusting her weight, he couldn't help but chuckle a little to himself. Damn, she was adorable. He carried her down and over to the gunwale, slow and easy, and was grateful to see that Killian's fishermen had turned their backs to give them privacy.

"Nireed? Reid?" Someone was calling their names, but it wasn't coming from anywhere on deck.

Nireed eagerly patted his shoulder and pointed. He leaned over the side.

Four mermaids stared up at them from the water below.

"We're okay!" she shouted, sagging against him with relief. The other mermaids were too far down for him to make out their expressions, but if Nireed's response was anything to go by, he'd bet they felt the same.

One by one, Nireed named each of them: Melusina, Delphine, Aersila, and Undine. Friends. Family. Leader. The one who'd called out their names was Nireed's older sister. Not only did she know his name, she knew enough to recognize him. While Nireed said her sister knew about them, damn, that he'd been important enough to bare mentioning was only just now sinking in.

Nireed slid from his back.

Clambering onto the gunwale, she perched there, gazing down, no doubt preparing to dive. But she didn't go just yet, and instead, turned to look back at him, her eyes red-rimmed and swollen by grief. There was something warm there, too, something that made his chest tighten and his breath catch. Something he'd seen in himself—unspoken feelings reflected in the shimmering pools of her eyes. "Thank you for coming for me."

"I'll always come for you," he said, stepping in closer. *I love you, Starfish.* But he didn't say it out loud, not yet. Not on the heels of the horror she'd seen.

A smile overtook her face, coupled with a happy glow. Had she heard his unsaid words anyway? Threading her claws through his hair, she leaned in, kissing him soft and sweet.

"I'll see you soon." Those were her parting words before joining her merfolk kin.

THIRTY-FIVE

REID RIFFLED THROUGH THE FILES TAKEN FROM THE factory ship's captain. Some of the work orders and sales directives contained the CEO's name and signature, directly tying him to the company's black market operations. A little dumb to leave a paper trail like this, but Reid wasn't about to look a gift horse in the mouth. This had to be the final nail in the coffin for Nautic.

And then there was the satellite phone. It had called one phone number over and over in the last three weeks. Soon after *The Merry Mariner* sunk, in fact. If Reid dialed it, who would pick up on the other end? Nautic's CEO? A frequent buyer?

"Killian, do you recognize the other man in this picture?" Jackie held up her phone, a pair of wire-frame glasses perched on the end of her nose. "I'm trying to figure out if he's another one of Nautic's fishermen."

Killian leaned forward, peering at the screen. "Can't say I do. Where'd you get this?"

"A friend of *The Merry Mariner's* captain. I put out a call for photos when I was working on a story about the crew, and this guy emailed it over—used some nondescript email like 'flyboy1998.' Wouldn't give me his name, but it was more of an obit piece, so I didn't push."

"Mind if I show the guys? The independent crews don't mingle with Nautic's—you'll never find them drinking at the same bar—but we work the same docks. Unless he's brand new, someone will have seen him."

"By all means." Jackie passed her phone to Killian.

One by one, he showed his crew, but they all shook their heads.

"Either *flyboy1998*'s brand new, or he's not a fisherman at all." Jackie took back her phone. "I wouldn't have thought twice about this, if it weren't for the military haircut, and how cagey he was about identifying himself further."

Military haircut? Reid had been a quiet observer of the exchange, but this snagged his full attention. There wasn't a huge Coast Guard presence in Haven Cove, or any other military branch for that matter, so if this guy was one of them, there was a decent chance he'd have seen him in passing, even if he didn't know him personally. Maybe one of the Yeomen or ITs. "Can I see the picture?"

She held the phone face out for him to see.

A prickling sensation rolled across his skin, all at once numb and tingling. *This couldn't be right.*

Flick Rockland, *The Merry Mariner*'s captain, stood on the left, a lake in the backdrop. And beside him, with his arm across the fisherman's shoulders, holding up some kind of trout, was Petty Officer Jake Hatcher.

Reid's crewmate. *His friend.*

All this time, Hatcher knew Flick Rockland, one of Nautic's fleet captains, and he hadn't said a word. Not when they were responding to the boat's emergency beacon. Not when Reid was in the water. And not when Nireed yanked Flick below the surface, never to be seen again, or any time after that.

Why wouldn't Hatcher say that he knew someone on the case? That he'd lost someone?

"You know him." It wasn't a question. And Reid wasn't going to insult the reporter with a denial. But he wasn't about to throw Hatcher under the bus either. There had to be a reasonable explanation, but something about this made Reid's brain damn right itchy.

None of them knew what Nautic was doing to the merfolk at the time. Maybe the more they found out, the harder it got for Hatcher to admit he'd been friends with one of the fishermen. Or maybe to him that information didn't feel pertinent to the investigation, especially if it didn't impact how he did his job...

Reid gripped the phone tighter, the numb feeling burning away for something red hot.

A firm hand clasped his shoulder. Killian. "Reid, are you okay?"

No. No, he was not.

It *had* affected how Hatcher did his job, hadn't it?

Dropping the evidence collected from *Gale's Promise*. The cheap flip phone. The secretive calls.

It only made Reid's brain itchier, his skin hotter.

He turned on the microphone of his aviation headset. "Perez, where's Hatcher? Did he get recalled too?"

"Nah. He's on leave."

"So he doesn't know we've detained *The Seriphus*?"

"No...why?"

"Might be nothing."

Only, he didn't think it was nothing. And what he wanted to do next would probably get him in trouble with the Coast Guard and the FBI. He wasn't supposed to insert himself into an active investigation. He didn't have the authority.

Fuck it. He reached for *The Seriphus's* satellite phone.

"*The Seriphus* called a number repeatedly from their sat phone. I'm going to see who it is."

"Kruetz, I don't think you should..."

"I don't care." Reid dialed the number. "I have to know."

"Know what? What's going on?"

"Shh. It's ringing. Just listen." Reid held the sat phone receiver close to the mic.

It rang four times before there was a click on the other end, a familiar voice answering, "Hatcher."

Reid's blood flashed hot, then cold. It was one thing to suspect, another to hear it confirmed. This was real, the ugly math added up and shoved in his face. Nautic had an inside man, a mole, and it was Jake Fucking Hatcher. Someone he thought he knew.

Before he could pile stupid on top of stupid, like tell Hatcher he was a lying, traitorous sack of shit, Reid quietly hung up the satellite phone and set it aside. Threading his fingers behind his head, he tilted his face to the sky and sucked in a deep breath. *Fuck!*

How long had Hatcher been working for these murderers? And what kind of information was he feeding them? He had access to ship tracking information, all of NOAA's "be on the lookout" orders and fly over plans, and he'd know the whereabouts of Coast Guard assets. There were any number of things he could've tipped Nautic off about.

They needed to tell command.

"Perez, did you get that?"

Silence followed, then a quiet, "Yeah, I got that."

HOURS PASSED WAITING FOR THE FBI TO ARRIVE. TEN LONG, sleepless hours for the news about Hatcher's betrayal to stew and fester. Reid should've pressed him harder when things felt off, and he should've questioned why Hatcher always seemed to have something to say in defense of Nautic or its fishermen. The signs had been there. He just missed them.

Perez passed the information on to Lieutenant Commander Griffin, who then informed the FBI. Aside from an order to stand down on any further action, there was no word yet on what consequences Reid would face for taking matters into his own hands, but his conscience was clear, even if his stomach churned.

The FBI agents shuttled over from the cutter to *The Seriphus* with a Coast Guard boarding team on a smaller boat. Night had fallen, but the factory ship's deck was lit up like a football stadium, and the ladder Lorelei had thrown still dangled over the side. They used it to climb onboard.

Reid wasn't in Coast Guard orange or blue, but he must've exuded some air of authority, because the lead FBI agent didn't hesitate to approach him.

"Petty Officer Reid Kruetz," he said, offering the woman his hand.

She shook it with a firm, brusque grip, eyeing all thirty-five members of *The Seriphus's* crew, huddled together on deck. "Special Agent Clarice Sterling."

With the help of Killian and his crew, Reid had gotten the group down from the net Nireed had strung them in and spent much of the wait delivering first aid care. Bumps, bruises, and cuts mostly, but there were a few dislocated wrists and shoulders to set, and one orbital bone fracture that needed cold compresses.

Seeing what he had onboard *Gale's Promise*, the wholesale evisceration and dismemberment, these minor injuries spoke volumes about Nireed's restraint. The ship, and the ship alone, had taken the brunt of her wrath.

"You're the one who called Nautic's informant."

"Yes, Ma'am."

Agent Sterling pinned him with a hard, dispassionate stare. "Why?"

"I was afraid it might be one of us." No excuses, just truth, and for fuck's sake keep it to the point. That much had been drilled into him since basic training. If she wanted more information, she'd ask.

Reid braced himself for a chew out.

Agent Sterling studied him for a long, agonizing moment, no doubt making him sweat, or waiting to see if he'd fill the silence. When it became apparent that he wasn't going to, rather than dial up the signature FBI glower, she eased off. "So Lieutenant Commander Griffin said. I could give you an earful about following protocol, but I'll let your commanding officer do that. We've got more important work to do. Tell me, what'd we miss? Seems rather calm over here."

"In a word? Mermaid." No point trying to hide it, the claw marks and security footage would reveal as much, and besides, there was nothing to hide. Nireed had only been protecting her friends and had done a damn good job of it.

Special Agent Sterling arched a brow but nodded for him to continue.

"I wasn't here when it happened, but I imagine she sung to them. It's why they've been so cooperative."

"Sung to them?" The agent folded her arms. "Siren song's a real thing?"

"Apparently." He'd questioned its efficacy before, the day he helped Nireed break into Nautic's warehouse, but now he wasn't so confident. "Nautic's been using its fleet to capture and kill her kind—you can see their operations below decks. Have the ship's log and buyers lists, too. They were divvying up mermaid parts onboard and packaging them for sale. Bottom half to underground restaurants. Top half to organ traffickers."

"I see." Disgust flickered across the agent's features before her mask of imperviousness fell back in place. "We're going to get these folks detained, but when we're done, can you give me the walk through?"

"Of course."

Reid stood back with Killian as the FBI and Coast Guard boarding team marched *The Seriphus's* crew across the deck, each member still well and truly entranced. "Does siren song wear off?" It struck him that he didn't know.

"No," Killian answered, a little too quickly. "They have to release you."

Reid side-eyed his brother-in-law. That was firsthand knowledge talking—Killian's reddening cheeks and awkward shuffling signs of a guilty man—but he wasn't going to think too hard about that, for both of their sakes.

Clearing his throat, Killian continued, "Lorelei's going to have to snap them out of it."

"Is she open about what she is?" Reid tried imagining his sister marching up to the FBI and introducing herself as a shoreside siren, but it just seemed too brazen.

"It's kind of an open secret around here." Killian became grim. "She got outed at her job, so people know, but she never acknowledges it, except with family and friends. This is an extenuating circumstance, though, so I'm sure she'll make an exception. The crew won't talk, otherwise, and we need them to. Plus, there's cameras all around. I'd be surprised if one of them didn't catch her in action. There's no hiding or pretending anymore. Not for her."

God, his sister had just lost what was left of her already flimsy privacy.

One by one, *The Seriphus's* crew went down the ladder and into the small boat that would shuttle them over to the much larger Coast Guard cutter. And the fishermen who'd barricaded the factory ship in began dispersing, heading home, the action over.

It was well into the night when the FBI returned to do their initial sweep of the boat, taking pictures, collecting evidence, and interviewing Killian and his crew. When all was said and done, the ship would be driven to shore where the investigation would continue, but for now, it seemed like they were hitting all the obvious stuff.

Later that night, as they were preparing to leave, Special Agent Sterling pulled him aside. "Why didn't the mermaid just slaughter everyone?" she asked, some mixture of bafflement and suspicion coloring her tone.

Reid was exhausted, going nearly twenty-four hours without sleep, and emotionally overwrought. Not even the coffee Killian brought him off *The Lovely Lorelei* was doing him much good, so he was a little curt when he finally replied, "Because they're not mindless, murderous monsters. They're people."

CHAPTER

THIRTY-SIX

I𝚃 𝚆𝙰𝚂 𝙷𝙰𝚁𝙳 𝚃𝙾 𝙿𝙻𝙰𝚈 𝙸𝚃 𝙲𝙾𝙾𝙻 𝚆𝙷𝙴𝙽 H𝙰𝚃𝙲𝙷𝙴𝚁 𝚂𝙷𝙾𝚆𝙴𝙳 𝚄𝙿 for morning quarters, breezing in with a smile and a cup of coffee, like nothing had changed. But Lieutenant Commander Griffin wanted to, one, see if he would even show up, and two, observe his behavior with a CGIS agent present. If Hatcher hadn't checked the news, it was possible he didn't know the game was up.

"Agent Bentley from CGIS is joining us today," Lieutenant Commander Griffin announced, his tone light and cordial as he introduced the man standing next to him. "Just need to conference in his colleague, Agent Burke." He punched a number into the station's landline.

The pocket of Hatcher's utility blues lit up, the telltale sound of a vibrating phone filling the silent room. His face went sheet white.

"Go on. Answer it."

The traitor dropped his coffee and ran, but Agent Bentley didn't waste a second sprinting after him. Hatcher didn't get far. Within seconds, the CGIS agent brought him back into the room, wrists cuffed behind his back.

Reid toed the fallen thermos upright, a pool of spilled coffee staining the drab gray carpet. Watching Hatcher get caught didn't bring him the satisfaction he thought it would. He just felt tired. And kind of sad. The anger was still there, of course, but today it was buried under grief.

Beside him, Perez's impassive act fell. She clenched her jaw so hard he could hear her teeth grinding, and tears welled at the corners of her eyes. They hadn't just lost a colleague today, but a friend. Someone they thought they trusted.

Perez hastily swiped a hand over her eyes, before clenching it in a fist at her side. "Hatcher, how could you?"

"The mermaids, they killed my Uncle Flick."

He sounded so small, so lost.

A pang of sympathy came and quickly went. Yes, Hatcher lost a family member and was grieving, but that family member was one of the fishermen hunting merfolk to extinction. Whatever Hatcher knew and loved about his uncle didn't make up for that evil.

Lieutenant Commander Griffin folded his arms, all amicability gone. "Why didn't you come to me and say you knew the captain?"

Hatcher's shoulders sagged. "I thought if I did, I'd get taken off the case, and we'd waste time getting a replacement."

"And Nautic?" Agent Bentley pressed. "How'd you wind up being their informant?"

"I went to a bar my uncle used to frequent." Hatcher stared at the floor, unable to look any of them in the eye. "Got to talking to some of the guys—other Nautic fishermen—and they told me the mermaids were destroying their nets, losing them catch, but this was the first time they'd killed anyone. I just couldn't stand by and let that happen to more people. I had to do something, and the Nautic guys were the only ones being serious about taking action."

"And then?"

"And then, they introduced me to *The Seriphus's* captain, and he worked out a way for me to help. Just letting him know what we were putting in our reports, and some evidence tampering, too, but I never told him anything about our assets or where they were. That was a hard limit, I swear." Hatcher lifted his head, finally meeting Reid's eyes. "And I never shared anything personal. I just wanted to keep everyone safe."

Everyone but the merfolk.

Was Reid supposed to be grateful for Hatcher's "discretion?"

Fuck tired, fuck sad. Hatcher was just as complicit as the rest of Nautic. He was on the radio when Reid reported what he saw on *Gale's Promise*. Maybe he didn't know what fucked up shit Nautic had been up to before then, but he certainly did after, and yet he still continued helping them.

It was all Reid could do to keep his voice calm and his feet firmly planted in place. "Do you know what your new fishing buddies and good ol' Uncle Flick did with the bodies?"

"What are you…"

"After Nautic executed them with cattle guns." Reid spoke more slowly, and it was a test of his restraint. All he wanted to do was grab Hatcher by his collar and wring his worthless neck. "Do you know what they did with the bodies?"

"I don't…what, what did they do?"

Lieutenant Commander Griffin swiped a file folder from the desk behind him. Inside, there were printed out pictures of *The Seriphus's* fish processing hold. He opened it for Hatcher to see, shuffling photo after photo, and to the guy's credit, he didn't turn away from the truth this time. He looked, really looked, first frozen by surprise, then horror.

By the time Lieutenant Commander Griffin closed the folder, tears tracked Hatcher's cheeks.

For what little it was worth, his reaction seemed real.

CHAPTER

THIRTY-SEVEN

WITHIN THE SAFETY OF HOME, NIREED CURLED UP ON A BED
of seaweed with Aersila, just holding each other and soaking in the quiet
comfort of sisterhood. *Just like old times.*

No, not exactly like old times.

They were grieving. By Undine's count, one hundred merfolk had
been slain, about a fifth of their community. So many lives lost. Nautic
had been stopped but at a steep price.

What came next, beyond rebuild and repopulate, Nireed wasn't sure.
Would they get their loved one's bones back like Reid hoped? Would
there be more interaction with Surface Dweller leadership, some kind of
attempt at discourse and diplomacy? Or would the marine sanctuary
finally bring peace and quiet to their waters, her people left to dwell in
the deep, undisturbed?

But those were questions for another day. Nireed snuggled in closer
to her sister, taking comfort in the feeling of Aersila's claws running
through her hair.

Days later, Lorelei brought news.

"Nautic is being prosecuted." It was an unfamiliar word, but to
clarify, Lorelei added the sign for punishment. "All their boats were
taken away."

Relief, elation, spiked the water—Nireed's, Lorelei's, Aersila's. It was done. Thank the Twenty-Armed Goddess, they were safe once more.

"And the story our friend Jackie told has won a lot of support for merfolk. It's not just Cure Creator's colleagues and friends on your side, everyday Surface Dwellers too." Lorelei's smile only grew. "There's more. Merfolk waters have been officially declared a marine sanctuary."

Nireed pulled her friend into a fierce hug, bioluminescence flashing wildly, and while Aersila didn't join in, she was wearing one of her rare smiles. *Thank you, thank you, thank you.*

It was everything they had hoped for.

When Lorelei left, Nireed signed to her sister. "Reid kept his promise. Lorelei too."

Aersila's smile faltered, expression growing solemn. "They did."

"We have good allies among the Surface Dwellers."

"We do." She inclined her head. It was a quiet admission that she'd been wrong. "And I'm glad you saw that even when the rest of us couldn't. This is a victory for our whole pod, but you're the one who won this battle for us. I know I don't say it enough, but I'm proud of you, Nireed."

Tears burned her eyes. Just when she thought she didn't have any left to cry, there were a few more. "Thank you."

"Our very own emissary to the Land Above the Water." Aersila said it with such awe and wonder. "You go where few dare to tread. It's...I don't know how you do it."

"You understand more than you think." Nireed cupped her sister's cheek, weathered by hardship and time. Aersila bore so many scars for this pod. Many that could be seen and many that could not. "It's for my friends on shore, and my loved ones here."

Aersila dipped her head in understanding. A beat of stillness passed before she signed, "Your mate, seems..." She scrunched up her face, fighting for a word.

"Fit? Handsome? Perfectly suited to me?" Nireed teased.

Aersila scowled, swatting her with her tailfin. "Well, now I don't want to say anything."

"Come on." They hadn't gotten to meet, but Aersila had seen Reid with her onboard *The Seriphus*. "What did you think?"

"Fishing for compliments gets you nowhere with me."

"One won't kill you."

"Fine. I like the way he looks at you."

"Aquilus looks at you like that."

"You know what?" Aersila flopped down on their seaweed bed, patting a spot next to her. "Let's keep talking about Reid. Tell me all about the Surface Dweller who's ensnared your heart."

CHAPTER

THIRTY-EIGHT

Days had passed since Reid had last seen Nireed, perched on the gunwale of Nautic's factory ship. Work got in the way, and Hatcher's arrest, but now Reid was off duty, and he needed to see his siren. Make sure she was okay. Hold her, even if only for a little bit, if she wasn't. She had her sister and her friends and her pod, but he wanted to be there for her, too, in any way he could.

Reid hitched a ride offshore on *The Lovely Lorelei*. They couldn't enter mermaid territory, now officially a marine sanctuary, but Killian could get him close.

"Thanks for letting me tag along."

Killian was out on deck with him, watching as Reid triple checked his gear. "Does she know you're coming?"

"No. I'm hoping she'll smell me."

"All the way from the underwater city?" Killian folded his arms. "Not much of a plan."

"It's not," Reid agreed. "But I need to try. I won't go far."

Killian heaved a sigh, swiping a hand over his scruff. The captain hated this idea, that was plain to see. "You've got an hour. That's all I can give. If we don't work, we don't get paid."

"I'll take whatever I can get. And the tank can't hold more than that anyway."

"God help me. You and your sister sure find funny ways to stress me out."

This dive was more unnerving than the last. It was just him and the open ocean. No helicopter overhead, ready to yank him out at a moment's notice. No Lila tracking his location on GPS. No Lorelei in the water with him, showing him the way.

He wouldn't go far, or nearly as deep. Desperate as he was to see Nireed, he wasn't going to risk getting nitrogen narcosis again. It was still foolhardy, no doubt about that.

Reid descended to fifty feet and hovered there.

Waiting and hoping and utterly lovesick.

It wasn't Nireed who came, but his presence was noted. A small group of merfolk rose from the deep, green and blue light winking softly in the dark. They ascended to his level, but hung back, maintaining some distance.

He slowly, and clumsily, signed, "I'm looking for Nireed."

The group's collective bioluminescent brightened, and one of them began to sign back, a merman with golden scales, but his hand movements were fast, and Reid didn't recognize all the signs.

The merfolk watched patiently as Reid fingerspelled, "I don't understand."

This time, the merman fingerspelled the words, graciously keeping his movements slow. "Are you Reid?"

He nodded.

"I'm Aquilus. We'll get her for you."

The group returned to the deep, Aquilus leading the way, their lights fading and fading, until they winked out of sight. Reid checked his pressure and depth gauges and kept an eye on his watch. Ten minutes was a long time alone fifty feet below the surface, plenty of time to think and overthink, but to his relief, he saw a glimmer of amber, growing brighter and brighter as its bearer rose from the abyss.

Nireed streaked through the dark like a shooting star, and he braced himself for another tackle, but she mercifully drew up short, eyes wide with surprise and wonder.

"You okay, Starfish?"

Her expression softened, lingering traces of grief still there. Carefully minding his hose and respirator, she wrapped her arms around him, nuzzling her face into the crook of his neck. As he hugged his girl back, her body heaved a sigh of relief in his arms, all the tension ebbing. After everything, finally some peace. She was safe and sound, at last. Her mission accomplished.

They stayed like that for a long time. Long enough that he had to start thinking about ascent. But he soaked in every single moment they had, imprinting the feel of her into his flesh—his breathing limitations would grant them so few like this.

Reluctantly, he drew back just enough to repeat his question, but this time, when he asked, "Are you okay?" her cheeks were glowing a happy amber.

"I am now."

A WEEK PASSED, THEN TWO, BEFORE HIS SIREN RETURNED TO shore. Her grief was still there, and always would be, but her smiles came a little quicker and her laughter a little fuller. Not forgetting but moving forward.

Tucked behind him on his motorcycle, Reid brought Nireed to his favorite stretch of woods at twilight, the star-encrusted sky chasing away the last remnants of sunset. Where forest opened to the bay beyond, the ocean's glassy surface sparkled in the fading light. There was something he wanted to show her. Two somethings, but he was saving the second for later.

Beneath her helmet's face shield, she wore a black silk blindfold, to help him time the reveal just right, but if he was being perfectly honest with himself, he loved seeing her wrapped in silk. Pressed up against his back with her arms hugged around his waist, Nireed nuzzled into him, using him for warmth and stability. God, it was one of his favorite ways to feel her.

I love you.

Ever since *The Seriphus*, those three little words were a ball of fire in his chest, but he wanted the moment to be right when he told her.

Someplace quiet, calm, and just the two of them. Nowhere poisoned by Nautic's evil touch.

His stomach was a fluttery mess of excitement and adrenaline when he parked his motorcycle in the empty grove and shut off the engine. So much so that his hands shook when he gently lifted the helmet from her head and withdrew the plugs from her ears. Taking her by the hand, he led her to the picnic table, seating her at the bench that faced both forest and water.

He climbed up behind her, sitting on top of the table so that she sat wedged between his knees. Smoothing his fingers over the silk and lightly brushing her skin, he asked softly, "You ready, Starfish?"

She nodded eagerly, vibrating with excited energy.

Tugging the tie loose, Reid slipped the blindfold from around her eyes.

Fireflies flitted in and out in between the trees, their flashing amber bodies dotting the approaching night in an ever-shifting constellation. The bioluminescence of his world.

She gasped, clawed hands clasping over her mouth. As she watched, he enfolded her in his arms, resting his chin on top of her head.

I love you.

But he didn't say it. Didn't want to interrupt.

When she twisted around, brow adorably creased by wonder, her eyes sparkled with their luminescent light. "It's beautiful."

He cupped her face with both hands and kissed her, taking his time, caressing her throat with his thumbs. Savoring the decadent push and pull of her lips, the way she grasped his wrists, holding him close. *I adore you. I crave you. I want you to be mine. Always.*

Releasing her with a smile, he said, "Go on. See if you can catch one."

A wicked grin twisted her lips, equal parts amused and baited by the challenge. Slipping from his arms, she walked toward the trees, shedding his spare leather jacket, letting it fall from her shoulders to the ground.

Lifting her arms in line with the horizon, palms facing up, the bioluminescent nodes along her arms flickered to life. She dimmed their glow and matched it to the fireflies' slow, lazy blinking. Drawn to her light, the fireflies flew in close, hovering, investigating.

One landed on her palm, and moving so carefully, each step unhurried, she spun to face him. "I only thought such light existed in the sea," she marveled, turning her hand as the glowing beetle crawled to the other side. "Glows just like me."

I love you.

Shrugging out of his leather jacket, he stood to join her.

"They only come out this time of year." He stopped just in front of her, the toes of his boots nudging hers. Smoothing his hand along her outstretched arm, he drew back the strap of her tank top and pressed a soft kiss to her bare shoulder. "Reminds me there's still magic left in the world."

She smiled, a sweet contrast to the fangs it revealed.

The firefly flew away, and she rose on her tiptoes to kiss him, her claws skimming his sides as she drew up his shirt. "Swim with me," she whispered against his mouth.

Heat prickled his skin, every inch pleading for her touch. Piece by piece, they shucked their clothes, leaving them in a heap on the ground. Reid paused only to pluck a condom from his wallet before taking her hand. Together, they picked their way over the boulders lining the shore, wading into the water.

Letting go of his hand, she dove in, slipping seamlessly into her mermaid form, silver scales shimmering in the moonlight. He set the foil packet on a rock near the water's edge, then dove in after her, letting the sea take him whole. A cold, but invigorating plunge.

He followed her into deeper water.

All his life he chased the sea. That desire, that draw was always there, living deep in his soul, from his first kicks in a pool to long summer days spent at the lake. His life's path was always bringing him here to this moment. *To her.*

She circled back, twisting around him in graceful, artful spirals, her tailfins caressing his skin with every pass.

Expelling the air from his lungs, he sank down to watch her and the mesmerizing ripple of amber starlight across her skin. She slowed, floating in front of him, waiting to see what he'd do. What wouldn't he do, for her, to her, with her?

He was going to take the job Lila offered him. Get his technical diving certification. And he was going to live on that research ship so he could see Nireed every single day for as long as she'd have him.

Taking her by the hips, he pushed himself down, staring up into her lambent predator's gaze as he pressed a kiss to belly, just below her navel. And there, he considered a what-if. No, a secret hope. *A someday.*

Would their kids have his dark brown eyes? Or would they be luminescent like hers? Would they be able to breathe underwater and shift between human and merfolk forms? Would they like human things, too, like shoulder rides? He hoped so. He could picture himself giving plenty of those. Little ankles clasped in his hands. Joyful giggles and squeals.

He hoped they'd get the very best of both worlds.

A burning in his lungs forced him up for air. He sucked in a deep lungful, heart hammering as Nireed bobbed to the surface beside him.

A loon called out into the night, its haunting melody echoing from the opposite shore, sending shivers down his spine. Another answered, and they both paused to listen, smiling softly as they drifted into each other's arms.

One of nature's best sounds this side of the world had to offer. And Nireed got to hear it.

"Thank you for bringing me here," she murmured, nuzzling his neck. "It's becoming my favorite place."

"I think the kelp forest is mine."

Pulled into the deep by his sea goddess, hers was the only light in that dark abyss. Ravished. Bespelled. Utterly ensnared. The memory brought a new surge of heat.

Her amber gaze flashed, smile turning wicked once again. "Which part?"

"All of it."

Clasping his hips, she dipped beneath the water, his heart racing at a million beats per minute as she kissed down his torso, his belly tensing beneath her lips. She nipped at the tender skin at his hip.

"Taste me," he pleaded, guiding one of her claws.

It was unhinged, asking a flesh-eating siren to swallow him, but fucking hell he wanted it and nicked himself anyway. Giving his hip a light squeeze, she took him in the smooth glide of her mouth, chasing away the sting of salt, her tongue worrying over the tender spot where he bled. He groaned, fingers curling in her hair. He knew from their second meeting that she could retract her fangs, and she had done so for this.

It had been a gamble, but if he could trust her at one hundred feet beneath the surface, he could trust her now.

She sucked him down further, far, far deeper than expected, and when her throat convulsed around his tip, he almost blacked out from the pleasure of it.

Releasing him, she popped back to the surface, staring at him with a self-satisfied smirk, knowing that trick alone had him seconds from coming. *Wicked, wicked tease.* He seized her in a hard, demanding kiss, pulling them both back to shore where he could get some goddammed leverage.

It was his turn to ravish her with the land at her back.

Splaying her out on a smooth, sandy patch—his legs entwined with her tail in water—he tore into the foil packet he'd left on shore with impatient ferocity and sheathed himself. He tossed the wrapper away from the leisurely lapping tide—something to grab on their way out— and plunged his tongue into the plush seam beneath her parted scales, attacking her clit.

"Reid!" She gasped, back arching off the shore as she grabbed onto his hair, bioluminescence a rapid, erratic flashing.

He worked her with punishing strokes of his tongue, making her quiver and sing his name some more. Each moan dragged from her lips took on an enchanting lilt, just as eerie and haunting as the loon song they'd heard, but this made his mind fuzzy with euphoria.

Didn't matter that he'd pinned her to the sand, demanded dominance, one word, and he was hers to command. Anything she wanted. She'd always bewitched him, had him wrapped around her pretty little claws, but this was something new, and he never wanted to escape her thrall.

"You singing for me?" He rolled his tongue where she liked it best, nice and slow.

"Yes," she said, with a heavy-lidded nod. "Do you like it?"

"I love it."

Her song began as a low hum, one he felt in his skin, his marrow, his very soul, thrumming in time to his beating heart. Building, building, until a soft crooning fell from her lips, dreamy as a lullaby, and yet seductive in its deeper, richer pitch. He loved watching her pretty throat work to make the sound as her body quaked for him.

A hard, well-placed suck made her song falter. "Keep singing," he whispered to her slick flesh.

Her brow pinched, his name a breathy plea, the sweetest note.

I know, sweetheart. Almost there.

But she sang, even though her voice trembled. She sang just for him.

A little more pressure and Nireed came with a sharp, melodic cry. He stroked his fingers over her lips, down her throat, watching her face fall into bliss. Such a perfect sound.

When her breathing evened, she opened her eyes with a sleepy blink. "I want more."

"Good. Not done with you yet." With a quick kiss to her cheek, he slotted himself in place. She was tight, having just come, but she spread her seam, and nodded for him to continue.

"You sure?"

"You won't hurt me."

He pushed in slowly, carefully, her channel slick but squeezing him something fierce. And all the while, he watched her expression for any sign of discomfort. None came.

A soft, contented sigh escaped her lips.

NOTHING FELT SO PERFECT AS THIS NIGHT. ABOVE, TREE limbs heavy with needles swayed, their silhouettes visible against the backdrop of the starry night sky. Below, water lapped at her tail, and the man she loved took her where land met sea.

Reid's arms were braced to either side of her, fingers curling in her hair, face turned into her neck. And there he kissed her skin, smoothed his tongue over her gills, teasing the folds. He quickly learned that they were sensitive—each stroke shot a lovely electric jolt to her tail, her pleasure a continuous tide coating them both—and he had been lavishing them with attention ever since.

Sliding her claws up Reid's thighs and over the round of his backside, Nireed pressed him into her, urging his hips on, now flying at a furious pace.

His breath came out in harsh pants, the finish close. Then, when he punched into her for one final thrust, his forehead fell to hers, their skin sticky with sweat. Lying here, their bodies locked together between land and sea, Reid whispered, "I love you, Starfish. I love you so damn much, and I've been meaning to say it all night."

She pulled back, staring into his eyes, and knowing she'd seen that look many times before, but had never known what it meant. Now she did. All this time, he loved her.

She was smiling so hard it hurt.

"You love me, Coast Warrior?"

"I love the ever-loving shit out of you."

It was an odd phrase, but it must be Surface Dweller for the deepest sort of love there was, if his beaming smile was anything to go by. Hugging him tight, she said, "I love the ever-loving shit out of you too."

A joyful scent was rolling off Reid in waves. He planted a kiss on her cheek, her lips. "What do merfolk do to make this official?"

"Official?" she repeated back, confused.

"Yeah, do I ask you to become my mate? Or is girlfriend more appropriate?"

Her heart skipped a beat. *His mate.*

He was always hers, her one and only, but she had kept that tucked away in her heart, secret and safe, waiting for him to know it and want it too. And now he was asking, eyes bright with hope, and the promise of new beginnings. A life of happiness and devotion.

"The first one," she whispered. "The second, whichever. Both."

He laughed, nuzzling her nose. "Will you make me the luckiest Surface Dweller on this planet and be my mate? My girlfriend too?"

"I'll be both." She sealed the promise with a kiss.

When she pulled away, he tapped the tip of her nose. "I've another surprise for you."

"Another?" A giddy, bubbly feeling filled her chest.

"Yes, another. I wanted this to be a night to remember."

It already was. What more could there be?

When Reid brought her back to his houseboat and pulled away the tarp draped over the side, she saw it, painted in big blue letters across the hull.

Starfish.

Thank you for reading! Did you enjoy? Please add your review because nothing helps an author more and encourages readers to take a chance on a book than a review.

Find more from Desirée M. Niccoli at www.dmniccoli.com

And read THE BINDING STONE, by City Owl Author, Lizzy Gayle. Turn the page for a sneak peek!

Also be sure to sign up for the City Owl Press newsletter to receive notice of all book releases!

SNEAK PEEK OF THE BINDING STONE

BY LIZZY GAYLE

The magic is palpable. It tingles as it radiates up and down my arms. My eyes snap open the moment I feel it.

I let the power drift over and through me, soaking it up like a human does sunlight. My fingertips crackle with it. Voices become clear now, and sounds assault my ears like daggers after the blissful silence of nothingness. I prefer to sleep. When I do, there is no need to think. Or remember.

Whoever dares disturb my century-long slumber will suffer my wrath. That's a promise.

"Really? Only ten?" The voice of a young man attracts my attention.

He is close, but my senses remain dulled from my sleep inside the gemstone, so I choose to be cautious, staying invisible to human eyes. His voice, warm like honey, soothes the edges of my anger. But some qualities can be deceiving. I know from experience.

"Jer, remind me not to bring you along when I buy a used car," comes the voice of another young man. "Your haggling skills need some serious work."

I stand in the center of a modern marketplace. It is small but cluttered, centered in front of a brick house with several people milling about the lawn and walkways. Whatever time I'm in, the women wear far less clothing than I remember. Near the outskirts of the unkempt grass, I spy a girl who is closest in appearance to me. A small child tugs at her arm, but the woman is distracted. A smile pulls at the corners of my mouth, and I quickly change from the draped fabrics of my last master's time, mirroring her outfit. I nod in approval. I'm going to enjoy this century.

Now to locate and destroy the source of the threat. It is not difficult. I follow the same girl's blushing gaze toward the honeyed voice I'd heard before.

"I'll take it."

He stands a mere table's width from me, and it is clear he is indeed the One. His aura glows like none of the others. A rainbow of iridescent colors pulsates and bleeds around him like a force field. This is too easy.

A gasp draws my attention. It's the young mother, frozen in a state of horror. I've seen that look before, so I follow her stare to find the toddler examining a flower growing in a crack in the concrete. A machine of some sort zooms toward her, so big it will surely crush the child in seconds. Time slows as I raise my fingers and invisible hands lift the young one out of harm's way, setting her securely back near her mother. No one has seen, save the woman who will likely never again be so negligent.

Focusing on the rainbow aura, I raise my hands. All it will take is one blast, directed at the handsome man busy handing a piece of green paper to an elderly woman. He will cease to exist. But I feel it as I let go, and even before it bounces harmlessly off his aura, I know. So I scream. It is not as though anyone can hear it. Not yet.

"Never figured you'd go for the whole bling thing," says the one with glasses and a dull, human aura. "Try it on."

I watch helplessly as Jer slips the ring on his middle finger. The large opal in the center gleams a little too brightly, and I tug at the choker around my neck, running my thumb along the matching stone. I hope the ten-paper is worth more than it appears. Why must I care so much for the innocent after all these years? If I'd let that machine crush the child…

No. I am not, nor will I ever be, one of the human Magicians. It is what sets me apart, and the only thing that may make up for some of my past sins. The ones that were within my control.

"Great. Can we go now please?" It seems by his rush that the friend does not like it here. I cannot blame him. My nose wrinkles up as I scan the rest of the market—a few scattered tables covered in odd objects, dusty boxes stacked and interspersed between them. Most things I don't recognize, but it all looks like junk to me. So how did I end up here? Just one more indignity to add to the list.

I trail behind as the two boys move away and down the wide street. The homes surrounding the market are similar to each other, yet closer together than in my last master's time. It saddens me to find far fewer trees and greenery to balance all the brick and mortar surrounding us as we walk.

The chilled wind carries the ozone-tinted scent and humid feel of a body of water nearby, which pleases me. It is refreshing after my sleep. I let my bare arms stretch out behind me, allowing goose bumps to prickle along my skin. A few buildings away, the men amble up the uneven brick walk, scattering fall's last crisp leaves from the single maple tree in front, before bursting inside the four-story rectangle. I've seen worse. Although I'm certain this "Jer" will be upgrading soon. I continue following them up creaking metal steps and into a small room, containing a sagging, cushioned seat big enough for two, a square table and chairs, a well-worn bed, dresser, and a desk.

"Do you think it's real?" Jer's friend inspects the ring.

"I don't know, Gabe. There was something about it. Like I couldn't put it down."

Of course not. You sensed the power. My power.

I suppose I should reveal myself. If I do not, the stone will force me, and at least this way I can have a little fun with the friend.

I loosen the invisibility and freeze Jer's friend before he can touch the ring. I will teach him not to touch things that do not belong to him. I grin and let my eyes glow green with power so there can be no doubt as to my nature.

My new master's reaction is immensely satisfying. About to sit in the chair near the desk, he spies me and misses, falling to the floor with a *thud*. His face is pale, his eyes huge as his gaze darts between me and his friend. I would not be surprised if he fainted. Instead, he licks his lips and clears his throat.

"Hel...hello?"

Well, that's different.

Don't stop now. Keep reading with your copy of THE BINDING STONE, by City Owl Author, Lizzy Gayle!

And sign up for the latest news, giveaways, and more at www.dmniccoli.com

Find more from Desirée M. Niccoli coming soon! All the details at
www.dmniccoli.com

And discover THE BINDING STONE, by City Owl Author, Lizzy
Gayle!

A thousand years of servitude left Leela more than a little jaded.
Betrayed by the man she loved only begins her lessons on the
wickedness of humanity.

Her hope for freedom for herself and her fellow Djinn from the magical
stones that bind them has dimmed to a barely-there glimmer.

But it hasn't yet been extinguished.

When the young, handsome, and idealistic Jered inadvertently becomes
her new master, Leela wonders if his tenderness and concern may be
real.

And despite her years of suffering, her heart begins to open to him. And
the chance at romance.

As she inches closer to trusting Jered, the past and the enemies that
come with it, resurface, threatening the small spark of happiness in
Leela's long life.

After a millennium of pain what—and who—is Leela willing to sacrifice
for freedom?

Please sign up for the City Owl Press newsletter for chances to win special subscriber-only contests and giveaways as well as receiving information on upcoming releases and special excerpts.

All reviews are **welcome** and **appreciated**. Please consider leaving one on your favorite social media and book buying sites.

For books in the world of romance and speculative fiction that embody Innovation, Creativity, and Affordability, check out City Owl Press at www.cityowlpress.com.

ACKNOWLEDGMENTS

First, I want to thank my husband Kyle for fielding every one of my 1,000 questions about the Coast Guard—the ins and outs of search and rescue missions, radio communications, and all the nitty gritty details about logistics and standard procedure. He's also a fantastic storyteller in his own right, and an excellent brainstorming buddy, as good at plotting books as he is charts. I wanted to portray Reid's on the job scenes as accurately as possible, but any mistakes made, or any creative liberties taken, are my own. Also, I'm sorry ASTs get all the limelight. So let me say it here for anyone who picks up this book: *my* forever love interest is a Boatswain's Mate.

To my agent Kaitlyn Katsoupis of Belcastro Literary Agency, thank you for having my back at every step. I breathe easier knowing you're in my corner.

The last round of developmental editing is always the hardest. At least, it is for me. To my editor Tee Tate, thank you for your encouragement and getting me over that last hurdle.

To Agatha Andrews, I appreciate everything you do. Thank you for being a Hype-Queen for this series and all things vicious merfolk; for sensitivity reading *Ensnaring the Siren*; and for championing cozy horror and horror romance, our favorite genre blends, on the She Wore Black Podcast.

To my extraordinary alpha and beta readers, Alexandra, Casey, Katie Erin, Katelyn, Morgan, Rania, and Sarah, thank you for simultaneously whipping this story into shape and reenergizing me when I was overwhelmed and drowning in edits. *Ensnaring the Siren* was simultaneously the easiest and hardest Haven Cove book to write, each chapter a breeze to write but an emotional rollercoaster ride to edit.

To my friends and family, and to my fellow authors and book community—especially Charish Reid, Colleen Delaney, Dani Frank, Ingrid Pierce, Katie Erin, Katie Rose, Morgan T. Jackson, Paulette Kennedy, Rania Hanna, and @agoblinofsorts—thank you for every kind word, every check-in, and bit of encouragement. I hold each one close to my heart. Publishing is a hard road to travel, fluctuating wildly between highs and lows, joys and disappointments—writing the book itself is only the beginning—but you make this worth doing.

xoxo,

Desirée

ABOUT THE AUTHOR

By night, Desirée M. Niccoli writes a blend of vicious romance and cozy horror, featuring monsters, villains, and the supernatural, often served with (mostly) emotionally intelligent characters and heart. By day, she is a public relations professional living the nomadic military life with her husband and two cats Pawdry Hepburn and Puma Thurman. Although born and raised in Pittsburgh, Desirée has since lived in coastal Maine (where her spooky heart truly lies), Maryland, and Connecticut.

Want to be the first to get a look at covers, sneak peeks, and more? Sign up for her newsletter and find more at www.dmniccoli.com.

 facebook.com/dmniccoli
 x.com/dmniccoli
 instagram.com/author_dmniccoli
 tiktok.com/@dmniccoli

ABOUT THE PUBLISHER

City Owl Press is a cutting edge indie publishing company, bringing the world of romance and speculative fiction to discerning readers.

Escape Your World. Get Lost in Ours!

www.cityowlpress.com

facebook.com/YourCityOwlPress
x.com/cityowlpress
instagram.com/cityowlbooks
pinterest.com/cityowlpress